SOOT AND STEEL
DARK TALES OF LONDON

SOOT AND STEEL
DARK TALES OF LONDON

Edited by Ian Whates

NEWCON
PRESS

NewCon Press
England

First edition, published in the UK August 2019
by NewCon Press
41 Wheatsheaf Road, Alconbury Weston, Cambs, PE28 4LF

NCP 212 (hardback)
NCP 213 (softback)

10 9 8 7 6 5 4 3 2 1

ISBN: 978-1-912950-37-9 (hardback)
978-1-912950-38-6 (softback)

Cover layout and design by Ian Whates
Text layout by Storm Constantine

CONTENTS

In memory of John Whates
(1932 – 2019)
My uncle, and a true Eastender

SOOT AND STEEL: AN INTRODUCTION

A few years back I stumbled on a slender novel called *The Hole in the Wall*, written by one Arthur Morrison and published in 1902. It told of a young lad, orphaned and subsequently raised by an uncle who ran a shady East End pub in docklands, where small-scale smuggling was not unknown. Within these pages lurked murder, mystery, a colourful cast of characters, and a powerful evocation of a bygone age that I found enthralling.

I suspect my decision to compile a London-inspired anthology stems in large part from reading that book.

My intention at outset was to publish a volume consisting entirely of original stories – as with so many previous anthologies – one that recalled London in former days. The brief was simple: I asked authors for genre-flavoured stories that focused on the capital's industrial past, the docks, Victoriana, the Blitz and the War; I asked them to expose the city's grim and sooty underbelly.

I reckon they've done me proud.

However, as submissions began to arrive, another thought occurred to me: in setting such a task, was I attempting to reinvent the wheel? After all, there have been many writers over the past 150 years who have written about the London of their day, who set ghost stories and murder mysteries in the capital's alleyways and night-shrouded streets. I started to delve, and after many glorious hours lost in old books and the far newer websites that reference them, I came up with seven pieces that could almost have been written for the anthology, though clearly they weren't – unless, that is, you give credence to the conjectures regarding the nature of time and our perception of it as featured in E.F. Benson's "The Tube". What a remarkable story this is. First published in 1922, it examines concepts that, decades later, would provide fertile ground for the imaginations of many a science fiction writer.

All seven 'classic' pieces featured here are worth noting, from

7

Henry Mayhew's simple but oh-so-revealing interview with a young girl selling watercress, to George Gissing's tale of a Camden bibliophile whose obsession puts his wife's life at risk, from Arthur Morrison's keenly observed "The Street" and "Behind the Shade" – the latter a cautionary tale of how pernicious the gossip of wagging tongues can be – to T.G. Jackson's chilling story of a family split asunder by a well-intentioned will and the unexpected terms it sets out. I owe Storm Constantine thanks for bringing Hume Nisbet's "The Phantom Model" to my attention. As with Benson's "The Tube", this is to some extent a ghost story, but again it delivers a good deal more than that broad label might imply.

These works from the Victorian and Edwardian eras sit comfortably beside the original stories, providing texture and context which the new pieces expand on. Indeed, Reggie Oliver's "A Maze for the Minotaur" might almost have been lifted from the Victorian age itself, so effectively does the author evoke the period. Set primarily in St John's Wood – a part of London I frequented a fair bit once upon a time – the story features a genuine historical resident of the area and is perfectly judged. Rose Biggin's contribution also has a historical figure at its heart, Dr Samuel Johnson, in a tale of deceit involving a supernatural hoax with a man's life at stake, as told by a ghost.

Juliet E. McKenna's "The Hand that Rocks the Cradle" was originally submitted for another project entirely, which sadly never came to fruition. The tale of a children's governess dismissed for no good reason and without recourse, who is directed to an institute with surprisingly progressive attitudes, it features cameos from a character or two who may seem familiar…

Paul Di Filippo delivers a delicious Sherlock Holmes tale, told from the perspective of Wiggins, leader of the Baker Street Irregulars – the Detective's network of street urchin informants – while Bryony Pearce tells of a man whose sustenance requires unique measures. Fortunately, on the streets of the capital the dead and the dying are never in short supply. David Rix takes us beneath those streets, to the malodorous world of the sewer rats and the mudlarks, while Terry Grimwood spins a steampunk fairy tale featuring a young Prince Albert, not long into his marriage with

Queen Victoria. This story also references the ancient spirit of the land, a theme that resonates with Susan Boulton's "Blood and Bone". Set during World War II, it recalls the halcyon days of high society and also the grim reality of the Blitz. The narrative focuses on efforts by the fire watch to protect St Paul's Cathedral and a reporter's determination to capture the perfect picture. Paul StJohn Mackintosh brings the volume right up to date with a contemporary tale of young love between two students in Southall, with more at stake than one of them could possibly realise.

Arthur Morrison's *The Hole in the Wall* certainly provided incentive for this book, but it was by no means the only catalyst. I come from London stock. My parents were both born and raised in the East End, my father within the sound of Bow Bells which officially qualifies him as Cockney. By the time I arrived they were financially stable and comfortably middle class, but that had not always been the case. My dad was one of five children, his father walking out on them while he was still a boy, leaving Nan to raise the family on her own – holding down four jobs in order to do so. Dad's first paid work involved fetching mugs of tea for the dockers. His career blossomed after he left the RAF, having survived WWII.

I vividly recall the annual pre-Christmas gatherings when the whole clan – the five children, their respective spouses and spawn – would descend upon Nan Whates' home: a council house in Barking. Woe betide anyone who couldn't make it; no excuses acceptable – *everyone* had to be at Nan's on that day. Later, it would be weddings and then funerals, but at that time these were the only occasions the whole family came together.

In addition to familial roots, my affinity with London owes much to the seven years I spent attending school in the City. From the age of ten onwards, I travelled in by train each morning to Farringdon Street and later Moorgate before walking to school, which faced the Thames at the foot of Blackfriars Bridge. I have fond memories of a rag-tag gang of us piling onto a convenient bus or charging down Farringdon Street – ties and jackets akimbo – on those rare occasions when school ended a little early, and leaping on the tube to King's Cross. We did so in hope of catching the early train, the 4.03, thereby reaching northern suburbs and leafy Hertfordshire ahead of schedule. Sometimes we made it, sometimes not, more than once watching in despair as the last carriage trundled away from the platform, tantalisingly out of reach, while we panted our frustration in its wake.

I have a kaleidoscope of memories relating to those schooldays in London – Royal Institute lectures in which I would invariably get drowsy despite them often being fascinating, ducking out of the opportunity to hear Tolkien speak because I'd yet to read *The Hobbit* and had never heard of him, the surreal wonder of singing in the Temple Church at Christmas, turning down an invitation to audition for the Chapel Royal because acceptance would have meant missing out on playing football at lunchtimes, the dreaded cross-country runs at Grove Park, downing a pint of beer without swallowing – falling short of the school record for doing so by fractions of a second – travelling in on a half-empty train for a Saturday morning detention due to some misdemeanour or other, winning the Lord Mayor's Prize for English for an essay titled "London the Living City", and being presented with said prize by the Mayor at Mansion House (£10.00 cash, which I spent before even returning home, stopping off at the much-missed Temple Records in Chancery Lane to buy *Yessongs*, a triple live LP by Yes)…

London has played a substantial role in shaping who I am, and I continue to savour each visit. It evolves constantly, as any city should, but that has never threatened the deep connection I feel with the Old Smoke, which manifests most obviously in my own writing through the character Chris – protagonist of the novella *The Smallest of Things* (PS Publishing, 2018) and several short stories. Chris can step between different realities, different versions of London, earning his keep as an investigator and fixer: finding things, making connections, solving problems.

In many ways, it was perhaps inevitable that at some point I would compile an anthology that focusses on London, its character, its charm, and its foibles. Here it is. I hope you enjoy.

Ian Whates
Cambridgeshire
May 2019

HUNGER

Bryony Pearce

The girl could have been no more than fourteen; body contorted from years of factory work, three fingers missing from her right hand. She had left the machinery, I assumed, as she grew less nimble and that had led her to Hyde Park after dark. Anything for a few shillings. Now she lay half in and half out of a pool of gaslight, tattered clothing stained with a mixture of blood and stagnant water, her remaining fingers stretched towards the gloom, reaching for comfort that would never arrive.

Perhaps for the first time in her life she had space. The horror of her end had forced even the hardened night-time crowd to give her a wide berth, preferring to splash through running sewage rather than tread on her spread skirts.

She had the face of an angel; grainy with soot, creased with habitual pain, but an angel nonetheless. Her eyes were a shocked blue, her nose straight, her mouth lax now but still perfectly rosy. It was the sound of her dying that had called me from my lodgings and now I knelt in the circle of repulsion her last moments had created, as the shoving, shuffling crowd surged around us.

To my relief, I was just in time. As I crouched, a spark flickered in her eyes; not hope, which had died long ago, but confusion. I imagined she saw my doctor's bag and, despite her injuries, remained able to wonder why such a fine gentleman might be risking his trousers by joining her in the dirt.

Hastily I removed an empty jar from its case and unscrewed the lid. Already the light in her eyes was fading as her breath hitched, once then twice. Blood foamed on her lips as she exhaled a third and final time. I pressed the maw of the jar to her fluttering mouth and the lamp above us hissed and flickered. As her chest stopped moving, we were plunged into noxious darkness, leaving me unsure:

had the jar filled? What if I had left a gap between the seal and those rosy lips? With infinite care I slid the jar sideways and over the upturned lid, which I turned on its thread until it groaned. With the trembling hands of a starving man, I held the jar, as if it were a piece of bread, tightly to my chest. Restraint was agony, but I would have to wait until I reached my laboratory to find out if I had succeeded.

Anticipation drove me to my feet as a solid stench slammed into me. I looked up into the eyes of the gong man, wheeling his barrow towards the Thames.

"She dead?" He tilted his head towards the girl. I nodded and raised my bag a little as I put the jar inside, knowing it would be explanation enough for him. I couldn't open my mouth to answer; the barrow trailed shit, its stained wood piss-soaked and reeking; already I wanted to retch. The man hawked and spat. "She'll be bound for St Brides then. I'll come back with me barrow. Unless you want the Peelers to see to 'er?"

I shook my head, watching with quiet horror as the man staggered on towards the river. So, a shit-soaked barrow was to be my angel's hearse, and her grave an open pit. I, more than anyone, should know how little it mattered, but I felt the bite of obligation. I strode after the man and with a shudder, made myself touch him on the shoulder. "Not St Brides." I pressed three shillings into his flaccid fingers.

The man blinked, then recovered, tucking the coins into a crusty handkerchief. "I'll treat her like me own daughter," he whispered hoarsely. "Bunhill Fields all right?"

I nodded and watched him as he coughed and sniffed his way into the soot-soaked night, then I turned and headed back towards my temporary home. Lamps cast shadows onto soot blackened walls, and the calls of prostitutes mingled with cries of street hawkers, doors slamming on arguments and the noise of revellers tumbling from public houses. Somewhere the girl's murderer sat, nursing a beer. Part of me wanted to hunt him down but, honestly, I saw no point in such theatrics. A heavy carriage rumbled towards me and I was forced to jump to one side, into the press of humanity. I felt hands in my jacket, and groping fingers nudged the clasp on my bag. I twisted and tightened my grip.

"Thieves!" I swung around, but the boys had melted into the crowd, vanishing like mist on a sunny day. Heart thumping, I checked the bag. The jar remained intact, my wallet was gone. The jar was the important thing; if they had only known. I wiped my brow and, with a curl of my lip, strode back over the road, wishing once again that I had never left the Auvergne, but knowing that I'd had no choice.

The dead and dying were never in such great supply as they were in London in this new age and I was so very, very hungry.

My man closed the door behind me and quiet wrapped us like a blanket. I shucked my coat. "I'll be in my workroom, Robert." I took the lidded jar from the bag and held it to the light, knowing as I did that no matter how full, I would see nothing with my naked eye.

"A successful outing, Master Roquetaillade?" Robert didn't meet my gaze. He never did. I nodded nevertheless.

"I believe so." My stomach rumbled and I reached a finger to my face. Creases beside my nose and wrinkles around my eyes: how long had they been there? No point in asking Robert. I glanced in the mirror. Grey at my temples. No wonder I felt half-starved.

My feet caught in the loose carpet as I strode towards the hall door, my left hip seized suddenly with an awful aching. I gasped as I staggered into the wall and gripped the jar to my chest. What if I had dropped it? I pictured the glass smashed on the flagstones. The horror.

I forced myself to limp slowly to my workroom. I had time to do this properly, no matter what the mirror told me. I had rushed before, but my angel deserved careful treatment.

The still was dripping just as I had left it. I placed the jar beside the bowl and slowly prepared mercury, vitriol and saltpetre, smiling as I remembered writing in my book all those centuries ago *'tout le secret est dans le sel'*: *'the whole secret is in salt'*. I had truly believed it. Now I grinned as I the joke struck me. *Sel* I had written. It sounded so much like *Soul* in the bastard English. Perhaps I had known, even then.

I dropped the crystals into the aqua vitae. They absorbed the liquid until glimmering white sand sat in the centre of the bowl. It was a process I had carried out a thousand-thousand times. I hesitated. Had it really been so many? I shook my head: no matter. Holding the jar upside down, I unscrewed the lid and attached the thread to the glass tube. Gently, I applied suction from the warmed bellows, if I had captured the soul, it would now be drawn down the tube and over the silt.

I watched avidly, my eyes watering from the intensity of my scrutiny. There would be a colour change when the soul was absorbed. Each time it was different, some turned the mixture gold, or gleaming copper; some blue, or red. I believed it was much to do with who the person had been. I felt sure that my angel would be gold. I pressed closer to the bowl. It had been years since I had created gold. "Please," I whispered.

The grit sat untouched, unchanged. "No." I stared. "I captured you. I know I did." But I remembered the darkness and my chest tightened. I worked the bellows again, my arms aching in time with my hip. My eyes were watering now, my vision blurring.

I blinked, refocused and there, finally was a transformation. The white sheen faded from the silt in the bowl and it dulled, almost as if a corruption was creeping over it. When the colour settled, I had a lumpen grey-brown mixture, pale and stippled with white, barely changed at all.

My yell of rage brought Robert running. "Master?"

"It happened again." I turned to the wall, shuddering as I suppressed the need to smash the equipment that had failed me.

"The soul escaped?" Robert stared at his hands.

"Non." I closed my eyes. "Transformation occurred. But it was... corrupt, weak. Like all the others have been recently. I don't understand." I spun around. "One soul is no longer enough to create a stone. I need another, quickly."

"The slums?" Robert asked as I limped towards the door. My hand twitched, muscle memory demanding I complete the final step in the process. My stomach growled. I needed to devour the soul, but if I did, it would be water to a starving man. I clenched my fists.

"Is there still cholera in Broad Street?" I turned as I reached the door and Robert nodded, still without meeting my eyes. "Then that is where we shall go."

I returned with a further two jars. They had been easy enough to fill. Posing as a doctor in an area plagued with disease allowed me into any of the tiny crowded rooms that took my fancy. More problematic was taking the soul in front of the family, but I told them it was a way to stop the illness spreading. The poor were credulous. So were the rich I suppose, when their lives were on the line; there was little to divide them in the fear of death.

In my bag I carried a small boy and his grandmother. I had never created a stone with mixed souls before, it had seemed disrespectful, and there had never been a need. But desperate times...

I watched as first one and then the next darkened the silt. Then I compressed the grit into a tablet, took it from the bowl and turned it over in my hand. It sat lumpen in my palm, the colour of old char. It was hardly appetising, yet my gut twisted and I wrapped an arm around the emptiness inside me.

"Master?"

"Leave me, Robert." I put the stone in my mouth and sucked. It was salty, like tears. Nevertheless, even as Robert closed the door, the ache in my hip subsided. I crunched, and the sour crystals dissolved between my teeth. Three souls spread through my body and yet... it was drinking stagnant water when used to champagne. Bile smashed back up my throat and I bent double, splashing vomit into the corner of the room. What, in the name of heaven, was happening?

"It's the disease," I snapped as I sat shivering by the fire. "How can I expect to be restored by diseased souls?"

"But Master," Robert placed a steaming mug on the table beside me. "The soul should remain untouched by the travails of the body. You took the plague-touched in France with no difficulties."

"Could the physical translate into spiritual pain perhaps?" I stroked my eyes. The creases had plumped out, but I felt traces of them, under the skin, ready to return.

"It hasn't before."

"No." I stared into the flames. "Then what has changed, Robert? What has weakened these souls, made them worthless?"

"Perhaps we should leave London – return home?" There was hope in his voice.

I shook my head. "I need souls, Robert, in greater numbers than ever. Where else would I find enough to feed me, but in a city of a million people?" I sipped my toddy. "Perhaps it is my own age." I gazed into the flickering depths. "I am so very old now."

Robert fixed his own gaze on the portrait above the fireplace. "You *will* solve this problem."

I nodded. "I need more souls." I whispered. "More souls."

The man was showing no signs of illness. In a city where death stalked every corner, he was hale as an oak. I stood in the doorway and watched. He carried a fiddle under one arm and his voice, when he spoke, was mellifluous. I imagined he sang beautifully. His face was homely; pox-scarred and broken-nosed, but there was something about his broad grin that called people to smile back. He had smiled at me when I was in Broad Street and called me, not to smile but, to follow.

I was so very hungry.

It had been a century since I had thrown off my monk's habit, but I still believed I was being guided and I had found *this* man. After all, Plato said *music gives soul to the universe.* This was a musician. His soul would feed me for a month, more perhaps. And yet... he was not sick.

I fingered my bag. What if he were to have an accident? A mugging, a fight, a fall? He might contract an infection or be knocked over by a horse – there were so many ways to die in London. I watched the people around him closely. None seemed any more criminal than the others. He laughed in the centre of the group, tossing his shaggy hair back, light catching his eyes.

I turned and walked away.

"May the Lord save you."

I looked up. I had limped blindly as far as the mill works in Soho, my hip a burning pain, my bag of jars knocking against my leg. Around me, the walls were black and the sounds of human misery mixed with the roar and creak of machinery.

Why had I come here? Deaths in this place were sudden and bloody. Too sudden for my work; a last breath been and done before the body knew the soul was fleeing. A line of exhausted, partially deformed, soot-grimed workers straggled through a side-door; their eyes dull, coughing as they marched or spitting blood into the overflowing gutter. I pictured my angel among them, her back twisted, her aching hand clutched to her chest.

"Lord save you." The voice repeated and I turned. There was a priest by the factory gate, a Bible held to his breast like shield. "You're a doctor?"

I lifted my bag in silence and he gasped and stepped forward. "There is so much work to be done here. If a *doctor* were to speak to the foreman about the conditions –"

"Stick it up yer arse, priest." A trio of men were marching towards us. "You want to stop these men and women getting paid? You're going the right way about it."

"No, that's not –"

"Leave. Go on, take yer whining and yer pet *doctor* and get!"

The priest straightened his back. "I have the Lord to protect me," he quavered. His face was flushed and he trembled like an ash in a gale, but he stood his ground.

One of the men bent, scooped a rock from the muck and threw it. The Priest ducked too slowly. The missile struck the side of his head with a hollow thud. I moved without thought and caught him before he hit the ground.

"Go on, git." Two of the men were laughing, the third was pale and staring from his throwing hand to the muddy Bible that lay fluttering in a puddle by my feet.

I put a shoulder under the groaning priest and started to walk. His feet dragged, his head nodded and he was a dead weight, but his black robe hid a frail and skinny frame and, despite the pain in my hip, I was able to carry both him and my bag of jars, which clattered as we staggered like drunks towards Waterloo.

The priest came-to once we were out of sight of the belching factory, and I helped him to sit on a sagging bench in a little square. He was barely able to focus his gaze, bleary and confused, and sudden heat filled my palms with sweat.

17

"Are you all right?" I wiped my hands on my trousers and the priest nodded carefully but the right side of his face was bloody and he touched his fingers to the gash.

"You're... French?" He asked after a long moment. "Your accent..."

I nodded. "A long time ago."

"So –" he stopped and looked at his fingers. "The conditions in those factories." He groaned. "They're beasts... eating people, chewing them up and spitting them out. Children... men and women. They arrive here from the countryside thinking they'll have a better life, full of hope and hunger and in weeks they're nothing but fodder for the machines. Dead inside. It has to stop."

"Dead inside?" I echoed.

"Yes," the priest focused on me with difficultly. "You were there to help, weren't you?"

"I was... lost," I said sadly. "But I think you may have found me." I looked, really *looked* at the sickly wall of smog; it clung to the thick mist from the river, creating a miasma that covered the streets with haze. I strained my ears, listening to the sounds around us: children's cries, shouts of anger, barking coughs, sporadic cruel laughter. I turned my face up and realised that I couldn't see the sky through the belching smoke. How long had it been since I had seen the sun? "Dead inside," I repeated. And I thought back: was it possible that the souls I had been collecting had started to fail at around the time the factories... I stared at the priest. "But... you're not," I said and my stomach growled.

He shook his head. "I'd like to think that I –"

I stopped listening; the blood pounded in my ears, drowning out all other sound. I could see his lips moving but heard nothing but the drumming of my own pulse. I looked at my hands, age-spotted and starting to curl arthritically. I touched my face; carrying the man had tired me.

"How old do you think I am?" I interrupted him, and he blinked.

"I don't want to offend –" he started.

"How old?" I rasped.

"Perhaps... sixty." The priest stammered. "You carried me here, yet you're not a young man. I'm so grate –"

"Sixty." I touched my face again. "Sixty!" I had never before appeared a day over forty-five.

The gnawing in my stomach grew until it seemed my belly would erupt. I moaned and folded over.

"Are you all –?"

I had only ever taken the souls of the dying, those my travels had led me to. Those the *Lord* had led me to. Now He had led me here. I had never injured another man. But I was so *hungry*.

I lunged.

I was old but the priest was frail and his head still bleeding.

There were so many ways to die in London; so much the smog could hide. I heard others in the square, but saw only ghostly shapes which moved no closer, repelled rather than called by the priest's choking cries.

His heart beat against my chest as he tried to tear my hands free. My face pressed against his, in an embrace so intimate that I felt the moment he gave up and his heart slowed to almost nothing. I gave one final tight squeeze and then released his throat, letting him sag back on the bench. I opened my bag, took out a jar and pressed it to his lips. "I'm sorry!" I whispered.

As I sucked the gold stone, life returned to my limbs and the priest's soul faded into the thousands that had already fed my own.

"Has it occurred to you, Master, that the priest's work might have saved your own?" Robert said afterwards, his eyes pinned to the floor.

I refused to consider his question. "Why do you never look at me, Robert?" He kept his eyes on the flagstones. "Never mind." I licked my lips. "I feel better than I have in years and now I know what I have to do." I looked around my workshop until I located a particularly wicked looking hook. "There's a musician I need to find. I believe that his soul too, would make gold."

I marched from the laboratory and, for the first time, as I climbed the stairs with my bag and hook, I felt Robert's eyes burn into my back. He was finally looking at me. The heat of his gaze was searing, but I did not turn around.

After all, I was getting hungry.

A STREET

Arthur Morrison

This street is in the East End. There is no need to say in the East End of what. The East End is a vast city, as famous in its way as any the hand of man has made. But who knows the East End? It is down through Cornhill and out beyond Leadenhall Street and Aldgate Pump, one will say: a shocking place, where he once went with a curate; an evil plexus of slums that hide human creeping things, where filthy men and women live on penn'orths of gin, where collars and clean shirts are decencies unknown, where every citizen wears a black eye, and none ever combs his hair. The East End is a place, says another, which is given over to the Unemployed. And the Unemployed is a race whose token is a clay pipe, and whose enemy is soap: now and again it migrates bodily to Hyde Park with banners, and furnishes adjacent police courts with disorderly drunks. Still another knows the East End only as the place whence begging letters come; there are coal and blanket funds there, all perennially insolvent, and everybody always wants a day in the country. Many and misty are people's notions of the East End; and each is commonly but the distorted shadow of a minor feature. Foul slums there are in the East End, of course, as there are in the West; want and misery there are, as wherever a host is gathered together to fight for food. But they are not often spectacular in kind.

Of this street there are about one hundred and fifty yards – on the same pattern all. It is not pretty to look at. A dingy little brick house twenty feet high, with three square holes to carry the windows, and an oblong hole to carry the door, is not a pleasing object; and each side of this street is formed by two or three score of such houses in a row, with one front wall in common. And the effect is as of stables.

Round the corner there are a baker's, a chandler's, and a beer-shop. They are not included in the view from any of the rectangular holes; but they are well known to every denizen, and the chandler goes to church on Sunday and pays for his seat. At the opposite end, turnings lead to streets less rigidly respectable: somewhere 'Mangling Done Here' stares from windows, and where doors are left carelessly open; others where squalid women sit on doorsteps, and girls go to factories in white aprons. Many such turnings, of as many grades of decency, are set between this and the nearest slum.

They are not a very noisy or obtrusive lot in this street. They do not go to Hyde Park with banners, and they seldom fight. It is just possible that one or two among them, at some point in a life of ups and downs, may have been indebted to a coal and blanket fund; but whosoever these may be, they would rather die than publish the disgrace, and it is probable that they very nearly did so ere submitting to it.

Some who inhabit this street are in the docks, some in the gasworks, some in one or other of the few shipbuilding yards that yet survive on the Thames. Two families in a house is the general rule, for there are six rooms behind each set of holes: this, unless 'young men lodgers' are taken in, or there are grown sons paying for bed and board. As for the grown daughters, they marry as soon as may be. Domestic service is a social descent, and little under millinery and dressmaking is compatible with self-respect. The general servant may be caught young among the turnings at the end where mangling is done; and the factory girls live still further off, in places skirting slums.

Every morning at half-past five there is a curious demonstration. The street resounds with thunderous knockings, repeated upon door after door, and acknowledged ever by a muffled shout from within. These signals are the work of the night-watchman or the early policeman, or both, and they summon the sleepers to go forth to the docks, the gasworks, and the ship-yards. To be awakened in this wise costs fourpence a week, and for this fourpence a fierce rivalry rages between night-watchmen and policemen. The night-watchman – a sort of by-blow of the ancient 'Charley', and himself a fast vanishing quantity – is the real professional performer; but he goes to the wall, because a large connection must be worked if the pursuit is to pay at fourpence a knocker. Now, it is not easy to bang at two knockers three-quarters of a mile apart, and a hundred others lying between, all punctually at half-past five. Wherefore the policeman, to whom the fourpence is but a perquisite, and who is content with a smaller round, is rapidly supplanting the night-watchman, whose cry of "Past nine o'clock," as he collects orders in the evening, is now seldom heard.

The knocking and the shouting pass, and there comes the noise of opening and shutting of doors, and a clattering away to the docks, the gasworks and the ship-yards. Later more door-shutting is heard, and then the trotting of sorrow-laden little feet along the grim street to the grim Board School three grim streets off. Then silence, save for a subdued sound of scrubbing here and there, and the puny squall of croupy infants. After this, a new trotting of little feet to docks, gasworks, and ship-yards with father's dinner in a basin and a red handkerchief, and so to the Board School again. More muffled scrubbing and more squalling, and perhaps a feeble attempt or two at decorating the blankness of a square hole here and there by pouring water into a grimy flower-pot full of dirt. Then comes the trot of little feet toward the oblong holes, heralding the slower tread of sooty artisans; a smell of bloater up and down; nightfall; the fighting of boys in the street, perhaps of men at the corner near the beer-shop; sleep. And this is the record of a day in this street; and every day is hopelessly the same.

Every day, that is, but Sunday. On Sunday morning a smell of cooking floats round the corner from the half-shut baker's, and the little feet trot down the street under steaming burdens of beef, potatoes, and batter pudding – the lucky little feet these, with Sunday boots on them, when father is in good work and has brought home all his money; not the poor little feet in worn shoes, carrying little bodies in the threadbare clothes of all the week, when father is out of work, or ill, or drunk, and the Sunday cooking may very easily be done at home – if any there be to do.

On Sunday morning one or two heads of families appear in wonderful black suits, with unnumbered creases and wrinklings at the seams. At their sides and about their heels trot the unresting little feet, and from under painful little velvet caps and straw hats stare solemn little faces towelled to a polish. Thus disposed and arrayed, they fare gravely through the grim little streets to a grim Little Bethel where are gathered together others in like garb and attendance; and for two hours they endure the frantic menace of hell-fire.

Most of the men, however, lie in shirt and trousers on their beds and read the Sunday paper; while some are driven forth — for they hinder the housework — to loaf, and await the opening of the beer-shop round the corner. Thus goes Sunday in this street, and every Sunday is the same as every other Sunday, so that one monotony is broken with another. For the women, however, Sunday is much asother days, except that there is rather more work for them. The break in their round of the week is washing day.

No event in the outer world makes any impression in this street. Nations may rise, or may totter in ruin; but here the colorless day will work through its twenty-four hours just as it did yesterday, and just as it will to-morrow. Without there may be party strife, wars and rumors of wars, public rejoicings; but the trotting of the little feet will be neither quickened nor stayed. Those quaint little women, the girl-children of this street, who use a motherly management toward all girl-things younger than themselves, and toward all boys as old or older, with 'Bless the child!' or 'Drat the children!' — those quaint little women will still go marketing with big baskets, and will regard the price of bacon as chief among human considerations. Nothing disturbs this street — nothing but a strike.

Nobody laughs here — life is too serious a thing; nobody sings. There was once a woman who sang — a young wife from the country. But she bore children, and her voice cracked. Then her man died, and she sang no more. They took away her home, and with her children about her skirts she left this street forever. The other women did not think much of her. She was 'helpless'.

One of the square holes in this street — one of the single, ground-floor holes — is found, on individual examination, to differ from the others. There has been an attempt to make it into a shop-window. Half a dozen candles, a few sickly sugar-sticks, certain shrivelled bloaters, some bootlaces, and a bundle or two of firewood compose a stock which at night is sometimes lighted by a little paraffine lamp in a tin sconce, and sometimes by a candle. A widow lives here – a gaunt, bony widow, with sunken, red eyes. She has other sources of income than the candles and the bootlaces: she washes and chars all day, and she sews cheap shirts at night. Two 'young men lodgers', moreover, sleep upstairs, and the children sleep in the back room; she herself is supposed not to sleep at all. The policeman does not knock here in the morning – the widow wakes the lodgers herself; and nobody in the street behind ever looks out of window before going to bed, no matter how late, without seeing a light in the widow's room where she plies her needle. She is a quiet woman, who speaks little with her neighbours, having other things to do: a woman of pronounced character, to whom it would be unadvisable – even dangerous – to offer coals or blankets. Hers was the strongest contempt for the helpless woman who sang: a contempt whose added bitterness might be traced to its source. For when the singing woman was marketing, from which door of the pawnshop had she twice met the widow coming forth?

This is not a dirty street, taken as a whole. The widow's house is one of the cleanest, and the widow's children match the house. The one house cleaner than the widow's is ruled by a despotic Scotchwoman, who drives every hawker off her whitened step, and rubs her door handle if a hand have rested on it. The Scotchwoman has made several attempts to accommodate 'young men lodgers', but they have ended in shrill rows.

There is no house without children in this street, and the number of them grows ever and ever greater. Nine-tenths of the doctor's visits are on this account alone, and his appearances are the chief matter of such conversation as the women make across the fences. One after another the little strangers come, to live through lives as flat and colourless as the day's life in this street. Existence dawns, and the doctor-watchman's door knock resounds along the row of rectangular holes. Then a muffled cry announces that a small new being has come to trudge and sweat its way in the appointed groove. Later, the trotting of little feet and the school; the midday play hour, when love peeps even into this street; after that more trotting of little feet – strange little feet, new little feet – and the scrubbing, and the squalling, and the barren flower-pot; the end of the sooty day's work; the last home-coming; nightfall; sleep.

When love's light falls into some corner of the street, it falls at an early hour of this mean life, and is itself but a dusty ray. It falls early, because it is the sole bright thing which the street sees, and is watched for and counted on. Lads and lasses, awkwardly arm in arm, go pacing up and down this street, before the natural interest in marbles and doll's houses would have left them in a brighter place. They are 'keeping company'; the manner of which proceeding is indigenous – is a custom native to the place. The young people first 'walk out' in pairs. There is no exchange of promises, no troth-plight, no engagement, no love-talk. They patrol the street side by side, usually in silence, sometimes with fatuous chatter. There are no dances, no tennis, no water-parties, no picnics to bring them together: so they must walk out, or be unacquainted. If two of them grow dissatisfied with each other's company, nothing is easier than to separate and walk out with somebody else. When by these means each has found a fit mate (or thinks so), a ring is bought, and the odd association becomes a regular engagement; but this is not until the walking out has endured for many months. The two stages of courtship are spoken of indiscriminately as 'keeping company', but a very careful distinction is drawn between them by the parties concerned. Nevertheless, in the walking out period it would be almost as great a breach of faith for either to walk out with more than one, as it would be if the full engagement had been made. And love-making in this street is a dreary thing, when one thinks of love-making in other places. It begins – and it ends – too soon.

Nobody from this street goes to the theatre. That would mean a long journey, and it would cost money which might buy bread and beer and boots. For those, too, who wear black Sunday suits it would be sinful. Nobody reads poetry or romance. The very words are foreign. A Sunday paper in some few houses provides such reading as this street is disposed to achieve. Now and again a penny novel has been found among the private treasures of a growing daughter, and has been wrathfully confiscated. For the air of this street is unfavourable to the ideal.

Yet there are aspirations. There has lately come into the street a young man lodger who belongs to a Mutual Improvement Society. Membership in this society is regarded as a sort of learned degree, and at its meetings debates are held and papers smugly read by lamentably self-satisfied young men lodgers, whose only preparation for debating and writing is a fathomless ignorance. For ignorance is the inevitable portion of dwellers here: seeing nothing, reading nothing, and considering nothing.

Where in the East End lies this street? Everywhere. The hundred and fifty yards is only a link in a long and a mightily tangled chain – is only a turn in a tortuous maze. This street of the square holes is hundreds of miles long. That it is planned in short lengths is true, but there is no other way in the world that can more properly be called a single street, because of its dismal lack of accent, its sordid uniformity, its utter remoteness from delight.

A MAZE FOR THE MINOTAUR

Reggie Oliver

From the *Marylebone Gazette* December 15th 1897

Strange Disappearance Of Local Philanthropist

Mr Frederick Cooper has mysteriously disappeared from his home in Melina Grove NW. A wealthy commercial gentleman of, we are told, philanthropic interests, he was chiefly noted in the district for driving a smart two horse phaeton, usually with a groom in the dickey. On the afternoon of December 10th, despite a mist having descended, he went for his customary drive, leaving the groom behind in the mews at the back of his house. A little over two hours later, he returned to Melina Mews. The groom, Laird by name, saw Mr Cooper descend from the carriage and signal to him to unharness the carriage and stable the horses. Then Laird saw him walk round into Melina Grove, apparently to enter his house by the front door, but he never arrived. It was some hours before it was realised that something was amiss, the alarm being finally raised by Mr Cooper's wife, but by that time it was dark and very foggy withal. Intensive searches and enquiries were instituted by the local Constabulary in the surrounding area the following morning, but to no avail. Not a single clue as to his fate has as yet been made manifest. Mr Cooper has the reputation of being a man of somewhat eccentric habits and is known by some, for reasons we cannot ascertain, as The Minotaur. The only certainty is that he has vanished into the mists of a most baffling labyrinth.

"Does he come today?"

"I doubt it, my dear," said Mrs Belling, "the Minotaur rarely comes on Fridays. Surely you remember?"

"Oh, yes," said Mabel with a little sigh of relief. "I was forgetting."

"But Lord Arthur is due at any moment."

"Will, he wish to see *me*, Mrs Belling?"

"Of course, my dear. He always does."

Mabel seated herself in the window of Mrs Belling's 'drawing room', as she chose to call it (rather than a 'parlour'), and looked down onto the garden below. It was nothing very special in the way of front gardens, just a patch of lawn surrounded by a few disconsolate bushes, but Mabel viewed it with satisfaction. It was so different from what she had known before. It was a September afternoon in the year 1897 and the first sere notes were beginning to manifest themselves in the trees and shrubberies of St John's Wood.

The house, Number 2 Boscobel Place, stood in a street of similar white stucco houses, with small front gardens surrounded by high brick walls. The doors in the high brick walls were usually painted green and had in them small square metal grilles through which the visitor might see in and perhaps determine whether the occupants were at home.

It was a leafy, oddly secretive place, St John's Wood in those days: too grand to be called a London suburb, almost fashionable, but Belgravia or Mayfair it was not. It has been called 'a metropolitan oasis... with a peculiar moral and aesthetic character.'[1] Some successful artists inhabited 'the Grove of the Evangelist', as the more aesthetically inclined among them would call it, and theatre people of the better class, a smattering of writers, and some others of more dubious standing. The gentry, the aristocrats, the purple of commerce (as Oscar Wilde would say) did not often dwell there, but they visited.

It was a quiet place too, before the traffic came. There were the visiting carriages, the grocer's van, the butcher and baker with their deliveries. Every month or so the secluded streets would echo to the cry "Rag-a-bone! Rag-a-bone!" as the rag and bone man passed with

---

[1] From *St John's Wood, its History, its Houses, its Haunts and its Celebrities* by Alan Montgomery Eyre (Chapman and Hall 1913) A very brief and incomplete account of the legend of The Minotaur of St John's Wood may be found therein.

his open cart drawn by a single, shambling old cob. It was a cry that for Mabel brought back the streets where she was raised, and she did not welcome it, but today the afternoon avenues, muffled by the leaves of early autumn were all but silent. She was at peace, as far as one could be while waiting for the first client of the day. Lord Arthur was not an unpleasant man, and, though on the wrong side of forty years old, still within hailing distance of it. Not like The Minotaur.

Effie entered the room, young and high spirited. Many, herself included, would have said she was prettier than Mabel: certainly she dressed more flamboyantly; but, as Mrs Belling, said: "Many of my gentlemen prefer the quiet ones." Mabel looked up and smiled. She liked Effie's gaiety even though she could not always respond to it.

"Well, here I am," she said, performing a little pirouette to emphasize the fact.

"So I should think," said Mrs Belling. "Getting up at all hours, and your gentleman expected any minute. Have you eaten, my girl? Go down to Mrs Mason and get yourself something. There's bread in the crocket and tea on the hob."

"Oh, Mrs B, you have a heart of gold," said Effie, whirling Mrs Belling's stout form around in an impromptu waltz.

"Get along with you, girl!" said Mrs Belling, disengaging herself and puffing hard from the exertion. She did not seem altogether displeased, though. The quiet when Effie had left the room was palpable.

"Mrs Belling," said Mabel, "why do they call him the Minotaur?"

"Lord, what a question! Well in the first place, we don't know his true name, but Lord Arthur when I told him about his doings — he likes to hear about such things while he has his sherry — he says: 'My word, he sounds like a proper old Minotaur.' and then he says something in Latin. And every time after that, he asks after 'the Minotaur'. Maybe it's because of that mask he wears."

"I don't like that mask, Mrs Belling. It gives me the shudders."

"Well, he doesn't do no harm. Not really."

"And I don't like being all sticky afterwards."

"I know, dear, but you girls always get a good old rub down once he's gone." The bell rang. "Oh, gracious! That must be Lord

31

Arthur. Make yourself presentable, my girl."

Mrs Belling came over and pinched Mabel's cheeks to put a blush in them. She always did this before the arrival of a client and it did hurt a little. Mabel on the whole liked Mrs Belling, who could be kind as long as you did as you were told, but there were occasions when an underlying harshness was evident. The cheek pinching was one such example, but never in her previous existence had Mabel been treated with such consideration, so she made allowances. Maybe, too, Mrs Belling had not liked being asked too many questions about one of her most profitable clients.

"*I come from the haunts of coot and hern!*" said Lord Arthur Brook on being shown into the drawing room by the maid. It was a verbal sally with which he often made an entrance at Mrs Belling's, especially when, as on this occasion, he had just arrived from the country and was wearing tweeds.

"Oh, Lord Arthur, you are a one!" said Mrs Belling, her customary response.

Lord Arthur, a younger son of the Marquess of Martlesham, was not very distinguished in appearance: florid, balding, inclined to stoutness, but quite pleasant looking. Like many Old Etonians he gave the impression of having received an education more extensive than his capacity to do anything useful with it. Politics he had considered, but then, perhaps sensibly, had given up in favour of complete idleness. He was a man who had made no mark on the world beyond marrying a wealthy cousin and siring two sons, but he liked to think of himself as a bit of a character. He carried about with him the remnants of sound learning and a taste for the arts slightly in advance of the majority of his peers. The quotation with which he announced his presence was from Tennyson's "The Brook", and the implied pun was of his own devising. He prided himself on it, but he would never have deigned to explain it to the likes of Mrs Belling or her girls. Their ignorance was all part of the fun.

Effie entered the room with a flourish.

"Oh, Lord Arthur, this is an unexpected pleasure!"

"Hello, Effie," said Lord Arthur offhandedly before turning his attention to Mabel. "Miss Mabel, how have you been keeping?"

Mabel had risen and given Lord Arthur a demure little curtsey. "Pining away in my absence, what?"

"Thank you, Lord Arthur, I have been very well."

Effie gave a little pout and left the room. She could never understand why Lord Arthur preferred "Mousy Mabel" to her. Effie would have liked to have added a titled gentleman to her retinue. Mrs Belling looked on and understood perfectly.

"Would you care for some refreshment after your journey, Lord Arthur?" she asked. Like so many things at Number 2 Boscobel Place this speech was a formality which received the anticipated response.

"Thank you, Mrs B, I'm much obliged but I'll take a sherry and a biscuit with you afterwards. And now, Miss Mabel, if you would be so kind as to lead the way?"

Mabel took the proffered oil lamp from the maid and led the way up to the second floor bedroom which was their customary place of assignation.

After the business was done, Lord Arthur liked to dress slowly while Mabel lay stretched on the bed, naked. The dressing table mirror was so placed that he could adjust his necktie and watch her small languid movements on the bed at the same time. Lord Arthur flattered himself on the refined pleasure he took in these moments.

"You look like one of Mr Poynter's sea nymphs," Lord Arthur had said to her on one such occasion. It was an apposite remark. Mabel possessed an exquisite figure, and had worked as a model, though not for Mr. Edward Poynter R A. She knew how to pose on a bed, and had for a while been a model at the St John's Wood Art School. It was while working there that she came to the notice of Mrs Belling, who had offered her a more lucrative and less tiring means of employment.

"Lord Arthur, what do you know about the Minotaur?"

"Good gracious, girl, what a question!"

"I beg your pardon, Lord Arthur."

"No, no! No offence, little girl." Lord Arthur was in an emollient mood. He had performed to his own satisfaction, if to no one else's and was not indisposed to chat. He left the mirror and came to sit on the edge of the bed. His hand stroked Mabel's soft and perfectly shaped left thigh. It was another of those exquisite pleasures which seemed to him even more delightful than the act itself.

"I shouldn't trouble your pretty head over old *semibovemque virum semivirumque bovem.*" He laughed at Mabel's puzzled frown. "He's certainly a rum 'un and no mistake."

"Do you know who he is?"

"I do, Miss Mabel. As a matter of fact I made some enquiries, but the results are not for the likes of you, lassie. I will only say that he is a man of much substance, but not a gentleman, I fear. Made his money out of jute, I understand. Though what one does with jute, I have never been able to grasp. Does one eat it? Does one weave it? Import it? Export it? Who knows? Perhaps you should ask the fellow next time he calls." And with that he slapped her bare thigh and resumed his dressing. The rose coloured imprint of his hand stung for quite some time. Mabel wiped away a tear and waited for the pain (and the mark) to fade before she asked another question, but she was ignored. Lord Arthur was trimming his moustache in the mirror.

Mabel had learned to disguise her passions well, but once they had been aroused she would doggedly pursue them until they were satisfied. She was not sure why her curiosity about the Minotaur had been so stimulated, nor why she hated him so vehemently, but somehow the hatred and the curiosity were connected. The other girls just thought it was a lark, 'money for jam', as one of them had rather wittily put it, but Mabel did not.

When Lord Arthur had gone, Mabel told Mrs Belling that she would briefly go out for a walk, and to post a letter. Mrs Belling nodded approvingly: she considered Mabel to be a good girl, because she behaved herself demurely with clients and never went absent without leave as some of her girls did. As for Mabel, familiarity had not yet worn away the charm of pleasant surroundings and an absence of money worries for the first time in her life. She was only just beginning to chafe at her employer's restrictions. As for the nature of her work, it had been a part of her life for a long while, long before Mrs Belling, and not always in the safest of environments. Mabel had learned to bury its ugliness deep inside her, and yet a man like the Minotaur could arouse the latent horror. Why exactly?

Mabel finished the letter to her cousin. To Cousin Margery, the poor but respectable wife of a country schoolmaster, Mabel presented herself as an artist's model and a dancer in musical shows, both of which she had once been. Cousin Margery was not to know that St John's Wood was a rather grand address for a mere chorine.

It was still light when Mabel went out but a London fog was descending, in consequence of which the lamplighters were about their work. The street lights were surrounded by an aureole of bright mist, similar to that which Mabel had seen encircling the head of Christ in paintings. She reached the corner of Acacia Avenue where stood the pillar box and posted the letter. She felt a momentary pang as she committed her little budget of half-truths to the darkness beyond the scarlet lips of the post box.

"Hello, Mabel!"

The voice, immediately familiar yet not so quickly identified, made her gasp. She turned and saw a young woman, smaller than her and wrapped against the chill of the fog in a grimy plaid shawl.

"Lily! What are you doing here?"

"Ain't you pleased to see your little sister? My you're looking smart. We don't see you these days. Don't you want to know your own flesh and blood?"

Mabel felt cold. She knew how she must look to her sister. "How have you been?" she asked.

"Very kind of you to ask, I'm sure," said her sister, putting on an absurdly genteel voice. It occurred to Mabel that Lily might be imitating her accent, acquired partly through natural absorption, partly from Mrs Belling's deliberate tuition. To return her voice now to its old ways would be to insult Lily still further; she would have to continue to sound prim and proper.

"You look well," said Mabel.

"Ta very much, Mabel. I'm not so bad. Ma's the same. Maybe worse. I'm trying to look after her a bit, but everything I gives her goes on drink."

"Oh."

"Yes. That's all on yours truly now. Never a word from you, let alone a visit."

"I didn't know where you were. We lost touch."

"You could have tried to find out. I've found *you*."

"Yes, but that's…"

"Easier? Well, it would be, wouldn't it? Ain't no excuse."

"No," said Mabel. She looked in her purse and found a half sovereign. "Here," she said, proffering the coin. "It's all I've got just now. Could you use it, Lil?"

Mabel knew that if this were a melodrama, her offer would be greeted by an heroically indignant refusal; but, this being reality, Lily took the coin and said: "Thanks. And don't think I won't be back for more. Are you going to show me where you live?"

"This way. I'm afraid I can't ask you in. We will be receiving callers shortly."

"Not good enough for the likes of me, eh?"

"No, it's not that, Lil…" But perhaps it was. Lily was not bad looking, but her face and figure lacked Mabel's natural refinement. As for her clothes, Mabel could hardly bring herself to look at them, while feeling shame at her own fastidiousness. The two walked slowly up towards Boscobel Place, exchanging news. Lily was still 'at the game', "like you are," she added, looking accusingly at her sister.

They were approaching Number 2 when a two horse phaeton with a groom in the dickey came round the corner and stopped in front of the house. The driver, caped and hatted, was a large man in black who clambered awkwardly down from the driving seat, assisted by the groom, a swarthy little fellow who looked almost dwarfish by comparison. The big man threw the reins at the groom who proceeded to attend to the horses while his master rang the bell outside the gate of Number 2. Lily drew her sister against the high wall that ran along the street.

"'Struth almighty, I know that old rotter." So did Mabel. The big man was the Minotaur. Even in the thickening light he could be identified by his huge, barrel-chested bulk, and the leprous whiteness of his skin. "Looks like you know him too."

"I know he comes to us. He's known as the Minotaur. I don't know his real name or nothing."

"Nor do I. But we call him the Beast."

"Why?"

"You should know. A right nasty piece of work, that one. But he pays."

"I must get back, Lil, now he's here."

"Sooner you than me, Mabel love."

"Quickly, Lil: when, where can I see you again?"

"Oh, so you're not too grand to know your little sister after all. Most evenings you'll find me at the Empire Promenade. If I'm lucky not after eight. Don't look so shocked. I'm the same as you even if I don't do it in a swanky St John's Wood 'residence'. Well, tata for now."

The next minute Lily was gone, swallowed up in the deepening twilight and thickening fog. Mabel felt a peculiar revulsion at having to enter through the gate of Number 2 under the eye of the groom. She had barely noticed him before. He stared at her while he held the horses and breathed steam into their nostrils to calm them. Greying blackish curls sprang from under a greasy forage cap. His face was deeply lined; there was an old, hungry look about him.

When Mabel entered the house, Mrs Belling said: "Where have you *been*? Come on, girl, he's here."

"I know," said Mabel and hurried upstairs to undress.

She came downstairs with the other girls. There were four of them: Effie, Mabel, Rose and Charlotte, and they all wore thin robes of Chinese silk over their naked bodies. Effie, Rose and Charlotte were giggling but Mabel was silent. In the drawing room all the furniture had been moved to the edges of the room. Mrs Belling was sitting (fully dressed) at an upright piano. Candles in elaborate brass sconces illuminated the sheet music on the piano's stand. She was practising *Ta-ra-ra Boomdeay* which was giving her some trouble.

"Quiet now, girls," said Mrs Belling. "I can't hear myself play with you giggling away like that." There was silence while Mrs Belling launched into *Ta-ra-ra Boomdeay* once more, at a very sedate pace, but this time all her notes were correct. Her cheeks glowed in the light of the candles that flanked her. The parlourmaid entered with a large plate of jam tarts on a black lacquered tray and placed them on a side table. She paused for a moment as if she wanted to stay, but Mrs Belling looked up from her piano and nodded fiercely to dismiss her. Soon after she had left, the Minotaur entered the room.

His huge white body was naked save for a mask which covered

the upper part of his face. The mask was black and fringed with woolly black hair, and two black horns shaped like those of a bull emerged from the temples. Above the mask a shiny bald cranium streaked with a few reddish grey hairs emerged. Beneath was a large sensual mouth with loose engorged lips whose ruby redness contrasted hideously with the almost dead white pallor of his skin. The aggressive chin was partly obscured by pendulous jowls which hung like dewlaps from his veined cheeks. The whole effect might have suggested the Minotaur to a classicist; to anyone seeing it for the first time it would have appeared merely monstrous.

The man lowered his head and peered round the room. There was something bull-like about this gesture, as if he were preparing to charge. He sauntered over to the plate of jam tarts and examined them minutely, then, having selected one of them, he retreated into the centre of the room. His long member, hitherto flaccid, began to show signs of arousal. With an impatient, imperious movement of his left hand he gestured to the girls who slipped off their silken robes and stood naked for his inspection. The Minotaur strutted before them, the jam tart poised on the flat of his right hand. Mrs Belling turned round from the piano and looked enquiringly at him. He nodded and she immediately launched into *Ta-ra-ra Boomdeay*.

This was the signal for the girls to begin to dance about the room. Mabel was a better dancer than the others, and she deliberately showed off her skills while knowing that this was not what the Minotaur was looking for. The others followed her lead, and it did not please him. He stamped and growled, executing a few clumsy steps himself by way of example. He was looking for less refinement, more Bacchanalian abandon. Then, with one swift and surprisingly adroit movement the Minotaur hurled the jam tart at one of the dancing girls. It struck Rose on the left buttock with such force that she gave a little cry of pain which she rapidly converted into a whoop of abandon. That cry of pain seemed to jerk the Minotaur into full arousal. He gestured to Mrs Belling to play faster which she did, stumbling over the notes, this time of *Daisy Bell* while the girls began to cavort around the room uttering shouts of mock ecstasy.

Meanwhile the Minotaur had picked up the plate of jam tarts

and was hurling them in a frenzy at the passing girls. Then, quite suddenly, he gave a great roar, which was a signal for the music and the dancing to stop. For a space of half a minute nothing could be heard in the room except the exhausted gasps of the dancers and the Minotaur's stertorous breathing. Effie, involuntarily, let out a little giggle, and went pink with embarrassment and fear. She knew that any indication that their activities had been somehow a source of amusement displeased the Minotaur greatly.

There were three jam tarts remaining. Taking them from the plate, which he unceremoniously dropped on the carpet, the Minotaur advanced towards Effie while she stood naked and now trembling in front of Mrs Belling's upright piano. Cupping one of the jam tarts in his right hand, the Minotaur came very close to Effie until she could feel his hot malodorous breath on her forehead. Then he pressed the jam tart hard into her left breast. Effie let out a scream of pain and stumbled back, almost falling over Mrs Belling as she did so. Mrs Belling rose and held Effie steadily from behind by the shoulders while the Minotaur, with even greater force, slapped a jam tart onto Effie's right breast. Effie cried out even louder at the pain and burst into a torrent of sobs.

Mabel, who had been standing next to her, made an involuntary move forward to defend Effie from any further attack. The Minotaur turned upon her. He was almost a foot taller than she was and she could see his eyes staring down at her through the mask. She had never before seen his eyes so close to. The irises were a strange pale green colour, the whites bloodshot, the overall effect feral and malignant. Keeping his eyes on her, he slowly and deliberately ground the last jam tart into the space between her thighs. Mabel stared back defiantly, determined to show no sign of weakness, suffering, or even loathing. The satisfaction of a mirrored hatred would be denied him. All the same, some satisfaction must have been achieved, and the resulting emission spilt itself on the carpet.

Another few seconds of complete silence followed before the Minotaur stamped out of the room. Mrs Belling, who always kept her composure on these occasions, uttered a peremptory "Shh!" as soon as the client had slammed the door behind him. Then, putting her index finger to her lips she rang for the maid who was close at hand and carried a dustpan and brush. Having commanded her to clear away the fragments of jam tarts and other spillages, she sent the girls upstairs to wash and change without any further words.

In the upstairs room the maid had, as usual, filled a hip bath with hot water. All the girls crowded around Effie who was still in tears from the attack she had sustained. Tenderly they washed her bruised body before they attended to their own needs.

"That man must not come again," said Mabel.

"Oh, yes? And who's going to tell Ma Belling that?" said Effie still sniffling.

"I will," said Mabel. "If you'll all back me." There was a murmur of assent. It was not as wholehearted as Mabel had hoped, but she had to concede that their position was weak.

Mrs Belling frowned at their deputation, like a disappointed headmistress. She had always looked on Mabel as a favourite because of her good sense and genteel ways, and so, to find her leading what amounted to a rebellion saddened her. Perhaps it even enraged her, but Mrs Belling was a woman who kept her composure at all times. She told her girls that 'the gentleman' – she did not refer to him by his sobriquet, let alone name him – had acknowledged to her in private that he had been a little 'too rough'. Then she pointed to four sovereigns on the plate where the jam tarts had been and said that he had left 'a little extra present' for each of them, by way of recompense, and that he would be calling again as usual the following week.

Mabel was the last to take the gold and leave the room. She heard Mrs Belling call her back softly but she chose to ignore the summons. What else were they to do? The St John's Wood House was their home now.

The following Monday evening Mabel managed to get down to the West End. Monday was a day they often had off, because Sunday was usually busy. Many gentleman felt the need to escape from the oppressive domesticities of this 'day of rest'.

When Mabel arrived before the facade of the Empire in Leicester Square, she hesitated before she went in. She knew it to be foolish but she did not want to be associated with the kind of women, like her sister, who haunted the Promenade. As an unaccompanied young woman she must arouse suspicion despite the stern respectability of her dress.

A broad staircase of some grandeur, flanked on both sides by globes of electric light upon elaborate wrought iron lamp stands, led up to the promenade which encircled the stalls, separated from it by waist high balustrades and Corinthian columns. It was a broad, carpeted space, sufficiently well lit to give one a good view of the promenaders. The clock had struck six, but even at this early hour most of the men on the promenade or leaning against the bars that lined the back wall were clearly in search of company. Mabel avoided their glance.

A decorous ballet – the Empire was famous for its ballets – was proceeding on stage but nobody seemed to be paying it much attention. It was a woodland scene, painted in soft colours. Mabel allowed herself for a moment to be drawn into the landscape. Its utter unreality was what beguiled her, even its absurdity: it allowed her to believe for a moment in a better world.

She permitted herself only a moment of respite, then she was watching the promenaders. Some of the women were so well dressed that Mabel wondered how her sister could fare in such a company, but Lily did not lack boldness.

Mabel tried not to look at the women, or to attract attention, but she was looking for her sister. Guilt had been building up in her all through the week since he had seen Lily, the simple guilt of the more prosperous survivor.

"Hello, dearie, what you up to?" The woman who addressed her was tall and thin, her face heavily painted. Her evening gown was of red shot silk, not quite in the first blush of cleanliness, but still lavish.

"I'm looking for my sister," said Mabel. "Lily Jerome. You seen her?"

"So you're Mabel Jerome." The woman seemed genuinely curious. "Oh, yes. Lily talks a lot about you. 'St John's Wood Mabel' she calls you."

Mabel did not care for the sobriquet at all, but she did her best to conceal her distaste. "And who are you?" she asked.

"You can call me Julia. Or Julian." Julia laid her hand on Mabel's and she saw it was broad with strong well-formed fingers. She had no feelings of revulsion or even astonishment. The world she had entered was all mystery, and only the quest mattered.

"Have you seen Lil, today?"

"She was here earlier, dear. She found a customer."

"Where does she live?"

"She's got a gaff off Windmill Street, but he's probably taken her to a hotel."

"D'you know who? A regular?"

Julia bent down close to Mabel's ear. The breath smelt of gin and tobacco. Julia whispered: "The Beast!"

"Him! What's his real name?"

"Oh, we don't know that, dear. Nobody's saying."

The ballet was coming to an end but Mabel heard the music as in a dream. A man passing by made some remark to her but she did not hear it. Something in her had changed. Julia wandered off but Mabel pursued her and asked for further details of her sister's lodgings.

Julia's directions were vague but she found them in the end. A door in a dark alley in a cliff of dingy brick. The place reeked of bones and rubbish. Mabel found herself ashamed of her own fastidiousness. A woman in a red dress with a face to match and a jet black wig, set a little askew, opened the door and agreed reluctantly that Lily lived there but was not in at the moment and that she was behind with the rent. Mabel put a few coins into the woman's hand and followed her up a creaking wooden staircase. Other occupants looked out of their rooms as she passed and seemed troubled by her fine clothes and ladylike ways. Mabel felt equally uncomfortable, because she did not quite know what she was doing there.

The room was a shock to her, even though it was what she had expected. There was a mean threadbare rug upon the floor, a table and chair by the window, a washstand and a brass bedstead with a green tasselled silk shawl draped over the end. The gesture of flamboyance seemed curiously pathetic in these mean surroundings. Threadbare curtains of an indeterminate colour were drawn back from a grimy window. It looked out upon the alley in which someone was singing drunkenly. Mabel sat on the chair first to wait for her sister, then, when the discomfort of that became unbearable, on the bed. She felt at times as though she were staring into a mirror darkened by time, at a life that might one day be hers again.

She had waited for over an hour and the light was beginning to thicken into a foggy evening when she heard a noise upon the stairs outside. The footsteps staggered as they approached and sobbing could be heard. Mabel ran out onto the landing where Lily fell into her arms. Her face was streaked with blood and there was blood on her clothes. She had on a yellow silk shawl, tasselled, like the one draped over the end of the bed, but it was stained in several places with blood.

Lily was in such a state that she barely registered that it was her sister who was with her. Mabel laid her on the bed and gently removed her clothes. The wounds and bruises were hideous. She went downstairs and gave money to the woman in the red dress to go out and fetch bandages and hot water and a doctor if possible. Then she returned. Mabel was barely breathing, and it was a while before she could answer any of Mabel's questions.

Very little was coherent, but Lily mouthed the word "Beast" and gripped Mabel's hand in hers. Mabel felt the chill of her sister's hand pass through her: it was enough.

A doctor came, a poor excuse for a doctor if ever there was one, with the blush of gin on his face and cheeks, and bandages were applied to the wounds. Mabel gave more money, then had to go, leaving her address, somewhat reluctantly, in the hands of the woman in the red dress. She took her sister's bloodstained shawl with her, wrapped in brown paper.

When she arrived back at the St John's Wood house Mabel was chided by Mrs Belling for being late: Lord Arthur was waiting for her. Mabel said nothing but went upstairs to where Lord Arthur sat in an armchair complacently smoking a cigar. The smoke sickened Mabel. She contemplated Lord Arthur's soft, silly face for a moment then smiled and moved towards him. The fact that he was harmless made her feel suddenly warm towards him. She knew her feelings had been on a knife edge since she had last looked at her bloodstained sister. She could have turned away from all men;

43

instead she turned towards Lord Arthur, but with a purpose.

"Oh, how I've longed for you, Lord Arthur!"

"Have you? Have you, little girlie? Have you?"

She turned round and sat on his knee.

"Oh, please will 'oo undo us at the back?"

"With the greatest of pleasure, little girlie mine."

Lord Arthur did not see her grimace as he applied himself to her laces. Almost tenderly he undid them while Mabel sighed softly and turned back to him to bestow kisses and loving glances. Lord Arthur planted kisses on the back of her neck. Mabel knew she was giving a performance but like a good actress she also to some extent felt what she was acting. It was a paradox which she had encountered before but not in such an extreme form. This time she gave herself wholeheartedly to the expression of a pretended passion, though she always kept in sight its purpose. Lord Arthur responded with a more gentle and considered approach to lovemaking, less of the hearty rough and ready manner that he usually adopted. He slid off her bodice with a practised hand and let his fingers play gently with the nipples of her breasts.

The unexpected tenderness and fervour of Mabel's subsequent lovemaking had its desired effect. It put Lord Arthur in the mood for conversation, but she knew she must tread carefully and not make her intentions obvious. She allowed him to tell her the funny stories that he had told her before. She giggled and kicked her legs in the air which aroused his playfulness once again, but she never for a moment forgot the wretched bruised and bloody girl lying in the bare Soho bedroom. At last, as Lord Arthur was dressing, and she was helping him in the neat, fussy way that amused him, she said:

"I think I saw our friend the Minotaur in the West End, the other day."

"Oh, really! Old *semibovem*! What was he up to, then?"

"On the Empire Promenade."

"And what was a respectable little girlie doing there? You ought to be ashamed of yourself."

"I know some of the dancers. Do you know, they call him *The Beast* there?"

"Do they by Jove?"

"But they don't know his real name."

"Aha!"

"And you do."

"Do I, girlie?"

"You said so."

"Did I, Miss Mouse?"

"You did, Mr Big Black Pussycat. And you can tell your Miss Mouse because she won't tell a soul else."

"But why does little Miss Mouse want to know?"

"Just because she's a curious Miss Mouse who likes to share a secret with her big brave pussy cat. He can whisper it in her ear."

And he did, and she kissed him tenderly for it, but then wondered what it was she could possibly do with the information. The following morning a message was delivered to Mabel informing her that Lily had been taken to the poor hospital at St Giles's where she had died from her injuries.

Mabel told Mrs Belling merely that her sister had met with a fatal accident and was given time off to make arrangements for the funeral and attend it. Her mother was drunk at the grave side and Mabel spurned her when she attempted to beg a few shillings off her. She later sent her some money but her mind was all fire and ice. She spent her remaining free time in the local library with a gazetteer looking up a certain Mr Frederick Cooper whom she discovered to be living not far from Mrs Belling's in Melina Grove NW.

Mabel did not tell the police, knowing what a world of trouble to no good effect that would unleash, but she did confide in Effie. Effie, she knew, had conceived an almost equal hatred of the Minotaur and would faithfully infect the other girls. She made a suitably fervent and vindictive confidant, so much so that she became almost impatient with Mabel for the slowness and deliberation with which she matured her plans. Otherwise, business went on as normal. Clients came and went, but the Minotaur did not come. Effie acquired an admirer in an elderly Baronet. It was almost as good (in Effie's eyes) as Lord Arthur, but not quite.

One afternoon towards the end of October a very respectable-looking young lady carrying a brown paper parcel rang the front door bell of Number 1 Melina Grove. To the parlourmaid who opened the door she presented a card bearing the legend;

Mrs L. Prentice

Society for the Reclamation of Fallen Women

When she asked to see Mr Cooper the servant replied that he was out for a drive, but would be back shortly. The lady looked a little flustered and said that an appointment had been made: perhaps she could wait? Was Mrs Cooper at home by any chance? Perhaps she could see her: she was sure that Mrs Cooper would be acquainted with her husband's most generous and charitable patronage of her little society.

The maid seemed dubious, but the lady appeared so earnest and respectable that it was hard to refuse such an innocent request. Besides Mrs Cooper went about so little, saw so few people, that a little company might do her good. Those were the servant's thoughts as she ushered Mabel into the Minotaur's drawing room.

It was a pleasant enough room, lavishly furnished and decorated in a style which was now becoming distinctly unfashionable. Rich and sombre colours predominated. A profusion of ornaments decorated available surfaces. Oil paintings depicting cattle basking in sunlight or drinking from tranquil pools and other rustic scenes all but obliterated the heavily patterned, sage green wallpaper.

In a corner, by the window in the sunlight sat a plump little woman doing embroidery. She looked up startled when Mabel entered. Mabel caught a smell of fear and smiled at a reaction which she might have predicted.

"I'm afraid my husband —"

"Mrs Cooper, how delightful to meet you at last. I have heard so much about you from your husband."

"Oh, have you? Oh, really?" It would seem that this innocent remark had intensified Mrs Cooper's agitation.

"May I be seated?" Mrs Cooper nodded nervously.

Mabel proceeded to explain very gently how Mr Cooper had been taking a great philanthropic interest in the Reclamation of Fallen Women. Mrs Cooper was very surprised at this.

"I am afraid, Mrs Prentice, I was not aware —"

"Ah! Such is the way of some philanthropists, Mrs Cooper. They are too modest for their own good; they hide their light under a bushel. Does not the bard say: 'The evil that men do lives after them, the good is oft interred with their bones'?"

Mabel did not quite know why she had made the last remark. It just seemed appropriate to the occasion, and the genteel piety of her assumed character. She had picked it up from Lord Arthur who was fond of his little tags. At that moment the door opened and the Minotaur entered the room. As soon as he saw Mabel the pale, flabby face became suffused with spots of colour, the eyes were enraged.

Both women rose but Mabel advanced swiftly towards him extending her hand.

"Lily Prentice, the Reclamation of Fallen Women. So nice to meet you at last, Mr Cooper, on your 'home territory', as it were!" She gave a genteel little laugh.

The Minotaur stood astonished, baffled, almost fearful. At last he said: "Mary, my dear. Would you excuse us? This lady and I have some business to discuss."

Mrs Cooper picked up her embroidery and hurried from the room. Several seconds of silence followed the closing of the door. The Minotaur went to open it and looked out. Only the parlourmaid was standing in the hall and he shooed her away with an impatient gesture. Then he turned and bore down on Mabel who stood her ground.

The man's extraordinary pallor had restored itself. At a distance the Minotaur's face might have resembled a lump of dough with a gash in it for a mouth and above it two currents buried rather too close together, for eyes.

"What the devil is all this about?" He scrutinised her. "Have I seen you before?"

"Oh, yes, Mr Cooper. At Number 2 Boscobel Place. Why do you no longer visit us?"

"What do you want, damn you?"

"Oh, Mr Cooper! That is no way to talk to a lady."

"You're not a lady, you're a damned little whore!"

"And you are no gentleman, sir. You're nothing but a beast, a Minotaur!"

The Minotaur stared at her in silence as Mabel coolly turned her back on him and went to the chair on which she had laid her brown paper parcel.

"I have something for you," she said. Turning again she held the parcel out to him. "Open it!" She could see the hesitation, the stubbornness in his eyes. He was afraid of surrender. "Open it, please, Mr Minotaur!"

He snatched the parcel from her, tore it open and drew out a yellow, tasselled silk shawl. It was smeared with the brown stains of dried blood.

"What the devil-?"

"It belonged to my sister Lily. Do you remember her? The Empire Promenade?"

"What is it you want, damn you? Money, I suppose?"

"No. I want you to have it cleaned and then return it to me."

"What? Why?"

"And then I want you to start coming to Boscobel Place again."

"But why, damn you? Why?"

"Why do you like jam tarts so much?"

By this time, the fury in him was eating him up. Mabel could see that he was longing to seize her and hurl her through the window, but the surroundings held him back. The slight fear that he might break into violence added something piquant to the pleasure Mabel felt at the sight of this twitching, defeated lump of a man.

"I will call for the shawl at this precise hour in a week's time when you will receive further instructions," she said. "And now, if you will excuse me?"

The Minotaur put his vast bulk between her and the door.

Mabel said: "What would you like me to do? Shall I call for the servant? I am sure she cannot be far away."

The Minotaur stepped aside. "Be very careful, little girlie," he said.

"Thank you, Mr Minotaur. I will be." A pleasant fleeting smile and she was out of the door. As she had expected, the parlourmaid was on hand in the hall to open the street door for her. Mabel told her that she had made an appointment to call on her master at the same time next week, and would be glad to see Mrs M – Mrs

Cooper also. Then Mabel was out into the light misty air of autumn. She breathed heavily and fought back the spasm of hysterical laughter that threatened to overwhelm her.

During the following days Mabel barely ventured out of Boscobel Place. Mrs Belling noticed that she was even more docile and well-behaved than usual, but that if she ever entered a room when Mabel and some other girls were present, their conversation stopped or became more subdued. Fortunately Mrs Belling was not a suspicious woman. She remained confident of maintaining one of the most successful and 'respectable' houses of assignation, as she chose to call it, in London. Had they not been visited on several occasions by Royalty?

The following Wednesday Mabel rang the bell at Melina Grove at the hour appointed.

"Mrs Prentice to see Mr Cooper." It was a fine, coppery autumn evening in the Wood. The parlourmaid smiled as she let Mabel in and studied her curiously. But she knew nothing, surely: she could not.

"Mr Cooper is in the drawing room," she said.

"And Mrs Cooper?"

"Upstairs, ma'am. Would you like to see her, ma'am?"

"No. I shall not stay long. But if you would remain in the hall to let me out."

"Very good, ma'am," and she opened the drawing room door and announced Mrs Prentice to its occupant.

The Minotaur stood with his back to the fire, hands clasped behind him. He had taken up a position where his gigantic frame might be seen to its best advantage. Mabel was so amused by this assumption of threat that she almost forgot her loathing of the man. Over these last days her mood had become steadier, less febrile.

The Minotaur pointed to a brown paper parcel on a low table before him.

"I have had it cleaned as you requested. Now take it and go." The venomous contempt with which he spoke aroused Mabel's hatred again. Coolly, taking her time, she opened the parcel and examined the shawl.

"There are still traces of blood, here and here," she said,

pointing to them. "Not good enough! Have it cleaned again!" She threw the shawl in his face and drew back two paces, knowing the risk she had taken. The Minotaur did not deign to catch it; the shawl fell from his face to the ground. For a brief moment it looked as if a monument were being unveiled.

He stood still, paralysed by the shock of her affront. Fiery threads of blood vessels pulsated in his cheeks. His eyes glistened darkly like two tiny shards of pure jet.

Quickly, before he could speak or move, she said: "This time next week you will come to us in Boscobel Place. Bring the shawl, clean this time, and come alone. Do not bring the groom. We can mind the horses while you are with us if you choose to drive. Then we can bring this matter to a conclusion. Fail to obey these instructions and you know what the consequences will be. Good afternoon, Mr Minotaur!"

Mabel left the room without a backward glance, closing the door behind her. She was relieved to find the parlourmaid in the hall.

"I am afraid I must leave. Will you give my very warmest regards to Mrs Cooper?"

The parlourmaid dropped a curtsey. "Yes 'm!" And she led her to the front door. Just then both of them distinctly heard a howl of rage coming from beyond the drawing room door.

"Mr Cooper is much vexed," said Mabel in a confidential undertone to the maid. "One of our *protegées* has met with a most distressing fatality. I would advise you not to disturb your master for as long as possible."

The parlourmaid nodded her head and dropped another curtsey. Her hand was white and trembling as she opened the front door for Mabel.

Mabel informed Mrs Belling of the proposed visit of the Minotaur the following Wednesday. Naturally she was asked how this had come about, to which Mabel replied, with a certain cool politeness with which Mrs Belling had begun to be familiar, that she was sorry, but she was not at liberty to say. With the other girls she was more forthcoming about what was to occur. To Mrs Belling she only said that the customer would be arriving by carriage without a groom and that Mrs Mason the housekeeper could attend to the horses during his stay. Mrs Belling nodded, but made no comment.

And he came at his usual time of three in the afternoon. Mrs Belling smiled upon him and the girls smiled to themselves. One incident puzzled Mrs Belling. As he encountered Mabel in the hallway he thrust a brown paper parcel into her hands with such an aggressive gesture and such a dark look that even Mabel's composure was shaken, if only for a moment.

When, having disrobed and put on his mask, the Minotaur entered the drawing room, he felt, as all did except Mrs Belling, a certain tension. She began to play *After the Ball is Over* while the girls shed their silken robes. On the side table, as before, was the plate of jam tarts. The Minotaur clapped his hands and the girls began dancing slowly around him, nodding and winking at him as they passed by. He clapped again, a signal for the music and the dancing to become more abandoned. Mrs Belling changed to *Ta-ra-ra Boomdeay*. The Minotaur threw his first jam tart. It hit Effie on the thigh and she let out a little shriek. This was enough to arouse the Minotaur who bellowed his satisfaction. He picked up another jam tart to throw, but just then somebody behind him stripped him of his mask and blindfolded him. Before all went dark he could see the gold tasselled fringes of Lily's yellow shawl dance in front of him. He was about to raise objections when he found that a handkerchief was being stuffed into his mouth. Somebody clapped to increase the pace and volume of the music. Mrs Belling, oblivious to all else, applied herself diligently to her tune while the girls surrounded the Minotaur pressing their naked flesh to his and leading his staggering body onwards he knew not where.

A strange sensation overcame the Minotaur, a mixture of bafflement, fear and arousal, but above all of a complete absence of power which almost seduced him. Soft hands caressed him; soft breasts pressed against him; a tongue was at work as he was drawn away from the music in the drawing room towards a wider, cooler space. The hallway? Then something struck him on the back of the head and he was tumbling down some stairs. There was a moment of bleak, intense revelation before the void swallowed his shrivelled soul.

The girls contemplated the great white body crumpled at the foot of the stairs.

"Do you think he's gone?" said Effie.

Mabel laid down the poker she had just wielded and said. "I will go and make certain." So, still naked, she walked down the stairs. On reaching the bottom she crouched over the body to feel for a pulse in his neck, pulling the handkerchief from his mouth as she did so, and removing his blindfold. Then she straightened up, nodded solemnly and said: "He's gone all right."

In the sitting room Mrs Belling had not ceased from hammering away at *Ta-ra-ra Boomdeay*.

She only did so when the shocked girls interrupted to inform her of what had happened: apparently the Minotaur had chased some of them out into the hall, then lost his balance, tripped and fell down the uncarpeted stone steps leading to the servants' quarters in the basement. Mrs Belling reacted at first with hysterics, but her agitation was alleviated by the fact that her girls, despite being still dressed only in their silken robes, were behaving so calmly. No suspicion entered her head at that moment. When it did, later on, it was far too late to do anything about it and was quickly suppressed.

The idea of summoning the police was soon rejected. Mrs Belling's, as she insisted, was a 'respectable house', and such a discovery would do irreparable damage to her reputation and that of her girls. It was then that Mabel intervened.

She reminded them that the Minotaur's phaeton was still outside their house guarded by Mason, the housekeeper. She therefore suggested that Charlotte, the tallest of the girls, should dress in the Minotaur's clothes and drive the phaeton round to Melina Grove and leave it in the mews behind the Minotaur's house – Mrs Belling never thought at the time to question how Mabel knew his home address. Charlotte was not as vast in size as the Minotaur, naturally, but it was a misty afternoon and she was a big girl. She could pass for Mr Cooper in the twilight. Moreover, she had the advantage of knowing something about horses, her father having been an ostler before the drink took him.

The rest of the girls, under the supervision of Mabel, would take care of the body. The servants would have to be informed, if they did not know already, for the body had fallen into their domain, but they would be discreet. It was in their interest as much as everyone else's. This, as Mrs Belling had so often said, was a respectable house.

The corpse was dragged into the pantry and lifted with much difficulty into a capacious butler's sink. Then the kitchen maid was sent round to borrow a saw from their local butcher's. She told the butcher it was to cut up some game presented to them by a noble client. The butcher offered to perform the task himself, but the kitchen maid, with a nervous smile, said that they were quite adequate to the task themselves.

It was Mabel who did most of the sawing. Mrs Belling, who never actually ventured down into the servant's quarters herself, was surprised that Mabel was so willing to undertake this sordid task, but she was beginning to become used to the girl's surprising qualities and even, though Mrs Belling had not quite admitted this, to rely on them.

Parts of the Minotaur were then boiled or minced and fed to the kitchen cat. The rest of him was put piecemeal into the great stove which had recently been installed to heat the new hot water boiler for the house. The calcined bones were raked out and placed in a sack along with some mutton bones that also needed to be disposed of. The Minotaur's clothing was cut up and either made into dishcloths or put into another sack for the rag and bone man. All this was conducted under Mabel's patient and untiring supervision.

About four days after the Minotaur's disappearance, the Police called to make enquiries. They spoke to Mrs Belling respectfully in the knowledge that the local Commissioner was an occasional visitor to her establishment. Mrs Belling, with Mabel seated beside her, had of course known of the man in the phaeton and had seen him pass by on frequent occasions, but not on the afternoon of his vanishing. The Police went away unsuspecting.

Then came the afternoon, bitter cold it was and misty as usual, when the rag and bone man called. His chant, heard from afar off, was to Mabel like a summons to the last rites or to a funeral. Rather to Mrs Belling's disapproval, Mabel helped the kitchen maid take out the sacks of rag and bone which were the final remnants of the Minotaur and place them on the old man's cart. To Mabel, this last act was a necessity, the curtain call to the drama in which she had played such a prominent role.

This done, she came indoors, poured herself a cup of tea and sat at the drawing room window to watch the light die in the street outside. *When it is spent, a great passion — hatred or the other kind — leaves behind an emptiness.* "The evil that men do lives after them…" No. Lord Arthur, or Shakespeare, or whoever it was, was wrong. Nothing lives after them: good or evil: it is all carried away by the rag and bone man.

"Rag-a-bone! Rag-a-bone!" cried the man on the cart as he disappeared into the mist. Mabel turned away from the window. Her eyes were moist.

"Dry your tears, lovey," said Mrs Belling. "Look, there's Lord Arthur come to see you."

"Give me a few minutes, and then show him up, Mrs Belling," said Mabel. Mrs Belling was surprised, even a little indignant. Mabel's tone had not been imperious, but it was firm and indicated a certain authority. An irrevocable change had taken place. Mrs Belling hesitated for a moment, wondering whether she should reassert herself by pinching Miss Mabel's pale cheeks as she had done so often before, but she thought better of it. She merely nodded and went down to usher in Lord Arthur.

Mabel turned back to the window. The mist had thickened. Long after all sight of the man and his cart were gone, the chant of "Rag-a-bone! Rag-a-bone!" echoed through the twilit Grove of the Evangelist.

THE PHANTOM MODEL
A WAPPING ROMANCE

Hume Nisbet

I
The Studio

"Rhoda is a very nice girl in her way, Algy, my boy, and poses wonderfully, considering the hundreds of times she has had to do it; but she isn't the model for that Beatrice of yours, and if you want to make a hit of it, you must go further afield, and hook a face not quite so familiar to the British Public."

It was a large apartment, one of a set of studios in that artistic barrack off the Fulham Road, which the landlord, himself a theatrical Bohemian of the first class, has rushed up for the accommodation of youthful luminaries who are yet in the nebulous stage of their Art course. Each of these hazy specks hopes to shine out a full-lustred star in good time; they have all a proper contempt also for those servile daubsters who consent to the indignity of having R.A. added to their own proper, or assumed, names. Most of them belong to the advanced school of Impressionists, and allow, with reservations, that Jimmy Whitetuft has genius, as they know that he is the most generous, as well as the most epigrammatical, of painters, while Rhoda, the model, also knows that he is the kindest and most chivalrous of patrons, who stands more of her caprices than most of her other masters do, allows her more frequent as well as longer rests in the two hours' sitting, and can always be depended upon for a half-crown on an emergency; good-natured, sardonic Jimmy Whitetuft, who can well appreciate the caprices of any woman, or butterfly of the hour, seeing that he has so many of them himself.

Rhoda Prettyman is occupied at the present moment in what she likes best, warming her young, lithe, Greek-like figure at the stove, while she puffs out vigorous wreaths of smoke from the cigarette she has picked up at the table, in the passing from the daïs to the stove. She is perfect in face, hair, figure and colour, not yet sixteen, and greatly in demand by artists and sculptors; a good girl and a merry one, who prefers bitter beer to champagne, a night in the pit to the ceremony of a private box, with a dozen or so of oysters afterwards at a little shop, rather than run her entertainer into the awful expense of a supper at the Criterion or Gatti's. Her father and mother having served as models before her, she has been accustomed to the disporting of her charms à la vue on raised daïses from her tenderest years, and to the patois of the studios since she could lisp, so that she is as unconscious as a Solomon Island young lady in the bosom of her own family, and can patter 'Art' as fluently as any picture dealer in the land.

They are all smoking hard, while they criticise the unfinished Exhibition picture of their host, Algar Gray, during this rest time of the model; Rhoda has not been posing for that picture now, for at the present time the studio is devoted to a life-club, and Rhoda has been hired for this purpose by those hard-working students, who form the young school. Jimmy Whitetuft is the visitor who drops in to cut them up; a marvellous eye for colour and effect Jimmy has, and they are happy in his friendly censorship.

All round the room the easels are set up, with their canvases, in a half-moon range, and on these canvases Rhoda can see herself as in half-a-dozen mirrors, reflected in the same number of different styles as well as postures, for these students aim at originality. But the picture which now occupies their attention is a bishop, half-length, in the second working upon which the well-known features and figure of Rhoda are depicted in thirteenth-century costume as the Beatrice of Dante, and while the young painter looks at his stale design with discontented eyes, his friends act the part of Job's comforters.

"There isn't a professional model in London who can stand for Beatrice, if you want to make her live. They have all been in too many characters already. You must have something fresh."

"Yes, I know," muttered Algar Gray. "But where the deuce shall I find her?"

"Go to the country. You may see something there," suggested Jack Brunton, the landscapist. "I always manage to pick up something fresh in the country."

"The country be blowed for character," growled Will Murray. "Go to the East End of London, if you want a proper Beatrice; to the half-starved crew, with their big eyes and thin cheeks. That's the sort of thing to produce the spiritual longing, wistful look you want. I saw one the other day, near the Thames Tunnel, while I was on the prowl, who would have done exactly."

"What was she?" asked Algar eagerly.

"A Ratcliff Highway stroller, I should say. At any rate, I met her in one of the lowest pubs, pouring down Irish whiskey by the tumbler, with never a wink, and using the homespun in a most delectable fashion. Her mate might have served for Semiramis, and she took four ale from the quart pot, but the other, the Beatrice, swallowed her dose neat, and as if it had been cold water from one of the springs of Paradise, where, in olden times, she was wont to gather flowers."

"Good Heavens! Will, you are atrocious. The sentiment of Dante would be killed by such a woman."

"Realistic, dear boy, that's all. You will find very exquisite flowers sometimes even on a dust-heap, as well as where humanity grows thickest and rankest. We have all to go through the different stages of earthly experience, according to Blavatsky. This Beatrice may have been the original of Dante in the thirteenth century, now going through her Wapping experience. It seems nasty, yet it may be necessary."

"What like was she?"

"What sort of an ideal had you when you first dreamt of that picture, Algy?"

"A tall, slender woman, of about twenty or twenty-two, graceful and refined, with pale face blue-veined and clear, with dark hair and eyes indifferent as to shade, yet out-looking – a soulful gaze from a classical, passive and passionless face."

"That is exactly the Beatrice of the East End shanty and the

Irish whisky, the sort of holy after-death calm pervading her, the alabaster-lamp-like complexion lit up by pure spirits undiluted, the general dreamy, indifferent pose – it was all there when I first saw her, only a battle royal afterwards occurred between her and the Amazon over a sailor, during which the alabaster lamp flamed up and Semiramis came off second best; for commend me to your spiritual demons when claws and teeth are wanted. No matter, I have found your model for you; take a turn with me this evening and I'll perhaps be able to point her out to you, the after negotiations I leave in your own romantic hands."

II
Dante in the Inferno

It is a considerable distance from the Fulham Road to Wapping even going by bus, but as the two artist friends went, it was still farther and decidedly more picturesque.

They were both young men under thirty. Art is not so precocious as literature, and does not send quite so many early potatoes into the market, so that the age of thirty is considered young enough for a painter to have learnt his business sufficiently to be marketable from the picture-dealing point of view.

Will Murray was the younger of the two by a couple of years, but as he had been sent early to fish in the troubled waters of illustration, and forced to provide for himself while studying, he looked much the elder; of a more realistic and energetic turn, he did not indulge in dreams of painting any single magnum opus, with which he would burst upon an astonished and enthusiastic world, he could not afford to dream, for he had to work hard or go fasting, and so the height of his aspirations was to paint well enough to win a note of approval from his own particular school, and keep the pot boiling with black and white work.

Agar Gray was a dreamer on five hundred per year, the income beneficent Fortune had endowed him with by reason of his lucky birth; he did not require to work for his daily bread, and as he had about as much prospect of selling his paint-creations, or imitations, as the other members of this new school, he spent the time he was not painting in dreaming about a possible future.

It wasn't a higher ideal, this brooding over fame, than the circumscribed ideal of Will Murray; each member of that young school was too staunch to his principles, and idealized his art as represented by canvas and paints too highly to care one jot about the pecuniary side of it; they painted their pictures as the true poet writes his poems, because it was right in their eyes; they held exhibitions, and preached their canons to a blinded public; the blinded public did not purchase, or even admire; but all that did not matter to the exhibitors so long as they had enough left to pay for more canvases and frames.

Will Murray was keen sighted and blue-eyed, robust in body and forever on the alert for fresh material to fill his sketch book. Algar Gray was dark to swarthiness, with long, thin face, rich-toned, melancholy eyes, and slender figure; he did not jot down trifles as did his friend, he absorbed the general effect and seldom produced his sketching-block.

Having time on their hands and a glorious October evening before them, they walked to Fulham Wharf and, hiring a wherry there, resolved to go by the old waterway to the Tower, and after that begin their search for the Spiritual, through the Inferno of the East.

There is no river in the world to be compared for majesty and the witchery of association to the Thames; it impresses even the unreading and unimaginative watcher with a solemnity which he cannot account for, as it rolls under his feet and swirls past the buttresses of its many bridges; he may think, as he experiences the unusual effect, that it is the multiplicity of buildings which line its banks, or the crowd of sea-craft which floats upon its surface, or its own extensive spread. In reality he feels, although he cannot explain it, the countless memories which hang forever like a spiritual fog over its rushing current.

This unseen fog closes in upon the two friends as they take up their oars and pull out into mid-stream; it is a human fog which depresses and prepares them for the scenes into which they must shortly add their humanity; there is no breaking away from it, for it reaches up to Oxford and down to Sheppey, the voiceless thrilling of past voices, the haunting chill of dead tragedies, the momentous hush of acted history.

It wafts towards them on the brown sails of the gliding barges where the solitary figures stand upright at the stern like so many Charons steering their hopeless freights; it shapes the fantastic clouds of dying day overhead, from the fumes of countless fires, and the breaths from countless lips, it is the overpowering absorption of a single soul composed of many parts; the soul of a great city, past and present, of a mighty nation with its crowded events, crushing down upon the heart of a responsive stream, and this is the mystic power of the pulsating, eternal Thames.

They bear down upon Westminster, the ghost-consecrated Abbey, and the history-crammed Hall, through the arches of the bridge with a rush as the tide swelters round them; the city is buried in a dusky gloom save where the lights begin to gleam and trail with lurid reflections past black velvety-looking hulls – a dusky city of golden gleams. St. Paul's looms up like an immense bowl reversed, squat, un-English, and undignified in spite of its great size; they dart within the sombre shadows of the Bridge of Sighs, and pass the Tower of London, with the rising moon making the sky behind it luminous, and the crowd of shipping in front appear like a dense forest of withered pines, and then mooring their boat at the steps beyond, with a shuddering farewell look at the eel-like shadows and the glittering lights of that writhing river, with its burthen seen and invisible, they plunge into the purlieus of Wapping.

Through silent alleys where dark shadows fleeted past them like forest beasts on the prowl; through bustling market-places where bloaters predominated, into crammed gin-palaces where the gas flashed over faces whereon was stamped the indelible impression of a protest against creation; brushing tatters which were in gruesome harmony with the haggard or bloated features.

Will Murray was used to this medley and pushed on with a definite purpose, treating as burlesque what made the dreamer groan with impotent fury that so dire a poverty, so unspeakable a degradation, could laugh and seem hilarious even under the fugitive influence of Old Tom. They were not human beings these breathing and roaring masses, they were an appalling army of spectres grinning at an abashed Maker.

"Here we are at last, Algy," observed Will, cheerily, as the pair pushed through the swinging doors of a crammed bar and approached the counter, "and there is your Beatrice."

III
The Picture

The impressionists of Fulham Road knew Algy Gray no more, after that first glimpse which he had of Beatrice. His studio was once again to let, for he had removed his baggage and tent eastward, so as to be near the woman who would not and could not come West.

His first impressions of her might have cured many a man less refined or sensitive; – a tall young woman with pallid face leaning against the bar and standing treat to some others of her kind; drinking furiously, while from her lips flowed a husky torrent of foulness, unrepeatable; he was in luck when he met her, and enjoying a holiday with some of her own sex, and therefore wanted no male interference for that night, so she repulsed his advances with frank brutality, and forced him to retire from her side baffled.

Yet, if she offended his refined ears, there was nothing about her to offend his artistic eyes; she had no ostrich feathers in her hat, and no discordancy about the colours of her shabby costume; it was plain and easy-fitting, showing the grace of her willowy shape; her features were statuesque, and as Will had said, alabaster-like in their pure pallor.

That night Algar Gray followed her about, from place to place, watching her beauty hungrily, even while he wondered at the unholy thirst that possessed her, and which seemed to be sateless, a quenchless desire which gave her no rest, but drove her from bar to bar while her money lasted; she appeared to him like a soulless being, on whom neither fatigue nor debauchery could take effect.

At length, as midnight neared, she turned to him with a half smile and beckoned him towards her; she had ignored him hitherto, although she knew he was hunting her down.

"I say, matey, I'm stumped up, so you can stand me some drink if you like." She laughed scornfully when she saw him take soda water for his share, it was a weakness which she could neither understand nor appreciate.

"You ain't Jacky the Terror, are you?" she enquired carelessly as she asked him for another drink.

"Certainly not, why do you ask?"

"'Cos you stick so close to me. I thought perhaps you had spotted me out for the next one, not that I care much whether you are or not, now that my money is done."

His heart thrilled at the passivity of her loneliness as he looked at her; she had accepted his companionship with indifference, unconscious of her own perfection, utterly apathetic to everything; she a woman that nothing could warm up.

She led him to the home which she rented, a single attic devoid of furniture, with the exception of a broken chair and dilapidated table, and a mattress which was spread out in the corner, a wretched nest for such a matchless Beatrice.

And as she reclined on the mattress and drank herself to sleep from the bottle which she had made him buy for her, he sat at the table and, while the tallow candle lasted, he watched her, and sketched her in his pocket-book, after which, when the candle had dropped to the bottom of the bottle which served for a candle-stick, and the white moonlight fell through the broken window upon that pure white slumbering face, so still and death-like, he crept softly down the stairs, thralled with but one idea.

Next day when he came again she greeted him almost affectionately, for she remembered his lavishness the night before and was grateful for the refreshment which he sent out for her. Yes, she had no objections to let him paint her if he paid well for it, and came to her, but she wasn't going out of her beat for any man; so finding that there was another attic in the same house to let, he hired it, got the window altered to suit him and set to work on his picture.

The model, although untrained, was a patient enough sitter to Algar Gray when the mood took her, but she was very variable in her moods, and uncertain in her temper, as spirit-drunkards mostly are. Sometimes she was reticent and sullen, and would not be coaxed or bribed into obedience to his wishes, at other times she was lazy and would not stir from her own mattress, where she lay like a lovely savage, letting him admire her transparent skin, with the blue veins intersecting it, and a luminous glow pervading it, until his spirit melted within him, and he grew almost as purposeless as she was.

Under these conditions the picture did not advance very fast, for now November was upon them with its fogs. Very often on the days when she felt amiable enough to sit, he had no light to take advantage of her mood, while at other times she was either away drinking with her own kind or else sulking in her bleak den.

If he wondered at first how she could keep the purity of her complexion with the life she led or how she never appeared overcome with the quantity of spirits she consumed, he no longer did so since she had given him her confidence.

She was a child of the slums in spite of her refinement of face, figure and neatness of attire; who, six years before had been given up by the doctors for consumption, and informed that she had not four months of life left. Previous to this medical verdict she had worked at a match factory, and been fairly well conducted, but with the recklessness of her kind, who resemble sailors closely, she had pitched aside caution, resolved to make the most of her four months left, and so abandoned herself to the life she was still leading.

She had existed almost entirely upon raw spirits for the past six years, surprised herself that she had lived so long past her time, yet expecting death constantly; she was as one set apart by Death, and no power could reclaim her from that doom, a reckless, condemned prisoner, living under a very uncertain reprieve, and without an emotion or a desire left except the vain craving to deaden thought, and be able to die game, a craving which would not be satisfied.

Algar Gray, for the sake of an ideal, had linked himself to a soul already damned, which still held on to its fragile casement, a soul which was dragging him down to her own hell; her very cold indifference to him drew him after her, and enslaved him, her unholy transparent loveliness bewitched him, and the foulness of her lips and language no longer caused him a shudder, since it could not alter her exquisite lines or those pearly tints which defied his palette; and yet he did not love the woman; his whole desire was to transfer her perfection to his canvas before grim Death came to snatch her clay from the vileness of its surroundings.

IV
A Lost Soul

December and January had passed with clear, frosty skies, and the picture of Beatrice was at length ready for the Exhibition.

When a man devotes himself body and spirit to a single object, if he has training and aptitude, no matter how mediocre he may be in ordinary affairs, he will produce something so nearly akin to a work of genius as to deceive half the judges who think themselves competent to decide between genius and talent.

Algar Gray had studied drawing at a good training school, and was acknowledged by competent critics to be a true colourist, and for the last three months he had lived for the picture which he had just completed, therefore the result was satisfactory even to him. Beatrice, the ideal love of Dante, looked out from his canvas in the one attic of this Wapping slum, while Beatrice, the model, lay dead on her old mattress in the other.

He had attempted to make her home more home-like and comfortable for her, but without success; what he ordered from the upholsterer she disposed of promptly to the brokers, laughing scornfully at his efforts to redeem her, and mocking coarsely at his remonstrances, as she always had done at his temperate habits. He was not of her kind, and she had no sympathy with him, or in any of his ways; she had tolerated him only for the money he was able to give her, and so had burnt herself out of life without a kindly word or thought about him.

She had died as she wished to do, that is, she had passed away silently and in the darkness, leaving him to discover what was left of her, in the chill of a winter morning, a corpse not whiter or less luminous than she had been in life, with the transparent neck and delicate arms, blue-veined and beautiful, and the face composed with the immortal air of quiet which it had always possessed.

She had lasted just long enough to enable him to put the finishing touches upon her replica, and now that the undertakers had taken away the matchless original, he thought that he might return to his own people, and take with him the object which he had coveted and won. The woman herself seemed nothing to him while she lay waiting upon her last removal in the room next to his, but now that it was empty, and only her image remained before him, he was strangely dissatisfied and restless.

He had caught the false appearance of purity which was about her, but all unaware to himself, this constant communication of the more natural part had been absorbed into his being, until now the picture looked like a body waiting for the return of its own mocking spirit, and for the first time, regretful wishes began to tug at his heart-strings; it was no longer the Beatrice of Dante that he wanted, but the Beatrice who had mockingly enslaved him with her vileness, and whom he had permitted to escape from him for an ideal, she who had never tempted him in life, was now tormenting him past endurance with hopeless longings.

He had gone out that afternoon with the intention of returning to his studio in the West End, and making arrangements for bringing his picture there, but after wandering aimlessly about the evil haunts where he had so often followed his late model, he found that he could not tear himself from that dismal round. A shadow form seemed to glide before him from one gin-palace to another as she had done in life; the places where she had leaned against the bars seemed still to be occupied by her cold and mocking presence, no longer passive, but repulsing him as she had done in the early part of the first night, while he grew hungry and eager for her friendship.

She was before him on the pavement as he turned towards his attic; her husky, oath-clogged voice sounded in his ears as he passed an alley, and when he rushed forward to seize her, two other women fled from him out of the gloom with shrieks of fear. All the voices of these unfortunates are alike, and he had made a mistake.

The ice had given way on the morning of her death, and the streets were now slushy and wet, with a drizzling fog obscuring objects, so that only an instinct led him back to his temporary studio; he would draw down his blind and light his lamp, and spend the last evening of the slums in looking at his work.

It appeared almost a perfect piece of painting, and likely to attract much notice when it was exhibited. The dress which Beatrice had worn still lay over the back of the chair near the door, where she had carelessly flung it when last she took it off. He turned his back to the dress-covered chair and looked at the picture. Yes, it was the Beatrice whom Dante yearned over all his life – as she appeared to him at the bridge, with the same pure face and pathetic eyes, but not the Beatrice whom he, Algar Gray, passed over while she lived, and now longed for with such unutterable longing when it was too late.

He flung himself down before his magnum opus, and buried his face in his hands with passionate and hopeless regret.

Was that a husky laugh down in the court below, on the stairs, or in the room beside him? – her devil's laugh when she would go her own way in spite of his remonstrances.

He raised his head and looked behind him to where the dress had been lying crumpled and away from his picture. God of Heaven! His dead model had returned and now stood at the open door beckoning upon him to come to her, with her lovely transparent arm bare to the elbow, and once more dressed in the costume which she had cast aside.

He looked no more at his replica, but followed the mocking spirit down the stairs, into the fog-wrapped alley, and onwards where she led him.

Down towards Wapping Old Stairs, where the shapeless hulks of the ships and barges loomed out from the swirling, rushing black river like ghosts, as she was, who floated towards them, luring him downwards, amongst the slime, to the abyss from which her lost soul had been recalled by his evil longings.

THE GHOST OF COCK LANE

Rose Biggin

There's going to be another séance! and you cannot move for people crammed together in that narrow road, the crushing of shoulders as they shove, seeking to peer in at the windows. These people stand in the snow-slush without a care in the world for the chill creeping up their legs, soaking around the edges of their skirts, and some enterprising soul has set up a stall to sell them roasted nuts.

It is the year of our Lord (*my* Lord, the Light-bringer) 1762: we are five minutes' walk from St Paul's and scandalously close to Gin Lane. To prevent ambiguity let me declare that your narrator is dead, and a ghost (though not resident in Cock Lane); but be assured this will in no way encumber our tale, and know that every word is true.

Voices can be made out through the bustle: 'If you want *my* opinion we shouldn't be having another séance at all.' That's a young woman wearing her fair share of powder, leaning nonchalantly against the dark brick wall. She underscores her point by spitting into a puddle.

"I agree," says a woman in a ragged shawl, tapping her foot impatiently. "Why speak to the ghost yet *again*? She's already been quite clear."

Jostling to the front, closer to the house, a pair of fellows with canes give their input.

"Aye, the ghost has spoken, therefore they should hang him and be done with it!"

A newly-arrived woman, panting for breath, worried she might have missed it, says: "Hanging's too good for a wife-poisoner!"

Everyone joins in, except me.

"I hear this house is alive with the horror of that ghastly scratching!"

"I heard the daughter never sleeps these days, for the horror of the wailing!"

"Aye well, it's her who's *doing* the wailing, ain't it."

The reply is given suspiciously through narrowed eyes: "Be that as it may..."

"Have you heard who is attending today?"

"Who's that then?"

"It's that pedantic bloke that knows about spellings."

"Says he's going to put a stop to it!"

"They always say that."

"Any nuts left, Mary?"

"Oh, yes please!"

The crowds fill almost the whole of Cock Lane but their attentions are centred on only one residence. It's been a palpable frustration to be one of the neighbours, these past few months.

From the dusty window of the narrowest room on the top floor of the thin tall house standing spindly in the middle of Cock Lane – from up on high it's possible to make out the felt hats and woollen scarves of the onlookers, to chart their dance through the sodden streets. Shouts and calls rise above the general din.

"Hang William Kent!" is the cry to be heard the most by now.

A bit of explanation for you, since you're here. This house in the middle of Cock Lane is owned by a man called Richard Parsons, his wife Carrots (as she is known most affectionately by all, on account of her hair colour) and their little daughter Elizabeth. Until recently, the landlord has been renting out the house to two of your upstanding tenants, the Kents: William and Fanny... but that was until poor Fanny died of the smallpox. William tried to cope however he could, however you can – but however he coped, the fact remains that shortly after and not even before poor Fanny's funeral could occur, there began to come a-scratching on the walls and the doors of the house in Cock Lane, and a series of dreadful knocks, and the little girl Elizabeth began to have difficulty sleeping.

The day William and Fanny moved in to the house on Cock Lane – only a matter of months ago, how things change – they had been sitting shivering at the kitchen table, while the landlord leaned forwards most helpfully and enthusiastically stated his case for hospitality. The child Elizabeth stood in the corner of the room, sucking her fingers and dangling a rag doll by one leg, watching these strangers negotiate the details of where they would live.

The landlord threw his empty bottle into the basket by the fire and said:

"Well, never mind that your previous landlord threw you out, or why – I'm sure that's none of my business!"

Just as they grow unsure of where exactly he's going with this, his face widens into a generous smile.

"I can tell from here you're upstanding citizens, no doubt in m'mind. Elizabeth!"

He turns to his daughter. "Take Fanny upstairs and show her the rooms." He spreads his arms wide. "Welcome!"

The landlord waits for the footsteps to take them all the way up the rickety staircases, until they are safely away at the top of the house. He swills a sentence around in his mouth, then casually speaks into the air:

"I've a thought for you."

"A thought?"

"A little one. By which I mean nothing so urgent as to become a *question*. It's a matter concerning money."

"Of course," says William earnestly. "Rest assured we've enough for a few months in advance."

"All for the good," says the landlord. He takes a moment to gently drum his fingers on his thighs.

"Can I ask: do you happen to have any more besides?"

William looks up and for a moment the gaze between them sticks.

"I'm sorry?"

"It's a money matter."

William nods in agreement, confused.

"Merely a few guineas, that's all I'm talking about."

William's mouth moves without sound, as if counting what could be bought with these few guineas.

"Can you lend me twelve guineas?"

The landlord's expression is placid.

"What?"

The landlord sits back, as if the matter were already agreed. "We'll call it a loan. Imagine: you'll be in the loaning game!"

William rouses himself. "Now just a moment –"

"I know, I know," the landlord waves his hand about as if performing a magic spell to eliminate all troubles. I'm aware it makes the first payment feel a little heavier."

"That's certainly a concern –"

"Come now, William," he says, softly holding his hand between both of his. "I'll pay you back regular as clocks. A guinea a month."

And the landlord breaks off and wanders freely around the kitchen, eventually coming in close to throw his arm over William's shoulder.

"I can see this is going to work out for us both. You seem like my kind of fellow. Who'd've thought you'd be looking to move into a lovely new set of lodgings – in a nice house – with your lovely family? And it's so convenient because I was really scratching my head about sorting out that loan, and the fact that the two situations can work together couldn't be any neater, could it? Well that's just fantastic. I'm glad you agree. It's lovely to have you both moving in."

So William Kent loans money to his landlord.

Back to the bustling street, then. And you're just in time, because the séance party is about to arrive. In the throng of people, as the new arrivals – in their dark coats with buttons of silver – push through the waiting onlookers, you must try to keep an eye out for three figures in particular: the priest; the great and famous man of letters brought in to aid proceedings; and the tragic, tensely striding figure of the accused man, William Kent, whom you've just met.

The priest is highly esteemed in this part of town, since he has been conducting the séance at Cock Lane for several weeks now. Each one draws a larger crowd.

There is a reason for the repeated séances. This is because there can be no mistakes. This is a city of reason, and of utmost reasonableness; and as people of reason the investigation must be conducted in the most logical manner, and please no one get overexcited, as is explained in the priest's new pamphlet.

The first thing a person of reason should do is try to establish what the ghost actually wants.

Through a slow and scientific method, the priest has developed a means of impressive communication with the ghost, and found that the spirit of Cock Lane is none other than Fanny herself: that she is newly dead but not of smallpox; that she seeks vengeance for her foul and most unnatural murder. The spirit of Fanny claims her widower William poisoned her with arsenic in her broth, and calls for revenge.

Naturally. You can see why everybody in the street is calling for the hangman.

Back to the road, then – Cock Lane close-pushed with eager onlookers. More arriving, fresh flecks of snow arching past the gas lamps as another cloud opens. And there's the carriage pulling up, there's the grand buckled shoes getting out. It's Dr Johnson! There's the first people to notice his approach; the increase in the general intensity of the buzzing. He is not alone, of course, he is surrounded by folk of near-to-close social standing, a small clump of darkly-dressed respectable gentlemen of this parish, including the priest himself who will be communicating with the ghost – but really it is *he*, Samuel Johnson, the people are excited to see – esteemed composer of the Dictionary and occasional call-upon for civic matters, it's *he* they've heard of, mostly for the former – and now he strides through the Cock Lane crowds chest forward, eyes on the peeling paint door on the wooden front entrance to the house he seeks, the knocker glowing before him like the end of the alphabet – pushing open the door and standing confidently in the parlour of the haunted house, his eyes gazing briefly about the rafters before coming to rest with the heaviness of a millstone in the soft superstitions of the masses; it's the man himself, the very definition.

"We've a hoax to expose, let us hurry up and get about it," says Dr Johnson.

The priest pinkens about the cheeks as they all go upstairs.

The understanding that had somehow been keeping the crowd outside is abandoned, and people spill in through the entranceway, bringing the snow-chill in with them. Since the house is smaller than the street, soon people are squashed in the doorway.

There's a sudden surge in the shouts from below.

Dr Johnson interprets. "That must be our final participant."

The crowd jeers at the accused, William, as they politely part to let him by – from the front door all the way up to the top bedroom. There's really not a lot of space.

A stately woman in brocade speaks from the crowd: "We'll have answers to-day, Mr Kent. No more guesswork, no more approximation."

The whole party ascends to the top of the house and soon the whole building is filled to the rafters. Much of the occupation goes to groups of friends who always look to do their catching up at the Cock Lane séances, due to the social ambience.

The smallest room, right up in the dusty attic-space of the house, contains a small bed with crumpled sheets. In the bed sits Elizabeth, the daughter of the landlord of the house, looking pale and resolute. This whole thing by now is an accustomed ritual. Above her bed towers the landlord, an image of concern and haggardness.

A row of chairs line the walls and Dr Johnson sits in the centremost, facing the occupied bed. The priest looks around for support, aggrieved at the new seating arrangements. He eventually perches on a chair at the far end – opposite to William.

There is a moment of heavy, full silence, as if they all sit within a giant ball of snow. I look from one face to another, and observe the airs of concentration and anticipation. Johnson is looking quizzically at the door lintels.

The priest leans forwards slightly on his chair and clears his throat. It resonates in that thickly-quiet room.

He closes his eyes, and everyone holds their breath.

"Remember the system, O spirit; please knock once for yes, twice for no." He raises his arms slightly. "As per the usual."

This news is echoed in excited whispers all the way down the stairs.

The girl screws her eyes closed and tosses her head around a bit.

Someone hollers: "It's Fanny – she's with us!"

The priest catches the moment and launches into his first question, his knuckles clasped.

"Are you the ghost of the wife of Mr William Kent here – by which I mean, do we address the spirit of Fanny Lynes?"

One knock.

The crowd gasps.

"And did you die naturally?"

Knock. Knock.

"By poison?"

Knock.

The crowd hiss, newly riled. William looks irritated.

"And do you know which poison?"

Knock...

Knock.

"I see. Would you be willing to hazard a guess?"

Knock.

"Arsenic?"

Knock.

The crowd whoops. The priest looks serious.

"And was this poison administered, without your knowledge or desire, by Mr William Kent here?"

Konckhm.

That's the simultaneous sound of the knock in response to the priest's question and William rising angrily from his chair where it bangs heavily against the wall.

"I will not have this go on any further!" he cries. "This is slander upon my life and I shan't idly sit by!"

"Your life is exactly what's at *stake*, sir – pray calm yourself and sit down!" The priest's eyes are starting to glaze over with the stress of an interruption.

"I'm telling you this is ridiculous, I didn't kill her," says William. "I don't want to be back in Cock Lane. I'd be away grieving if you hadn't dragged me here."

The landlord rises from his chair: he and William now stare at each other across the room. It's a game of tennis and contempt is the ball. "Ridiculous, sir? Are we wasting your time?" says the landlord. His voice is as thick as coffee house dregs. "It's making my daughter suffer, sir, and I don't find *that* ridiculous at all."

They turn to Elizabeth, who shrugs and does a little cough.

William concedes. "Of course not."

The landlord's hands are fists by his sides. "So let the ghost say what she has to say!"

"Kind words, I'd hope!" cries William. "I loved Fanny and she me. For what reasons would I poison her?"

"If you were so in love, sir, why weren't you married?"

A gasp sweeps through the crowd.

"Mr Kent," says the priest, his voice level. "Is this true?"

William Kent looks down at his shoes. "Not through any lack of will. But through difficult circumstances."

"Oh yes, you heard what I said," continues the landlord, looking around at the shocked company. "Drummed out of their previous lodgings for ungodly behaviours. I didn't judge though, did I? Took 'em in out of my own charity, and get repaid with a murder under my own roof and a daughter forever channelling spooks."

William points to his landlord with his full arm. "You, sir, are horrendous."

The landlord points to himself, innocently. "Am I on a murder charge?"

"Neither am I!"

"*They* all think you are." A round gesture, taking in the audience. The priest mutters something vague about jurisprudence.

"His first wife even had the same name as my little girl!" cries the landlord. "Perhaps we are dealing with a serial wife-poisoner!"

"What?" William looks around indignantly. "That hasn't even anything to do with this. She died in childbirth!"

"Interesting," he mutters.

William's mouth moves but no sounds emerge. The priest takes the opportunity to jump back in. He claps his hands together and rubs them.

"Shall we carry on?" he says brightly, as if everyone has just returned from taking a break for lunch. "To be honest I do think we are nearly finished."

Without turning to look at his daughter in the bed the landlord speaks. "Bring her back to us, Elizabeth." He looks again at William, standing there seething by the wall. "This'll be the final chat we'll need, I have a *very* good feeling."

Silence settles again as the company turns its attentions to the girl in the bed, and she closes her eyes to channel the ghost. It's irrelevant now, anyway, whether William and Fanny shared the surname Kent; what's in question is solely whether William will live to mourn her.

Silence once more descends, and the reverend opens his mouth to speak.

He is interrupted by someone else. This time it's the renowned composer of the English Dictionary.

Dr Johnson holds up his hand.

"I have a thought," he says.

The priest throws both his arms up at the interruption. "Is it necessary to declare your thought *right now?*"

Dr Johnson raises both hands before him as if in surrender and looks around, making sure everybody observes his apparent humility. Instead of lowering them, he addresses the room: "This is my gesture." Everyone looks at him bemused. He continues: "With my arms in this position I am saying: *I will not intervene, I will not interrupt, I surrender to whatever comes.* And I would like everyone on these chairs to do it with me."

The priest hits his thighs with his hands several times. "Will you stop it, sir! You are making mischief with my spirit. This matter is incredibly serious. Pray desist!"

Another thought strikes him.

"And added to that, this motion of yours not to disturb proceedings is indeed an utmost hypocrisy, as it is in itself an interruption!"

Dr Johnson remains placid, hands gently wiggling in the air. After a brief standoff the priest is surprised to find himself mirroring the gesture.

The collective of séance-followers look to the priest for guidance. He looks back at them, pasting an expression of wisdom over his face like a poster for the circus.

"Let us all follow along with Dr Johnson's idea," he says. His face registers serene calm, but there is a slight waver to his voice that indicates Dictionary Johnson has taken him a few miles beyond the end of his tether.

The people standing together in the door frame immediately raise their hands, then turn to check everyone behind them is doing the same.

The gesture travels down the stairwell and across the rooms, resulting in the rustling of hundreds of arms taking on their new positions. In no time, hands are raised all through the house in solemn promise. Hands of various shapes and sizes, all pleased to be in the air.

The landlord tries to protest, but his objections are already stale as old beer. "Can't we just continue on without any of this sort of nonsense?" But the social pressure is too much as he looks around at all the forest of excited fingers, and eventually he too raises his arms with a laboured sigh.

Dr Johnson turns his gaze to the small child in the bed. His eyes twinkle with kindliness as he waggles his raised hands at her.

The landlord glares at Dr Johnson and addresses his daughter. "*You* don't have to," he says. "You're the one suffering here, don't let him boss you around."

The priest, having now given himself fully over to the sense of community Dr Johnson's instruction has instigated, is positively jolly. His hands wave about enthusiastically in the air. "Oh let's not leave anybody out! It's all about demonstrating our commitment to getting to the bottom of this whole issue. Good idea, Johnson."

The girl looks towards her father. He looks back at her and she slowly begins to slide her hands out from under the bedsheet; the landlord follows the movement, whilst willing the hands backwards with his eyes. Reality wins and the hands eventually come up over the sheet and are raised slowly up either side of her concerned face.

The landlord looks about the place, his eyes flicking from door to windows and back, over and over, perhaps wondering which route would provide the least difficult escape. The only swift route is out the window; but at what angle is the drainpipe? Too high to leave it to chance... certainty slips away from him, as he feels himself to be the unfortunate owner of a property who is pitifully ignorant of his own floorplan.

The priest clears his throat, finally ready to begin again with the ghost. But then a strange thing happens and it would appear Dr Johnson is now leading the proceedings.

"O spirit," he says, "sorry for the wait. Please do speak with us again."

A look flashes across the priest's face, the briefest of protests, but no one else seems to mind Dr Johnson's takeover.

"We're all wanting to know if you're here to see justice done for your murder?"

No knock comes.

"Do you wish William Kent to be disgraced and surely hanged for the crime of your murder?"

No knock.

"Are you still there?"

Nothing.

"O spirit?"

Nothing at all.

Looks are thrown around at this unusual development.

"Right," says Dr Johnson. He is already tidying his personals into his bag. "I trust this settles the matter. Do you think that carriage will still be outside?"

Dear reader, I am *so* tempted to deliver a single *knock* at this point, I cannot tell you.

The priest pays keen attention to the frost gathering in the corners of the window frame.

"Elizabeth?" he says, innocently, not looking at her. "Is there anything you would like to share with the group?"

Wincing a little, the girl reveals a small wooden block from about her skirts. The priest takes it from her hand, getting a sense of its heaviness, and attempts a few trial knockings 'pon the bedframe. The ghost's voice, exactly.

With the look of a man who has just guessed someone's card in a pack, the priest glances excitedly around the room, as if to say, *Ooooh.*

"Well that's a result," says William.

The crowd all drop their hands down again, and let out a collective despondent groan followed by tuts and scuffing shoes as they make their way back down the stairs.

In truth I feel despondent myself, as if we've all been taken round the bloody houses.

The priest stands fully upright. "I for one am glad," he says, looking around the assembled company, "for we have uncovered an act of utmost deception using approaches of reason and fact. It seems clear to me now —" he raises his voice to shout over the sound of droves of people leaving — "that this is the real crook, here." He points at the landlord. "Shame on you, sir, for inducing your daughter to act the ghost for you. It's a blasphemy to go about imitating the presence of spirits."

Dr Johnson has pulled on a pair of dark brown gloves and is already at the door. "Call trial on the landlord and let's get out of here."

The priest is fastening his collar. "I think this has gone smoothly, considering various factors, interruptions and so on," he says. "Well done everyone."

Dr Johnson nods politely in receipt of varying acknowledgments, then addresses the newly-uncondemned man.

"You must be feeling suitably relieved. I do hope you have a good afternoon."

"Thank you. I suppose I shouldn't expect him to ever return my twelve guineas."

Dr Johnson raises an eyebrow.

"In future, William Kent, I would advise against loaning money to your own landlord. Most unconventional a direction for debt to flow."

And he leads the party out of the house.

And Dr Johnson and the others stand triumphant in the front doorway, framed by a rectangle of light, the glare of winter sun on half-melted snow; and he cries to the awaiting crowds that the so-called Ghost of Cock Lane has finally been revealed as a dreadful hoax, and now to get out of his way please — for they'll have their chance to read about it in the papers and pour over the etchings and see it enacted in the popular dramas... and in time, of course, there go the crowds: disappointed in truth, realising that what they really preferred was speculation; and there goes the landlord in the grip of the constables, which is just as well, because Fanny's tragic story of arsenic before marriage was in danger of blossoming into a cautionary tale against indulging in the old pre-marital. But now we know it was never Fanny scratching there, only a small girl with a block of wood, enlisted through pressure and persuasion by a man who was a sort of block of wood himself in his own way, who'd rather see an innocent man hang than give up any of his money owed. It's all property and the exchanging of coin, in the end.

Beware landlords!

THE HAND THAT ROCKS THE CRADLE

Juliet E. McKenna

Charlotte woke. The five chimes from St Barnabas' soot-blackened tower faded with her dreams of the summer countryside. The memory of meadows sweetly scented with flowers was replaced with the reek of slops from the alley which her grimy window overlooked. Despite this early hour, with the May sun barely risen above the rooftops, carts rattled, horses neighed and draymen shouted in the brewery yard on the far side.

Even in the dead of night, London was never silent. Charlotte obstinately screwed her eyes tight shut. She wished that she could find herself back in Eastridge Parva by means of some unforeseen miracle. Even as she did so, her conscience pricked her. What sort of behaviour was that for a governess? Such self-indulgence was shameful in a young woman offering moral and spiritual guidance to impressionable girls.

Besides, why did she deserve such a miracle? Charlotte knew what her father would have said. She had her health and her strength and her good character. She should thank The Good Lord for His blessings and do His bidding with dutiful humility, trusting that His divine mercy would pour down on those in genuine need.

She opened her eyes and blinked away tears springing half from grief and half from anger. She missed her father so sorely; his unfailing kindness, his patience with his own pupils and his modesty, whether parsing Virgil with a true scholar's aptitude or preaching with quiet authority from the St Michael and All Angels' pulpit.

The thought of Lord Palgrave's feckless third son Albert standing in her father's place prompted Charlotte's anger. Where was divine providence when that chinless wastrel held the keys to the church and the rectory? Henry VIII might have rewarded his ancestors' loyalty with the long-dissolved abbey's lands, but where was the justice in his father using his right to appoint the parish priest to give this otherwise useless young man the pretence of an occupation and income?

Where was divine mercy now that her mother and her three younger sisters and two hopeful brothers had been turned out of the only home they had ever known, dependent on distant relatives' cold charity?

Charlotte drew a deep breath and threw back the threadbare sheet and equally worn blanket. She had declared she had no need of such grudging benevolence. She would earn her own living like countless other respectable and blamelessly impoverished women. So if she wasn't to be forced into a humiliating return, begging for forgiveness, she had better make haste.

She sat on the edge of the sagging mattress, straining her ears for any sound of the slatternly maid-of-all-work's feet on the stairs. Nothing. Another morning when she must go without the hot water supposedly included in her rent. Well, at least a brisk wash in the cold water from her basin's ewer helped wake her up.

St Barnabas' clock struck the half hour as she made her way downstairs, dressed in her sober grey dress. She had long since given up hope of the buttered bread and coffee which Mrs Foster invariably promised but so rarely provided. No matter. Charlotte had saved a roll from her dinner the night before, now wrapped in a linen napkin inside her purse. It would be somewhat stale but she could break her fast on the walk to her first pupil. No one in London would give her a second glance and there was no one who knew her to tell her mother that her eldest daughter was so lost to propriety that she had been seen eating in public.

Charlotte halted in the ill-swept hallway to raise her brown cloak's hood over her bonnet. The morning would still be chilly and besides, hiding her face saved her from errand boys' impertinences.

She paused and looked at the closed door at the foot of the stairs. She could hear Mrs Foster moving around in her own apartment in the basement but there was no sound at all from Miss Lewes who had this ground floor room. Belatedly Charlotte recalled that the door had been closed yesterday morning and the previous two mornings as well. But last week she had always passed a few words with Miss Lewes as she left the house. The kindly old lady was always awake before six after a lifetime spent educating recalcitrant children. The silence took on an ominous tone.

Charlotte walked to the top of the stairs leading down to the kitchen. "Mrs Foster?" When a genteel call won her no reply, she shouted more loudly. "Mrs Foster!"

"I was just coming up. The fire won't draw, you see –"

Charlotte wasn't interested in the shifty-eyed landlady's excuses. "Is Miss Lewes away?"

Mrs Foster stared upwards, her toothless mouth gaping in momentary surprise. "Gone away? She said nothing to me."

She came stumping up the stairs, one hand fumbling in her grimy apron's pocket as her face darkened wrathfully. "Done a flit? We'll see about that."

"I didn't say she's gone away," Charlotte protested, "I only asked if she had."

"She must have left Sunday. That's when I last seen her." Mrs Foster sorted through her keys before thrusting one into the lock and twisting it furiously. "Sly cat. Calls herself a lady –"

They both heard Miss Lewes' key fall from the lock to land with a sharp bang on the bare boards on the inside of the door. Mrs Foster sucked at her gums before reaching for the knob. She shoved the door open, only to baulk on the threshold.

A head taller, Charlotte could see past the landlady into the room. It was as meanly furnished as her own but at least Miss Lewes had mementos of her long life to brighten the walls and adorn the mantelshelf. Sunlight glinted on the frame of a daguerreotype showing the grand house where she had first served as a governess.

Miss Lewes would never look fondly on such memories again. Charlotte pressed a trembling hand to her mouth as she contemplated the figure slumped motionless in the chair by the window. There could be no question that the old lady was several days dead with the greenish pallor of her face only relieved by the bruise-like darkness of her lips and eyelids.

"Turned up her toes?" Mrs Foster screeched. "Who's to be put to the trouble of dealing with this, might I ask?"

"Her family —" But even as Charlotte spoke, she recalled Miss Lewes speaking of her parents and only brother, all long dead of the Asiatic Cholera, and of her brother's widow and son, whom she had so faithfully supported with her own earnings after the bank where all their legacies were invested had failed through unwise speculation.

The widow had died three years ago of a broken heart after her son had fallen in the Crimea. The regiment's repayment of the hundreds of pounds spent purchasing his cavalry commission had gone to settle the profligate young man's debts. Charlotte looked around the room and wondered if Miss Lewes had ever begrudged such lifelong sacrifice of her own daily comfort and any prospect of a secure old age.

Walking stealthily, as though the dead woman was only sleeping and might wake, she crossed the room to look at the cup and saucer on the sill. The stain of a last drink of tea was dry as a bone. Charlotte looked around the room. There was no sign of any food.

There was a neat stack of letters on the small writing desk. She moved a little closer, trying to read the topmost without openly intruding.

Dear Miss Lewes,
Thank you for your letter concerning our advertisement in The Times.
Regretfully I must inform you that the position has been filled —

Charlotte didn't need to read any more. She had her own collection of such letters. Miss Lewes had seen her distress when she had made the mistake of opening one in the hall, in her first week in London.

She knew that Miss Lewes had been trying in vain to secure a position since Michaelmas last year, with skills and testimonials far superior to Charlotte's own. In her youth, before such subjects were deemed unsuitable for girls, the older woman had learned Latin and Greek alongside her lost brother, together with Mathematics and Natural Philosophy. She had been governess to three titled families until her charges had married, all to advantage naturally. Each time

Miss Lewes' services had been dispensed with, her future of no concern to her erstwhile employers.

Charlotte looked at the dead woman again. "She just gave up. She locked herself in and sat in that chair and closed her eyes until her trials ended."

How truly desolate Miss Lewes must have been, for her hopelessness to outweigh whatever torments of hunger and thirst she must have suffered. Charlotte shuddered.

In the next moment, she stiffened as Mrs Foster bustled across to the mantelshelf and began examining the candlesticks and picture frames.

The landlady sniffed with contempt. "Brummagem ware. Not a hallmark to be seen. Might fetch a few bob all together, I suppose."

"What are you doing?" Charlotte's question was as curt a rebuke as any she might offer an impertinent pupil.

Mrs Forster turned to her, brazen. "You want to see her buried by the parish? Thrown into a pauper's grave? If she's to go to her rest with some dignity someone will have to pay and it won't be me, my girl."

Before Charlotte could find a response, the woman smiled, slyly. "Shouldn't you be on your way? Don't want to lose your place, do you?"

St Barnabas's clock chimed the third quarter. A chill ran through Charlotte. "I –"

Her feet were already carrying her to the front door and down the stained steps to the stinking street. She ran, hitching her skirts up above her ankles in shameless fashion, with no thought of trying to eat her bread. Even so, she knew it was well past the hour as she rounded the corner into Parmenter Street.

"Oh!" Charlotte barely escaped disaster as she came face to face with a chimney sweep's boy carrying a bundle of rods and brushes over one shoulder, his suit and face alike as black as pitch.

"I beg your pardon, miss." The lad stepped aside with a bow and flourish of his free soot-stained hand, as elegant as any gentleman on a Sunday in the park.

"You are excused," Charlotte said breathlessly.

She forced herself to slow to a ladylike walk, not least in case she was spotted from some upstairs window before she reached the Warringtons' house. Opening the gate in the black iron railings, she made haste down the basement steps, already scrubbed to gleaming whiteness this morning.

"Miss Cheriton."

"Mr Leigh." Charlotte was surprised into an unseemly squeak.

Why was the tall butler answering her ring on the kitchen door bell? He should be above stairs, directing the footmen about their duties while he stood ready to receive cards and callers at the house's pillared entrance.

"Mr Warrington has instructed me to give you this." He handed Charlotte a letter sealed with wax dark as blood. "Good day to you, Miss Cheriton."

"I'm sorry I am late, but –" She stood, aghast, as the butler closed the door in her face.

She looked down at the letter. The seal was so fresh that smeared wax stained her glove. She would never get the mark out of the pale kidskin, Charlotte thought numbly, and she could not afford a new pair.

She unsealed and unfolded the letter. She read the few curt lines in Mr Warrington's sweeping script. At least, Charlotte discovered, she had not been dismissed for being late this morning.

Mr Warrington regretted that he had been so foolish to concede to his wife's importuning. There could be no possible need for his daughters to amuse themselves learning French and Italian and History. Their own mother could perfectly well instruct them in the genteel manners and artistic and musical accomplishments desirable in a wife.

As a loving father, he rejected the cruelty of cramming his cherished children's heads with unnecessary knowledge and corrupting their innocence with notions they could have no use for in their future lives.

Anger momentarily overwhelmed Charlotte's anguish. Did Mr Warrington mean to slight her so thoroughly? Did he realise how grievously he insulted her father?

The Reverend Cheriton had not scorned to educate his own daughters. Indeed, her own governess had lived under the family's roof, bed and board all found with a respectable salary besides. Miss Andrews had not been paid a miserly penny per pupil per hour for the onerous task of disciplining and instructing three vain and spiteful little girls while their mother made her leisurely breakfast and prepared herself for a day of selfish indolence.

Charlotte screwed the letter into a wrathful ball and hurled it at the closed door. Mr Warrington was no gentleman He was a coward if he couldn't even dismiss her from his service in person. As for his daughters, let him see how their marriages prospered once they burdened their husbands with debt for lack of the basic arithmetic to count their pin money.

She climbed the steps back to the pavement and strode purposefully away. As she reached the far end of the street, though, her furious pace slowed. It wasn't as if she had anywhere to go until mid-morning; to the Martin house where she was engaged to instruct their four daughters from ten till twelve, before the Barlows' two girls benefited from her tuition from half past the hour until half past three, leaving Charlotte barely enough time to reach the Armitage residence to commence lessons promptly at four until the three fractious children were swept away to their nursery at seven.

Apprehension weighed her down as she walked aimlessly onwards. How soon would she be able to find another family to employ her at the start of each day? Charlotte's pace slowed still further as she realised her unguarded feet were already taking her towards the elegant square where the Martins lived. She really didn't want to arrive early. Master Robert Martin and his brother George were both home from school and fancied themselves great flirts even though they were barely whiskered. Charlotte had already made the mistake of treating them as familiarly as her own brothers. She had suffered a most unjust reprimand from the Martin's housekeeper, accused of seeking to lure one or other of the young masters into an illicit entanglement.

Had the vinegar-faced woman told her mistress of such scandalous suspicions? Weary tears stung Charlotte's eyes. She would be unable to help her mother, sisters and brothers without the Warringtons' money. If the Martins dismissed her, she would be hard pressed to keep body and soul together.

"You're better off out of that house, miss. The master takes liberties with the parlour maids and old Leigh cheats the mistress by selling off the linens what he claims the laundry has spoiled."

Startled to hear a voice so close behind her, Charlotte spun around. She gaped, astonished to see the chimney sweep's boy whom she had so nearly collided with in her earlier hurry.

"I been going into that house since I was a climbing boy," he assured her. "You hear no end of secrets when no one realises you're up a flue."

Charlotte's surprise was overtaken by indignation. "How dare you address me?"

"No need to cut up rough with me, miss," he chided her mildly. "I've done you no wrong."

Charlotte drew a sharp breath but could not deny the truth of his words. "No, indeed." It was unjust to vent her fear and anger on this luckless youth.

"I might be able to do you a good turn, miss," he ventured.

She had already turned her back on him. Now Charlotte stood stock still save for a tremor running through her.

Mr Barnett, her mother's remote cousin, had warned her of the countless perils lurking in London. Indeed, he had prophesied disgrace and disaster when Charlotte had announced her intention of making her own way in the metropolis, although, abruptly red-faced, he declined to explain precisely what catastrophes might befall unprotected young women.

"There's help for young ladies like yourself, miss."

Charlotte turned to look warily at the sweep. "The Governesses Benevolent Fund."

She had heard rumour of such charity but making any application meant admitting the abject failure of all her hopes.

The sweep grinned, his teeth startlingly white against the soot blackening his face. "Wouldn't you rather have help finding a good position? I know a governesses' registry office."

Charlotte shook her head. "They won't want me."

She had visited several such offices when she had first arrived in London, only to be looked up and down disapprovingly by those whiskered gentlemen. Governesses must bring more maturity to a schoolroom, they had explained in quelling tones, in order to impose adequate authority.

"Never mind, they cannot hold your youth against you forever." Miss Lewes had comforted her with typical kindness even though those same officious gentlemen had rejected her on account of her advanced years.

The chimney sweep was still grinning. "You should meet these ladies before you're so sure of that."

"Ladies?" Faint hope kindled in Charlotte's heart. Surely gentlewomen would have a better appreciation of her plight.

"Come along with me." The sweep was already crossing the road, heading towards a narrow entry.

Charlotte followed, suddenly resolute. *Audaces Fortuna iuvat*, as her father would have said. Fortune favours the bold. Though as she belatedly recalled the Reverend Cheriton reading Mr Dryden's translation to the family in the parlour, she rather thought the heroic young gentleman proclaiming such sentiments in Virgil's Aeneid had come to an unfortunate end.

She thrust away unbidden recollection of the tales of deceit and stealthy murder which she had glimpsed in those illustrated papers read illicitly below stairs in the Warrington and Barlow households. It was broad daylight after all with plenty of respectable men and women about their business on the streets and lanes which the sweep led her through.

Granted, after turning the fifth or sixth corner, Charlotte realised she had lost her bearings. No matter. These scholarly ladies could doubtless direct her to a thoroughfare she would recognise. All Charlotte needed to do was keep an ear cocked for the sound of a church clock's bells in order to leave in good time to reach the Martin's house at her appointed hour.

"Here we are, miss." Rounding a final corner, the youthful sweep pointed to the end house of the neat brick-built terrace.

Charlotte looked up the steps to see a modest brass plate on the wall beside the black-painted door.

The Alice Street Educational Registry.

It certainly looked a respectable house. The brass was polished, the paint was gleaming and the steps were scrubbed clean. The muslin curtains hanging at the windows were crisp and fresh.

"Go on, miss," the sweep urged.

"One moment." Charlotte reached into her purse, steeling herself to part with a thruppeny piece to reward the boy, but when she looked up, he was nowhere to be seen.

Indeed, she realised somewhat nervously, there was no one on this street at all. The pavements and road alike were deserted, unlike the thronged streets they had been walking through. There was no sign of life anywhere, until she looked up at the house and saw a muslin drape twitch.

Charlotte squared her shoulders and marched up the steps. She grasped the polished brass knocker in her gloved hand and rapped a brisk request for admittance.

Alea jacta est. The die is cast. She frowned as she recalled Julius Caesar had said that. Were there no Latin proverbs from stories with more promising outcomes?

"Good morning." A small, stout lady dressed in rusty black opened the door to reveal a hallway tiled in black and white with a staircase immediately ahead and a door to the left standing ajar.

Even to call the stout lady plain would be stretching truth to breaking point. In all honesty, she was breathtakingly ugly with her face as round and wrinkled as a discarded apple, her complexion coarse and brown and her eyes as black as boot buttons. Her nose was as bulbous and round as a misshapen potato.

"I —" Charlotte realised she was staring, transfixed by the sight of the single front tooth protruding over the woman's lower lip. Blushing, she turned as though to indicate the chimney sweep even though she knew full well he wasn't there.

She got herself in hand and cleared her throat as she looked back at the ugly woman. "Good morning. I understand this is an educational registry. I am a daily governess at present and am seeking a permanent position in a private household or perhaps in a school. I was directed here." She chose not to say who had led her to this door.

The ugly woman in black looked at her unsmiling. Charlotte lifted her chin and looked back at her. After a moment, she raised her eyebrows in mild enquiry.

The black-gowned woman's lips twitched, though Charlotte was unable to decide whether that signified amusement or contempt.

The woman rapped sharply on the tiles with the stick she had been leaning on. Startled, Charlotte thought she was being dismissed. Then she realised the woman was opening the door wider, using her stick to beckon Charlotte inside.

"Our Principal will wish to interview you." The black-gowned woman stumped towards the half-open door.

"Naturally." Charlotte followed, bracing herself for an encounter with someone even more formidable as the ugly woman ushered her into the sitting room.

Entering the room, however, she was disarmed to see a small and slightly-built woman seated behind a substantial leather-topped desk. Charlotte could not have guessed at her age; her face was as unlined as a doll's and her shiny black hair showed no hint of grey.

"Please, be seated." The woman leaned forward to indicate the empty chair on the other side of the desk.

Other than that, there was no furniture in the room beyond a hat stand in the corner, with a sensible black hat perched above a plain coat and an umbrella with an unexpectedly frivolous handle tucked into the base along with a large bag.

As Charlotte took the empty seat, the Principal folded her rather large hands on the desk before her. Charlotte wondered if she was near-sighted since she seemed to be peering intently at her. Perhaps, perhaps not. Regardless, the woman's bright blue eyes looked shrewd.

"I can provide references –" Charlotte began.

"Oh, we make it a rule never to give references," the Principal said firmly.

"Never?" Charlotte gaped.

The Principal smiled. "We find it unnecessary with our particular clientele. Tell me about yourself. Where have you come from? Why seek employment as a governess?"

"I was born and raised in Hampshire." Unaccountably, Charlotte found herself telling this stranger all the trials and tribulations which had beset her since her father's untimely death. Blushing as she realised she was imparting unseemly confidences, she hurriedly explained her hope of finding work in London.

"My mother was a governess before her marriage and she continued to help my father teach the pupils whom he prepared for the Universities –"

"Do you believe that women should be admitted to the Universities?" The Principal cocked her head to one side, bird-like.

"I do." Charlotte hesitated before continuing boldly. "I see no reason why women shouldn't be educated alongside their brothers. I believe that women could be doctors or scientists to equal any man. That we could run shops and railways and factories and anything else we put our minds to."

Charlotte didn't read the blood-curdling tales of murder and mayhem when she could abstract a newspaper from an employer's kitchen but the social and political writings of Mr Dickens and his fellow thinkers.

"I believe in reform of education and of the franchise and of the Poor Laws and the mines –" Her courage abruptly failed her and she bit her lip.

"Good," the Principal said firmly. "We have no time for old-fashioned attitudes here."

Charlotte was startled. "Your clientele accept such radical –?" She couldn't think how to frame her question without offering unintended insult.

"Our clientele accept us for who we are and for the particular services we can render them." The Principal smiled mysteriously. "Do you think that you can teach kindness and consideration for the rest of humanity to the over-indulged children of the blinkered and foolish?"

"I can try," Charlotte ventured. Before she could find a way to ask how exactly she might do so, she heard the clangour of church bells a few streets away.

"Excuse me, I must –" she broke off, puzzled to hear the bells ringing a peal rather than sounding the hour.

"Did you wish to attend divine service today?" The Principal enquired. "I believe you will have to wait for Evensong."

"Today?" Charlotte stared at her.

"It is Sunday, after all." The Principal raised her fine black brows.

Charlotte frowned. "Sunday? No –"

"Of course it's Sunday. Didn't you see how empty the streets were?" That mysterious smile still curved the Principal's lips.

Charlotte shook her head. "Forgive me –"

"You are excused." The Principal rose to her feet and offered Charlotte her hand. "Call again tomorrow if you wish to join our register. I hope you will. You are precisely the sort of young woman who will do very well with our help."

"I –" Charlotte drew a deep breath and stood up. "Thank you. Good day."

The ugly woman in black opened the door. Had she been listening at the keyhole, Charlotte wondered as she went out into the hallway.

"Good day," she said politely as the stout woman opened the door.

"Do call again." The woman's smile rendered her more hideous than ever with that protruding tooth.

Charlotte forbore to say she had no intention of returning to this strange place where people didn't even know what day of the week it was. She smiled with meaningless politeness and hurried down the steps.

It was only when she reached the end of the street that Charlotte realised she had neglected to ask for directions to some more familiar district. She had no idea which way to go to reach the Martin house. She didn't even know what time it was. Those dratted church bells were ringing another peal.

Charlotte's heart began to beat more quickly, her mouth dry with apprehension as all her cares came flocking back. Looking desperately this way and that, she saw a top-hatted gentleman approaching at a leisurely pace. She hurried towards him, heedless of propriety.

"Sir, I beg your pardon, but could you direct me towards Parmenter Street?" Retracing her steps was surely the swiftest way of returning to some recognisable locale.

"Parmenter Street?" The gentleman politely doffed his hat. "By all means. If you follow that road over there and then take the first left and the second right and carry straight on, you'll find it soon enough."

"Thank you." Charlotte broke off as the bells rang through the air again. "Excuse me, is there some celebration to prompt those peals?"

"Celebration?" The top-hatted man looked puzzled. "Not beyond celebrating the Sabbath and a day of rest from our labours."

"Day of rest?"

Charlotte stared at the man for so long that he coloured uncomfortably.

"Good day to you." He took a step.

"No, wait." Casting decorum to the winds, Charlotte seized his arm. "Please, I beg of you, what is the date?"

He stared at her, bemused. "It's the fifth of the month."

"The fifth?" Charlotte repeated faintly. "Then it really is Sunday."

"What other day would it be, to come after Saturday and before Monday?" The top-hatted man was growing distinctly uneasy.

"Then she's still alive." Charlotte didn't attempt to explain. She didn't bother trying to fathom this mystery. All such considerations could wait. She took to her heels.

With her back to the Alice Street house, Charlotte hadn't seen the muslin curtain twitch aside to give the sitting room's occupant a clear view of her encounter.

"Who brought her here, Mary?" As the woman in rusty black entered, she grew taller and more slender. Her shapeless gown was transformed into an elegant golden-brown dress while her complexion and features were smoothed into gentle loveliness.

"Tom, the sweep." The small woman with keen blue eyes continued to watch Charlotte running pell-mell down the road which the top-hatted man had indicated. She smiled as he looked up and doffed his hat before heading back the way he had come. "Was there something you wanted, Matilda?"

The transformed woman came to stand at the window beside her. "Ursula has written again. She says that while they are undoubtedly darling children, she is finding life as a Newfoundland dog increasingly tedious."

"Tell her it won't be for much longer. Peter will arrive soon."

Mary crossed the room to the hat stand. She shrugged on the plain coat and secured her sensible black hat with a pin.

Matilda was still looking out of the window. "Do you think we will see her again?"

"I believe so." Mary smiled, leaning down to pick up the large bag and the umbrella with the parrot's head handle.

"Do you suppose she will bring the old woman with her?" Matilda drew the curtains aside.

"Let us hope so." Mary took a moment to admire her reflection in the window. "We can do a great deal as nurses and nannies but it's time we found suitable governesses to continue our work."

"Indeed." Matilda threw up the heavy sash to open the window wide and the briskly blowing east wind carried Mary away.

WATERCRESS GIRL

Henry Mayhew

The little watercress girl who gave me the following statement, although only eight years of age, had entirely lost all childish ways, and was, indeed, in thoughts and manner, a woman. There was something cruelly pathetic in hearing this infant, so young that her features had scarcely formed themselves, talking of the bitterest struggles of life, with the calm earnestness of one who had endured them all. I did not know how to talk with her. At first I treated her as a child, speaking on childish subjects; so that I might, by being familiar with her, remove all shyness, and get her to narrate her life freely. I asked her about her toys and her games with her companions; but the look of amazement that answered me soon put an end to any attempt at fun on my part. I then talked to her about the parks, and whether she ever went to them. "The parks!" she replied in wonder, "where are they?" I explained to her, telling her that they were large open places with green grass and tall trees, where beautiful carriages drove about, and people walked for pleasure, and children played. Her eyes brightened up a little as I spoke; and she asked, half doubtingly, "Would they let such as me go there – just to look?" All her knowledge seemed to begin and end with watercresses, and what they fetched. She knew no more of London than that part she had seen on her rounds, and believed that no quarter of the town was handsomer or pleasanter than it was at Farringdon-market or at Clerkenwell, where she lived. Her little face, pale and thin with privation, was wrinkled where the dimples ought to have been, and she would sigh frequently. When some hot dinner was offered to her, she would not touch it, because, if she eat too much, "it made her sick," she said; "and she wasn't used to meat, only on a Sunday."

The poor child, although the weather was severe, was dressed in a thin cotton gown, with a threadbare shawl wrapped round her shoulders. She wore no covering to her head, and the long rusty hair stood out in all directions. When she walked she shuffled along, for fear that the large carpet slippers that served her for shoes should slip off her feet.

"I go about the streets with water-creases, crying, 'Four bunches a penny, water-creases.' I am just eight years old – that's all, and I've a big sister, and a brother and a sister younger than I am. On and off, I've been very near a twelvemonth in the streets. Before that, I had to take care of a baby for my aunt. No, it wasn't heavy – it was only two months old; but I minded it for ever such a time – till it could walk. It was a very nice little baby, not a very pretty one; but, if I touched it under the chin, it would laugh. Before I had the baby, I used to help mother, who was in the fur trade; and, if there was any slits in the fur, I'd sew them up. My mother learned me to needle-work and to knit when I was about five. I used to go to school, too; but I wasn't there long. I've forgot all about it now, it's such a time ago; and mother took me away because the master whacked me, though the missus use'n't to never touch me. I didn't like him at all. What do you think? He hit me three times, ever so hard, across the face with his cane, and made me go dancing down stairs; and when mother saw the marks on my cheek, she went to blow him up, but she couldn't see him – he was afraid. That's why I left school.

The creases is so bad now, that I haven't been out with 'em for three days. They're so cold, people won't buy 'em; for when I goes up to them, they say, 'They'll freeze our bellies.' Besides, in the market, they won't sell a ha'penny handful now – they're ris to a penny and tuppence. In summer there's lots, and most as cheap as dirt; but I have to be down at Farringdon-market between four and five, or else I can't get any creases, because everyone almost – especially the Irish – is selling them, and they're picked up so quick. Some of the saleswomen – we never calls 'em ladies – is very kind to us children, and some of them altogether spiteful. The good one will give you a bunch for nothing, when they're cheap; but the others, cruel ones, if you try to bate them a farden less than they ask you, will say, 'Go along with you, you're no good'. I used to go down to market along with another girl, as must be about fourteen, 'cos she does her back hair up. When we've bought a lot, we sits down on a door-step, and ties up the bunches. We never goes home to breakfast till we've sold out; but, if it's very late, then I buys a penn'orth of pudding, which is very nice with gravy. I don't know hardly one of the people, as goes to Farringdon, to talk to; they never speaks to me, so I don't speak to them. We children never play down there, 'cos we're thinking of our living. No; people never pities me in the street – excepting one gentleman, and he says, says he, 'What do you do out so soon in the morning?' but he gave me nothink – he only walked away.

It's very cold before winter comes on reg'lar – specially getting up of a morning. I gets up in the dark by the light of the lamp in the court. When the snow is on the ground, there's no creases. I bears the cold – you must; so I puts my hands under my shawl, though it hurts 'em to take hold of the creases, especially when we takes 'em to the pump to wash 'em. No; I never see any children crying – it's no use.

Sometimes I make a great deal of money. One day I took 1s 6d., and the creases cost 6d.; but it isn't often I get such luck as that. I oftener makes 3d. or 4d. than 1s.; and then I'm at work, crying, 'Creases, four bunches a penny, creases!' from six in the morning to about ten. What do you mean by mechanics? – I don't know what they are. The shops buys most off me. Some of 'em says, 'Oh! I ain't a-goin' to give a penny for these;' and they want 'em at the same price as I buys 'em at.

I always give mother my money, she's so very good to me. She don't often beat me; but, when she do, she don't play with me. She's very poor, and goes out cleaning rooms sometimes, now she don't work at the fur. I ain't got no father, he's a father-in-law. No; mother ain't married again – he's a father-in-law. He grinds scissors, and he's very good to me. No; I don't mean by that that he says kind things to me, for he never hardly speaks. When I gets home, after selling creases, I stops at home. I puts the room to rights: mother don't make me do it, I does it myself. I cleans the chairs, though there's only two to clean. I takes a tub and scrubbing-brush and flannel, and scrubs the floor – that's what I do three or four times a week.

I don't have no dinner. Mother gives me two slices of bread-and-butter and a cup of tea for breakfast, and then I go till tea, and has the same. We has meat of a Sunday, and, of course, I should like to have it every day. Mother has just the same to eat as we has, but she takes more tea – three cups, sometimes. No; I never has no sweet-stuff; I never buy none – I don't like it. Sometimes we has a game of 'honeypots' with the girls in the court, but not often. Me and Carry H carries the little 'uns. We plays, too, at 'kiss-in-the-ring.' I knows a good many games, but I don't play at 'em, 'cos going out with creases tires me. On a Friday night, too, I goes to a Jew's house till eleven o'clock on Saturday night. All I has to do is to snuff the candles and poke the fire. You see they keep their Sabbath then, and they won't touch anything; so they gives me my wittals and 1½d., and I does it for 'em. I have a reg'lar good lot to eat. Supper of Friday night, and tea after that, and fried fish of a Saturday morning, and meat for dinner, and tea, and supper, and I like it very well.

Oh, yes; I've got some toys at home. I've a fire-place, and a box of toys, and a knife and fork, and two little chairs. The Jews gave 'em to me where I go to on a Friday, and that's why I said they was very kind to me. I never had no doll; but I misses little sister – she's only two years old. We don't sleep in the same room; for father and mother sleeps with little sister in the one pair, and me and brother and other sister sleeps in the top room. I always goes to bed at seven, 'cos I has to be up so early.

I am a capital hand at bargaining – but only at buying watercreases. They can't take me in. If the woman tries to give me a small handful of creases, I says, 'I ain't a goin' to have that for a ha'porth', and I go to the next basket, and so on, all round. I know the quantities very well. For a penny I ought to have a full market hand, or as much as I could carry in my arms at one time, without spilling. For 3d. I has a lap full, enough to earn about a shilling; and for 6d. I gets as many as crams my basket. I can't read or write, but I knows how many pennies goes to a shilling, why, twelve, of course, but I don't know how many ha'pence there is, though there's two to a penny. When I've bought 3d. of creases, I ties 'em up into as many little bundles as I can. They must look biggish, or the people won't buy them, some puffs them out as much as they'll go. All my money

I earns I puts in a club and draws it out to buy clothes with. It's better than spending it in sweet-stuff, for them as has a living to earn. Besides it's like a child to care for sugar-sticks, and not like one who's got a living and vittals to earn. I ain't a child, and I shan't be a woman till I'm twenty, but I'm past eight, I am. I don't know nothing about what I earns during the year, I only know how many pennies goes to a shilling, and two ha'pence goes to a penny, and four fardens goes to a penny. I knows, too, how many fardens goes to tuppence – eight. That's as much as I wants to know for the markets."

QUEEN RAT

David Rix

As she washed off the mud of an entire day in the Thames, Long-Fingered Lissy was feeling more than a little melancholy. Her muddy trousers, jacket and everything else were in one tub, her day's findings in another, herself in a third, and the water in all three was roughly the same, stained as brown as tea and filling the room with a strong whiff of the Thames. A whiff of corruption, death and sewage that she hardly smelt any more.

It was impossible to get completely clean, but there was no denying that this felt good.

"Pass me the cloth," she said, standing up, feeling the grit and sludge beneath her feet. Her father did so with a brief wordless grumble and she wrapped it around herself then shook out her hair, spraying water droplets everywhere.

"Mind what you're doing," he said, moving his cup.

She was about to respond with something caustic when she heard a voice outside yelling her name. She swore and stepped out of the tub as the door opened, revealing a black and faintly menacing figure in a filthy long velveteen coat and a wide floppy hat. He held a staff considerably taller than himself and had a dark lantern fastened firmly to his chest. The lantern was closed but she could make out a faint crack of illumination. A stink radiated off the man – a stink so strong that it blasted even her rather desensitised nose.

"Evening, Tidy Tom," her father called.

"Oh, Tom," she said. "Couldn't you have tidied up a bit more?"

"I came straight here from the sewers."

"I can smell you did. Well, look away for a minute while I git dressed."

The figure turned about with a rather flamboyant gesture and she reached for her clothes – a well-patched and mended dress rather than her mudlarking gear.

"All right sweetheart, what do you want? I can see you want somethink more than the usual."

He spun around again, removed his hat and his face emerged into the light – a younger face than one might have expected from the outfit, and wearing a wide grin. "Bless your heart but such a day I've had."

"Well I'm glad someone's happy. I'm totally done up."

"No luck?" he asked.

"Oh I've been in luck. Come 'ere and I'll show you."

She hustled Tom over to what she thought of as her workshop – a small desk with various tools and pots. She slung the water out of the bucket of findings and replaced it from her washtub – a process she repeated twice. Then she drew out something large. He opened his dark lantern and shone the bulls-eye of light on it, and whistled. It was solid, glassy, opaque and a vivid sky blue in colour.

"Nice bit o' slag," she said. "No idea what they were smelting to make this. Some new 'sperimental... metal thing. An' this dumped on the bank of the Thames. But I know some people who'll love this. I could make some beautiful jewellery."

"Excellent," he said, then leaned forward with a hint of conspiracy. "But look what I found."

"If it's better than this," she said, "it'll win you a kiss."

"Oh, it's much better than that," he said eagerly. "'Ere, look. An' I wouldn't show jist anybody."

He fumbled in his bag and drew something out. There was a flash of gold.

"Ooohhhh," she murmured as he spat and rubbed the filth off. It was a sovereign – a whole sovereign. She stared at it in awe.

"When I change this, I'm going to buy you somethink nice."

"Where did you find it?"

He flashed her a huge grin. "There's the thing – that's why I'm here. I need your help."

"Hm?"

"There's more down there. So much more. I know places down there where the roads are paved with gold," he said. "Enough to make us both rich."

She stared at him dubiously. It was not unknown, she realised, to pick up coins of this value in the sewers, but they were events that tended to be whispered about in breathless excitement. The idea of more of them just there for the taking felt improbable. That wasn't how scavenging worked. Except in dreams.

"Help?" she asked with a frown.

"Yes. Come with me."

She had never ventured into the sewers before, even though the pickings were supposed to be good. Even though among the scavengers, the sewer hunters or toshers were the elites. Even though, when you got down to it, the stench and the shit weren't so different to that of the whole city these days. The sewers had always seemed too enclosed, too suffocating. Too many stories of people savaged to death by rats or flushed out when the flushermen opened the sluices of the tidal containment ponds upstream to wash out the system. Or stranger stories. Legends of rampaging feral pigs in the dark depths or wisps of eerie supernatural legend – female figures that haunted the darkness, now here, now gone again.

And she herself, picking around in the mud, had occasionally stumbled upon the resultant bloated corpses...

"I ain't going down there," she said. "The mud's my place, the sewers yours. And besides, I'm not putting my gas-pipes on any more today."

"It'll be perfectly safe. And I know the place like the back o' my 'and. I know the tides, I know the sluicing times – I know the places to go if anything goes wrong... it'll be safe as the bellows."

"Yes, I'm sure. All right, what is it you found?"

He leaned in conspiratorially. "In there... way, way in there, father than I ever went afore, there's a great big mass o' sewer metal. Biggest I ever seen. Maybe the works dislodged somethink and it all came tumbling down there and piled up. They are digging all around London now – Mr Bazalgette's interceptor sewers an' others. The railways... But serious, I need some 'elp. There's more, but I can't manage it by myself."

"Then git one o' the teams to 'elp you."

"No," he said. "I doesn't trust them. Too many o' them to

whack it as well. I…" He nudged her in the ribs. "I'd much rather whack it with you."

She glanced at him, the mischievous grin on his face confirming the small innuendo.

"And who knows," he continued. "Mr Bazalgette has already started work all over. There might not even be any sewers for us when he's done. No smell, they say – but no pickings either. So if there is somethink, I want to find it first."

She smiled dubiously. "I'm doing fine," she said. "No mudlark in London but me is selling blue jewellery. Only I know the finding o' it."

"A place o' your own? Out o' this court forever? Git this thing and we wouldn't care how the wind blows for the rest of our lives."

She froze, listening again to the racket from outside, glanced across at her father sitting at the table staring into his mug. "As much as that?" she whispered.

He shrugged. "Maybe. It's a big one. And I could see the gold. At least enough for a bit of luxury. And I want it afore the other hunters can git it."

She fell silent, idly turning over some of the stones on her desk – the blue slag, as well as some Thames flints. Nice though they were, and regular though the sales were, you couldn't ask much for a piece of Thames slag glass.

"Anything down there as I could make into some rum jewels?" she asked.

"Think any o' the toffs would like some polished sewer metal?"

She hesitated. He was grinning, but that was such an odd idea that it might even work. She had seen some of this material before – rusted and fused deposits that had built up over many years, filled with many different bits and pieces, including money – gold coin. Some people, she knew, had the taste for such unusual things. It was not all diamonds and pearls, antiques or orientalist curios. People collected all sorts, sometimes precisely because they were obscure and different rather than conventionally precious – precisely because the world they were from was alien to their own. She glanced at the ancient brown hacksaw on her desk, imagining it cutting out neat shapes, patterned with many colours of metal, maybe fixed and filled with shellac if needed. Then polished. Would that work? There was a temptation there. There was only so far you could go with blue slag glass.

"I am afeared o' the stink," she grumbled.

"Bless your heart, but it smells as bad out 'ere as it does down there these days."

"Hm."

"No – the stink niver done me no 'arm. Do I look sick?"

She had to admit that he didn't. Tidy Tom was small, wiry, strong and his complexion was good – certainly no pallid spectre.

"It's good for you," he said with a big grin. "Toughens you up. You jist don't git bit by the rats and you'll be fine."

She sighed. "All right, let's go. But if this is a fool's errand I swear I'll batty-fang you."

She grabbed her bag and shook it out, then quickly loaded today's pickings back into the bucket. A couple more pieces of blue glass joining the first – subtly varying colours.

He eyed them with another of those wide grins. "Hey – you owe me a buss."

She wrinkled her nose in disgust. "You stink."

"So do you. So does all o' London. You know, they even had to evacuate the toffs from parliament a while back, it stunk so bad."

She chuckled. "No great loss." She had to admit that was true, however. The air had never felt so foul. A constant inescapable miasma lurking over the river and the surrounding city, the source right there in the mud through which she waded. A soup of shit seasoned by the occasional bone and bloated animal carcass – or even the occasional human one.

"Well, wait till you've 'ad a wash," she said.

"I want to leave now. We'll wait till we're underground," he said with a lewd grin.

"No we damn wont. I'm no bangtail. And I am not going to pay a call on the local dressmaker either." She gave a groan and rubbed her eyes. "What do I wear down there? I have to git my gas-pipes on ag'in?"

"Yes." His grin widened. "You can't wear that lot down in the tunnels. And you got a dark lantern?"

"I have."

"A hammer?"

She hesitated. "Father," she called. "We still 'ave a hammer?"

"Yes," he said, pointing to a corner.

"Put it in your bag," Tidy Tom said. "And bind your knees."

"Why?"

"In case we need to crawl."

"Oh…"

She hurried across the room and dragged open a large basket, taking out a clean pair of trousers. She tugged them on beneath her dress, then dragged the floppy and still rather damp fabric off over her head and tossed it away. Shirt and thick jacket went on. Two cloths added to her bag for her knees.

"You got an 'at?" he asked.

"Not… that kind of 'at."

"We can pay a call at my place – you can have my spare. Jacket as well."

"All right, All right, let's go."

The stench always seemed worse nearer the river, the great brown slithering snake that was the Thames. Eventually the nose got used to smells, but that only lasted until something changed or increased – until you approached its source. Then it would come thundering back, almost a physical sensation in the air, almost a hallucinatory shimmer.

This was a black on black but clamouring world, pierced by only the occasional light. Voices, shouting, an endless bustle of people on the move to who knows where and who knows what. The thorns of masts rising up against a shadowy sky, their shapes pained and twisted – dark hulks of boats of all sizes, the tangle of building sites and constructions that filled the city like fungus.

Lissy was feeling a little nervous, however, for Tidy Tom's mirror had revealed a strange figure – almost unrecognisable as a woman, or indeed as anything. She was wearing the full sewer-hunter regalia now – a large floppy hat and long velveteen jacket a few sizes too large with a dark lantern fixed firmly to the chest. She had worn all sorts of things in her life – one had to when relying on whatever one could scavenge or pilfer – and when poking around in the mud, she had to do whatever it took. Trousers were a norm for her at least, in spite of the occasional glance they received. Sometimes, sensational news would filter down about some toffer wearing trousers and causing a flutter or scandal – even getting arrested. But they seemed like news reports from a distant country. She had been wearing trousers in the mud for much of her life. There was little choice. And as far as modesty was concerned, the filth of the Thames was a good barrier against any lecherous glances.

"This is Mr Bazalgette's interceptor," Tom said at last, as they approached another building site. Everywhere things were being built or torn down, the city seeming to change by the day, heaving and festering like a carcass in the sun. In the low light, it looked as though the street had exploded, a massive trench fenced off with wooden railings – and in the depths, hints of brick tunnel – twin slot-black holes leading off into oblivion. It was a time of turmoil, that was certain – and a time of uncertain future as well. Maybe Tom was right that the days of the sewer hunters and even the mudlarks could be numbered – a chilling thought. Thinking of Tom's discovery, she allowed herself a flicker of hope. Maybe something could be gained from this, if handled with sense.

"We – go down here?" she asked, looking round uneasily.

"No. Too well guarded. They really doesn't like us getting into the tunnels now. They say it's too dangerous, though they niver care how we starve or freeze. We'll slip into the old tunnel entrance jist down the river and git through that way."

"Okay," she muttered, feeling an upswell of nervousness.

"Keep your lantern closed," he added as they descended the steps to the Thames. This was familiar territory, of course, and she walked quickly, quicker than most would have.

"Tell me some more," she said. "Are there really wild hogs that live down there?"

He laughed a somewhat theatrical laugh. "Lor' bless you, no. I doesn't believe a word on it."

"And the ghosts?"

"You do see strange things."

"You ever seen the Queen Rat?"

He glanced at her and she could feel him grinning in the dark. "Oh yes. She appears sometimes as a fine lady in the sewers."

"And what would a fine lady be doing down there?"

He gave her a knowing look. "Wouldn't you like to know," he said.

"That's why I asked."

"They say as you won't guess who she really is – except that her eyes, if you catch them with your lantern, they shine like an animal's. And if you see her feet, her toes have claws."

"See her feet?" she asked with a laugh. "So this fire ship is down there, splashing through the shit, in bare feet?"

"Maybe," he said. "And you see a lot more than her feet."

"Yes?"

"They say she – if you guv her a really good time, she'll bring you luck. Plenty o' valuables to whack. But it has to be a really very good time."

Her laughter went a little shrill. "So that's how you found your great hoard? Having a tiff with strange wagtails in the shit?"

"Why would I when there's such a good time on the surface?" he said with a mischievous grin. She brushed that off, despite the warm feeling his words evoked. Her mood abruptly switched to chill again as Tom came to a halt. Ahead was a mouth of utter black in the wall that fringed the river. A faint sound of trickling water.

"Here we be," he said.

She nodded slowly. "What kind o' windward passage is this?"

"Hold still for a while and listen – and look. You sense anybody around?"

She froze for a while, ears and eyes straining, trying to analyse the familiar background murmur of the riverside city.

"I can't hear nothing."

"Nor can I. Okay – quickly inside."

With barely a sound, in spite of the squelching mud, Tom flitted forward and plunged into the dark. She followed, stumbling awkwardly. A hand took hers. "Walk forward ten paces," he said, and she allowed herself to be led, completely blind, trying not to think about any unexpected obstacles her feet might encounter or what would happen if she fell into whatever it was that was flowing around her boots.

Then they waited again – and a thin ray of light blazed, picking out ancient brick. It was a relief to cut through that utter black and she opened her own lantern and stared around with interest. The tunnel dwindled into the dark – ancient arching brickwork, soft and decayed, or occasionally fallen entirely, leaving rotten sockets behind them. It was pretty much as she had imagined it: a long thin world of wet and rot and stench. A concentrated essence of the stink that hung over London.

There was no time to stand still and stare, though, for Tom was already marching onwards at some speed. She followed without any real difficulty, the two lantern beams lighting up the sewer with a dreamlike quality. Walking here was if anything easier than out on the Thames mud. She knew the ways of the river intimately – knew which surfaces would take her weight and which would have her wading through a deep sucking morass. Here though the ground was a uniform swamp of sewage on brick – some debris but no major surprises.

"You ever seen her?" she asked,

"The Queen Rat?" He shrugged and grinned a dark, theatrical grin. "I might have. Well, maybe. I think I saw her king."

She stared at him in surprise. "You telling the truth?"

"I swear. Some say it's nothink more than some bored toffer or other who goes swanning around down there looking for excitement – you hear stories about what they git up to. But..."

In spite of herself, she felt a prickle and her eyes flashed up and down the sewer. "But what?"

He nodded. "I doesn't know," he said. "But one day... one night..." His voice dropped to a whisper and she looked at him in surprise. "One day, when I was down here, a'walkin the tunnels, I did catch a look o' someone. Somethink."

"Her?" she asked breathlessly.

"Naw. 'twas a man. An' I know that 'cause he was full nakked."

Her eyebrows rose.

"White as cloth, he was. Eyes very dark. And the moment he saw me, he slipped away so quick an' so quiet I thought I'd dreamed him."

She was silent, her skin still thrilling. Tom was a theatrical character and this might well be just another of his tall tales. But here in the utter darkness, it was hard to be sure.

"Close your lantern," he said. "Grating."

She did so, and became aware of a glimmer of light from overhead – a sound of voices and bustle that penetrated eerily into this underworld. She stared up in surprise at this glimpse of the street – a mundanity seen through an impassable crack. Sometimes the light would flash off as a figure passed overhead – the flicker of a pair of male feet or the complete eclipsing of a woman's dress. Passers-by totally oblivious of the watchers below.

"Shouldn't let them see nothink going on down here, in case anyone calls the peelers," he whispered.

She would have liked to pause and watch for a moment but Tom marched on, just fractionally faster than was comfortable, and soon the twin beams again pierced the dark. Conversation flagged and Lissy was starting to wish she'd had no part in this. It would have been nice to be in bed, listening to her parents snoring, then sleeping off a long day's work. This tunnel was unchanging, save for the occasional inlet pipe or overhead grating, necessitating the closing of their lanterns. It felt as though you could walk forever here – and indeed would have to. A continuous nightmare of wet brick. That was, if anything, more disturbing than the smell or the feeling of enclosure.

"How far do we have to go?" she asked at last.

"Way way in," he said. "Deeper in o' where the hunters usually go. Beyond the familiar tunnels."

"Fuck."

"We have to move fast to clear the tide. Normally we'd git in and out afore the tide comes in. This time, we go deeper to places where the water doesn't reach.

"What?" she demanded. "How long is this going to take?"

"We can take a rest in an hour or so. Can even sleep, if you wish."

"You niver told me it would be an all-night job," she said crossly.

"Think about what we might find," he said. "It's worth the effort."

She subsided, grumbling. But she felt surprisingly little urge to back out. Maybe there was indeed something hypnotic about these tunnels. They drew you onwards into another world. She was reluctant to admit it, but she was beginning to see why the sewer hunters were so strangely proud of what they did and where they did it. Even the smell was reasonably static, and by now her nose was becoming numbed to it.

"This had better be worth it," she said, breaking into a run for a few steps to keep up with him.

It was a long walk – very long. Sometimes, the tunnels narrowed frighteningly – at one point they even had to crawl on hands and knees. The reasons why this area was off the usual paths of the sewer hunters were becoming very clear – and the prospect of being caught in this narrow pipe when the flushermen opened the sluices was almost unthinkable.

Eventually, though, the way became easier again and they could rise to their feet. And a few minutes later, Tom came to a stop with a triumphant shout.

Here there was a step in the sewer, where the flow dropped about two feet. And right below the ledge, an amorphous mass. She stared at it, brain ticking over, trying to work out what she was seeing, her experienced mudlark's eye picking out plenty that fired her interest. To most it might have seemed unprepossessing, but there was definitely a gleam in there. Many gleams.

Metal.

Rusty, but very clearly metal.

She drew a deep breath. "Not bad," she murmured, bending down and poking it with her hammer. It must have been building up here for years, undiscovered by the scavengers, slowly growing and fusing almost as though alive. The sewer would sort the materials that it carried much as the tide would in her own river world. The heavier metals would accumulate in certain places, the lighter materials in others. And if you could read that, then sometimes, as here, there was treasure to be found. And how much might this be worth? Hints of copper and brass were promising, but it was the coins that were especially interesting. A few of them would be very welcome indeed. And could some of them really be gold?

"We can carry this out?" Tom asked.

"We can guv it a damn good try," Lissy said quietly.

"We can break it up with our hammers and fill as much as we can."

He swung his hammer and hit the mass a hard blow — a shockingly loud sound that echoed up and down the tunnel. A part of the mass cracked off and a stream of filthy water trailed from it. Tom picked the piece up, studying it. Lissy was trying to visualise what it would look like polished. The colours were interesting — hints of red and inky black, while no doubt polishing would reveal shining metal as well, all merged into a fused and complex mass. There was potential here, assuming she could find a way to clean this up and work it.

Her eyes wandered to her feet, where the water was still flowing strangely dark — some sediment or other released from its prison by the breakage. Her eyes and lantern followed the stain downstream… then she gave a huge yelp of shock. Tom looked at her, followed her eyes, and echoed it, dropping the chunk of metal with a solid splash.

There was a figure standing behind them, pale and naked. Still as a statue, like a paper cut-out, framed by the filthy brick and backed by darkness — watching them with deep black eyes. Lissy gave a faint wail, feeling a preternatural strangeness. Fear froze her into immobility — and Tom likewise beside her. As the terror flowed through her, she aimed the lantern at the figure's feet to check for claws, but they were submerged. For a moment, she wanted to collapse into the shit in obeisance and start praying.

But then, with a faint unlatching breath, something more rational began to surface in her mind. The figure was clearly female, the skin ghostly pale under the dirt that smeared her, but Lissy could recognise small details that spoke of flesh-and-blood reality. A few scars, delicate silky body hair, her chest rising and falling with a speed that indicated tension and wariness. And also her tools — hammer, pick, crowbar, awl and various pouches and bags, all suspended from a tough strap over her shoulder. Her hair was tied up tightly into a solid mass and Lissy could make out the slight pull of each individual strand on her forehead. Why she was naked, she couldn't begin to imagine — but she was definitely human.

"Who are you?" Lissy asked at last.

The woman just stared at them, her face blank.

"Bloody 'ell," Tom muttered, and Lissy refocused her eyes, realising that more figures were approaching down the tunnel. At a sound behind them they whirled round, to find yet more of these strange folk; at least a dozen of various ages and sizes. Women. Men. Even children. All naked save for their utility straps or belts – all the same ghostly pale skin. They may not have been supernatural, but terror swept through her again – the terror of being caught, pinned, trapped, by something she really didn't understand.

"Who are you?" Tom echoed, his voice high-pitched. "What do you want with us?"

The only response was a sudden movement – almost a pounce – as white arms lunged out and grabbed them from both sides. Many arms. Tom shrieked – a harsh raw sound that frightened her almost as much as the figures themselves.

"This," one of the men said in a quiet, light voice, "must be ours." He had long hair that had once been sandy-coloured, also tied up. Lissy hadn't a clue what he meant for a moment, then realised he was pointing at the metal deposit.

"Take it," Tom cried, his voice filled with terror. "Sir. Take it. I'll nawt stand in your way."

There was a flash of metal as Lissy was forced down first onto her knees, then flat on her face in the sewage. Tom likewise. It wasn't deep enough to choke her but it splashed around her mouth and chin horrifically.

Then the feeling of something cold and hard and very sharp at her throat. Lissy gave a long, closed-mouthed scream. It was the woman they had seen first, bending over her and staring down with an expression that was simultaneously implacable and... sad. Regretful? Behind her, stood the man with sandy hair. Both of these seemed to radiate an aura of authority – the rest of the group looking to them for directions.

"One must live how one can," the woman said. "This will allow us to buy many things." Her voice was strange – almost gentle. Perfectly enunciated, refined yet tinged with just a hint of the London streets as well – really quite beautiful. Even in that intense moment, it came as a surprise.

A flurry of bangs rang out in the tunnel and Lissy's terrified eyes could just make out some of the pale figures already working at the deposit with hammers and picks, hacking off lumps of fused metal and loading it into bags.

"There is nothing on the surface but a failed, poisonous world," the woman continued, her voice going dull. "So... our need is strong."

"Yes," Tom spluttered. "I agree... ma'am."

"We have no wish to hurt you, but at the same time, we must survive."

"We... we, we'll go," she said, trying to keep her mouth above the sewage. "Please, ma'am..."

"Nah, we can't 'ave you telling anybody," the sandy-haired man said – his voice very different, much more familiar from the streets. It was a startling contrast.

"We won't tell nobody, sir," she wailed. "I doesn't even know who you are."

"Right, sir," Tom said. "The sewers are my world too. You... This is your area? Why would I betray my fellow sewer people?"

"We must preserve ourselves," the pale woman said. "We cannot take risks."

Lissy closed her eyes, waiting for the blade to slice, her stomach feeling as liquid as the shit that sloshed around her.

"But... but... soon the sewers'ill be no more," Tom said. "Do you know this?"

"What are you speaking of?"

"Doesn't you know about the great interceptors, ma'am?"

There was a silence.

"The sewers may soon be cut off entirely," Tom continued, speaking urgently. "No more toshers then. No more sewer hunters. That's me gone. That's you gone – sir. Ma'am. We're fellows here. I can help you, not hinder you. Jist let us go."

More silence, and then the pale woman spoke. "What can you tell us of Mr Bazalgette?"

There was a shifting among the crowd and Lissy was finally allowed to sprawl over and sit up. She felt soaked from top to toe now in the reeking fluid, matter smeared over her coat and oozing within – the stench so strong that it was completely overwhelming her previously deadened nose. She desperately searched for some clean part of her clothes to wipe her face with, but there was nothing. She spat and spat again. Tom was in no better state, but he was staring around with gleaming, urgent eyes.

"I speak the truth," he said. "I'm no friend o' the surface, sir. Ma'am. They tell us what to do all the time yet let us starve and die without a thought. And... This is your area – that's fine, sir. The mudlarks 'ave the Thames, and we sewer hunters don't pick up stuff there. You 'ave the deep tunnels and we'll leave you alone as well. You have to trust us..."

"What of Mr Bazalgette?" the sandy-haired man echoed.

"Plenty," Tom said. "His great plan is to intercept all the sewers so they no longer flow into the Thames. Instead they'll flow east, out o' the city to the new pumping stations. And you ain't getting in and out o' there through a giant steam pump."

There was a hint of worry in the crowd now, Lissy could read it very clearly.

"Yes, sir," she chimed in. "This is a time o' change. Everything. In a few years... who knows where any o' this'll be?"

"Tell us more," the pale woman said.

Lissy just remained sitting in the sewage, listening as Tom talked in surprising detail – flow rates, diameters, rough outlines of the routes of the great new sewers, the new Thames Embankment where trains and sewers would coexist, the marvel of engineering that would soon be the Crossness containment system and outflow...

"Now I doesn't know," he was saying. "I doesn't know whether all ways'll be closed off straight away, or jist the Thames outfalls we usually use. You may know of ways out as I doesn't. But it's certain that one day the sewers'll be out of reach. They build, and build, and build – and it's fine and grand. But our world is fading away, and I doesn't know what else there is for us."

Lissy swallowed. The pale figures were looking much more human now, faces filled with unease and hints of fear. She stared in discomfort at the naked bodies – especially that of the sandy-haired man. He seemed very naked, disturbing her eyes every time they settled on him. Then she glanced at Tom. He appeared to be taking this in his stride at least – talking with both of them, man and woman, as though it was the most natural thing in the world. In a way that she would have to consider later, that caused her heart to beat faster.

To her surprise, the sandy-haired man extracted a cloth from his pouch and handed it to her, and at last she could wipe her face a little cleaner.

"I never saw a woman sewer hunter before," he said.

"Oh… I work the Thames, sir. Mudlark. Though – I also make jewellery o' what I find. There are heaps o' slag dumped by the river in the finest colours."

The sandy-haired man actually smiled at that – and held up his hand. Lissy focused on a bracelet he was wearing – made of woven leather but with a large round stone on it. She stared with interest, trying to make out the colours in the dim flickering light. It was dark – black with swirls and bands of reddish hue, as well as flashes of metallic sheen.

"Is that…?" She waved at the metal mass that some of the pale figures were still excavating and carrying off.

The sandy-haired man nodded and Lissy smiled back, wryly remembering her plan to try making just such jewellery. She didn't say anything about that, though – that plan was completely dead, at least as far as this expedition was concerned. "It's beautiful."

"We occasionally manage to whack some o' it," he said. "Though mostly nowt but raw metals an' the occasional gold."

She nodded slowly. That made sense. If certain people were fascinated by her slum jewellery from the Thames mud, they'd only be more so from a source such as this. "Um," she said shyly, "if you wish, sir, I might have some connections. The same people who buy my… river pieces might be very interested in somethink like this."

"Maybe. Though we 'ave to keep our secrets. As long as we can. Though if what your friend says is true…"

"It's true," she said. "I've niver known things changing so fast. Railways, canals, sewers… The only thing as doesn't change is that nobody cares what happens to us."

"We may have to return to the surface," the pale woman said. "I fear that would be bad."

"I... suppose," Lissy said, nodding. "Though, you know, there is always mudlarking."

He nodded slowly.

"If you wish," Tom said, "I can return here on occasion. While I can. And bring you news."

Lissy stared at him in surprise, trying to read his face. Was he putting on a massive act to try and get them to trust him? Or was there something in his eyes that said he meant it? If so, maybe she could see why. It was there in the sense of community among the mudlarks and sewer hunters – the sense that it was them against an unfriendly world. The sense that, whatever may have happened, these pale figures might be closer to them than most others on the surface. They occupied more or less the same place, after all.

And did they believe him? She wasn't sure. Maybe they weren't sure either.

"Aye," the pale man said at last.

"That is a good offer, and we thank you for it," the woman said. "And for everything you have told us."

"You can rely on me," Tom said.

"And we wish you good speed to the outside."

"Thank you," Tom said, "and... I also wish you an undisturbed future – for as long as possible. I wasn't fooling you. You ever need anything on the outside, you come and pay a call on Tidy Tom. Six Napier Court."

Again, Lissy stared in surprise at the familiar address.

"As long as I'm alive," he added with a hint of darkness in his face. "One shouldn't afear change. It's jist that them as doing the changing have never cared about us."

The pale woman nodded.

Tom cautiously rose to his feet. "So," he said, as though asking permission, "we shall be on our way?"

"By all means," the pale woman said. "Thank you."

He glanced down at his shit-drenched coat and lantern. "Apologies, but would you mind relighting our lamps? They've been flooded."

The pale woman held up her own rough lantern and Lissy met wick with wick. It spluttered for several seconds, then caught alight and she carefully transferred it to Tom's as well.

"Thank you," she mumbled.

With a certain awkwardness, they turned away. "Goodbye," she said, her voice still shaking. The two hurried down the tunnel, Lissy glancing over her shoulders every so often at the figures standing in their island of light, until they rounded a bend in the pipe and the darkness was complete again.

Tom was marching at full speed – so fast that she was almost running to keep up – and they walked for several minutes before he swung into a side passage and sat down heavily on a ledge.

"What are we doing?" she asked, breathing hard.

"No sense running. The tide's still up. Jist a bit."

Long-Fingered Lissy closed her eyes – the thought of much more time stuck here underground seemed barely endurable and tiredness gnawed at her mind. She sat down and pulled miserably at her clothes – but she had no way of cleaning herself. All she could do was rub at the drying filth on her face and try and wring it out of her hair.

If Mr Bazalgette really managed to take all this far far away, then so much the better.

It was not until several minutes later that she finally broke the silence. "I suppose... there is your Queen Rat."

He nodded.

"And... King Rat. Funny that," she murmured. "Makes you think. What actually... where these stories come from. And... other stories as well... who knows what... causes them."

She stumbled to a halt, too tired to express this.

"Her voice," he said.

She nodded slowly. "A fine lady."

There were stories here as well, it seemed. Confusing, impenetrable ones. She remained there listening to the trickle and drip of water, trying to imagine how someone could make the transition from the upper rarefied echelons of society to walking the sewers.

"Did you mean what you said?" she asked. "Would you come back?"

"Maybe I did, maybe I didn't," he muttered. "I... don't fancy 'aving my throat cut. Jist... We in this kind of life 'ave to stick together. An' I'm curious."

She nodded, not sure either. Then Tom abruptly shifted and grinned one of his huge grins in the lantern light.

"Bless your heart but I'll come back," he said. "Course I will. Those sewers are still paved with gold an' no Queen Rat is going to keep me away for long."

CHRISTOPHERSON

George Gissing

It was twenty years ago, and on an evening in May. All day long there had been sunshine. Owing, doubtless, to the incident I am about to relate, the light and warmth of that long-vanished day live with me still; I can see the great white clouds that moved across the strip of sky before my window, and feel again the spring languor which troubled my solitary work in the heart of London.

Only at sunset did I leave the house. There was an unwonted sweetness in the air; the long vistas of newly lit lamps made a golden glow under the dusking flush of the sky. With no purpose but to rest and breathe, I wandered for half an hour, and found myself at length where Great Portland Street opens into Marylebone Road. Over the way, in the shadow of Trinity Church, was an old bookshop, well known to me: the gas-jet shining upon the stall with its rows of volumes drew me across. I began turning over pages, and – invariable consequence – fingering what money I had in my pocket. A certain book overcame me; I stepped into the little shop to pay for it.

While standing at the stall, I had been vaguely aware of someone beside me, a man who also was looking over the books; as I came out again with my purchase, this stranger gazed at me intently, with a half-smile of peculiar interest. He seemed about to say something. I walked slowly away; the man moved in the same direction. Just in front of the church he made a quick movement to my side, and spoke.

"Pray excuse me, sir – don't misunderstand me – I only wished to ask whether you have noticed the name written on the flyleaf of the book you have just bought?"

The respectful nervousness of his voice naturally made me suppose at first that the man was going to beg; but he seemed no ordinary mendicant. I judged him to be about sixty years of age; his long, thin hair and straggling beard were grizzled, and a somewhat rheumy eye looked out from his bloodless, hollowed countenance; he was very shabbily clad, yet as a fallen gentleman, and indeed his accent made it clear to what class he originally belonged. The expression with which he regarded me had so much intelligence, so much good-nature, and at the same time such a pathetic diffidence, that I could not but answer him in the friendliest way. I had not seen the name on the flyleaf, but at once I opened the book, and by the light of a gas-lamp read, inscribed in a very fine hand, "W. R. Christopherson, 1849."

"It is my name," said the stranger, in a subdued and uncertain voice.

"Indeed? The book used to belong to you?"

"It belonged to me." He laughed oddly, a tremulous little crow of a laugh, at the same time stroking his head, as if to deprecate disbelief. "You never heard of the sale of the Christopherson library? To be sure, you were too young; it was in 1860. I have often come across books with my name in them on the stalls – often. I had happened to notice this just before you came up, and when I saw you look at it, I was curious to see whether you would buy it. Pray excuse the freedom I am taking. Lovers of books – don't you think –?"

The broken question was completed by his look, and when I said that I quite understood and agreed with him he crowed his little laugh.

"Have you a large library?" he inquired, eyeing me wistfully.

"Oh dear, no. Only a few hundred volumes. Too many for one who has no house of his own."

He smiled good-naturedly, bent his head, and murmured just audibly:

"My catalogue numbered 24,718."

I was growing curious and interested. Venturing no more direct questions, I asked whether, at the time he spoke of, he lived in London.

"If you have five minutes to spare," was the timid reply, "I will show you my house. I mean" – again the little crowing laugh – "the house which *was* mine."

Willingly I walked on with him. He led me a short distance up the road skirting Regent's Park, and paused at length before a house in an imposing terrace.

"There," he whispered, "I used to live. The window to the right of the door – that was my library. Ah!"

And he heaved a deep sigh.

"A misfortune befell you," I said, also in a subdued voice.

"The result of my own folly. I had enough for my needs, but thought I needed more. I let myself be drawn into business – I, who knew nothing of such things – and there came the black day – the black day."

We turned to retrace our steps, and walking slowly, with heads bent, came in silence again to the church.

"I wonder whether you have bought any other of my books?" asked Christopherson, with his gentle smile, when we had paused as if for leave-taking.

I replied that I did not remember to have come across his name before; then, on an impulse, asked whether he would care to have the book I carried in my hand; if so, with pleasure I would give it him. No sooner were the words spoken than I saw the delight they caused the hearer. He hesitated, murmured reluctance, but soon gratefully accepted my offer, and flushed with joy as he took the volume.

"I still have a few books," he said, under his breath, as if he spoke of something he was ashamed to make known. "But it is very rarely indeed that I can add to them. I feel I have not thanked you half enough."

We shook hands and parted.

My lodging at that time was in Camden Town. One afternoon, perhaps a fortnight later, I had walked for an hour or two, and on my way back I stopped at a bookstall in the High Street. Someone came up to my side; I looked, and recognised Christopherson. Our greeting was like that of old friends.

"I have seen you several times lately," said the broken gentleman, who looked shabbier than before in the broad daylight, "but I – I didn't like to speak. I live not far from here."

"Why, so do I," and I added, without much thinking what I said, "do you live alone?"

"Alone? oh no. With my wife."

There was a curious embarrassment in his tone. His eyes were cast down and his head moved uneasily.

We began to talk of the books on the stall, and turning away together continued our conversation. Christopherson was not only a well-bred but a very intelligent and even learned man. On his giving some proof of erudition (with the excessive modesty which characterised him), I asked whether he wrote. No, he had never written anything – never; he was only a bookworm, he said. Thereupon he crowed faintly and took his leave.

It was not long before we again met by chance. We came face to face at a street corner in my neighbourhood, and I was struck by a change in him. He looked older; a profound melancholy darkened his countenance; the hand he gave me was limp, and his pleasure at our meeting found only a faint expression.

"I am going away," he said in reply to my inquiring look. "I am leaving London."

"For good?"

"I fear so, and yet" – he made an obvious effort – "I am glad of it. My wife's health has not been very good lately. She has need of country air. Yes, I am glad we have decided to go away – very glad – very glad indeed!"

He spoke with an automatic sort of emphasis, his eyes wandering, and his hands twitching nervously. I was on the point of asking what part of the country he had chosen for his retreat, when he abruptly added:

"I live just over there. Will you let me show you my books?"

Of course I gladly accepted the invitation, and a couple of minutes' walk brought us to a house in a decent street where most of the ground-floor windows showed a card announcing lodgings. As we paused at the door, my companion seemed to hesitate, to regret having invited me.

"I'm really afraid it isn't worth your while," he said timidly. "The fact is, I haven't space to show my books properly."

I put aside the objection, and we entered. With anxious courtesy

Christopherson led me up the narrow staircase to the second-floor landing, and threw open a door. On the threshold I stood astonished. The room was a small one, and would in any case have only just sufficed for homely comfort, used as it evidently was for all daytime purposes; but certainly a third of the entire space was occupied by a solid mass of books, volumes stacked several rows deep against two of the walls and almost up to the ceiling. A round table and two or three chairs were the only furniture – there was no room, indeed, for more. The window being shut, and the sunshine glowing upon it, an intolerable stuffiness oppressed the air. Never had I been made so uncomfortable by the odour of printed paper and bindings.

"But," I exclaimed, "you said you had only a *few* books! There must be five times as many here as I have."

"I forget the exact number," murmured Christopherson, in great agitation. "You see, I can't arrange them properly. I have a few more in-in the other room."

He led me across the landing, opened another door, and showed me a little bedroom. Here the encumberment was less remarkable, but one wall had completely disappeared behind volumes, and the bookishness of the air made it a disgusting thought that two persons occupied this chamber every night.

We returned to the sitting-room, Christopherson began picking out books from the solid mass to show me. Talking nervously, brokenly, with now and then a deep sigh or a crow of laughter, he gave me a little light on his history. I learnt that he had occupied these lodgings for the last eight years; that he had been twice married; that the only child he had had, a daughter by his first wife, had died long ago in childhood; and lastly – this came in a burst of confidence, with a very pleasant smile – that his second wife had been his daughter's governess. I listened with keen interest, and hoped to learn still more of the circumstances of this singular household.

"In the country," I remarked, "you will no doubt have shelf room?"

At once his countenance fell; he turned upon me a woebegone eye. Just as I was about to speak again sounds from within the house caught my attention; there was a heavy foot on the stairs, and a loud voice, which seemed familiar to me.

"Ah!" exclaimed Christopherson with a start, "here comes someone who is going to help me in the removal of the books. Come in, Mr. Pomfret, come in!"

The door opened, and there appeared a tall, wiry fellow, whose sandy hair, light blue eyes, jutting jawbones, and large mouth made a picture suggestive of small refinement but of vigorous and wholesome manhood. No wonder I had seemed to recognise his voice. Though we only saw each other by chance at long intervals, Pomfret and I were old acquaintances.

"Hallo!" he roared out, "I didn't know you knew Mr. Christopherson."

"I'm just as much surprised to find that *you* know him!" was my reply.

The old book-lover gazed at us in nervous astonishment, then shook hands with the newcomer, who greeted him bluffly, yet respectfully. Pomfret spoke with a strong Yorkshire accent, and had all the angularity of demeanour which marks the typical Yorkshireman. He came to announce that everything had been settled for the packing and transporting of Mr. Christopherson's library; it remained only to decide the day.

"There's no hurry," exclaimed Christopherson. "There's really no hurry. I'm greatly obliged to you, Mr. Pomfret, for all the trouble you are taking. We'll settle the date in a day or two – a day or two."

With a good-humoured nod Pomfret moved to take his leave. Our eyes met; we left the house together. Out in the street again I took a deep breath of the summer air, which seemed sweet as in a meadow after that stifling room. My companion evidently had a like sensation, for he looked up to the sky and broadened out his shoulders.

"Eh, but it's a grand day! I'd give something for a walk on Ilkley Moors."

As the best substitute within our reach we agreed to walk across Regent's Park together. Pomfret's business took him in that direction, and I was glad of a talk about Christopherson. I learnt that the old book-lover's landlady was Pomfret's aunt. Christopherson's story of affluence and ruin was quite true. Ruin complete, for at the age of forty he had been obliged to earn his living as a clerk or something of the kind. About five years later came his second marriage.

"You know Mrs. Christopherson?" asked Pomfret.

"No! I wish I did. Why?"

"Because she's the sort of woman it does you good to know, that's all. She's a lady – *my* idea of a lady. Christopherson's a gentleman too, there's no denying it; if he wasn't, I think I should have punched his head before now. Oh, I know 'em well! why, I lived in the house there with 'em for several years. She's a lady to the end of her little finger, and how her husband can 'a borne to see her living the life she has, it's more than I can understand. By –! I'd have turned burglar, if I could 'a found no other way of keeping her in comfort."

"She works for her living, then?"

"Ay, and for his too. No, not teaching; she's in a shop in Tottenham Court Road; has what they call a good place, and earns thirty shillings a week. It's all they have, but Christopherson buys books out of it."

"But has he never done anything since their marriage?"

"He did for the first few years, I believe, but he had an illness, and that was the end of it. Since then he's only loafed. He goes to all the book-sales, and spends the rest of his time sniffing about the second-hand shops. She? Oh, she'd never say a word! Wait till you've seen her."

"Well, but," I asked, "what has happened. How is it they're leaving London?"

"Ay, I'll tell you; I was coming to that. Mrs. Christopherson has relatives well off – a fat and selfish lot, as far as I can make out – never lifted a finger to help her until now. One of them's a Mrs. Keeting, the widow of some City porpoise, I'm told. Well, this woman has a home down in Norfolk. She never lives there, but a son of hers goes there to fish and shoot now and then. Well, this is what Mrs. Christopherson tells my aunt, Mrs. Keeting has offered to let her and her husband live down yonder, rent free, and their food provided. She's to be housekeeper, in fact, and keep the place ready for any one who goes down."

"Christopherson, *I* can see, would rather stay where he is."

"Why, of course, he doesn't know how he'll live without the bookshops. But he's glad for all that, on his wife's account. And it's none too soon, I can tell you. The poor woman couldn't go on much longer; my aunt says she's just about ready to drop, and sometimes, I know, she looks terribly bad. Of course, she won't own it, not she; she isn't one of the complaining sort. But she talks now and then about the country – the places where she used to live. I've heard her, and it gives me a notion of what she's gone through all these years. I saw her a week ago, just when she had Mrs. Keeting's offer, and I tell you I scarcely knew who it was! You never saw such a change in any one in your life! Her face was like that of a girl of seventeen. And her laugh – you should have heard her laugh!"

"Is she much younger than her husband?" I asked.

"Twenty years at least. She's about forty, I think." I mused for a few moments.

"After all, it isn't an unhappy marriage?"

"Unhappy?" cried Pomfret. "Why, there's never been a disagreeable word between them, that I'll warrant. Once Christopherson gets over the change, they'll have nothing more in the world to ask for. He'll potter over his books –"

"You mean to tell me," I interrupted, "that those books have all been bought out of his wife's thirty shillings a week?"

"No, no. To begin with, he kept a few out of his old library. Then, when he was earning his own living, he bought a great many. He told me once that he's often lived on sixpence a day to have money for books. A rum old owl; but for all that he's a gentleman, and you can't help liking him. I shall be sorry when he's out of reach."

For my own part, I wished nothing better than to hear of Christopherson's departure. The story I had heard made me uncomfortable. It was good to think of that poor woman rescued at last from her life of toil, and in these days of midsummer free to enjoy the country she loved. A touch of envy mingled, I confess, with my thought of Christopherson, who henceforth had not a care in the world, and without reproach might delight in his hoarded volumes. One could not imagine that he would suffer seriously by the removal of his old haunts. I promised myself to call on him in a day or two. By choosing Sunday, I might perhaps be lucky enough to see his wife.

And on Sunday afternoon I was on the point of setting forth to pay this visit, when in came Pomfret. He wore a surly look, and kicked clumsily against the furniture as he crossed the room. His appearance was a surprise, for, though I had given him my address, I did not in the least expect that he would come to see me; a certain pride, I suppose, characteristic of his rugged strain, having always made him shy of such intimacy.

"Did you ever hear the like of *that*?" he shouted, half angrily. "It's all over. They're not going! And all because of those blamed books!"

And spluttering and growling, he made known what he had just learnt at his aunt's home. On the previous afternoon the Christophersons had been surprised by a visit from their relatives and would-be benefactress, Mrs. Keeting. Never before had that lady called upon them; she came, no doubt (this could only be conjectured), to speak with them of their approaching removal. The close of the conversation (a very brief one) was overheard by the landlady, for Mrs. Keeting spoke loudly as she descended the stairs. "Impossible! Quite impossible! I couldn't think of it! How could you dream for a moment that I would let you fill my house with musty old books? Most unhealthy! I never knew anything so extraordinary in my life, never!" And so she went out to her carriage, and was driven away. And the landlady, presently having occasion to go upstairs, was aware of a dead silence in the room where the Christophersons were sitting. She knocked – prepared with some excuse – and found the couple side by side, smiling sadly. At once they told her the truth. Mrs. Keeting had come because of a letter in which Mrs. Christopherson had mentioned the fact that her husband had a good many books, and hoped he might be permitted to remove them to the house in Norfolk. She came to see the library – with the result already heard. They had the choice between sacrificing the books and losing what their relative offered.

"Christopherson refused?" I let fall.

"I suppose his wife saw that it was too much for him. At all events, they'd agreed to keep the books and lose the house. And there's an end of it. I haven't been so riled about anything for a long time!"

Meantime I had been reflecting. It was easy for me to understand Christopherson's state of mind, and without knowing Mrs. Keeting, I saw that she must be a person whose benefactions would be a good deal of a burden. After all, was Mrs. Christopherson so very unhappy? Was she not the kind of woman who lived by sacrifice – one who had far rather lead a life disagreeable to herself than change it at the cost of discomfort to her husband? This view of the matter irritated Pomfret, and he broke into objurgations, directed partly against Mrs. Keeting, partly against Christopherson. It was an 'infernal shame', that was all he could say. And after all, I rather inclined to his opinion.

When two or three days had passed, curiosity drew me towards the Christophersons' dwelling. Walking along the opposite side of the street, I looked up at their window, and there was the face of the old bibliophile. Evidently he was standing at the window in idleness, perhaps in trouble. At once he beckoned to me; but before I could knock at the house-door he had descended, and came out.

"May I walk a little way with you?" he asked.

There was worry on his features. For some moments we went on in silence.

"So you have changed your mind about leaving London?" I said, as if carelessly.

"You have heard from Mr. Pomfret? Well – yes, yes – I think we shall stay where we are – for the present."

Never have I seen a man more painfully embarrassed. He walked with head bent, shoulders stooping; and shuffled, indeed, rather than walked. Even so might a man bear himself who felt guilty of some peculiar meanness.

Presently words broke from him.

"To tell you the truth, there's a difficulty about the books." He glanced furtively at me, and I saw he was trembling in all his nerves. "As you see, my circumstances are not brilliant." He half-choked himself with a crow. "The fact is we were offered a house in the country, on certain conditions, by a relative of Mrs. Christopherson; and, unfortunately, it turned out that my library is regarded as an objection – a fatal objection. We have quite reconciled ourselves to staying where we are."

I could not help asking, without emphasis, whether Mrs. Christopherson would have cared for life in the country. But no sooner were the words out of my mouth than I regretted them, so evidently did they hit my companion in a tender place.

"I think she would have liked it," he answered, with a strangely pathetic look at me, as if he entreated my forbearance.

"But," I suggested, "couldn't you make some arrangements about the books? Couldn't you take a room for them in another house, for instance?"

Christopherson's face was sufficient answer; it reminded me of his pennilessness. "We think no more about it," he said. "The matter is settled – quite settled."

There was no pursuing the subject. At the next parting of the ways we took leave of each other.

I think it was not more than a week later when I received a postcard from Pomfret. He wrote: "Just as I expected. Mrs. C. seriously ill." That was all.

Mrs. C. could, of course, only mean Mrs. Christopherson. I mused over the message – it took hold of my imagination, wrought upon my feelings; and that afternoon I again walked along the interesting street.

There was no face at the window. After a little hesitation I decided to call at the house and speak with Pomfret's aunt. It was she who opened the door to me.

We had never seen each other, but when I mentioned my name and said I was anxious to have news of Mrs. Christopherson, she led me into a sitting-room, and began to talk confidentially.

She was a good-natured Yorkshirewoman, very unlike the common London landlady. "Yes, Mrs. Christopherson had been taken ill two days ago. It began with a long fainting fit. She had a feverish, sleepless night; the doctor was sent for; and he had her removed out of the stuffy, book-cumbered bedroom into another chamber, which luckily happened to be vacant. There she lay utterly weak and worn, all but voiceless, able only to smile at her husband, who never moved from the bedside day or night. He, too," said the landlady, "would soon break down: he looked like a ghost, and seemed 'half-crazed'."

"What," I asked, "could be the cause of this illness?"

The good woman gave me an odd look, shook her head, and murmured that the reason was not far to seek.

"Did she think," I asked, "that disappointment might have something to do with it?"

Why, of course she did. For a long time the poor lady had been all but at the end of her strength, and *this* came as a blow beneath which she sank.

"Your nephew and I have talked about it," I said. "He thinks that Mr. Christopherson didn't understand what a sacrifice he asked his wife to make."

"I think so too," was the reply. "But he begins to see it now, I can tell you. He says nothing but."

There was a tap at the door, and a hurried tremulous voice begged the landlady to go upstairs.

"What is it, sir?" she asked.

"I'm afraid she's worse," said Christopherson, turning his haggard face to me with startled recognition. "Do come up at once, please."

Without a word to me he disappeared with the landlady. I could not go away; for some ten minutes I fidgeted about the little room, listening to every sound in the house. Then came a footfall on the stairs, and the landlady rejoined me.

"It's nothing," she said. "I almost think she might drop off to sleep, if she's left quiet. He worries her, poor man, sitting there and asking her every two minutes how she feels. I've persuaded him to go to his room, and I think it might do him good if you went and had a bit o' talk with him."

I mounted at once to the second-floor sitting-room, and found Christopherson sunk upon a chair, his head falling forwards, the image of despairing misery. As I approached he staggered to his feet. He took my hand in a shrinking, shamefaced way, and could not raise his eyes. I uttered a few words of encouragement, but they had the opposite effect to that designed.

"Don't tell me that," he moaned, half resentfully. "She's dying – she's dying – say what they will, I know it."

"Have you a good doctor?"

"I think so – but it's too late – it's too late."

As he dropped to his chair again I sat down by him. The silence of a minute or two was broken by a thunderous rat-tat at the house-door. Christopherson leapt to his feet, rushed from the room; I, half fearing that he had gone mad, followed to the head of the stairs.

In a moment he came up again, limp and wretched as before.

"It was the postman," he muttered. "I am expecting a letter."

Conversation seeming impossible, I shaped a phrase preliminary to withdrawal; but Christopherson would not let me go.

"I should like to tell you," he began, looking at me like a dog under punishment, "that I have done all I could. As soon as my wife fell ill, and when I saw – I had only begun to think of it in that way – how she felt the disappointment, I went at once to Mrs. Keeting's house to tell her that I would sell the books. But she was out of town. I wrote to her – I said I regretted my folly – I entreated her to forgive me and to renew her kind offer. There has been plenty of time for a reply, but she doesn't answer."

He had in his hand what I saw was a bookseller's catalogue, just delivered by the postman. Mechanically he tore off the wrapper and even glanced over the first page. Then, as if conscience stabbed him, he flung the thing violently away.

"The chance has gone!" he exclaimed, taking a hurried step or two along the little strip of floor left free by the mountain of books. "Of course she said she would rather stay in London! Of course she said what she knew would please me! When – when did she ever say anything else! And I was cruel enough – base enough – to let her make the sacrifice!" He waved his arms frantically. "Didn't I know what it cost her? Couldn't I see in her face how her heart leapt at the hope of going to live in the country! I knew what she was suffering; I *knew* it, I tell you! And, like a selfish coward, I let her suffer – I let her drop down and die – die!"

"Any hour," I said, "may bring you the reply from Mrs. Keeting.

Of course it will be favourable, and the good news –"

"Too late, I have killed her! That woman won't write. She's one of the vulgar rich, and we offended her pride; and such as she never forgive."

He sat down for a moment, but started up again in an agony of mental suffering.

"She is dying – and there, there, that's what has killed her!" He gesticulated wildly towards the books. "I have sold her life for those. Oh – oh!"

With this cry he seized half a dozen volumes, and, before I could understand what he was about, he had flung up the window-sash, and cast the books into the street. Another batch followed; I heard the thud upon the pavement. Then I caught him by the arm, held him fast, begged him to control himself.

"They shall all go!" he cried. "I loathe the sight of them. They have killed my dear wife!"

He said it sobbing, and at the last words tears streamed from his eyes. I had no difficulty now in restraining him. He met my look with a gaze of infinite pathos, and talked on while he wept.

"If you knew what she has been to me! When she married me I was a ruined man twenty years older. I have given her nothing but toil and care. You shall know everything – for years and years I have lived on the earnings of her labour. Worse than that, I have starved and stinted her to buy books. Oh, the shame of it! The wickedness of it! It was my vice – the vice that enslaved me just as if it had been drinking or gambling. I couldn't resist the temptation – though every day I cried shame upon myself and swore to overcome it. She never blamed me; never a word – nay, not a look – of a reproach. I lived in idleness. I never tried to save her that daily toil at the shop. Do you know that she worked in a shop? – She, with her knowledge and her refinement leading such a life as that! Think that I have passed the shop a thousand times, coming home with a book in my hands! I had the heart to pass, and to think of her there! Oh! Oh!"

Someone was knocking at the door. I went to open, and saw the landlady, her face set in astonishment, and her arms full of books.

"It's all right," I whispered. "Put them down on the floor there; don't bring them in. An accident."

Christopherson stood behind me; his look asked what he durst not speak. I said it was nothing, and by degrees brought him into a calmer state. Luckily, the doctor came before I went away, and he was able to report a slight improvement. The patient had slept a little and seemed likely to sleep again. Christopherson asked me to come again before long – there was no one else, he said, who cared anything about him – and I promised to call the next day.

I did so, early in the afternoon. Christopherson must have watched for my coming: before I could raise the knocker the door flew open, and his face gleamed such a greeting as astonished me. He grasped my hand in both his.

"The letter has come! We are to have the house."

"And how is Mrs. Christopherson?"

"Better, much better, Heaven be thanked! She slept almost from the time when you left yesterday afternoon till early this morning. The letter came by the first post, and I told her – not the whole truth," he added, under his breath. "She thinks I am to be allowed to take the books with me; and if you could have seen her smile of contentment. But they will all be sold and carried away before she knows about it; and when she sees that I don't care a snap of the fingers!"

He had turned into the sitting-room on the ground floor. Walking about excitedly, Christopherson gloried in the sacrifice he had made. Already a letter was despatched to a bookseller, who would buy the whole library as it stood. But would he not keep a few volumes? I asked. Surely there could be no objection to a few shelves of books; and how would he live without them? At first he declared vehemently that not a volume should be kept – he never wished to see a book again as long as he lived. But Mrs. Christopherson? I urged. Would she not be glad of something to read now and then? At this he grew pensive. We discussed the matter, and it was arranged that a box should be packed with select volumes and taken down into Norfolk together with the rest of their luggage. Not even Mrs. Keeting could object to this, and I strongly advised him to take her permission for granted.

And so it was done. By discreet management the piled volumes were stowed in bags, carried downstairs, emptied into a cart, and conveyed away, so quietly that the sick woman was aware of nothing. In telling me about it, Christopherson crowed as I had never heard him; but methought his eye avoided that part of the floor which had formerly been hidden, and in the course of our conversation he now and then became absent, with head bowed. Of the joy he felt in his wife's recovery there could, however, be no doubt. The crisis through which he had passed had made him, in appearance, a yet older man; when he declared his happiness tears came into his eyes, and his head shook with a senile tremor.

Before they left London, I saw Mrs. Christopherson – a pale, thin, slightly made woman, who had never been what is called good-looking, but her face, if ever face did so, declared a brave and loyal spirit. She was not joyous, she was not sad; but in her eyes, as I looked at them again and again, I read the profound thankfulness of one to whom fate has granted her soul's desire.

FROM THE CASEBOOK OF MASTER WIGGINS, ESQ.

Paul Di Filippo

Utter the song, O my soul! the flight and return of Mohammed,
Prophet and priest, who scattered abroad both evil and blessing,
Huge wasteful empires founded and hallowed slow persecution,
Soul-withering, but crushed the blasphemous rites of the Pagan
And idolatrous Christians.

— Samuel Taylor Coleridge

It features that I am just tuppeny over Nancy in love with Miss Vivianne Pye. I estimate that you would be too, if you could only see her the once, and then share her exquisite company at length, as I have done, while we both labored, off and on, at the behest of the Great Detective, aiding him in one case or another as his wiles and needs demanded.

First off, Miss Vivianne Pye is, quite impressively, all of five and half feet in stature, uncommon tall for a girl of fifteen years of age. She pretty much resembles a buggy-whip in point of slimness – thanks in part to the stern and intermittent diet afforded those of us who happen to be without reliable room and board, denizens of street or alley or church basement – although of late I have thought to notice certain mature curves blossoming beneath her usual colourful layered habiliments that consist of this and that castoff garment cadged from stalls and tips. (How she keeps these articles so clean and fresh while I and the rest of the Baker Street Irregulars tend to resemble ambulatory hampers of table linens after a feast at the Tankerville Club is a point of science far beyond me!) Her flaxen hair and dark flashing eyes are just as alluring as the rest of her perfectly assembled phiz. And I do not agree with her that her smile is spoiled by the smallish knurled scar that runs upward from the left juncture of her lips, a souvenir of her brave and daring exploits during one of Mr. Holmes's more challenging assignments.

When you add to this bodily sum her sharp wits and eagerness to please those whom she privileges with her friendship, and her easy laugh and sprightly manner, then you will confess, I daresay, that Miss Vivianne Pye is a charming package indeed.

I have more than once pledged to her my full troth and fealty, declaiming myself her total slave and lackey. But she only chooses to laugh in a not unkindly fashion and respond thus: "Oh, dear Wiggins, you are just thirteen years old and a mere child yet. It's not that I disdain or underestimate your affections and character, but it's just that you are far from mature enough to understand what such an avowal must mean."

"Thirteen-and-a-half!" I answer back. "Old enough by far to know what love is! And ain't I had far more educational experiences than the average lad of my years?"

But all my protestations are of no use. Miss Vivianne Pye merely says, "Save such declarations for when you are a bit older, Wiggins, and then I might consider them. Meanwhile, let us remain simply comrades and friends as we have long and staunchly conspired to maintain these several years."

What can I do then but sigh and make cow-eyes at her and go about my business?

But little did I wot that before I turned fourteen or Miss Vivianne Pye passed sixteen, both of us would be working with Mister Holmes as spies in the covert London establishment of that notorious heathen, Muhammad Ahmad bin Abd Allah, Mahdi of the Sudan, in danger of our lives, all to ferret out the lineaments of a plot that threatened to plunge London into chaos, and produce carnage such as this tired old city had never before seen.

That intemperately warm June day in the year of our Lord 1882 when the whole affair began, found me hanging about on the London Docks near the Ratcliffe Highway, seeking honest work if possible, and the main chance for some stomach-filling petty larceny if no sanctioned labours obtained. As has been oft averred of the Docks, they was always "one of the few places in the metropolis where men can get employment without either character or recommendation," and at least the latter part of that capsule description certainly applied to me. (I does like to think that despite outward appearances and lack of social ranking, my personal character is as noble as that of any highborn whelp.)

I had already blagged some potted meat from a grocer's and enjoyed a greasy unheated breakfast, the hem of my shirt serving as my napery, so I was replete and ready to perform any task, however lowly, that I might be assigned. So I began to amble the docks.

The forest of masts all about me, the tall chimneys vomiting clouds of black smoke, and the many-coloured flags flying in the air provided the background for what seemed utter flux and chaos.

The courts and alleys in the vicinity of the London Docks swarmed with low lodging-houses, and they had seemingly disgorged all their tenants at once. The aimless duffers ogled all the maritime goods in the many shops: bright brass sextants, chronometers and huge mariner's compasses, with their cards trembling with the motion of the cabs and wagons passing in the street. At the sail makers, the show windows were stowed with ropes and lines smelling of tar. The corners of the streets featured mostly slopsellers, their windows parti-coloured with bright red and blue flannel shirts, the doors nearly blocked up with hammocks and well-oiled norwesters, canvas trousers, and rough pilot coats. A satin-weskitted mate, accompanied by a black sailor with his large fur cap, fingered the weave of a dreadnought coat. A Customs-house officer in his brass-buttoned jacket was interrogating a sailor whose face was streaked with permanent indigo lines, a big green *parroquete* sitting atop his shoulder.

As I myself strolled along the noisy quay, I smelled tobacco and rum, then the stench of hides and huge bins of horns, and a bit further along, coffee and spice.

I intruded myself earnestly amongst several parties busy unloading cargo, but got no assignments whatsoever, not even to run an errand to the grog shop. So I perched myself high atop a crate of copper ore whence I could command a good vantage, and sought to amuse myself at the expense of the passing parade.

After a time, my eye was caught by a small altercation in progress.

A gaggle of exotically be-robed Mussulmen was hastening down the docks, plainly intent on getting somewheres quickly, and averse to any public displays. The several leaders of the group, their faces concealed beneath silken wraps that nearly met the lower edges of their turbans, leaving just slits for their midnight eyes, could be easily distinguished by a certain snootiness and lack of burdens. Their servants, weighed down with trunks and bundles and more plainly attired, followed behind. Bringing up the rear were what I took to be several heavily swaddled womenfolk, though no feminine distinctions showed forth to confirm my suspicions. And last, not quite of the party, came a bare-chested, mahogany-skinned beggar type, a dirty loincloth his only concession to dignity.

This obsequious, barefooted, crook-backed beggar, I could see, was trying his mightiest to ingratiate himself with the Mussulmen. Crouching half-doubled up, he scampered all around them like a pesky kid annoying a flock of elder goats.

"But oh, my honourable emirs and mullahs," the beggar whined in his accented English, "I can be of so much service to you! You are new to these foreign shores, and I am not! I know all the ways and wiles of this wicked city! Take me into your service, and I will prove infinitely valuable as advisor and guide!"

The leaders of the party ignored him for several yards, until finally one of them could stand his importunings no longer. The tall, fiery-eyed, beak-nosed fellow whirled upon the beggar and declaimed in harsh tones, "Begone, you wretch! We need no corrupt apostates who have been contaminated by life in the Dar al-Harab in our midst!"

"But, oh, my exalted mawlawi, just give me a chance to be of service —"

The angry Mussulman peeled off a heavy cord that belted his robe and began to lash the beggar. "Away with you! Begone!"

Whimpering and cringing under the blows, the hapless mendicant scuttled to the relative safety of the niche between my crate and the adjacent one, and the party of foreigners hastened away.

I peered down over the edge of my perch, expecting to see the chastised mumper muttering and soothing his sores.

So imagine my surprise when I confronted a pair of highly intelligent and somehow familiar eyes looking up at me, accompanied by an ironic grin that seemed out of place on that bronze phiz.

"Hello, Wiggins," said the beggar, in a commanding voice completely distinct from his prior whinging tones.

I must have goggled silently like a virgin dollymop confronted with her first client's exposed willy. It was only the resonant laughter from the beggar – who had now straightened up to a height utterly incompatible with his former distorted stature – that loosed my frozen tongue.

"Why, curse my soul, if it ain't Mister Holmes!"

"No need so cavalierly to seek damnation, Master Wiggins. And not so loud, if you please. I know my prey has passed out of earshot, but I still don't care to advertise my presence so broadly." Holmes pulled a rag from his loincloth and began to rub the dye from his hands and arms. "I need to restore my civilized appearance, Wiggins, a process that should take me no more than thirty minutes at most. Add in some transit time – well, what say you swing round to my lodgings in an hour or so, to learn of a new assignment?"

"Yes, sir!" I was already anticipating the generous emoluments that might be forthcoming, especially if I could aid Mister Holmes in a substantial fashion. I could quit sleeping rough for a week or two, and eat rabbit stew and fancy cakes instead of air pie.

I jumped down from the crate, and was halted by Holmes's oddly contrary white hand on my arm. He looked suddenly sober and dire.

"Oh, and Wiggins – please round up Miss Vivianne Pye and bring her with you."

I hastened off, for locating Vivianne would take me some little time, and I did not want to keep Holmes waiting.

I found my heart's desire in Borough Market, where I had suspicioned she might be. Last heard from, Vivianne had been desirous of securing employment with Uncle Ducky, who operated several carts what offered hot sheep's trotters at the market. Uncle

Ducky weren't no true kin to Vivianne, but merely a bloat-bellied, bewhiskered, cozening and self-serving goat of a businessman who liked to get a day's labour for half-a-day's wages.

"Vivianne, my beauty, 'tis I, bold Wiggins, your knight errant, with news of adventure and glory to share!"

Vivianne finished passing over a hot sloppy trotter out of the steaming pot to a beshawled and harried mother burdened down with three snotty brats and a trug full of leeks. Pocketing coins in her smeared apron, my love looked down her pert and pretty nose at me.

"Knight errant! I like that! If you really had my welfare to heart, you'd have spared me the tender offices of Uncle Ducky and seen me set up in some nicer job than doling out mutton."

"You know I've tried my best, Vivianne, but plum jobs don't drop into the laps of such Job's Turkeys as us the same easy way they do for Eton boys. But listen to this! I do have some work lined up, and it's for the Great Detective hisself!"

This detail caught Vivianne's fancy, for she was, I knew, half-besotted with the elegance and savoury fare and awesome brainworks of the Great Detective.

"Did he ask for me personal like?"

"Indeed!"

Vivianne hastily stripped off her apron and, putting her fingers twixt her lips, gave a piercing whistle. Before too long, a lad I recognized as little Jemmy Tingle showed up.

"Jemmy, take over for me for the rest of the day, won't you. That's a love!"

My jealousy at this term of endearment flared up, but I tamped it down manfully. The day I regarded Jemmy Tingle as my rival was the day I would qualify as a gulpy mug.

Taking Vivianne by her costermonger-clammy hand – and astonished that she allowed such intimacy – I trotted us crosstown to the ream flash lodgings of Mister Sherlock Holmes, 221B Baker Street.

We was let in smartly and without quibble by the affable Mrs. Hudson, who howsomever could not restrain from sniffing in muted disgust at our mutual pong. I was so unchivalrous, at least in my own thoughts, as to attribute to bulk of that offensive odour to Vivianne's mutton scent, rather than to my own unwashed condition.

Up in Holmes's curious and overstuffed study, we found the Great Detective, restored to his conventional appearance and tailoring, ensconced in a high-backed chair, working thoughtfully at his pipe. His comrade in crime-fighting, Doctor Watson, had half his buttocks resting on a desk corner, opposite leg extended, and was playing with a phial containing some almost-colourless liquid, tipping it back and forth to watch it slosh about like a child with a seashell at the beach.

"Ah, Wiggins," said Holmes with true affection, I thought. "And Miss Vivianne Pye. Welcome, welcome, please take your seats."

Vivianne gathered her dirty skirts like a duchess and plumped herself onto a low cushioned stool beside Holmes, while I dropped to the carpet at her feet, like a true knight at his lady's beck and call.

Holmes regarded us with a sober eye that couldn't help but transmit a sense of ominous importance to what he was about to say. But his words, when they came, were in the form of a surprising question.

"My young friends, how much do you love your country?"

To be honest, I had never given much thought to matters of patriotism, being generally too busy trying to keep my carcass yoked to my soul to consider flummut threats against the nation and my proper yeoman's response. But upon a moment's reflection, I said, "Well, Mister Holmes, not having had no experience of living abroad, I still feel confident in saying that Old Blighty, for all her obvious faults, strikes me as a glorious abode and well worth protecting. I'd have to rank my loyalties high, when push come to shove."

Vivianne nodded in agreement. "Wiggins has my own thoughts down pat, Mister Holmes."

"Good, good, very good. Because the assignment I have in mind for you, while extremely dangerous, is dedicated to preserving our nation – this city – from a calamity of unprecedented magnitude."

"Does it revolve around that sheik what you was trying to inveigle earlier?"

"Yes, Wiggins. Allow me to explain. That 'sheik' as you dub him is none other than Muhammad Ahmad bin Abd Allah, the Mahdi of the Sudan."

"The bugger what's staging a prater's revolt and harassing our own General Gordon around Khartoum?"

"None other."

"What's he doing here then?"

"The Mahdi has entered the country surreptitiously, for purposes I have yet to discern. But his motives and objectives cannot be of a nature beneficial to the Empire. He would not leave his prized rebellion to the care of even his three favourite deputies unless he thought he could strike a dreadful blow against us on our own hallowed ground, and thus advance his cause. I was trying to insinuate myself into his household, in order to monitor his schemes. But as you saw, Wiggins, I was unsuccessful. Yet inserting a spy into the Mahdi's establishment is still the only way we can possibly obtain information about his plans before he can bring them to fruition. Their cabal is too close-mouthed and tightly interlaced to betray themselves to outside observers."

I leaped to my feet and struck a heroic posture that I was sure would impress Vivianne. "I sees exactly where you're a-driving to, Mister Holmes! Well, paint me up like a walnut, and I will get myself hired by the Mahdi as a dogsbody. Just teach me some of that Arab lingo, and I'll be ready!"

Mister Holmes patted me on the shoulder in an avuncular manner that I felt was somewhat unbefitting of my valour. "I applaud your courage and willingness, Wiggins. But I have other tasks in mind for you. The person I would like to plant in the Mahdi's establishment is none other than Miss Pye."

"And where would she fit amongst those dangerous heathen rogues?"

"I intend to sell her to the Mahdi as a white slave and she will go straight into his harem."

Before I knew what I was doing, I had hurled myself on Holmes with fists a-flailing. But prior to me landing so much as one blow, he had me immobilized by some devilish arts and pinned upside down in the chair he had vacated with impossible quickness, my face scrooged into the upholstery.

"Wiggins! Calm down now! Do you seriously think I would offer such a plan without features for the protection of Miss Pye's virtue?"

The blood rushing to my topsy-turvy head seemed to restore my trust in Holmes, and I was able to make my surrender known around a mouthful of horsehair fabric, and thus I was released.

"Miss Pye, I take it that you are conversant with the facts of life, with regards to male desires."

Vivianne had the grace to blush a bit. "I've had a fair number of ungentlemanly hands questing up my skirts, Mister Holmes, without losing my honour entire. And you cannot live in such gutter-dwelling circumstances as Wiggins and I do without seeing human nature – and the human body – at its most unadorned and flagrant."

"So I assumed. Well, I am fairly confident that the indignities you would experience in the Mahdi's harem would amount to little more than you have already been subjected to in the course of daily living. And the reason for that guarantee lies with Doctor Watson."

Watson got up off the desk and flourished the phial of liquid before us. "This, my children, is hyoscine hydrobromide, a preparation of *Hyoscyamus niger*, or the common henbane. It has what is dubbed an anaphrodisiac effect when administered in the proper doses. And it is our intention to make sure the Mahdi's entire household is dosed properly. Holmes and I have infiltrated the victualler whom the Mahdi has hired to supply his crew. Wishing to remain hidden, the foreigners are relying entirely on this catered source of foodstuffs, rather than go shopping themselves in the market and attract unwanted attention."

"So you see," Holmes said, "the Mahdi and his men will be physically unable to steal Miss Pye's maidenhood from her, although they might yet indulge in some casual and lackadaisical groping. But their natural impulses to recline amongst and confide in the inhabitants of the harem at day's end will remain – as will the gossip's grapevine among the women. And occupying the traditional subservient and slighted role of her sex in a Mussulman's entourage, Miss Pye can employ her sharp nose and wits to ferret out any preparations that will alert us to the nature of the plot to harm London."

I looked questioningly at Vivianne and she returned my silent interrogative with the same bold and even excited gaze that Boadicea probably showed just prior to battle.

"I'll do it, Mister Holmes! For England – and for you!"

"And what's to be my role again?" I queried.

"You, Wiggins, are going to perform some nightly aerial acrobatics!"

The Kensington High Road's a fair Bedlam, a bewildering, relentless, round-the-clock parade of every type of dray, carriage, rider, goods-trundler, pedestrian, and mock-crippled and creeping leg and lurker out to slit a weasand. The tightly packed buildings, adorned with as many hortatory signs as there's pigeons on a split sack of spilled oats, channel the flow like the walls of some stone canyon. Colourful flags on ropes extend high above the crowd, from one side of the street to t'other. Under the shade of scattered street trees can be found clots of gypsies, Haymarket Hectors and their girls. The random strolling hard-nosed Blue Bottle sees to it that disturbances and disorder are kept to a minimum, and that the wrong people – or rather, the right people, the toffs – don't get excessively gulled and abused.

Off the High Road at intervals are plenty of rookeries, cheap dwelling places crammed with stinking humanity of every race, age and condition, in all their forms of slovenly sloth, quiet dignity and desperate dreams. I often thought my own doorway lodgings were preferable to such noisome nests.

Market Court was one such, neither the most despicable nor the nicest. Naught but a congeries of scabbed-together, ill-sorted, shambling structures rearing at their highest some three stories tall and enclosing a litter-strewn muddy courtyard. But the cul-de-sac did feature the distinct advantage of strictly limited and controlled ingress and egress. Thus it suited the fortress mentality of Muhammad Ahmad bin Abd Allah, the Mahdi of the Sudan, and his crew of presumably cut-throat Mussulmen, who had taken over the establishment entire, permitting no one in save the victualler bearing his thankfully tainted, ballocks-blocking provender.

How I despaired of Miss Vivianne Pye's fortunes amidst such a den of blackguards! I awaited eagerly the moment when she might be released from her durance vile, as Mister Holmes swept in with a squad of crushers, bearing enough evidence garnered by his crack Irregulars to put paid to these plotters.

But the only trouble was, after two weeks of Vivianne scraping up every tidbit of information she could rumble, we were no closer to understanding the machinations of these Mussulmen than on the day of their arrival.

Perhaps tonight, I thought, as I prepared myself for my bold scarpering across sodden, slippery and shabby shingles, would be the night we gained the prize. Vivianne and I, of course, might not even recognise that we had attained our sufficiency of information. Only the mighty master mind of Mister Holmes, piecing together every scrap we relayed to him with that patented pattern-making big brain of his, would turn the key in this riddle.

At the edge of the nameless rookery some dozen yards away from Market Court, as London's smoky twilight descended fully upon us like a fat sow squishing her brood, I paused with my comrades, several of the regular Irregulars, namely Trosper, Pupshaw and Jernigan.

"You understand, men, what I need you to do, should I signal?"

Jernigan scratched a poxy blemish on his upper lip. "Indeed, Wiggins, indeed! Same as what we stood ready to do during your past excursions. You may rely completely on our capacity to wake the dead."

"All right, then, I'm off to climb Rapunzel's tower, so to speak."

After making sure the length of stout rope coiled around my waist was secured, I dashed toward the nearest drain pipe, leapt halfway up its lower reaches, and began to haul myself up to the rookery roof.

Once atop that tilting, daunting, many-levelled surface, I kept hunched so as not to arouse outcries from any nosy parkers below, and raced like a roach toward my appointed date.

When I began this mission two weeks ago, my course across these rooftops, where the geography bore no visible relation to the streets below, had proved a mite perplexing. But now the path to the roof's edge above the courtyard window of the harem where

Vivianne was immured was second-nature to my hands and feet. I would have made a prime snakesman to any snoozer, in and out with the chink and couter before any sleeping victim could even mumble and turn over.

At my destination, I unlooped the rope and secured one end around a sturdy chimbly. Then, holding the free end ready, I awaited Vivianne's whistle, a muted version of what she was wont to use to summon her replacement when in Uncle Ducky's employ.

After several hours or anticipatory crouching, during which I nearly dozed off, the signal came, and I lowered myself away.

My shoes found familiar purchase on a rim formed by some irregular bricks, and then I was feasting my lamps on my beloved.

Vivianne had been tarted up in silks and chiffons, scrubbed pink and painted, her hair coiled up like some hot cross bun, but she was still my tough boulevard princess.

"My little bird, how I've missed you!" I whispered. "Give us a kiss!"

Vivianne's shadowed face showed her a nervous nellie, as was only natural under the fraught circumstances, but I could tell that underneath her apprehension she had to be pleased at my bold love-making amidst such a parlous climate.

"Hold off there, Romeo! Let me tell you my news first." She looked back over her shoulder, to make sure that her fellow concubines in the next room were still fast asleep. "Nasif let it slip…"

My sudden emotions got the better of me, and I interrupted her, mayhaps a bit too loudly. "That damn sand-blackamoor! It galls me to picture you and him lying a-bed, with him pressing his flaccid todger into your virgin flanks!"

Astonishingly, Vivianne defended the rogue. "Nasif is the nicest one here. He's just a lad, after all, hardly older than us. He's very gentle and innocent, and I think he's been seduced by the charm and glamour of the Mahdi and his cause. But he has his doubts about what they call *jihad*, and that's why he confides in me." She paused. "And his willy, while not able to stand to attention, thanks to Doctor Watson's dosing, seems otherwise quite respectable."

I growled then. But, having satisfactorily jabbed my jealousy bone, Vivianne ignored me and continued. "You recall the shipment of chemicals that arrived here last week? Well, they have been fussing with them continuously in the basement, raising some horrid stinks. And now they have received an order of glass carboys. I saw the dealer's name stencilled on the crates. Geronimus Aspenshade and Sons. Perhaps Mister Holmes can learn more from that source."

I swung one-handed from my rope, leaning in to clasp my little bird with my free arm. I stole a snog, to which she assented not utterly unwillingly. Yet I could not help but wonder if she would have relished the precious affection from any of the familiar Irregulars under such dire and isolated conditions as obtained for a spy in the harem, or did she regard me as her special beau?

"This is big news, Vivianne, and I'd better hasten to Mister Holmes." I began to squirrel up the rope.

"Oh, one more thing," Vivianne called softly. "I happened to glimpse the Mahdi himself studying a map. From the snatch I got as he pinched my bum and shooed me away, I took it to be a plan of the Tube stations."

"Right-o!"

Partway up the rope, a hand encircled my ankle. Ah, sweet Vivianne could not bear to part yet!

But the sudden savage yank on my personal limb revealed that I was mistaken.

Looking down, I saw an angry bearded Arab face assigned to the hoary meat hook glommed onto my fetlock. Vivianne meanwhile had been pinioned by another man who was muffling her attempted screams of warning.

I loudly gave out with the Irregulars's secret hoot.

"Barney up, men, barney up!"

Immediately from the High Street side of the rookery came an enormous ruckus, bellowings and clatterings and bangings. A hail of stones flew over the roof into the courtyard.

The unexpected riot had its intended effect, momentarily disconcerting my assailant. I kicked wildly, and freed myself.

I hesitated only a moment, fantasizing I could plunge into the harem, rescue Vivianne and flee together. But instantly my common sense dissuaded me. If I attempted a rescue and were captured,

Mister Holmes would never learn the vital information I carried.

So, with my heart breaking at images of Vivianne's sordid plight, I monkeyed up my lifeline, across the rooftops, and bunked straight to Mister Holmes.

The cheery and trig establishment of Geronimus Aspenshade and Sons, hard by the smoky, ashy Falcon Glassworks on the banks of the Thames, appeared to be on the up-and-up, no secret headquarters of some international cabal of assassins. Nonetheless, as I entered the Ali Baba trove of sparkling pendants, multi-coloured goblets and faceted punch bowls behind Mister Holmes, I maintained a vigilant manner. Last night's fray had set my nerves on edge, and I had no wish for us to be ambushed here in this seemingly staid and frowsty shop.

Holmes had been awake and dressed at 221B when I arrived around midnight. Did that superhuman fellow never sleep like lesser men? As I poured out all my news to him in a frantic blurt, his calm and pointed questions had the effect of calming me down summat.

At last I concluded with my major worry. "But Mister Holmes, whatever will happen to my poor Vivianne?"

"Wiggins, my boy, I firmly believe that the child will be fine. You maintain that your conversation betraying your true interests was not overheard. So the Mahdi's men have no notion that you were conducting a prearranged confab centred on their machinations. Instead, they no doubt took you for a typically lusty local swain out to despoil their harem. Vivianne will doubtlessly suffer some kind of mild corporal punishment for her transgressions – a few strokes of the switch perhaps. But this presumed transgressive behaviour on her part is well-known among the inmates of the harem, and regarded as within the normal limits of turpitude. No, what we need to focus on is the game afoot. If only Watson could more speedily rustle up a list of those chemicals sold to the Mahdi. It's taking him forever to find their supplier. Ah, well, patience is a virtue we must always cultivate. And in the morning we can investigate the glassblower's shop whose identity you and Miss Pye have so ingeniously ascertained."

I hardly slept that night, being both too worried over some half-horrid, half-beguiling fantasies of Vivianne's tender bum receiving its lashes, and too unused to the luxury of resting on Mister Holmes' couch, swaddled in real woollen blankets thoughtfully supplied by a drowsily accommodating Mrs. Hudson.

We approached the counter now where Geronimus Aspenshade awaited us with the eagerness of any merchant anticipating a sale. Portly and balding and brawny, Aspenshade sported bare hairy arms that revealed dozens of coin-sized bare patches, scars from small healed burns encountered in his molten trade.

Holmes introduced himself, finding that his name met with no small recognition and respect. He stated his interests, and Aspenshade cogitated a moment before replying.

"Ah, yes, a most curious order. Generally, brewers and chemists take my carboys in the standard five-gallon size. Them's my best sellers by far. But these chaps wanted relatively tiny one-gallon thingamabobs. And they even specified the grade of glass."

"Extra strong?" ventured Holmes.

"Just the opposite! These had to be fashioned from stuff that was less strong than mere window glass! First off, they could hardly hold much liquid, and then, they were bound to shatter at the slightest shock! Whatever use could they have in mind? I had to pack the buggers in extra sawdust just to ship them safely! But they paid good money, and the customer knows best, I always says."

"Thank you for your help, Mister Aspenshade."

Outside, Holmes spoke reflectively, as if I weren't present. "Easy to shatter, only a gallon... It all depends on that list of chemicals! Come, Wiggins, we will haunt Doctor Watson's office till he returns."

But when we arrived at Watson's practice, he was already there.

"Here's the list, Holmes. They were deucedly clever, going far afield for these substances. Their supply house was all the way in West Ham. But I tracked them down at last. Potassium acetate, arsenic trioxide –"

Holmes stiffened and trembled like a hound. "My god, Watson! They are making cacodyl, or Cadet's fuming liquid! I see it all now. Quickly, there is not a moment to lose!"

**

Even after studying for many minutes this strange army assembled in a back room at King's Cross station, I was having the demnedest time convincing myself I wasn't inhabiting some queer story by that Frenchy fable-flogger, Mister Jules Verne. Maybe I had really been transported to the Moon, and was witnessing an army of Moon Men.

Three dozen of London's toughest rozzers had been rounded up by Mister Holmes on short notice and assembled here at King's Cross. Then, under the supervision of Doctor Watson, they had all been outfitted with the oddest kind of masks. Watson had explained to Holmes the nature of this scientific equipage – rubber and metal and glass getups with a canister perched smack dab in the middle of their lower faces – and as best I recall the Doctor had dubbed them "Barton's respirators," and said the canisters held "lime, glycerin-soaked cotton wool and charcoal."

Holmes studied the apparatus intently and said, "They are unproven against the cacodyl, but we will have to hope for the best."

Now the boss copper, a beefy redhead I knew from previous tussles named Bert Smudge, lifted his mask and addressed Mister Holmes.

"I sure hope you've accurately deduced the time and place for this supposed assault, detective. It would look awfully bad for us if those murdering heathens struck elsewhere while we were congregated here, or if they attacked on some other day when we had been lulled into complacency."

"No, Smudge, this is the place, and the day is now. King's Cross is the busiest station on the Circle Line, and we have to assume our murderous opponents are desirous of inflicting maximum casualties, as warped recompense for General Gordon's campaign against them. And the date could be no other, for this is the eighth of June."

Smudge itched at his brainpan. "And what makes the eighth of June so precious?"

"It is precisely the one thousandth and two hundred and fiftieth anniversary of the death of the Prophet Muhammad."

No-wise enlightened, Smudge replied, "Well, I will have to

accept your estimation of the importance of this date, Mister Holmes. Now, as to the matter of clearing out the citizens, I still feel–"

Holmes showed some small exasperation. "I have told you, Smudge, we simply can't empty the station of riders. That would alert the Mahdi's men to our presence and to our knowledge of their plans. It must appear to be business as usual here, to draw them out. We can't have them panicking and going into hiding elsewhere in the city, where we can't lay our hands on them. No, we shall have to rely on our superior forces intercepting the attackers in order to prevent harm to the innocent bystanders."

"And we can't raid the Market Court rookery because –"

Now Holmes's patience was positively exhausted. "Can't you comprehend simple strategy and tactics, Sergeant? My lord, what are they teaching you boys these days? Our plan is predicated on the simple fact that the team of attackers is already dispersed and in transit. Left at the rookery will be only the Mahdi himself, awaiting reports of his victory. We will mop him up afterwards."

I wanted to say, *But Vivianne is also at the Market Court rookery too, and needs rescuing!* But I knew that the cool and calculating mind of Mister Holmes would not give a yennap for Vivianne's fate until he had frustrated the Mahdi's plans and saved the larger number of souls.

"Now, Sergeant, if you would be so good as to emplace your men in the concealed positions I have previously denominated, we can await the incursion."

I kept close by Holmes and Watson as we took up our own blind.

Need I even say that the whole fracas transpired as the Great Detective foretold?

The Mahdi's men were deuced clever. They had doffed their native costumes of course and disguised themselves as peppermint-water sellers. But we recognized them by those unnaturally small carboys full of deadly liquid ready to explode as suffocating gas. As they trundled in their handcarts weighed down with poison, they were, one by one, instantly and quietly intercepted by the rozzers, whose alien appearance helped to disconcert, at least momentarily, the conspirators. Half of the subway riders within sight of the action never even noticed what was happening, while the other half thought they were witnessing a typical pinch of an illegal seller.

It was all bob's-your-uncle, and Doctor Watson was visibly relaxing, providing me a cue to do the same, when one lagging Arab, witnessing the apprehension of his fellows, managed to dash his carboy to the tiles, where it promptly shattered, releasing its hideous cargo.

Instantly three masked rozzers had him. Others ploughed through the lethal fog to swiftly lead to safety the helpless coughing citizens caught in the edges of the miasma. One copper went down to the floor, gasping and writhing, victim of a mask that didn't quite fit, or a bad filter canister. Other crushers let loose with hand-pumped sprayers filled with a water and baking soda mixture. I caught the faintest stench of the poison from a scarf of gas wafting our way, but soon King's Cross was restored to near-normal conditions.

Coughing a bit hisself, Mister Holmes nodded in satisfaction. "And now to put paid to the Mahdi!"

If I lives to be a hundred, I will never forget that mad dash across London in the hansom cab, Holmes as intent as an eagle on his prey, Watson running calculations in his brain as to how he might improve those masks for the next time we faced such a threat – and me all a-quiver over the unknown fate of my beloved Vivianne Pye!

The Market Court rookery looked odd to me from the ground level, after viewing it from above for so many nights, and I got slightly turned around. But Holmes dashed straight for the proper entrance, and I followed close behind.

Just inside, we came upon a most pathetic scene, like something from a domestic melodrama staged in a penny gaff.

Lying on the floor, bleeding from a deep gash in his shoulder, was a slim Arab youth clad in one of them white native bathrobes, now stained red. His wispy black moustache stood out more vividly due to his wound-blanched olive complexion. A long curving sword rested on the floor by his hand.

Kneeling beside him, cradling his head tenderly, her own harem outfit all besmirched, was my very own Vivianne Pye!

"Oh, Nasif, don't die! Hang on, my dear, hang on!"

"It is no use, Miss Vivianne, I am surely going soon to meet my many promised virgins, none of whom will shine as brightly as you."

Holmes brusquely interrupted this tender scene. "Miss Pye! Where is the Mahdi?!

"Nasif tried to stop him, but the Mahdi struck him down with his own sword, then dashed into the basement."

"These rookeries are threaded with tunnels," exclaimed Holmes, "but I know where he will probably debouch."

Holmes snatched up the fallen sword and raced off.

Torn between my allegiance to Vivianne and my fealty to Holmes, I chose the latter – a decision made a bit easier by the shocking infidelity of my beloved. "Nasif, my dear," my arse!

By the time I arrived on the High Street, the duel twixt West and East was on!

In the middle of a ring of shocked spectators, Holmes and the Mahdi were enveloped in a ferocious whirlwind of blades. The Mahdi's fierce face expressed utmost contempt for his opponent, while Holmes showed only a stern respect tinged with disdain for the Mahdi's cowardly means of waging war upon innocent civilians.

The fighters seemed evenly matched – until Holmes began to falter.

As I afterwards learned, he had inhaled a larger whiff of cacodyl than I back at the station, but shied from telling us, and the exposure had left him temporarily deficient in his wind.

The Mahdi struck Holmes heartily with the flat side of his blade upon his head, and Britain's champion was down!

The Mahdi dashed off, the awestruck spectators failing to intervene.

I rushed to the side of my mentor, and found him already coming round, resigned to this throw of the dice.

"He's gone, Wiggins. I intuit that he had a well-defined escape route out of the country planned well in advance. He's General Gordon's problem now. I don't give him more than a few years back home. And I doubt he or his co-religionists will try another such attack for many a year, having been defeated so soundly, thanks to the sterling efforts of you and Miss Pye."

Such praise stirred the cockles of my heart. And that warm feeling, recalled at intervals, along with the several sovereigns that Mister Holmes would later bestow on me, would do much to carry me through the rough times ahead, as Vivianne traitorously nursed the pardoned Nasif back to health, introduced him into the ways of his newly adopted nation, and then found herself tossed aside in favour of a bold Turkish tart employed as a dancer at Wilton's Music Hall in Whitechapel, who appealed more deeply to Nasif's foreign tastes.

And so, a year older, I approach that mature condition where my dream girl, the unmatched Miss Vivianne Pye, might deign to look favourably upon my earnest, Irregular suit!

ALBERT AND THE ENGINE
OF ALBION

Terry Grimwood

From:

Prince Francis Charles Augustus Albert Emanuel Saxe-Coburg-Gotha

To:

Baron Stockmar

Dated July 25th 1840.

Buckingham Palace, England

My Dearest Baron

So now I am a hero to my adopted race. A race hitherto suspicious of this foreigner who has dared marry their queen. It took only a moment; gun shots as we rode in our carriage among London's cheering crowds, my own body a shield protecting my beloved.[2]

The would-be assassin claims not to know what drove him. But I know and I must share this secret and terrible thing with you, my closest friend, a man who has seen the world and the one to whom I owe my present happiness with my beloved Victoria.

My hope is that you know me as a man of integrity and as proof that I am no seeker of sensation, I ask you to reveal this letter or its contents to no one else and to destroy it the moment you have read it.

Our wedding, in February, was a glorious occasion and, in my beloved's own words, an example to the nation over which she rules

---

[2] There was an assassination attempt on Queen Victoria in 1840 by one Edward Oxford. Shots were fired at her open carriage and Prince Albert heroically shielded his wife with his own body.

so dutifully of the sacredness of the matrimonial estate.

It has not been easy. I struggle to find a place. I am allowed to see no document or offer no word of advice. I am, however, alive with plans and have undertaken to effect improvements to this very Palace. It is a magnificent yet wretched place. The ventilation is poor. There are bad smells and it is cold in the winter because the fires are dampened for fear of filling the rooms with smoke.

Do not mistake this frustration for unhappiness. I have never known such bliss of the heart. I have never known such joy at the sight and presence of another human being.

But all this has been marred by that odious and strange day, the 31st of June in The Year of Our Lord, 1840.

Yes, the 31st of June. Know this Baron, that date is no slip of my pen.

On its eve, we had guests at the Palace, among them Lord Melbourne, the Prime Minister himself. He is a good man, always welcome. Melbourne is to Victoria what you are to me, dear Baron, a close friend and wise advisor.

We dined, and after cigars and serious conversation for the men and gossip for the women (an odd custom, one I have attempted to resist but have been vigorously defeated), we danced. How my Victoria loves to dance. On and on, hour after hour. It has been known for her to dance until the sun rises. Hardly appropriate behaviour for a sovereign you may say, but she is young and vigorous and it gives me joy to see her lay down the burdens of office and be merry, if only for a while.

As for me? Ah Baron, you know only too well that by ten in the evening I am weary and ready for my bed. That night, however, I danced, as often with my beloved as I was allowed. It was no chore. Her eyes shone, reflecting the light of the thousand candles illuminating the ballroom. Full of mischief they were. Full of the very spark of life.

I cannot say precisely when I noticed the stranger, neither can I recall his arrival or his presence at dinner. He was a singular character. His hair, longer than is appropriate for a man, his face gaunt, cheekbones Slavic. Russian perhaps. And his eyes, they were dark and piercing, as he watched our merriment. He was dressed in a fine dark-green coat and an ochre waistcoat. His outfit was more befitting of the age of the Prince Regent than our modern times, but he seemed unconscious of his outmoded style. Indeed, there was something of the dandy about him and an arrogance I did not much care for.

His smile was unpleasant, as if he mocked our foolish entertainment. His presence cast a stain upon the warmth of the room. I felt that I must keep my Victoria away from him and danced with her long after it was decent. For her part, my beloved seemed delighted.

"Are you not tired Bertie?" she asked.

"Not at all," I answered. "Tonight, I will outdo you. I will dance until dawn if necessary."

She laughed her free and delightful laugh. The stranger watched us. I drew Victoria closer and she protested, happily that I was making a public show of our affection. She was right, but I had to protect her from this visitor, who had, I must add, made no display of hostility and seemed ignored my most of the guests present.

Except one, and this was disturbing.

Lord Melbourne approached him even as I watched and suddenly they were speaking in low, conspiratorial tones. Perhaps this newcomer was some foreign diplomat. There was much nodding of heads. Then Melbourne moved away and suddenly, to my great alarm, the visitor stepped out of the shadows and glided towards us through the tightly-packed dancers, his dark eye fixed upon my Victoria.

There was nothing I could do. To refuse him would have been an unforgivable slight. He waited politely as the waltz ended, then bowed and addressed me as Prince and Victoria as Your Majesty. Close to him now, I noticed that he had about him a peculiar odour of earth and also of grease and machineries. I noticed, too, that the room had turned cold.

Before another word was spoken, Victoria was in his arms and whisked away into a fast polka. Their movements were so fluid I was sure they had danced together before, and often.

Humiliated, but maintaining my dignity, I retreated to the edge of the room. I watched as they danced. The music jangled and echoed through my skull. The room swam, I felt dizzy, ill-at-ease, hot and stifled. I searched for an exit, but was confused. The room was suddenly unfamiliar to me.

I saw Melbourne and strove to go to him, but my way was blocked by dancers, more than I remembered, couple-upon-couple spinning by. Some, I realised, were not human at all, but winged and delicate as butterflies, while others were hulking, beastlike, toppling chairs and upending candles.

And at the eye of this storm, Victoria and the Guest, caged against my interference by the other revellers. He held her close. She leaned her head against his chest, her eyes closed.

On and on it went, louder, wilder, faster, until the music beat me to my knees. An icy wind gusted through the room. Candles flared. Sheet music tumbled. And all the while Victoria and the Guest whirled about the room.

I could not bear this. I wanted to escape. There was no door. There was no relief. The ungodly horde capered and careered, a clumsy, crashing, terrifying maelstrom of wings and horns and hooves and talons. I cried out, but my voice was lost in the din. Shadows flickered and danced as if of their own accord. The floor thrummed to the stamp of their feet –

I woke.

Confused, out of breath, my head spinning, I sat up in the dark and knew that I was in our marital bed, but fully clothed, even down to my shoes.

I was not alone. There was the scent of a sweet-smelling perfume I recognised.

Victoria.

I lay down once more and now felt the heat from her. I whispered her name. She murmured and rolled over to face me.

"Bertie?" she said, her voice heavy with sleep.

"Who was he?" I asked. The question was forthright but I could not restrain myself. It was jealousy, my dear Baron, nothing more, nothing less.

"Who?"

"The gentleman with long hair."

Victoria looked round at me. "Which gentleman with long hair?"

"Do not toy with me Victoria. I am tired."

"I have no idea of whom you speak, Bertie."

"You danced with him."

"I did not. I danced only with you, then with Lord Melbourne. No one else. I was flattered that you kept me to yourself all evening." I felt her hand on my face, the touch, a tender one. "You showed your wicked side tonight, Bertie."

"Victoria, please be serious with me for a moment. You are telling me, you are swearing to me, that you have no recollection of dancing with that man?"

"None." She spoke more loudly this time and sounded angry.

"I must be mistaken." I lied. Something that went against the very grain of my nature. "I was feeling ill. Perhaps... I saw nothing."

"My poor Bertie," Victoria crooned, and she was in my arms and close to me.

Every care, every burden of life is puffed away as smoke when our arms entwine, when our lips meet... I am sorry Baron, you will think me far less than a gentleman for speaking of such things, but I must tell you of that night. Victoria you see is always... unrestrained in the bedchamber. That night, she was most urgent, willing and tireless.

Yet, something was missing. There was a distance between us, a gulf of spirit. She was mine, yet not mine.

Now, Baron, this you will not believe.

I could not sleep. Fatigued as I was, my eyes remained wide and my mind a tumble of thoughts that would not be ordered. The air was hot, stiflingly so. Unmoving and foul-tasting, it bore down upon me as I lay and stole my breath. The last of the candles in the room flickered and, in its last glimmer, I saw the pendant.

Its jewel rested at the base of my beloved's throat. Light pulsed, now green, now red, now blue, from deep within its crystalline heart. On closer examination I saw that the luminance was diffused by a mist that swirled about the interior of the stone.

The candle died but the pendant's glow remained to cast a small pool of illumination over Victoria's skin, lighting her face and flicking away the shadow. I made to pull the loathsome thing from her neck. She cried out, as if afraid. I tugged harder, panicked now, but not knowing why. The cry became a groan of pain. She rolled over, away from me, and sobbed bitterly, yet she was still asleep. I could see the ghastly shifting light of the pendant, radiating from the far side of her slumbering silhouette.

Do you fear for my sanity, dear Baron? I did, at that moment, as I lay awake, uneasy and disturbed in that crushing heat. But this was not all. There was worse to come.

The silence became whispers.

I tried to block them out, convinced that they were of my own imagining.

Then Victoria answered.

With a murmur, at first, the words unintelligible, but words nonetheless. My heart all but stopped in my chest. I shivered, despite the heat, shivered with fear. The whispers grew louder. The voices of many. Victoria's murmurs rose also. She rolled onto her back and chuckled softly. The moon was suddenly bright and, through the great window, painted the room's sumptuous drapery and furnishings silver. I saw my beloved reach up with her arms. The pendant too flared bright. Her body rose slightly. Her back arched. The whispers filled with laughter. Then a louder, commanding voice broke through.

"Who's there?" I demanded, my voice strong despite my fear. "Show yourself."

The voices stopped. Victoria moaned softly, as if upset, and slumped back into the bed. I nestled her in my arms. Her skin, yes, I must speak of it, Baron, her skin was damp with sweat. She was cold and tremulous, yet deeply asleep.

Disgusted, I made to tug the pendant free one more time, and was met by an outburst of horrible ferocity from my beloved. She spun about and lashed at my hand. Her nails tore my flesh so deeply I feared she had opened it to the bone.

I cried out and rolled away until I fell from the bed in an ungainly tangle of sheets and limbs.

Clutching my bloodied hand to myself I fled from the room. I am not a coward, but I could not endure this awful nightmare a moment longer.

Sunlight poured through the opened curtains. I was alone in my own chamber, and it was late. I sat up, and noticed myself to be drenched in sweat. I felt hollow and exhausted. My mind spun from a tangle of disturbing dreams. I felt a stab of pain and remembered my wound.

It was not as savage as I had feared. A mere scratch, the bleeding long staunched and dry.

I looked to the clock, the one given as a gift to me, dear Baron, that stands proud on the mantlepiece. Half the hour after nine. Victoria was, no doubt dressed and about her royal business.

Or fevered and ill on her bed. I would visit her room to ascertain her condition then, perhaps, call for a physician.

I rose, crossed to the pitcher of water on the washstand and undertook my ablutions. The face I saw in the mirror was haggard, the eyes dark-ringed. My hands shook as I shaved. A sharp and sudden pain bit into my neck. Blood mingled with the soap. I had cut myself. Of no great moment, but a sign of how disturbed I was.

As I dried my face I went to the window. The sky was a clear blue dome that encompassed and enclosed the capital. I could see little of the city other than the jumble of its rooftops and chimneys that cluttered the view beyond the lush green of St James's Park. London; I have never known such a noisy, teeming place. So many extremes. The grand house and the slum. The well-fed rich and the hungry poor. Wide streets and narrow lanes. Great wonders and foul alleyways defiled with human filth. You could hear the dull rumble and clatter of the city's breath at all times of day and night.

But not this morning. This morning the city was oddly quiet and still. As was the Palace where, surely, there should be the sounds of staff going about their business.

Instead there was a silence.

I felt an urgent need to seek the face of my God, so I kneeled by the bed.

I found no peace in the act, however. My mind was too distracted, my heart troubled. A miasma had formed between myself and Heaven.. A mist that absorbed every supplication even as it left my lips. It was as if, and I swear this to be true, an evil presence had entered the room and poisoned my mind with dark and blasphemous thoughts.

Prayer become a true spiritual battle that drew every ounce of strength from my soul.

There was sudden laughter. Like the tinkle of tiny bells. I opened my eyes to see light spiral in through the bedroom's open window. At first I thought it to be a sign from God, an angel perhaps. But then the glow resolved to become a column of sparkling shapes, dancing in the air like insects on a summer evening.

One of the intruders broke away to hover only a few inches from my face.

It was a woman, the size of a wren, her wings patterned like a butterfly's. She was dressed in robes so diaphanous as to be invisible and writhed wildly in the air, her face twisted in lewd mockery. I wanted to avert my eyes from the creature's wickedness. But, God forgive me, I could not.

Glimpsed through her translucent flesh were wheels and machineries like the workings of a pocket watch.

Mechanical or not, the creature's lewdness was undiminished. I batted it away as one would a fly, but it persisted, dancing about my face, offering vile temptations, unspeakable contortions and gesture. Tiny wings flickered over my skin.

I returned to prayer, agonised now, pleading for mercy and a release from temptation.

My pain and despair, my broken heart, all drew tighter then unleashed themselves as a sudden roar of rage that wrenched me to my feet. The creatures swirled upwards. Their tinkling laughter turned to shrieks of fear.

And they were gone.

Still partly-dressed, I rushed to Victoria's chamber. The great windows were open and the curtain billowed inwards despite the lack of breeze. My beloved was in her bed.

But not alone.

A figure stood over her. The stranger from last night. He looked up as I burst into the room and grinned, revealing teeth as pointed as those of a wolf. There was contempt in that grin.

"Victoria," he whispered, and the whisper filled the room.

"My Lord," she murmured back.

Enraged, I snatched up a Bible from the small table beside the bed, intending to hurl it at the stranger's head, but the tome erupted into flame in my hand. I cried out, cast the flaming mass aside and then, heedless of my own safety, threw myself towards the creature.

Eyes widened in surprise, he twisted about and leapt out of the window like a fleeing cat. Surely no man could jump from such a height and live. I made to look outside, to view the horror of his broken body on the paving below. However, before I could move, Victoria uttered a sigh, so bitter and sad that I thought my heart would break.

Tears rolled down her ashen cheeks. "I must go to him," she said, clearly, as one who is in full command of their faculties.

Go to him? "You cannot," I said sternly. "You must remain here, safe from that creature's power."

Before I could prevent her, she had rushed to the window. "My Lord!" she cried out. "I will come to you."

I drew her away. She began to weep, then suddenly grasped my arms and, eyes burning, swung herself about in a dance so abandoned, it shocked me to my soul. I joined in, not from desire, but from fear that resistance would throw her once more into some convulsion. We spun about the room, to a discordant melody that issued from her throat. And for a moment, I thought I heard the music echoed from outside.

"You must not fear!" she cried breathlessly. "This is as it should be. You must laugh and be glad."

Abruptly, she detached herself from me and hurried to the window. Again, I forced her back. This time she screamed and lashed with her fists. Then slumped in my arms and wept loudly.

I lay her on the bed, held her hands and uttered her name. She made no sign that she heard me. All the while, that vile gem pulsed and glowed against her skin.

Restless, uneasy, I paced the room. Outside, the sky had darkened with cloud.

"Bertie? Where are you?"

I looked round to see Victoria, out of the bed now, coming to me, her eyes alive with fear. "We must pray," she said. "As earnestly as possible."

She fell to her knees, urging me to join her. Though fearing a trick, I consented. Her hand found mine. "I am frightened," she said. "My mind is confused. What is happening to me Albert?"

I had no answer. Instead, I held her and we trembled in each other's arms. Our comfort was broken by a loud pounding at the door.

"Your Highness, quickly!" Melbourne, sounding distressed.

I let him in and was shocked to see that his clothes were disordered, and that he was bleeding from a wound to his forehead. I helped him to the nearest chair.

"The servants have him..." Melbourne gasped. "A terrible fight... struck me..."

"Who?"

"The uninvited guest from last night's ball. I thought him a friend to the Queen but..."

"Where is he?"

"The Chapel."

"Very well." I glanced at the window, uneasy, unsure. Then decided. "Stay here. I will send someone up to you. And lock the door."

I was away, as dishevelled a Prince Consort as ever you saw, running barefoot over the cold floors of Buckingham Palace. I called for help, but was answered only by echoes. Neither did I meet anyone, no servant or retainer, no maid, no document-laden officials.

It was as if the Palace was deserted...

Suddenly, a dread was upon me, and I was running once more, though not to the Chapel, but back to the bedchamber. I battered at its unyielding door. Calling for entrance.

It swung open, the way blocked by Lord Melbourne. Beyond him, the room was empty, the window open, curtains billowing. The sky was no longer clear. Thunder rumbled, lightning flashed.

I backed away. "What have you done, Melbourne?"

"It has to be," he said gently.

"What has to be... I do not understand..."

"This day," Melbourne said. "Is not a real day."

"A dream then. A terrible nightmare."

"This is no dream, but rather a day placed between those days we see as real, like an extra card added to a pack. And this day exists only for those who have a part to play in its dramas. Though why you…"

"Dramas? For the love of God –"

He laughed, a humourless sound. "God? Perhaps that is the reason you are here." His laughter became a frown. "I hope not. This has little to do with Him."

"Enough riddles Melbourne. You must tell me where Victoria is"

"The Centre, Your Highness, the very centre."

"If she has come to any harm, I swear –"

"He means only good. He is our ally."

"Satan is your ally?"

"Not Satan. Rather, the King of the Earth. He is the one whose power has armed and fuelled this nation's victories since the days of Arthur. Turn from him and this land and our Empire will fall. Every monarch must vow allegiance to him. Every royal firstborn must be his offspring."

I recoiled in horror.

I was away, Melbourne shouting after me. afraid now. "You must not interfere…!"

The sky was a heaving, dark ocean. Lightning tore it apart, striking through the clouds to reveal the titanic, roiling landscapes within. A strong wind blew, which almost swept me from my feet the moment I stepped, now fully dressed, through the grand doors of the Palace. The Mall stretched out before me, framed within the curved borders of the grand Marble Arch which fronts the palace.[3] A gale issued from the archway as if from a great mouth.

The Centre, Melbourne had said.

I wanted to run, but to where? I attempted to calm myself and tease the meaning from Melbourne's taunt. The centre. Of what?

---

[3] Marble Arch was originally constructed as the entrance to Buckingham Palace. In 1850 it was moved, piece-by-piece to its present position as the entrance to Hyde Park.

The Earth itself? The city?

Wait...

The new square, John Nash's creation, the memorial to Nelson's great ocean victory... Yes, because St Martin's, the church that stood on its north-eastern edge, was considered the very centre of London.[4] A foolish idea perhaps, but my only hope at that moment.

I broke into a shambolic run, out through the arch and onto the Mall. No carriage clattered along its tree-lined expanse on this day, no fashionable ladies promenaded in their finery. Today it was bleak and empty. The trees strained and hissed in the gale, their leaves silvered by the odd light that pierced the tumult above.

As I walked, a cloud of the tiny winged succubae I had encountered in the Palace unfurled themselves before me and circled about my head. Oh, such unwholesome whispers they poured into my ears. Their caresses were tiny but so many that my skin tingled and I felt my desire grow strong. But I must not. I batted at them as one would a troublesome insect and ran once more.

"Bertie!"

Victoria. My beloved. Her voice was plain above the storm and filled with fear. I stumbled to a halt and looked around wildly. Again, my name, cried out in distress. To my right, yes. The park. She must have escaped the creature and sought sanctuary in the park.

I entered at a run, calling out, searching desperately for one glimpse of her. Here the trees creaked and waved wildly as if shaken by giants. The waters in the lake rippled and surged like some miniature ocean tempest.

I struggled on against the gale which tore at my hair and clothes. The wind brought with it a terrible chill that seemed to eat its way into flesh and bone. The strange, mechanical fairie folk returned to dance about my face, seemingly impervious the wind which should have have blown them away like chaff.

---

[4] St Martin-in-the-Fields is considered to be the central point of London. It is thought to stand on the site of an ancient pagan temple.

There, a glimpse of white that darted between two trees, on the far side of the lake.

The first of the rain fell as I set off around the end of the waters. It swept out of the sky and was driven into my face like a million fragments of glass. It lashed at my skin and drenched my clothes into sodden weight on my back. Lightning splintered the gloom. The thunder was the relentless roar of cannon at the height of battle.

There, again, my beloved. I called her name, shouting to be heard above the tumult until I grew hoarse. She stopped. She turned to me, arms outstretched.

And was gone, leaving naught but shadow and the restless flicker of lightning.

A trick. A diversion to lead me on a merry chase while my beloved was... I dare not imagine what was happening to her. Cursing my own stupidity, I resumed my shambolic progress through the park, beset by the tiny succubae and stalked by dark, hulking things that lurked at the edges of my vision.

I heard her again, and again. Pleading with me to come to her aid. I tried to stop my ears, but her anguished cries forced themselves into my very mind and painted pictures of her cowering, broken and cold, as the shadow beasts closed in upon her.

Quite suddenly, I burst out of the park and found myself facing the grandeur of the Horse Guards barracks. Here, surely, there would be aid. A horse for me and a corps of soldiers to ride down the King of the Earth and rescue our monarch.

I crossed the parade ground with renewed spirits. Of the Horse Guards there was no sign, but I hadn't given up hope. Perhaps they were sheltering from the storm. I tried to call to them, but there was little breath left in my lungs.

I reached the nearest of the buildings and stood, fist raised and ready to pound its door. I sensed movement behind the nearest of the great arched windows. I turned to draw the attention of whoever was there, and paused.

There were noises from within, snorting and snuffling sounds. The noises of a pig, though I doubted that whatever lay behind that door was a mere farmyard swine. More sounds, a low growl. Then the very wood of the door thrummed and creaked as if under strain and about to shatter into a thousand splinters.

Alarmed, I stepped back. Shapes passed the windows, too large to be human.

I fled. Do not judge me, Baron. The things I saw were denizens of Hell that no man should gaze upon.

Victoria again, from behind me. I glanced back and saw her running across the parade ground, her night robes flowing, her hair caught by the wind. An object of desire –

No. I stopped my ears against her siren cry. Every part of me ached from fatigue. Assailed by the gale, by the relentless cacophony of the storm, lashed by the rain, wet and miserable, I hurried into the short arched passageway that would take me through the barracks.

There was no sanctuary here. True, the passage was dry and gave some respite from the wind, but the place was diseased, the very masonry blotched and corrupt. A grasping mass of tendrils grew from the wall and over its surface. The paving, too, was torn open by some rank, grass-like growth that clutched at my feet and threatened to bring me to the ground. Only God knows what horror awaited me if I fell.

I staggered free of the place and onto Whitehall, only a few yards from the new Trafalgar Square. Opposite stood the grandiose façade and domed turrets of the War Office. Beside it, numerous other great buildings. All around me was the seat of government, fine and imposing, yet as stained and corrupt as the passageway had been. Walls were cracked and overrun by rank foul-smelling vegetation that stank of death. Worse than this, festooned across the street were vast webs. Glimpsed within these ragged silken curtains were dark shapes, many-legged. Their bloated bodies pulsed like nightmare hearts.

And I must walk among them.

Summoning the last of my courage, I set off towards the square. I dared not look up. The sticky, silken skirts of the webs brushed my face and tangled with my hair. I sensed the beasts they contained stare down at me, jaws wet with venom. They twitched, and thrummed and watched.

Dear God, this was beyond endurance.

"Bertie, please help me!"

I did look up then. How could I not? There she was, my beloved, trapped in the next web I must pass, her arms outstretched as if crucified. She struggled but her movements only bound her further. I cried out for her to remain still, because her endeavours had attracted the attention of the owner of the web. Immense it was, and foul. Its obscenely furred outstretched legs drummed at the web. Its horrible, bloated body throbbed like a Hellish heart.

I ran to her. Her foot was within reach. All I had to do was drag her down to me and she would be free.

But it was a lie. A deceit. This beautiful creature, this image of the woman whom I loved more than life, was a trick. I shouted the fact out loud, trying to blot out Victoria's pleas.

I stumbled beneath her and as I did so the monster struck. I heard her shrieks of pain, and wept. The cries faded into the howl of the wind and clash of thunder.

Again, on the next web and the next, my beloved, hung as if on a cross, begging for release then consumed by the loathsome thing that had ensnared her.

I became certain that I too was being pursued. I looked back to see one of the beasts rushing along the street towards me. Oh, now I had strength. Now I had fire. I ran like a man fresh into a race. I ran driven by the engine of terror. I ran until I thought my heart would burst and my lungs catch aflame.

I ran into the square and there my strength gave out.

Trafalgar Square was in a state of chaos as it has been since the death of its architect, John Nash. There was much mud and piles of building material. There were ladders and tools, but no workmen. Some of the square had been laid with tarmacadam, other parts were soil and rubble. At its centre was a half-built column, its flanks encased in scaffolding.

Something was askew, even within the clutter and disruptions of building. All was distorted and turned unwholesome. As if some awful miasma had descended upon the place. The walls of the National Gallery, and of St Martin's church were blotched with what looked to be mould. The sky above was a storm of restless grey cloud that cast gloom relieved only by the incessant flicker of lightning.

But there was another luminance here. A globe of light before the steps that fronted the church, within which I saw two figures.

Victoria, still clad in her night gown, her hair loose and awry in the manner of a wanton, and the King of the Earth, who held her hands and faced her with the demeanour of one who was in love. She too, gazed at him with something akin to devotion.

I set off across the Square, stumbling and tripping over the uneven ground and hindered by the debris left by its builders. The King turned and scowled then yanked Victoria into the circle of his left arm.

"Go back," he snarled, his voice a booming roar. "I will return your beloved to you when I am done with her."

The world bucked under my feet as if shaken by an earthquake. I was thrown onto my back.

"No!" I gasped, my lungs afire, my throat raw. I was quickly on my knees, and strove to regain my feet. "England is a Christian land!"

He laughed. "Christian? By lip yes, but by heart?"

Victoria stared at me from the heart of the light. Willingly in the arms of that creature, but with torment in her eyes.

Then I remembered; the pendant.

I approached, slowly, murmuring a prayer.

"Stop," the King said. "No closer."

I dared to believe his warning to be born from fear of the Almighty. But I was wrong, because the ground about the pair was suddenly shaken with a violence I had never know or imagined. I glimpsed the grand edifices about me waver. I saw the ground rent open and soil and rock spew upwards in a huge filthy wave, then crash upon its surroundings in an avalanche of dirt and stony missiles.

A vastness emerged from the wound, a monstrosity beyond my ability to comprehend. A machine? Perhaps. There were wheels and mechanisms, pipes and great pistons that slammed back and forth with terrifying force. But there was flesh here too, through which pulsating and trembling organs could be seen. Running from its many surfaces and landscapes were cords that at one moment resembled the roots of a tree, then the strands of a cobweb, then the blood-filled vessels that give life to a living body.

These vessels, these tendrils, ran away from the thing into the earth. I saw them pierced into the walls of the buildings, as if giving to, or receiving sustenance from, them. A booming bell-like tolling thundered from within the object akin to the even rhythms of an immense heart.

I regained my feet and stood, trembling, before the vast engine. I saw, to my horror, that the King was climbing its face, drawing my beloved behind him. The wind plucked at his wild hair and at the white folds of Victoria's night gown. Their hold seemed precarious. If they fell, if Victoria fell…

Without thought I threw myself at the thing and, grasping those foul warm pulsing veins and metallic protrusions, hauled myself upwards. Battered by the gale and waves of stinging rain I pressed on. I looked up to see that the King stared down at me. He made an odd gesture with his free hand.

A globe of fire hurtled by. I felt its heat sear my face and heard it explode far below me. Another, and another. Only the outcroppings and distorted limbs of the machine hindered his aim and preserved my life.

Desperation drove me onwards. I was close now, near to my beloved. I had no breath with which to call her name but I saw the plea in her eyes.

Save me…

I hauled myself over yet another lip of iron, clasped at living flesh, flinched aside to avoid a stinging, whip-like tentacle, and found myself on the very peak of the thing. The surface was flat and some twenty feet from edge to edge. It was translucent and marbled with veins. The King held Victoria's hand. She made no effort to escape. It was as if her flesh desired to stay and be ruled by the creature, whilst her mind begged for release.

"You are ignorant," the King raged at me. "So treacherous and disloyal to your adopted land."

I made no answer but hurled myself at the fiend. He was too startled to cast another fireball. I collided with him and was bewildered for he had no weight. He was as a feather and fell away easily. Enraged, I hurled him from the platform. I saw his body fall from me, his face as shocked as mine must have been. Then he was gone, lost to the rain and spiralling storms of grit and dust.

Appalled at the murder I had committed, I turned back to my Victoria. She ran to me and I wrapped my arms about her, unable to speak.

Something bulged and swelled from the flesh of the platform behind her. It surged upwards, twisting and writhing like a serpent. I retreated, bringing my beloved with me. The thing took upon itself familiar lines and forms. No, this could not be...

There stood another King of the Earth, identical to the one I had slaughtered.

"Consort," he called to me and there was regret in his voice, rather than anger. "You have no idea what you are doing."

"Stay back from us," I retorted.

He raised his arm, his hand encased in flame, yet he paused, perhaps unwilling to risk harm to our Queen.

"This machine, this Titan," his voice had quietened and yet, despite the storm, I could hear him clearly, "is the heart of this city. London is a living thing, built upon a sacred place and settled since time immemorial. Why? Because the heart is here. The Engine of Albion.

"I mean no harm. The firstborn of all Albion's sovereigns since the very first, are of my line. It is a pact made long before history began."

"A lie! Most sovereigns have been kings and you are..."

"I am male and female and neither. I have both seed and womb."

Oh how this creature disgusted me. It was more loathsome than the lowest scavenger in Hell.

"Victoria," the King said softly.

The pendant flared and Victoria turned to him, eyes wide, glistening with tears. "I cannot..."

"You must," the King said. "Come with me."

I felt her pull away from me. I clutched at her more tightly and she began to struggle. I felt the sting of her nails as they raked my cheek. I felt the pain of her teeth as she tore at my wrist. I saw hatred in her eyes. That was the worst of it, my dear Baron. That hatred. The eyes of the one I loved beyond all, brimming with contempt and scorn.

"Help me," she cried suddenly.

I snatched at the necklace and tugged. It burned the flesh of my hand. Victoria screamed in rage and yet held my fingers in place about the slender chain. I felt her grip strengthen and her strength became mine. Our flesh aflame, we tore at the pendant and suddenly it came away. We held it aloft and, as one, endured the agony as it turned molten and dripped between our fingers and faded to dust.

The King merely shook his head, his demeanour one of unfathomable sorrow and, in a moment, he was gone from our sight.

I remember little of the descent from the Engine, or our journey back to the Palace, only that my beloved and I clung to one another for strength and for comfort. Above us the clouds boiled as if maddened by what they had witnessed. Lightning flared bright and struck downwards to sear the ground to left and right of us.

Safe at last, in our private chambers we knelt, silent, before the fire I had lit in the grate. We did not shed our sodden clothes, but rather let our own heat and that of the flames restore warmth to our flesh.

After a while, at the fading of the last light of that unholy day, I sensed that another had entered the room. I looked up to see Lord Melbourne, his face flushed with rage.

"What have you done?" he said. "What have you done to our kingdom?"

"Freed it," Victoria answered, her voice tremulous, but firm.

"Freedom?" Melbourne was almost amused, but my soul was chilled by his words. "This freedom will bring wars the like of which you cannot begin to conceive. There will be revolt and an end to the order of things and perhaps even the destruction of our Empire."

Then he sat down and spoke no more of it, an old man, weary with all he had seen.

I remember little more of that day. My next recollection is of waking on another, more wholesome, morning. My Victoria appeared not to remember any of what had happened to her. Her eye was clear and her mind fixed once more on the burden of her position.

And now, alive despite a madman's bullets. I take my place in this kingdom. There is work for me now, schemes and projects. I try to be a wise advisor, but shadows are forming. Our enemies gather, both in this world, and in others we cannot see. All at a distance for now, but the darkness is there and it will come.

Pray for us, my beloved Baron, and for your own soul. Pray and never cease.

Yours in deepest affection,
Albert.

IN THE TUBE

E.F. Benson

"It's a convention," said Anthony Carling cheerfully, "and not a very convincing one. Time, indeed! There's no such thing as Time really; it has no actual existence. Time is nothing more than an nfinitesimal point in eternity, just as space is an infinitesimal point in infinity. At the most, Time is a sort of tunnel through which we are accustomed to believe that we are travelling.

"There's a roar in our ears and a darkness in our eyes which makes it seem real to us. But before we came into the tunnel we existed for ever in an infinite sunlight, and after we have got through it we shall exist in an infinite sunlight again. So why should we bother ourselves about the confusion and noise and darkness which only encompass us for a moment?"

For a firm-rooted believer in such immeasurable ideas as these, which he punctuated with brisk application of the poker to the brave sparkle and glow of the fire, Anthony has a very pleasant appreciation of the measurable and the finite, and nobody with whom I have acquaintance has so keen a zest for life and its enjoyments as he. He had given us this evening an admirable dinner, had passed round a port beyond praise, and had illuminated the jolly hours with the light of his infectious optimism. Now the small company had melted away, and I was left with him over the fire in his study. Outside the tattoo of wind-driven sleet was audible on the window-panes, over-scoring now and again the flap of the flames on the open hearth, and the thought of the chilly blasts and the snow-covered pavement in Brompton Square, across which, to skidding taxicabs, the last of his other guests had scurried, made my position, resident here till tomorrow morning, the more delicately delightful. Above all there was this stimulating and suggestive companion, who, whether he talked of the great abstractions which were so intensely real and practical to him, or of the very remarkable experiences which he had encountered among these conventions of time and space, was equally fascinating to the listener.

"I adore life," he said. "I find it the most entrancing plaything. It's a delightful game, and, as you know very well, the only conceivable way to play a game is to treat it extremely seriously. If you say to yourself, 'It's only a game,' you cease to take the slightest interest in it. You have to know that it's only a game, and behave as if it was the one object of existence. I should like it to go on for many years yet. But all the time one has to be living on the true plane as well, which is eternity and infinity. If you come to think of it, the one thing which the human mind cannot grasp is the finite, not the infinite, the temporary, not the eternal."

"That sounds rather paradoxical," said I.

"Only because you've made a habit of thinking about things that seem bounded and limited.

"Look it in the face for a minute. Try to imagine finite Time and Space, and you find you can't.

"Go back a million years, and multiply that million of years by another million, and you find that you can't conceive of a beginning. What happened before that beginning? Another beginning and another beginning? And before that? Look at it like that, and you find that the only solution comprehensible to you is the existence of an eternity, something that never began and will never end. It's the same about space. Project yourself to the farthest star, and what comes beyond that?

"Emptiness? Go on through the emptiness, and you can't imagine it being finite and having an end. It must needs go on for ever: that's the only thing you can understand. There's no such thing as before or after, or beginning or end, and what a comfort that is! I should fidget myself to death if there wasn't the huge soft cushion of eternity to lean one's head against. Some people say – I believe I've heard you say it yourself – that the idea of eternity is so tiring; you feel that you want to stop. But that's because you are thinking of eternity in terms of Time, and mumbling in your brain, 'And after that, and after that?' Don't you grasp the idea that in eternity there isn't any 'after,' any more than there is any 'before'? It's all one.

Eternity isn't a quantity: it's a quality."

Sometimes, when Anthony talks in this manner, I seem to get a glimpse of that which to his mind is so transparently clear and solidly real, at other times (not having a brain that readily envisages abstractions) I feel as though he was pushing me over a precipice, and my intellectual faculties grasp wildly at anything tangible or comprehensible. This was the case now, and I hastily interrupted.

"But there is a 'before' and 'after,'" I said. "A few hours ago you gave us an admirable dinner, and after that – yes, after – we played bridge. And now you are going to explain things a little more clearly to me, and after that I shall go to bed –"

He laughed.

"You shall do exactly as you like," he said, "and you shan't be a slave to Time either tonight or tomorrow morning. We won't even mention an hour for breakfast, but you shall have it in eternity whenever you awake. And as I see it is not midnight yet, we'll slip the bonds of Time, and talk quite infinitely. I will stop the clock, if that will assist you in getting rid of your illusion, and then I'll tell you a story, which to my mind, shows how unreal so-called realities are; or, at any rate, how fallacious are our senses as judges of what is real and what is not."

"Something occult, something spookish?" I asked, pricking up my ears, for Anthony has the strangest clairvoyances and visions of things unseen by the normal eye.

"I suppose you might call some of it occult," he said, "though there's a certain amount of rather grim reality mixed up in it."

"Go on; excellent mixture," said I.

He threw a fresh log on the fire.

"It's a longish story," he said. "You may stop me as soon as you have had enough. But there will come a point for which I claim your consideration. You, who cling to your 'before' and 'after,' has it ever occurred to you how difficult it is to say when an incident takes place? Say that a man commits some crime of violence, can we not, with a good deal of truth, say that he really commits that crime when he definitely plans and determines upon it, dwelling on it with gusto? The actual commission of it, I think we can reasonably argue, is the mere material sequel of his resolve: he is guilty of it when he makes that determination. When, therefore, in the term of 'before' and 'after', does the crime truly take place? There is also in my story a further point for your consideration. For it seems certain that the spirit of a man, after the death of his body, is obliged to reenact such a crime, with a view, I suppose we may guess, to his remorse and his eventual redemption. Those who have second sight have seen such reenactments. Perhaps he may have done his deed blindly in this life; but then his spirit recommits it with its spiritual eyes open, and able to comprehend its enormity. So, shall we view the man's original determination and the material commission of his crime only as preludes to the real commission of it, when with eyes unsealed he does it and repents of it? That all sounds very obscure when I speak in the abstract, but I think you will see what I mean, if you follow my tale. Comfortable? Got everything you want? Here goes, then."

He leaned back in his chair, concentrating his mind, and then spoke:

"The story that I am about to tell you," he said, "had its beginning a month ago, when you were away in Switzerland. It reached its conclusion, so I imagine, last night. I do not, at any rate expect to experience any more of it. Well, a month ago I was returning late on a very wet night from dining out. There was not a taxi to be had, and I hurried through the pouring rain to the tube-station at Piccadilly Circus, and thought myself very lucky to catch the last train in this direction. The carriage into which I stepped was quite empty except for one other passenger, who sat next the door immediately opposite to me. I had never, to my knowledge, seen him before, but I found my attention vividly fixed on him, as if he somehow concerned me. He was a man of middle age, in dress-clothes, and his face wore an expression of intense thought, as if in his mind he was pondering some very significant matter, and his hand which was resting on his knee clenched and unclenched itself. Suddenly he looked up and stared me in the face, and I saw there suspicion and fear, as if I had surprised him in some secret deed.

"At that moment we stopped at Dover Street, and the conductor threw open the doors, announced the station and added, 'Change here for Hyde Park Corner and Gloucester Road.' That was all right for me since it meant that the train would stop at Brompton Road, which was my destination. It was all right apparently, too, for my companion, for he certainly did not get out, and after a moment's stop, during which no one else got in, we went on. I saw him, I must insist, after the doors were closed and the train had started. But when I looked again, as we rattled on, I saw that there was no one there. I was quite alone in the carriage.

"Now you may think that I had had one of those swift momentary dreams which flash in and out of the mind in the space of a second, but I did not believe it was so myself, for I felt that I had experienced some sort of premonition or clairvoyant vision. A man, the semblance of whom, astral body or whatever you may choose to call it, I had just seen, would sometime sit in that seat opposite to me, pondering and planning."

"But why?" I asked. "Why should it have been the astral body of a living man which you thought you had seen? Why not the ghost of a dead one?"

"Because of my own sensations. The sight of the spirit of someone dead, which has occurred to me two or three times in my life, has always been accompanied by a physical shrinking and fear, and by the sensation of cold and of loneliness. I believed, at any rate, that I had seen a phantom of the living, and that impression was confirmed, I might say proved, the next day. For I met the man himself. And the next night, as you shall hear, I met the phantom again. We will take them in order.

"I was lunching, then, the next day with my neighbour Mrs. Stanley: there was a small party, and when I arrived we waited but for the final guest. He entered while I was talking to some friend, and presently at my elbow I heard Mrs. Stanley's voice: 'Let me introduce you to Sir Henry Payle,' she said.

"I turned and saw my vis-à-vis of the night before. It was quite unmistakably he, and as we shook hands he looked at me I thought with vague and puzzled recognition.

"'Haven't we met before, Mr. Carling?' he said. 'I seem to recollect –"

"For the moment I forgot the strange manner of his disappearance from the carriage, and thought that it had been the man himself whom I had seen last night.

"'Surely, and not so long ago,' I said. 'For we sat opposite each other in the last tube-train from Piccadilly Circus yesterday night.'

"He still looked at me, frowning, puzzled, and shook his head.

"'That can hardly be,' he said. 'I only came up from the country this morning.'

"Now this interested me profoundly, for the astral body, we are told, abides in some half-conscious region of the mind or spirit, and has recollections of what has happened to it, which it can convey only very vaguely and dimly to the conscious mind. All lunch-time I could see his eyes again and again directed to me with the same puzzled and perplexed air, and as I was taking my departure he came up to me.

"'I shall recollect some day,' he said, 'where we met before, and I hope we may meet again. Was it not –?' and he stopped. 'No: it has gone from me,' he added."

The log that Anthony had thrown on the fire was burning bravely now, and its high-flickering flame lit up his face.

"Now, I don't know whether you believe in coincidences as chance things," he said, "but if you do, get rid of the notion. Or if you can't at once, call it a coincidence that that very night I again caught the last train on the tube going westwards. This time, so far from my being a solitary passenger, there was a considerable crowd waiting at Dover Street, where I entered, and just as the noise of the approaching train began to reverberate in the tunnel I caught sight of Sir Henry Payle standing near the opening from which the train would presently emerge, apart from the rest of the crowd. And I thought to myself how odd it was that I should have seen the phantom of him at this very hour last night and the man himself now, and I began walking towards him with the idea of saying, 'Anyhow, it is in the tube that we meet to-night.'... And then a terrible and awful thing happened. Just as the train emerged from the tunnel he jumped down on to the line in front of it, and the train swept along over him up the platform.

"For a moment I was stricken with horror at the sight, and I remember covering my eyes against the dreadful tragedy. But then I perceived that, though it had taken place in full sight of those who were waiting, no one seemed to have seen it except myself. The driver, looking out from his window, had not applied his brakes, there was no jolt from the advancing train, no scream, no cry, and the rest of the passengers began boarding the train with perfect nonchalance.

"I must have staggered, for I felt sick and faint with what I had seen, and some kindly soul put his arm round me and supported me into the train. He was a doctor, he told me, and asked if I was in pain, or what ailed me. I told him what I thought I had seen, and he assured me that no such accident had taken place.

"It was clear then to my own mind that I had seen the second act, so to speak, in this psychical drama, and I pondered next morning over the problem as to what I should do. Already I had glanced at the morning paper, which, as I knew would be the case, contained no mention whatever of what I had seen. The thing had certainly not happened, but I knew in myself that it would happen. The flimsy veil of Time had been withdrawn from my eyes, and I had seen into what you would call the future. In terms of Time of course it was the future, but from my point of view the thing was just as much in the past as it was in the future. It existed, and waited only for its material fulfilment. The more I thought about it, the more I saw that I could do nothing."

I interrupted his narrative.

"You did nothing?" I exclaimed. "Surely you might have taken some step in order to try to avert the tragedy."

He shook his head.

"What step precisely?" he said. "Was I to go to Sir Henry and tell him that once more I had seen him in the tube in the act of committing suicide? Look at it like this. Either what I had seen was pure illusion, pure imagination, in which case it had no existence or significance at all, or it was actual and real, and essentially it had happened. Or take it, though not very logically, somewhere between the two. Say that the idea of suicide, for some cause of which I knew nothing, had occurred to him or would occur. Should I not, if that was the case, be doing a very dangerous thing, by making such a suggestion to him? Might not the fact of my telling him what I had seen put the idea into his mind, or, if it was already there, confirm it and strengthen it? 'It's a ticklish matter to play with souls,' as Browning says."

"But it seems so inhuman not to interfere in any way," said I, "not to make any attempt."

"What interference?" asked he. "What attempt?"

The human instinct in me still seemed to cry aloud at the thought of doing nothing to avert such a tragedy, but it seemed to be beating itself against something austere and inexorable. And cudgel my brain as I would, I could not combat the sense of what he had said. I had no answer for him, and he went on.

"You must recollect, too," he said, "that I believed then and believe now that the thing had happened. The cause of it, whatever that was, had begun to work, and the effect, in this material sphere, was inevitable. That is what I alluded to when, at the beginning of my story, I asked you to consider how difficult it was to say when an action took place. You still hold that this particular action, this suicide of Sir Henry, had not yet taken place, because he had not yet thrown himself under the advancing train. To me that seems a materialistic view. I hold that in all but the endorsement of it, so to speak, it had taken place. I fancy that Sir Henry, for instance, now free from the material dusks, knows that himself."

Exactly as he spoke there swept through the warm lit room a current of ice-cold air, ruffling my hair as it passed me, and making the wood flames on the hearth to dwindle and flare. I looked round to see if the door at my back had opened, but nothing stirred there, and over the closed window the curtains were fully drawn. As it reached Anthony, he sat up quickly in his chair and directed his glance this way and that about the room.

"Did you feel that?" he asked.

"Yes: a sudden draught," I said. "Ice-cold."

"Anything else?" he asked. "Any other sensation?"

I paused before I answered, for at the moment there occurred to me Anthony's differentiation of the effects produced on the beholder by a phantasm of the living and the apparition of the dead. It was the latter which accurately described my sensations now, a certain physical shrinking, a fear, a feeling of desolation. But yet I had seen nothing. "I felt rather creepy," I said.

As I spoke I drew my chair rather closer to the fire, and sent a swift and, I confess, a somewhat apprehensive scrutiny round the walls of the brightly lit room. I noticed at the same time that Anthony was peering across to the chimney-piece, on which, just below a sconce holding two electric lights, stood the clock which at the beginning of our talk he had offered to stop. The hands I noticed pointed to twenty-five minutes to one.

"But you saw nothing?" he asked.

"Nothing whatever," I said. "Why should I? What was there to see? Or did you –"

"I don't think so," he said.

Somehow this answer got on my nerves, for the queer feeling which had accompanied that cold current of air had not left me. If anything it had become more acute.

"But surely you know whether you saw anything or not?" I said.

"One can't always be certain," said he. "I say that I don't think I saw anything. But I'm not sure, either, whether the story I am telling you was quite concluded last night. I think there may be a further incident. If you prefer it, I will leave the rest of it, as far as I know it, unfinished till tomorrow morning, and you can go off to bed now."

His complete calmness and tranquillity reassured me.

"But why should I do that?" I asked.

Again he looked round on the bright walls.

"Well, I think something entered the room just now," he said, "and it may develop. If you don't like the notion, you had better go. Of course there's nothing to be alarmed at; whatever it is, it can't hurt us. But it is close on the hour when on two successive nights I saw what I have already told you, and an apparition usually occurs at the same time. Why that is so, I cannot say, but certainly it looks as if a spirit that is earth-bound is still subject to certain conventions, the conventions of time for instance. I think that personally I shall see something before long, but most likely you won't. You're not such a sufferer as I from these – these delusions –"

I was frightened and knew it, but I was also intensely interested, and some perverse pride wriggled within me at his last words. Why, so I asked myself, shouldn't I see whatever was to be seen?

"I don't want to go in the least," I said. "I want to hear the rest of your story."

"Where was I, then? Ah, yes: you were wondering why I didn't do something after I saw the train move up to the platform, and I said that there was nothing to be done. If you think it over, I fancy you will agree with me... A couple of days passed, and on the third morning I saw in the paper that there had come fulfilment to my vision. Sir Henry Payle, who had been waiting on the platform of Dover Street Station for the last train to South Kensington, had thrown himself in front of it as it came into the station. The train had been pulled up in a couple of yards, but a wheel had passed over his chest, crushing it in and instantly killing him.

"An inquest was held, and there emerged at it one of those dark stories which, on occasions like these, sometimes fall like a midnight shadow across a life that the world perhaps had thought prosperous. He had long been on bad terms with his wife, from whom he had lived apart, and it appeared that not long before this he had fallen desperately in love with another woman. The night before his suicide he had appeared very late at his wife's house, and had a long and angry scene with her in which he entreated her to divorce him, threatening otherwise to make her life a hell to her. She refused, and in an ungovernable fit of passion he attempted to strangle her. There was a struggle and the noise of it caused her manservant to come up, who succeeded in overmastering him. Lady Payle threatened to proceed against him for assault with the intention to murder her. With this hanging over his head, the next night, as I have already told you, he committed suicide."

He glanced at the clock again, and I saw that the hands now pointed to ten minutes to one.

The fire was beginning to burn low and the room surely was growing strangely cold.

"That's not quite all," said Anthony, again looking round. "Are you sure you wouldn't prefer to hear it tomorrow?"

The mixture of shame and pride and curiosity again prevailed.

"No: tell me the rest of it at once," I said.

Before speaking, he peered suddenly at some point behind my chair, shading his eyes. I followed his glance, and knew what he meant by saying that sometimes one could not be sure whether one saw something or not. But was that an outlined shadow that intervened between me and the wall? It was difficult to focus; I did not know whether it was near the wall or near my chair. It seemed to clear away, anyhow, as I looked more closely at it.

"You see nothing?" asked Anthony.

"No: I don't think so," said I. "And you?"

"I think I do," he said, and his eyes followed something which was invisible to mine. They came to rest between him and the chimney-piece. Looking steadily there, he spoke again.

"All this happened some weeks ago," he said, "when you were out in Switzerland, and since then, up till last night, I saw nothing further. But all the time I was expecting something further. I felt that, as far as I was concerned, it was not all over yet, and last night, with the intention of assisting any communication to come through to me from – from beyond, I went into the Dover Street tube-station at a few minutes before one o'clock, the hour at which both the assault and the suicide had taken place. The platform when I arrived on it was absolutely empty, or appeared to be so, but presently, just as I began to hear the roar of the approaching train, I saw there was the figure of a man standing some twenty yards from me, looking into the tunnel. He had not come down with me in the lift, and the moment before he had not been there. He began moving towards me, and then I saw who it was, and I felt a stir of wind icy-cold coming towards me as he approached. It was not the draught that heralds the approach of a train, for it came from the opposite direction. He came close up to me, and I saw there was recognition in his eyes. He raised his face towards me and I saw his lips move, but, perhaps in the increasing noise from the tunnel, I heard nothing come from them. He put out his hand, as if entreating me to do something, and with a cowardice for which I cannot forgive myself, I shrank from him, for I knew, by the sign that I have told you, that this was one from the dead, and my flesh quaked before him, drowning for the moment all pity and all desire to help him, if that was possible.

"Certainly he had something which he wanted of me, but I recoiled from him. And by now the train was emerging from the tunnel, and next moment, with a dreadful gesture of despair, he threw himself in front of it."

As he finished speaking he got up quickly from his chair, still looking fixedly in front of him.

I saw his pupils dilate, and his mouth worked.

"It is coming," he said. "I am to be given a chance of atoning for my cowardice. There is nothing to be afraid of: I must remember that myself…"

As he spoke there came from the panelling above the chimney-piece one loud shattering crack, and the cold wind again circled about my head. I found myself shrinking back in my chair with my hands held in front of me as instinctively I screened myself against something which I knew was there but which I could not see. Every sense told me that there was a presence in the room other than mine and Anthony's, and the horror of it was that I could not see it. Any vision, however terrible, would, I felt, be more tolerable than this clear certain knowledge that close to me was this invisible thing. And yet what horror might not be disclosed of the face of the dead and the crushed chest… But all I could see, as I shuddered in this cold wind, was the familiar walls of the room, and Anthony standing in front of me stiff and firm, making, as I knew, a call on his courage. His eyes were focused on something quite close to him, and some semblance of a smile quivered on his mouth. And then he spoke again.

"Yes, I know you," he said. "And you want something of me. Tell me, then, what it is."

There was absolute silence, but what was silence to my ears could not have been so to his, for once or twice he nodded, and once he said, "Yes: I see. I will do it." And with the knowledge that, even as there was someone here whom I could not see, so there was speech going on which I could not hear, this terror of the dead and of the unknown rose in me with the sense of powerlessness to move that accompanies nightmare. I could not stir, I could not speak. I could only strain my ears for the inaudible and my eyes for the unseen, while the cold wind from the very valley of the shadow of death streamed over me. It was not that the presence of death itself was terrible; it was that from its tranquillity and serene keeping there had been driven some unquiet soul unable to rest in peace for whatever ultimate awakening rouses the countless generations of those who have passed away, driven, no less, from whatever activities are theirs, back into the material world from which it should have been delivered. Never, until the gulf between the living and the dead was thus bridged, had it seemed so immense and so unnatural. It is possible that the dead may have communication with the living, and it was not that exactly that so terrified me, for such communication, as we know it, comes voluntarily from them. But here was something icy-cold and crime-laden, that was chased back from the peace that would not pacify it.

And then, most horrible of all, there came a change in these unseen conditions. Anthony was silent now, and from looking straight and fixedly in front of him, he began to glance sideways to where I sat and back again, and with that I felt that the unseen presence had turned its attention from him to me. And now, too, gradually and by awful degrees I began to see...

There came an outline of shadow across the chimney-piece and the panels above it. It took shape: it fashioned itself into the outline of a man. Within the shape of the shadow details began to form themselves, and I saw wavering in the air, like something concealed by haze, the semblance of a face, stricken and tragic, and burdened with such a weight of woe as no human face had ever worn. Next, the shoulders outlined themselves, and a stain livid and red spread out below them, and suddenly the vision leaped into clearness. There he stood, the chest crushed in and drowned in the red stain, from which broken ribs, like the bones of a wrecked ship, protruded. The mournful, terrible eyes were fixed on me, and it was from them, so I knew, that the bitter wind proceeded . . .

Then, quick as the switching off of a lamp, the spectre vanished, and the bitter wind was still, and opposite to me stood Anthony, in a quiet, bright-lit room. There was no sense of an unseen presence any more; he and I were then alone, with an interrupted conversation still dangling between us in the warm air. I came round to that, as one comes round after an anaesthetic. It all swam into sight again, unreal at first, and gradually assuming the texture of actuality.

"You were talking to somebody, not to me," I said. "Who was it? What was it?"

He passed the back of his hand over his forehead, which glistened in the light.

"A soul in hell," he said.

Now it is hard ever to recall mere physical sensations, when they have passed. If you have been cold and are warmed, it is difficult to remember what cold was like; if you have been hot and have got cool, it is difficult to realise what the oppression of heat really meant. Just so, with the passing of that presence, I found myself unable to recapture the sense of the terror with which, a few moments ago only, it had invaded and inspired me.

"A soul in hell?" I said. "What are you talking about?"

He moved about the room for a minute or so, and then came and sat on the arm of my chair.

"I don't know what you saw," he said, "or what you felt, but there has never in all my life happened to me anything more real than what these last few minutes have brought. I have talked to a soul in the hell of remorse, which is the only possible hell. He knew, from what happened last night, that he could perhaps establish communication through me with the world he had quitted, and he sought me and found me. I am charged with a mission to a woman I have never seen, a message from the contrite… You can guess who it is…"

He got up with a sudden briskness.

"Let's verify it anyhow," he said. "He gave me the street and the number. Ah, there's the telephone book! Would it be a coincidence merely if I found that at No. 20 in Chasemore Street, South Kensington, there lived a Lady Payle?"

He turned over the leaves of the bulky volume.

"Yes, that's right," he said.

A ROMANCE OF THE PICCADILLY TUBE

T.G. Jackson

Old Mr. Markham lay dying in an upper room of a fine mansion in a great London square. The house was plunged in that oppressive stillness which reigns when sickness is there and death is near. Footsteps were stealthy, and voices subdued, and the ticking of the clock was audible in the silent room. By the bedside of the old man was Mr. Harvey, his confidential solicitor and old friend, come to attend the execution of the sick man's last will and testament.

"You are quite resolved then," said Mr. Harvey, "to dispose of your property thus? I have drawn the will exactly to your instructions, but as an old friend of you and your sons, you will forgive my putting this question again for the last time."

"Yes," said a feeble voice, "that's what I mean."

"You cut off your elder son, George, with a thousand pounds, and leave all the rest, except some minor legacies, to James. The old will, you remember, left them equal shares."

"Yes, yes," said the old man peevishly. "I have paid George's debts over and over again till I am sick of it, and what I might give him now would only go the way of the rest. He has a little money of his own from his mother, if he hasn't spent it, and he must make that do. James is a careful lad and the estate will fare better in his hands."

"Well, I have no right to say more, though I'm sorry. But of course, you must do what you please with your own."

The old man was propped up in his bed, a pen was put into his feeble fingers, a servant was called in as a second witness, the deed was duly signed and attested, and Mr. Harvey took it away with him.

The two sons were waiting in the dining room. They had

finished a late luncheon and were standing by the fire. They knew of Mr. Harvey's visit, and guessed its purpose, and various thoughts were passing through their minds. George indeed did not trouble himself much about the will. In his careless way, he thought things would be all right, and he need not worry himself about them beforehand. He was concerned for his father, whom he really loved, though he knew how often he had plagued and offended him, almost beyond forgiveness. James, on the contrary, being of a cooler and more calculating temper, could not help wondering what was meant by a new will, and an altered disposition of the property. The estate was a large one, with lands in the country, beside the house in town, and large sums in the funds, and he wondered how his interests would be affected by what was going on upstairs.

The door opened and Mr. Harvey came in to bid them goodbye. He had known them since they were boys, and had a regard for both of them, though in his secret heart he preferred the scapegrace George to his more careful brother.

"Well, sir," said George advancing to meet him, "how did you leave my father? I am sorry to say the doctor gives us little hope. Do you think he would like to see me?"

"I doubt it, George; you must ask the doctor or the nurse. He is very feeble."

"Was he able to attend to the business you came about?" asked James.

Mr. Harvey thought the question rather ill-timed and unfeeling, and answered a little curtly, that there had been no difficulty. He then took leave of them. George accompanied him to the door, and as they were parting, Mr. Harvey putting his hand on his arm, said: "Tell me, George, have you any debts?"

"Not a penny," said he radiantly, "my dear old father paid them all off last week before he fell ill. It was awfully good of him. I know I have behaved badly, and did not deserve it from him."

"Well, George," said Mr. Harvey, "let me give you a hint. There must be no more debts in future. You will have to be careful. I speak seriously for your good. Farewell, and don't forget what I say."

Left to himself, George wondered what was meant by this hint, connected, he supposed, with the new will, if indeed a new will had really been executed, as he and his brother believed. Mr. Harvey's words seemed to convey a friendly warning that things had not been going favourably for him upstairs. He had always understood that he and his brother were to share equally in the estate; was this arrangement now to be disturbed? That would be awkward, for he had only small means of his own, and his way of living had always been after an opulent fashion.

"Hang it all," he said, "it will be deuced hard on me, if James gets more than his share. After all, I'm the eldest son, and he has no right to cut me out."

Like the two sons of the Patriarch, the two Markhams differed entirely in character and pursuits; but in the modern case, the parental preference had been reversed, for it was the mother who had loved the Esau of the family best, and the father who favoured the Jacob. George Markham was lively and adventurous, a lover of pleasure and selfish and self-indulgent in its pursuit; but he had a kindly and generous vein in his composition which in the view of his friends went far towards compensating his faults. James was of a cautious and calculating nature, who did everything with deliberation, looking carefully after his own interests, and fencing himself round with precautions. He was married, and had children, and a business in the City which was doing well. Since his mother's death, George's influence in the family steadily declined: Esau sank into disfavour and the star of Jacob ascended; till at last, as we have seen, their father resolved that by leaving George free of debt and with a thousand pounds in his pocket, he might wash his hands of further responsibility for him.

In this perturbed state of mind, after parting with Mr. Harvey, George avoided rejoining his brother, and taking his hat, sallied forth to go to his chambers in the Temple. The justification for these chambers was a shallow pretence he made of reading for the Bar, though beyond eating his dinners he did little else to qualify himself for a forensic career.

However, it served as a pretext for establishing himself in bachelor's quarters, which was convenient for his way of living, and his father had long given up in despair any inquiry after his legal studies.

It was growing dusk as he descended to a station of the Piccadilly tube. There was the congestion of would be passengers usual at eventide when offices close and myriads of clerks and servants flock from the centre of London to the outskirts. Trains arrived crammed to suffocation, not a seat vacant, passages choked with strapholders, and entrance lobby solid with perspiring humanity. When the carriage doors were opened to discharge a few travellers, the mob surged desperately to force an entrance, half of them to be disappointed, and condemned to wait for another train, where they might be more fortunate. George was near one end of the platform where the crowd was a little less compact, though even there he had hardly room to move. A train was heard approaching and every head was turned in that direction. At that moment a gentleman in front of him dropped something, and stooped to recover it, though the crowd allowed him little room for movement. George saw it at his feet: it was a paper folded lengthways and lay more within his reach than that of the owner. "Let me get it for you, sir," he said, and stooped to pick it up and restore it. The roar of the train sounded close at hand; the crowd pressed on the stooping figures, as they rose together they were pushed violently against one another; the other man was close to the edge of the platform, and to his horror, George saw him lose his balance and fall over the edge. As he fell, George caught sight of his face; it was his old friend, Mr. Harvey. The train was upon him in a moment.

There was a shriek from the crowd, first a recoil and then a rush of agonised spectators; George was swept back to the far side of the platform and stood leaning against the wall, trembling and sick with horror. Officials arrived, the train was moved, and men went down on the line upon their ghastly errand. He could not bear to wait and see the recovery of the body, or witness the frightful details of the accident. Shaking in every limb, he found his way to the exit, half unconsciously; the lift was remote and news of the accident had not reached the attendant when George took his place, and there was no delay. As he reached the surface, he noticed that he had in his hand the fatal paper which had occasioned the disaster. It was too dark to see the address, and he put it in his pocket. It had belonged, he supposed, to his poor friend, and on the morrow he would forward it to the address it bore. It did not matter now, his only aim for the moment was to get to his quarters and try to recover his nerve. He called a cab and drove to the Temple.

Arrived at his rooms, he sank into an armchair and covered his face with his hands. The whole dreadful scene passed before him in imagination; the crush, the collision, the reeling back of his poor friend, the glimpse of his face and of the grey hair as his hat fell off, and then the train came upon him. It made him sick to think of it. By and by, as the first horror of the scene passed and left room for calmer reflection, he thought less of the accident, and more of the man. Harvey had long been his father's friend and adviser; he had always been kind to himself as a boy, and had often stood his friend when he had need of an advocate with his father. He thought of him with affection, and remembered how many times he had given him sound advice which had never been followed, but of which he now saw the value; and now that was all at an end, and what an end!

After a time he rose, and thought he would go and dine somewhere quietly. He could not bear to go to his club and face his friends with this horror fresh on his mind, and so he had a quiet chop at one of the old eating houses in Fleet Street, where he knew he should meet no one of his acquaintance, and it was late when he came back to his chambers.

When he had turned on the light, his eye fell upon something that lay on the table. It was the fatal paper, which he had taken from his pocket before going out. He took it up listlessly, to see if it bore any address to which he should send it in the morning. But it bore no address, and when he had read the endorsement, he stood some minutes motionless with the paper in his hand, as if he were turned to stone. He saw it was a will, or rather a codicil to the last will and testament of Richard Markham, which had been executed that very afternoon. After a time, he laid the paper again on the table, and stood with his back to the fire thinking what he should do.

So there really had been a new will, or a codicil to alter the old one, and from the hint dropped by his poor friend, Mr. Harvey, he gathered that the alteration had not been in his favour. The temptation was strong to open the paper and see how he stood, but he was restrained by a scruple, and continued to stand by the fire looking at it as it lay on the table before him. He supposed that his loss would be James's gain. James had always been his father's favourite, comparisons had been drawn between him and James, to James' advantage; James had been proposed to him as a pattern, though he hated James's cautious ways which seemed to him mere selfishness. The selfishness of his own idle extravagant life naturally did not occur to him. James, he thought, was a schemer, who had always got the better of him, and had robbed him of his birthright as eldest son. What would be the justice of James taking more than a fair share of his father's estate? The longer he thought about it the stronger grew the temptation to open the paper and see what provision it made for him. There it lay before him, as it were looking him in the face and inviting him to take it; a riddle awaiting solution, charged with fate and the whole current of his future life. He took it in his hand and weighed it: on this fatal sheet his fortunes depended. In a matter so vital it was folly to be over-scrupulous; as he gathered, he was the person most likely to be affected by its contents; surely he was entitled to know them, and it could not matter to anyone else whether he knew them or not.

He sat down and opened the paper. It was a codicil to the old will, very short, and it dealt almost entirely with the one subject of George's share in the disposition of the estate. He laid the paper down in dismay, and sat in silence looking into the fire.

"A thousand pounds and nothing more," he kept repeating to himself. "It is monstrous. What have I done to deserve to be treated thus?" Independently of the money, how was he to explain his position to the world, for his friends had always looked on him as his father's heir. How was he to live on the slender income inherited from his mother, which, luckily for him, she had so tied up that he could not touch the capital? All his habits and tastes were expensive; he constantly outran his father's liberal allowance, and as constantly had to appeal to him for money to clear his debts. There was no one now left to appeal to, for it would be idle to approach James, who he knew would stand on his rights and give him his thousand pounds and no more. Besides which, he could not bring himself to beg of his younger brother; no, that at all events was not to be thought of and there lay the accursed paper in his lap. What was to be done with it? He supposed it ought to go to Messrs. Harvey & Moor, his father's lawyers. But that might wait till tomorrow. And poor Harvey was dead. That however did not affect the matter, for the firm was there. He must send it to them tomorrow, he supposed.

It was then that some pestilent devil at his elbow seemed to whisper in his ear, "Why send it at all?"

The idea covered him with shame and he scotched it at first, for reckless as his life had been he had never stooped to anything dishonourable. But it would not be so dismissed, and kept pestering him with suggestions of the ease with which the codicil might be suppressed. Putting things together he made out that Mr. Harvey had taken the codicil to Mr. Markham, who had signed it, the witnesses being Mr. Harvey himself and the footman, whose names appeared in the document; that Mr. Harvey had taken the paper away with him, and had arrived at the station on the Piccadilly tube at pretty nearly the same moment when he got there himself. The rest of the story we know.

"Then," thought George, "one of the witnesses was dead, and the footman could only testify that he signed a paper, not knowing what it was, which might have been something quite different." The lawyers, of course, had instructions for drawing the codicil, and probably a rough draft of its contents, but what evidence could they produce that it had ever been executed? The only proof of that was the codicil itself and that now lay in his lap; and the fire was burning opposite him. It would only be an affair of a moment, the hateful deed would be reduced to a few ashes, and he would inherit the half of the estate to which he maintained he was entitled by every consideration of justice and fair play. James would have the other half, which was his fairly enough, and he was already doing well in business, and so would really be much better off than his elder brother. The temptation was strong; almost irresistible; the devil at his elbow kept urging him; and his very fingers itched to twitch the fatal paper from his lap on to the glowing coals. But his better self restrained him: he could not bring himself to do it, and locking the deed up in his drawer he went to bed.

He was roused next morning by a messenger from his father's

house, with a letter from his brother James, enclosing another addressed to himself.

"Dear George," it began, "You will not be surprised to hear that all is over here. Our dear father died quietly last night. You will, no doubt, come at once to help me make the necessary arrangements. I enclose a letter for you from Messrs. Harvey & Moor, which, as it was marked 'immediate,' I ventured to open. You will be shocked at its contents.

Your affectionate brother, *JAMES MARKHAM.*"

Messrs. Harvey & Moor's letter announced the unfortunate death of the elder partner from an accident on the railway. They thought, as he was engaged in business for Mr. Markham at the time of his decease, they ought to lose no time in communicating the sad intelligence to Mr. Markham's representative.

George had not expected his father's death so suddenly, and was much affected. He wished he had been with him at the end. Their relations had not always been friendly, but he admitted the fault had been his own, though the punishment in time end was unfairly severe, he went home therefore with mixed feelings of sorrow and resentment.

He alighted at the same station on the tube railway which had been the scene of the catastrophe the night before, and he looked with horror at the fatal spot. As he made his way to the lift he had an uncomfortable feeling that he was being followed. To be sure a crowd was going with him, but it was not that; he saw no one especially noticing him, and could not account for the feeling. He had given up his ticket and entered the lift, when the attendant said "Ticket, please," to some one behind him. He turned but saw no one.

"Old gentleman with you, sir?" asked the attendant. "Why, what has become of him?" he continued, looking about him.

"No. There is no one with me," said George, much surprised.

"Well, I'm dashed," said the attendant, staring about. "He's gone, anyhow. That's rummy"; and then he attended to his duty and started the lift.

George found the great house with all the windows darkened: the straw with which the street had been strewn during the late owner's illness deadened all sound from outside, and within was the silence of death. James met him, already attired in funereal weeds, and his wife was there whom George disliked, for he thought her intriguing and meddlesome, and mistrusted her influence on James himself. He knew instinctively he had no friend in her should any question arise about the disposition of the estate. He went and saw his father; the tears stood in his eyes as he thought of the unkindness that had grown up between them year by year, and he was touched with remorse as he recalled the many occasions on which he had given cause for his father's displeasure. He even, at that moment, forgave him that fatal codicil, though the feeling of resentment returned as he sat at luncheon with James and his wife, and thought how unfairly they were to benefit at his expense. He took his part in the arrangements for the funeral and other matters, but would not stay in the house, and returned in the evening to his chambers in the Temple, anxious and dispirited, and with a sense of impending calamity. And then he remembered that he was to have sent that paper to the lawyers in the morning, and had not done so. Well, it was too late tonight he would do it in the morning. He would be glad to be rid of it and be put out of his misery.

His sleep was not untroubled. He seemed to go back to the time when he was a boy, and his father a younger man, who had been kind to him and proud of his performances in his school games, at which James had always been a duffer; and then his father's face grew serious and displeased as it had become in later life; and then it melted away into another face, the face of his old friend Harvey, sad and warning, and oh, horror! there were streaks of blood, and with that he awoke. Morning was beginning, he could sleep no more; a cold bath restored his nerves, and a walk in the brisk morning air before breakfast braced him up somewhat for the coming day.

Days passed and the time came for the funeral, and after that he knew the executors would be moving in the matter of the will, and questions would arise about the codicil. It still lay in his drawer. He had put off from day to day taking the irrevocable step of sending it, which would deprive him at once of all claim to what he held was his rightful inheritance. He said to himself it was useless to put it off; it could make no difference to him whether he sent it now, or kept it a few days longer: the result would be the same; and yet he had not the courage to do the fatal act. The pistol was at his head as it were, and his finger on the trigger, and he dared not pull it, though he knew he was doomed. He grew pale and anxious and avoided society. Of James he saw as little as possible, though family arrangements made it necessary they should meet sometimes. He fancied his sister in law looked at him with an air of subdued triumph, though what could she know about the codicil and its contents? It raised his bile and hardened his heart, and he thought how easily if he pleased he could defeat her.

Mr. Markham's executors were two, Mr. Winter, a City magnate, and Sir Charles Mallet, a retired Indian civilian, and they were already in communication with the solicitor firm of Harvey & Moor. The only will in evidence was that made some years before, which gave the two brothers an equal share in the estate. But Mr. Moor produced the draft of the codicil which upset this arrangement, and which he believed had been duly executed, though at present it could not be found.

"What makes you think it was executed?" asked Sir Charles.

"I think so," said Mr. Moor, "because we had Mr. Markham's instructions to send it to him for signature, he being then ill in bed. It was therefore copied out fairly, and my partner, Mr. Harvey, took it with him to Mr. Markham's house. He was seen there by both the sons, and we know that Mr. Markham signed something, for a servant, whom we can produce, witnessed it, and we presume it was the codicil. Mr. Harvey, as you know, was unhappily killed on his way home, and the document which he no doubt had with him was, we presume, lost or destroyed in the accident."

"What the servant witnessed," said Mr. Winter, "may have been only a transfer of stock or something of that kind."

"Perhaps, but we are not aware of any such transfer being made at that time."

"On the other hand," said Sir Charles, "Mr. Markham may have changed his mind and altered the codicil before signing it. I confess it seems to me it was a monstrous piece of injustice from first to last."

"Well, gentlemen, what do you suggest?" said Mr. Moor.

The executors debated about the matter a little longer and at last it was agreed to have another meeting at which the two Markham sons, who were principally concerned, should be present.

"What could induce my old friend Markham to make such a change in his will as that unhappy codicil was to have done?" said Sir Charles as the two executors walked away together.

"I know he was much put out by his elder son's extravagance," said the other, "and had paid a deal of money at times to get him out of debt. I suppose he thought that should be brought into the account."

"Well, I should be sorry if George lost his share. He is a good fellow at bottom," said Sir Charles, "and I dare say he has sown his wild oats by now. But what about this tiresome codicil? Do you think it was really executed, and if so, shall we ever find it?"

"Goodness knows," said Mr. Winter. "At all events I think it will give us a lot of trouble.

Dear me! Who would be a trustee or executor?"

"I don't like James, the younger brother," said Sir Charles. "George is a much better fellow, though he has been playing the fool."

"And it is James," said Mr. Winter, "whose interest it is to put forward the codicil."

"You mean he will oppose the probate if we propound the old will without it?"

"Well," said Mr. Winter, "I know something of James in the City, and he is a good man of business."

"I see," said Sir Charles. "Goodbye; here I think our ways part." And then they shook hands and separated.

The proposed meeting at which the two brothers were to attend was fixed about a week later at Mr. Markham's house, where James Markham and his family were staying to see about the necessary domestic arrangements. Thither, at the time appointed, George Markham made his way, alighting at the tube station nearest the house as usual. He hated the sight of the place, which had such painful associations, and had he thought of it, he would have come another way, but from force of habit he had unconsciously followed the usual route. As he gave up his ticket at the lift the attendant looked hard at him, and then beyond him over his shoulder. The man's manner made George turn round to see what he was looking at. But he saw nothing.

"He's gone again," muttered the man. "I don't 'alf like it. Bill," said he to another attendant when he had discharged his living cargo at the top, "did ye see that grey-haired old gen'leman as come to the lift at the bottom, but didn't get in?"

"Not me," said Bill, who was not interested. "Well, but look ye here! He follers that gen'leman as you see there walking away, up to the lift, and when I arst 'im for 'is ticket, why he isn't there."

"Trying to bilk the company, very likely," said Bill. "If you can ketch 'im, p'rhaps you'll get a reward."

"Don't be a fool, Bill," said the other. "I tell you this has happened every time that same man comes 'ere. And I'll tell you another thing," said he, lowering his voice. "Do you remember that accident the other day when an old gentleman was killed?"

"Why, in course I do. What of that?"

"Why, as they carried 'im away, I see 'is face, and I see that face again just now at the foot of the lift."

"Oh, go along with you!" said Bill, as he walked away. "I don't believe in ghosties you've been drinking and got the horrors."

The meeting took place in the dining room. Both the executors were present with Mr. Moor, and George and James, by whose side his wife was sitting, with whom he frequently conferred in a whisper.

Both brothers had, of course, been formally made acquainted by the solicitor with the terms of the will, and also of the missing codicil.

But the solicitor stated the case afresh to make sure that it was understood in all its bearings by those concerned. The old will was obviously to be put forward for probate: about that there was no room for difference of opinion. The only difficulty was about the codicil. The codicil being missing, the question was one of proof that it had ever been executed.

Sir Charles Mallet said the whole thing was very uncertain. Even if the codicil had been duly executed, of which positive evidence seemed wanting, how were they to know whether it had been signed without alteration?

"It is not for me," he continued, "to criticise Mr. Markham's motive in making that codicil, but the effect of it, if I may be allowed to say so, is so unusual in the difference it makes between his sons, and so serious in the case of the elder brother, that it is quite conceivable that the testator may have changed his mind before signing. A stroke of the pen, for instance, might have converted Mr. George Markham's thousand pounds into ten or twenty thousand, or even more."

Mr. Winter, the other executor, seemed to concur with this view. He said he did not quite see his way to act on the draft codicil in the absence of the document itself. But, of course, he would be guided by the lawyers.

"I think," began James, "my dear father's last wishes…" but here he was stopped by marks of disapproval on the faces of his auditors.

"You were about to say something, Mr. Markham," said the solicitor. Mrs. James had been whispering to her husband, and obedient to her prompting he proceeded. "I was going to ask whether we should be doing right if we disregarded what we positively know to have been my father's last wishes as to the disposition of his estate."

"You mean that you should take my share as well as your own?" said George, who had not spoken before.

But James took no notice of this remark. "Do I understand," said Mr. Moor, "that you will oppose the probate of the will without the codicil?

"Well, I am of course in a somewhat difficult position," said James, "being an interested party. But I have to consider others as well as myself, who would be affected; for myself, I might be disposed to waive any claim, but there is my wife, and there are my children, who would have rights in the matter, and so well, gentlemen, you see the difficulty of my position."

His speech ended rather lamely, and it was received by the company in silence. Sir Charles looked at his colleague and raised his eyebrows. The other nodded, and the party broke up without any formal resolution, it being understood that the executors would be guided by legal advice in their procedure.

Sir Charles shook hands with George as they went out, and said it was an awkward business, and he was sorry for him if things went wrong. As for James, Sir Charles managed to avoid his parting salute.

"James showed very badly," he said to his colleague as they walked away. "He should have held his peace. That cant about his wife and children was in bad taste."

"You'll see James means to have his knife into his brother," said Mr. Winter. "We are in for a lawsuit over this business if I am not much mistaken."

Meanwhile the codicil still lay lurking in the drawer of George's writing table in the Temple. The longer he deferred sending it, the harder it seemed to be to do so. He still said to himself he supposed it had to be done, but the more he thought about it the more cruel did the necessity appear. It was monstrous injustice to rob him of what his father had intended to give him by the will. Sir Charles Mallet had almost said as much at the meeting, and when he shook hands with him at parting. And James, with his hypocritical pretence of shielding himself behind the absurd rights of his wife and children! If anything would make him keep back the codicil it would be a desire to defeat James and his odious wife. James, with half the estate and a flourishing business in the City, was a rich man already, richer than he himself would be, even if he got his share. James ought to be satisfied with that, and not try to rob his elder brother of his rightful inheritance. With these thoughts George worked himself up into a passion of resentment against his brother, his sister-in-law, the codicil, the lawyers who drew it, and everyone concerned about it, and persuaded himself that he was the injured victim of a conspiracy to defraud and beggar him. And all the while the same pestilent little devil at his elbow kept whispering, "Don't send it, don't send it; burn it, burn it."

And yet, when he got to his chambers, took it out of the drawer, and looked at it and at the fire, he could not do it.

"Not yet, not yet," he said to himself, and he put it back into the drawer and locked it up. But he had taken a step nearer the fatal act, and the next step would be a short one.

And James; he too was not quite happy. He had been greatly surprised to learn the contents of the codicil, which went far beyond any change he had imagined it would make in the disposition of the estate. He was not without affection for his brother, who had protected him at school, though he laughed at him and thought him a muff, and who had always acted generously to him as they grew up. Underneath a crust of cold selfishness still glowed the embers of their old friendship, and his first thought on reading the lawyer's communication had been: "It is very hard on poor George; what will he do?" It even occurred to him to let the matter of the codicil drop, especially as the document itself had been lost, and there was no positive proof of it ever having been executed. He was well off; the estate was a large one, and half of it with what he had would make him a rich man. He could afford to let George's half go as the old will had intended it should. But, unhappily, James consulted his wife, who overpersuaded him, and suggested the arguments which he had employed at the meeting, and by which, with her help, he at last succeeded in convincing himself. His father no doubt thought he was acting for the best, and his last wishes ought to be sacred; he had never cost his father a penny since he started in life, whereas George had bled his father's purse freely over and over again, and that surely ought to be taken into account. And then there were his wife and children but here he paused: the faces of the executors at the meeting when he used that argument recurred to his memory, and he felt it would not do. He even blushed slightly at the recollection, and felt he had lowered himself by stooping to such a shallow pretence, which deceived nobody, not even himself.

Had James at this point been left alone he was not incapable of a generous decision. He had half a mind as he left the meeting and realised the unfavourable impression his claims had made on the executors, to write to the lawyer and say he waived any claims he might have arising from the codicil, and was content to abide by the original will; but he reckoned without his wife. Her tears and reproaches overcame his weak leaning to the generous side, and he resolved to claim his legal rights under the missing codicil, if his lawyers advised him that he had a good case.

The matter therefore had to be decided in a court of law, for the executors decided on ignoring the draft codicil, and propounded the original will. There was a special jury empanelled, and the highest talent of the Bar was employed on either side. James and his wife were there throughout the whole proceedings. George would not go near the place. In a manner he was relieved by the course things were taking. If the court decided that the codicil was to be upheld, why he had done no harm by keeping it hidden; the result would only be the same as if it had never been lost. If, on the other hand, the codicil should be negatived, he would take it as his justification in suppressing what he held to be an unfair invasion of his rights as the elder son. He was not really satisfied with these arguments; his conscience told him he was guilty of a dishonest act, and so far prevailed that he could not bring himself to show his face in court. He therefore spent the day in the country; the trial, he was told, would certainly take all day, and he would hear the result when he returned in the evening.

He had a long tramp over the Surrey hills, from Epsom race course to Headley Common and Boxhill, returning by Mickleham and Leatherhead. The day was lovely, the larks singing in a sky of heavenly blue, the trees were still decked in the fresh virgin green of spring, and there was that delicious brisk buoyancy in the air that makes a man say life is worth living. But to George, at that time, it did not seem so. Life seemed to him a sordid affair. Take his own case; think of the choice before him: on one hand to be honest and a beggar, or on the other to be wealthy and a thief. Was such a life worth living in either case? Between the horns of this dilemma he was miserable. It haunted him as he walked, and as he ate his solitary luncheon at the wayside inn. His conscience troubled him; his honour in any case was smirched; whatever reparation he might make would not wipe off the stain; and that being so, that pestilent little tempter suggested, "Why worry about it? You have gone so far, you can't undo the fact that you have been guilty; it is too late to mend matters; go home and burn he deed. If the jury decide against you it won't be wanted, and if they decide for you it will be best in the fire to make things safe."

It was with this resolution finally fixed in his mind that George returned to town and sought his chambers. A telegram and some notes lay on his table, as he naturally supposed, containing a report of the result of the trial. He felt no impatience to learn what it was; he was disgusted with himself and the whole business.

The telegram was from the lawyers, and said: "Will maintained, codicil upset." A later note from them confirmed this, and offered congratulations. Another note from Sir Charles Mallet, warmly expressed, said how glad he was of the result: that for his part he could not believe his old friend Mr. Markham really had signed a deed which was so obviously unjust.

"If he only knew," said George to himself, "that the codicil lies at this moment in the drawer under my hand, what would he think of me?

He sat down to consider what he should do. He was now a rich man, but he felt no elation. It was however impossible to draw back. He must go on to the end. If ever the codicil were to be given up, it should have been done before the trial. The half of the estate was now legally his; to give it up would be quixotic. He half persuaded himself that his father, had he lived, would have reconsidered such an unfair division of the estate, and that the result of the trial, could he know it where he was, would not be displeasing to him.

He went to dine quietly at a City eating house, not feeling fit for society, and unable to face the congratulations of his friends if he went to his club. He sat an hour over his port wine, making up his mind. He now had what he held to be his just rights, and it was necessary to make them secure. If he had made a bargain with the devil, at least he would have the fruits of it. The codicil should be destroyed that night, and James, with his odious wife, should be finally defeated for good and all.

Having made up his mind he went back to his chambers. His mind was in a strange confusion, a sort of nervous oppression weighed on him as he opened the door and entered. A fire was burning in the grate sending flickering gleams about the room. He turned on the lights; unlocked the drawer, and laid the fatal paper on the table. He stood a minute looking at it, and then he suddenly discovered he was not alone. Seated by the fire with his back to him was a man, whose grey head was visible over the top of the easy chair. George was on the point of asking who he was and what he wanted, when something seemed to arrest his speech, and he could only regard his strange visitor in silence. The figure rose slowly and turned to confront him across the table. The face was the face he had seen in his dream, the face of his old friend Harvey, and it regarded him with an earnestness that penetrated his very soul. George was unable to speak, to act, or even to move. He seemed fixed in a trance and could only look piteously at that serious face and wait in terror for what was to come. Still keeping its gaze fixed on him, the figure advanced to the table and laid its hand on the paper that lay there. Its regard was severe, but not unkindly; it seemed even to express pity and sorrow. Resting its hand on the fatal codicil it seemed to ask a question. George knew what it was, and the answer it wanted. Fierce debate raged within him, greed and passion on one side, shame and remorse on the other fought for supremacy, and still that steady gaze penetrated his inmost being. Gradually his evil passions seemed to melt before those calm searching eyes; his conscience awoke to better things; the resolution to do right prevailed. He knew the question that was put to him, and in a passion of tears he stammered out, "I will," and sinking into a chair he covered his face with his hands. When he removed them he was alone.

When he recovered himself he rose with a lightened heart, for a weight seemed to have been lifted from him. Reparation, that was the question that he had answered; reparation was what he had promised. It could not be made too soon. It should be made that very night. He put the codicil into an envelope and sealed it, and addressed it to Messrs. Harvey & Moor. They need not know whence it came, and so his shame need not be exposed. And yet without confession the reparation would not be complete. He would write to James and tell him all. And in order that James should learn it first from him, and not officially from the lawyers, he would take the letter himself and put it in the letter box after posting that for the lawyers.

As he walked through the streets in the cool night air he felt happier than he had ever felt in his life. He had done right at last, and had been mercifully saved from consummating his shameful offence. He now looked back on it with horror. What had possessed him to act as he had done? Thank God he had been spared the worst. His heart was light and joyful, and he could even smile to think of the lawyers' surprise next morning.

He posted his letter and then walked on to his old home, and having dropped the letter for James in the letter box, found his way to the tube station, which had been the scene of poor Harvey's accident. Had he really seen his old friend that night, or was it a vision of his imagination? He could not tell; whichever it was, it was Harvey who had been his saviour; to Harvey he owed the recovery of his self-respect, the victory over his worse self. He thought of his old friend with love and gratitude, and thanked God for him.

The platform was congested with people from the theatres which had just closed. Never had he seen such a crowd. The train came up and George was carried in the rush to the entrance of the car. It was over full already; his foot was on the step when the gate was slammed in his face; he could not extricate himself from the crowd; the train began to move, his foot slipped, and was caught between the car and the platform; the train went faster and faster; he was dragged down and down, and he knew no more.

Two missives were put into James Markham's hand early next morning. One was George's letter:

"DEAR JAMES,

"I have had the codicil all the time. It came into my hands by a mere accident, and at first I did not even know what it was. Tonight I intended to destroy it, but I was prevented by my good angel. I have just posted it to Messrs. Harvey & Moor. They will not know whom it comes from. I ask you to keep my secret, to forgive me, and if you can to think kindly of your brother.

"GEORGE."

The other letter was from St. George's Hospital, to say that a gentleman, named Markham, had been brought there with injuries received in a railway accident, which it was feared would be fatal, and that he wished to see his brother, Mr. James Markham, before he died.

James was shocked and deeply affected. The old fraternal affection, which had been buried under a load of selfishness and greed, awoke within him. George's noble renunciation of the advantage he had won, and candid confession of the wrong he had done, filled him with admiration. He could not help asking himself how he would have behaved had he been subjected to such a trial.

When he stood by George's bedside it was too late. He had died during the night. The tears stood in James Markham's eyes as he took the cold hand in his, and bending over his brother whispered, "George, I forgive you; your secret is safe with me."

BLOOD AND BONE

Susan Boulton

RAF meteorologists report for 29th December 1940

Weather Low Countries and Northern France: Cloud mainly 8/10ths to 10/10 ths at 2,500ft in the West at first, at 1,500ft in the East and locally 800ft in occasional rain. Low cloud increasing rapidly at 1,000ft in North-west France early in the period and locally 300 to 600ft covering hills in a period of moderate rain. These conditions spreading eastwards over the whole of Northern France during the period with visibility generally poor. In the East winds WNW moderate in the West, wind freshening from the South-west becoming fresh or strong with gusts of gale force locally on the coast.

The weather looked bad, but was it bad enough to prevent them flying?

If only.

As he left the small café in Vannes with the rest of his crew, he scuffed the cobbles with the toe of his boot. They were slick with damp. The weather was closing in, he was sure of it. The mission this evening really should be cancelled. Not that it would be. None of the senior officers at the base had the balls to say no in the face of the pressure from high command. The Führer had issued an edict. Such things were not challenged. *Scheisse!* Earlier in the month they had sat in their aircraft with the engines running in a bloody snowstorm. Common sense had prevailed that day, but would it tonight? Dieter looked skywards. No chance of snow, but the visibility was not good. He was sure it would be worse over the channel.

"Come on, Dieter, are you driving, or am I?" Rainer said, turning round and looking at his crewmate. The rest of the crew were already milling round the vehicle.

"You." Dieter fumbled in his pocket for the keys. He pantomimed throwing them to Rainer. Rainer cupped his hands and caught the keys with precision. Afterwards giving his friend, and the pilot of their aircraft, a sketchy salute.

Dieter walked to the car and got into the front passenger seat of the Citroën Traction Avant. It was a lovely vehicle. It had been commandeered from the local mayor. When the mayor had delivered the vehicle to the airfield for the use of the valiant crews of the squadron, Dieter had noticed that though the man bowed his head, and smiled, there was a coldness about his demeanour. It was the same as the waiter's in the café, who had continually apologised for not having any decent wine due to the war and charged the earth for the vinegar he had served. For all the bowing and scraping, it was like living with a regiment of knives at your back. How long before the knives became real, Dieter wondered. Everything had happened so quickly. The victory promised against the French had been achieved. No one had expected the British to continue to fight. Six months ago Dieter would have sworn on a stack of bibles that the war would be over by Christmas, and that the British did not have the stomach for another long fight. Yet, once the British had retreated back to their small island, things had changed. Dieter felt as if he had been caught in a meat grinder which was slowly chewing through the best of them.

"Cheer up," Rainer said. His left hand tapped away on the polished wooden steering wheel, his wedding ring beating out an uneven rhythm. *Tap, tap... Tap, double tap.* Dieter found the noise unnerving. His heart stumbled and tried to match the beat. It was childhood rhymes that kept you awake when you were six, such as *die gar traurige geschichte mit dem feuerzeug.* And wasn't this just what he and his fellows were doing, playing with matches, and trying to set a city alight?

"Tonight we will hit it."

"You sure?" Dieter said.

Tap, tap... Tap, double tap. Dieter could almost hear voices chanting.

"*Scheisse*, you do know how to fly don't you?" Mandel joked from the back seat, adding, "With the *Knickebien* and a mouthful of

Stuka-tabletten, there will be no stopping us. We will set fire to that dome along with all the rest of the city."

The others laughed. Dieter joined in, but in his head the continued tapping of Rainer's ring unscored his thoughts: *Tap.* No matter how good the direction finding radio beacon was. *Tap…* No matter how many pills they popped. *Tap, double tap.* No matter how many tonnes of high incendiary bombs they dropped, he felt that the meat grinder would get them before they got St Paul's.

The weather looked bad, but was it bad enough to prevent an air-raid?

God. Claire, hoped not. It would just be her luck. Another wasted night.

She had schemed and planned, hell, she had sacrificed enough, hadn't she? Oh, she knew she was gifted, but having the eye for a good photograph wasn't of any use if you weren't in the right place. London was the right place. Here she would get that one perfect photograph. A city in flames. A city at war. One that would be on the front cover of every newspaper here and, more importantly, across the Atlantic. And to get it she would, no matter the cost. Tobias thought she was mad. But Tobias thought anyone who left the safety of the Savoy's basement during an air-raid to be mad, including himself. For the most part Tobias wrote fluff pieces for the folks back home in the states. Plucky Brits and all that. *Stupid.* Ordinary people were not what war was about. Still, Tobias had his uses. He was well-known and pretty well respected by the rest of the twenty plus posse of the US press corps which had made the Savoy hotel their headquarters. And he had contacts among the British press, and local authorities, but that was just because he had been here since the time of the so-called phoney war before France fell.

Claire carefully removed the last of her current photographs from the tray of water, and pegged it on the thin line strung above the table. Water dropped off the bottom edge, hitting the stained wood of the table. *Tap, tap… Tap, double tap.* She rubbed her temple with her left thumb. The sound, damn blast it, it set her teeth on edge.

The last reel had been near to useless. A waste of film. It was what she called general background shots. Street scenes. Pavements covered in broken glass. Londoners going about their daily routine. Children playing in bombed out streets. She leaned forward, looked again at the last photograph, and wrinkled her nose. Yes, maybe that one was all right. In the red light of her makeshift dark room she looked hard at the two girls in the picture. Their hands outstretched to each other. Caught in a single moment during their game. The rhyme they had chanted as they clapped still lingered at the back of her mind. What was it? No, the words eluded her. They were a little dark as many nursery rhymes were, of that much she was sure.

Tap. One thing was for sure: it wasn't what her mother back home would have considered suitable for young ladies to sing. But the Brits, especially Londoners, had a real liking for anything that sent a shiver down one's spine. Burt, one of the regulars in the pub situated a floor below her flat, had relished telling her and other occupants of the snug tales of Sweeny Todd. *Tap...* Not that she believed his embellishment of the story. He, after all, worked in the newspaper industry, as did a lot of the Rose and Crown's patrons, as it sat just a stone's throw away from Fleet Street. *Tap, double tap.*

She glared at the photo and was tempted to shake it to stop the dripping. It would be stupid to do so, that last one might be worth a few dollars. Not that she needed the money. It was never about that. The picture might get her noticed, but hell, it might not. It wasn't anything different than a hundred other photographs out there. It wasn't the shot she craved. That craving was one of the reasons she had moved out of the Savoy. Not that she had been one of the official press pack to begin with. They all looked down their noses at her, especially the women. *"Not paid her dues."* Why the hell should she? A tip off from one of Tobias' contacts had told her that after the docks, the area round St Paul's and the City, was high on Herr Hitler's list. Also it helped being close to the centre of the British newspaper industry. When the bombs started falling she would be right on the spot, and those so called female journalists in the Savoy would be left biting their badly cared for nails in frustration at her, Claire Fitzjohn's success. She looked round, checking everything. Goodness knows what Mrs Higginbotham, the landlady, would say if she knew that on top of her pub was a darkroom full of inflammable liquid. Still, if a bomb landed on the pub, it would be the least of her landlady's worries. Claire switched off the red light, and lifted the thick blackout curtain which separated her darkroom from the rest of her small sitting room. The light had already faded from the day. It was barely three forty-five pm in the afternoon. No street lights would be spluttering into life outside. Claire found she missed the way the soft yellow spread across the street, trying to replace the sun that was now fading fast. Not that the sun penetrated deeply into the haze of coal smoke that hung over London most days. Not like home. Boston, the part she had been brought up in, did not have industry that threaded its way into the heart of the city, like London did. There the sun this time of year was bright and brittle.

She glanced into her bedroom. The black cloth covered frame over the window was still in place. It hadn't been worth the effort of lifting it off. It had been gone noon when she had woken. It had been a heavy night last light. The young man, what was his name, Richard? Anyway, he worked in a lowly position at the American Embassy. Still, lowly or not, he had contacts, and the party they had ended up had had a high percentage of senior British Officers attending.

The room was getting colder. For a moment she considered switching on the third bar of the old electric fire. No. It would be a waste. The thriftiness that pervaded all of life in England had not begun to rub off on her, had it? No. It would impress her landlady if she resisted. Create a good impression. So she switched the fire off. *Tap.* The metal sheet behind the cooling metal element of the fire took up the chant of the dripping water as it contracted. She was going out soon anyway. *Thank God.* It was not the most comfortable of apartments. So many things here were different. *Tap...* Central heating, like an electric fridge, *God,* she missed being able to have ice in her whisky, were not part of what Mrs. Higginbotham or, Claire supposed, many Brits considered necessary items in a two-roomed furnished apartment. Mrs Higginbotham had made it plain that the inclusion of the broom-cupboard sized bathroom made the place highly desirable in the current market. Not that the hot water was plentiful. It was very hit and miss, more on the miss. *Tap, double tap.*

The noise from the metal plate went up an octave. Her teeth protested more. It felt like she was chewing on the top of a metal pen. Still, she was certainly better off than the occupant of the apartment on the other side of the narrow landing. He had to share the Higginbotham family's own ablutions downstairs. And her landlady never failed to mention it.

Claire had promised Tobias she would meet him for afternoon tea at the Savoy, and if there was a raid, this evening she would not be needing the contents of the half-empty milk bottle that stood on top of the small cupboard that acted as her pantry. She would be out and about, hunting that one, so desired shot, with or without Tobias. The milk was an excuse, of course. A good one, and the chocolate bars she had been given at the America Embassy on Christmas Eve would seal the deal. It was, after all, about contacts.

There would be a raid tonight.

A bad one. Luke knew it.

The fact pounded in his blood and bones. He rubbed at the back of his neck to ease the tension. His fingers began to throb. *Tap.* He tried to smile at Alice, Mrs Higginbotham, as she handed him a cup of tea. The fruit cake he had brought had gone down well with her and the girls. They didn't ask where he had gotten it from, and he didn't volunteer the information. The wrapping was smoked-stained, and the words, Fortnum and Mason, *export only,* on the silvered seal hinted that it had come from some half-burnt out building a few miles east of the Rose and Crown. His fingers felt swollen. *Tap...* He tried to ignore it as he took the tea from Alice and put the cup and saucer down on the table. The spoon knocked against his fingers, and the sensation dissipated, leaving an aching in his bones. *Tap, double tap.*

The meal Luke had shared with Alice and her two girls, Sally and Maude, had been theirs and his, main one of the day. It made sense to pool their rations, and Alice liked it that they ate as a family. Not that Luke was family as such, but he had boarded with the Higginbothams since 1937, and as time had passed Alice and her husband, Frank, considered him to be. Since Frank, a reservist, had been called up, Alice had made it a point to keep up with opening at lunch time. From reporters down to typesetters, a liquid lunch was as important as ever. A pie, with its unidentifiable meat content was an optional extra. Often midday was the only time she made any income. With the constant air raids her evening trade was non-existent some nights. Only the most hardened or foolhardy drinkers ventured out. Even though The Rose and Crown had a deep, brick-lined cellar, it did not often win over other places of refuge when the siren sounded.

"What time you due in?" Alice asked, as she covered the remains of the cake with a spare plate.

"Between four and five." Luke said. "Heard from Frank?"

She nodded. "Rang this morning. Had a quiet night, hoping for the same tonight. His gun has seen a lot of action of late. He said he is due a day's leave end of next week."

"Hopefully –" Luke replied, but his tone was not convincing.

"You got a feeling…?" Alice looked towards her two daughters. The girls were sitting on the small rug in front of the fire, looking through a magazine.

"Just – get downstairs, no better still, make for one of the public shelters, or St Paul's, if things get hairy."

"They won't let us in St Paul's, you know that." Alice tried not to look worried.

"Maybe they will," Luke replied. The feeling in his blood and bones began again. It felt stronger. *Tap, tap… Tap, double tap.* The rhythm of the rhyme. The clapping of children's hands one on another. Stone and brick. Timber and metal. The city's blood and bones. He could feel the city drawing in its breath as it braced for the coming onslaught. Why him? He wasn't London born. He hadn't set foot in the smoke until he began his apprenticeship with Mr. Thomas. Luke's father had been a bricklayer in the Midlands, who had benefited from the housing boom in the early 1930s. Sending Luke to study architecture could in his father's eyes be of great benefit to the future of the family business. Luke certainly wasn't suited to the outdoor building life, as were his two younger brothers. He had suffered from a bad chest since he was a child.

What Luke had not bargained on was developing this, *instinct,* as his employer called it. A unique gift, Mr. Thomas said. Not that

Luke felt it was. But Mr. Thomas had pooh-poohed that, saying Luke would soon realise that for an architect it was a boon. He wasn't the first, and he wouldn't be the last. It was just every now and then someone in the profession would begin to show signs of it as they learned the trade. A feel for what type of building the city might accept, and allow to grow deep into its bones and blood. There was no logic with regards to which building knitted itself into the city's body. Some that were built barely lasted twenty years before they were torn down. The city shed them like a dried out skin, emerging new and bright underneath. Yet some, altered, changed, or rebuilt, had roots that extended deep into the heart of the city. One of those was the Cathedral a mere street away, and Luke could feel its power and strength from here.

Luke could see the worry in Alice's eyes. Frank was part of the crew on one of the Ack Ack guns that formed the backbone of the city's protection. She did not know where, didn't want to know. Alice changed the subject. "Do you want me to put you some of the cake up to take with you?"

"Thanks, but best not. Won't have enough to go round. And they do feed us, you know."

"Who feeds you?"

Luke turned round to look at the young woman who had asked the question. Miss Claire Fitzjohn had entered the kitchen of the Rose and Crown without even a polite knock on the half-open door. For a moment Luke toyed with the idea of answering that it was none of her business. Miss Fitzjohn was what his mother would have called 'a nosy parker, and not in a nice way'.

"Miss Fitzjohn, how can I help you?" Alice got up and walked towards the new arrival.

"I was going to be out, and wondered..." Claire held out the half pint of milk. "It won't keep until tomorrow."

Alice frowned. Luke tried not to snort. The milk was only yesterday's put on the windowsill this weather and it would last until at least Tuesday, maybe Wednesday.

"Can you use it?" Claire asked.

"Errr yes, of course," Alice said, and took the bottle.

"And," Claire continued, "I was wondering if the girls..." She began to open her handbag.

"No," Alice said sharply.

"No? But you don't know?" Claire answered, her eyes narrowing.

Yes, *not in a nice way*. Any gift would have a price tag.

"I know that you mean well, but it doesn't do the girls any good." Both of Alice's daughters had looked up from the magazine, their gaze going from their mother's face to the almost exotic one of the American lady in her well-made woollen coat, with its fox fur trim, and matching hat. It was as if one of the models in their magazine had stepped off the page.

"I see, well, I'd best get going." Claire said, giving the occupants of the room a bright, brittle smile, before she turned and left.

Sally, the eldest of the two girls, gave a big sigh, and got to her feet.

"No you don't, young lady," Alice said, sharply.

"I wasn't going to..." Sally said looking sheepishly at her mother.

"It's not that... You know what happened last time. The questions..." Alice began.

"Questions?" Luke frowned.

"Yes, about Daddy, where he was stationed and... I didn't tell, honestly... 'cause, I don't know, but the chocolate was... and if she had more chocolate..." Sally began to look even more sheepishly, and scuffed at the worn hearth rug with her right foot.

"Chocolate or not, I've half a mind to ask the young woman to leave. She has annoyed half my customers with her pestering. Burt is convinced she is fifth column."

"Well, if Burt thinks she is fifth column ..?" he began, then burst out laughing. "Anyway, I'd best be going." Luke stood and gathered his belongings.

News Chronicle 31/12/1940.

"Around a hundred fire watchers: altogether, the crypt gave sanctuary to three hundred."

The Dean and his team, from their vantage point high up in the roofs of the Cathedral had watched the rapid progress of the flames. The cloth warehouses of St Paul's churchyard, and book stores of Paternoster Row were well ablaze. So it did not come as a surprise that permission was asked to use the Cathedral crypt as a temporary shelter for the hundred or so fire watchers, first aiders and other workers on their way from the firm of Hitchcock, Williams and Co, as well as others coming in from nearby shelters, being overwhelmed by the fierce pace of the fires.

There was at that time no prospect of evacuating those gathering in St Paul's to a place of genuine safety. It was as much an act of faith as anything else by all concerned, underscored by the fact that the refugees were welcomed by a mug of hot cocoa, rather than the usual cup of tea.

Tap. The barman put down the glass he was holding, and listened. The sound of the air raid siren echoed through the cocktail bar of the Savoy. Claire looked at her watch. It was 6.10 pm. The conversation in the room stopped for all of a minute, then continued. No one moved. Claire took out a cigarette from the packet lying before her on the bar, accepting a light from the blond-haired fellow countryman sitting beside her. *Tap...* He dropped the lighter onto the bar, and Claire watched as it skittered across the polished wood. Their on off conversation petered out. Claire turned in her seat to watch the rest of the bar's occupants. At 6.30 pm the bar manager announced that if the patrons wished to retire to the shelter it was now open. As if his announcement had given them permission, a steady trickle of people picked up their drinks, and ambled in the direction of the door. It swung back and forth. *Tap, double tap.*

A couple of the US press pack began to gather together their belongings, shuffling on coats and winding scarves round their necks. They were going out on the hunt for a story. She began to get up and smiled at the lanky blond. He smiled back. Called to the barman to put his last drink on his tab, picked up his lighter, put on his hat, and left the room totally ignoring her. Damn him. He had promised to take her with him. Not that she needed any protection out on the London Streets. On the contrary she could be useful to him. The police and especially the ARP wardens were, on occasions, inclined to act like 'little Hitlers'. And she knew from past experience that by thickening her American accent, and bating her eyelids; nine times out of ten she could get herself through any cordon. By tagging along with one of the reporters it gave her leverage over them. A favour she could call in.

She opened her handbag, then closed it. "Put it on his tab," she told the barman, and not waiting for an answer she picked up her coat, camera, and followed the reporter out. As she stepped out of the Savoy the sky in the direction of St Paul's, just over a mile away, was already aglow. "Damn him to hell," she muttered. The lanky blond had vanished into the night.

"Who?"

Claire turned; it was Tobias. She tried to hide her surprise, but she was sure he had spotted her expression. "You going out?"

"I do, you know," Tobias replied, as he turned up the collar on his coat.

"Do you?" she retorted, and stepped onto the pavement looking for a black cab. She could try to walk, but a cab, if she could get one, would be quicker. She wanted buildings ablaze, not firemen damping down fires.

Tobias shook his head. "Been here since February. I know my way around." Was he being sarcastic? Was there an edge of disapproval in his voice? No, Tobias liked her, he looked at her legs often enough. He was joking, of course he was.

"And my being here just a month makes me a novice?" she replied, smiling.

Tobias did not answer, but joined her on the pavement, and looked at his watch, then down the street. A black cab was coming towards them.

"About time." Claire put her hand out.

"Sorry, my dear. That's mine," Tobias said, as the cab pulled alongside him.

The cabby leaned out the window. "Evening, Mr. Cross, you ready?"

"Evening, Albert, do you think we will get through?" Tobias asked, as he opened the back door of the vehicle.

"Not sure. Getting pretty fierce round Fleet Street and St Paul's, but I will if I can."

"You are not going to leave me stranded? Besides, I need to check on Mrs Higginbotham and her girls. The Rose and Crown is just off Fleet Street," Claire said, trying to appeal to his chivalrous side.

Tobias gave a sigh, stepped aside and allowed her to get into the cab ahead of him. Did he believe her? Not that it mattered anyway.

The cabby looked back at them and grinned, then pulled away from the kerb. They were not the only vehicle heading down the Strand towards Fleet Street. Twice they were overtaken by convoys of fire engines of all types, from the standard London fire brigade machine, to civilian cars pulling small tenders and manned by volunteers. The air began to fill with flickering sparks which drifted down from roof tops. Small bursts of light ignited on the road and pavements. Some were put out by shadowy figures, armed with buckets of sand, and stirrup pumps. Others continued to burn, spreading their flames into doorways, down alleys, and up walls. Smoke billowed round the cab. Halfway down Fleet Street a policeman stood amid a tangle of fire hoses. The street was slick with water. Fires raged in the buildings on either side and were reflected in the wet, black glassy surface of the road. The cab stopped. Claire began to inwardly fume. She pulled her camera case open. All around her was a city on fire. No way was she being sent back.

Tap. The bobby knocked on the driver's window. Albert lowered it. Thick acrid smoke rushed in. It caught at the back of Claire's throat. She tried to stifle a cough.

"And where do you think —?" the Policeman began.

"US press! We are trying to get through to St Paul's. I have permission from the dean." Tobias pulled his press credentials from his pocket and stuck them against the glass that separated him from Albert. The policeman leaned in and peered at the papers.

"Both of you?" He looked at Claire.

"Of course," Claire said, earning herself a glare from Tobias.

"All right, but really you should be in a shelter. Things are getting a bit hairy. I won't be responsible if things take a bad turn."

"We understand," Tobias said.

"You will have to make your way from here on foot." Claire could see that the Policeman would rather have told them to bugger off.

"Very good, officer" Tobias opened the cab door and got out. Claire followed. "Albert, best you try and make it back home." He then moved towards the open window of the cab, and pulled a large white note out of his pocket, handing it to Albert.

"If I can't get down here, I doubt I'll make it to Blackfriars, but you never know," Albert said, taking the note. "Thanks, Mr. Cross. Same time tomorrow if the Jerries come calling?

"Same time, Albert." Tobias stepped back. Albert swung the cab round, hardly grazing the right kerb with his offside tyre as he did so. *Tap...*

Claire stood there watching the cab vanish into the smoke.

"Keep to the centre of the road and if anyone, and I mean anyone, working down there directs you to a shelter, or tells you to run, you run, understand?"

"Yes, officer," Tobias said.

The policeman looked at Claire and shook his head. He straightened his tin helmet and began to jog down the road towards a fire engine, where the men were starting to run out their hoses to mingle with the writhing mass already on the ground.

Claire pulled the belt on her coat tight, straightened her hat, and looked at Tobias. He said nothing and set out towards St. Paul's. She swore he had a look of exasperation on his face. At her? Surely not. She opened her mouth to speak, but before she could a dull bang vibrated down the street. A shockwave of hot air fought to open the coat she had just fastened.

"That sounded like a big one." Tobias shouted, and hurried in the direction of the sound.

Clair pulled her camera out of its case. It was the newly improved Kodak 35. An ugly looking thing, with its external linkage to the rangefinder, but Claire liked the feel of it. She pulled off her leather gloves and ran her fingers over the cold metal.

As they moved down Fleet Street Claire felt her skin begin to tingle. Not from the warm air that buffeted her, nor the smouldering motes of burning buildings. She knew she was close to getting the picture she so desired. The thought was setting her on fire.

"Jesus Christ! The Associated Press Building, the roof has gone!" Tobias was looking upwards, shielding his eyes with his hand. The street was now clogged from one side to the other with fire engines. The firemen were trying to stop the flames from spreading by soaking a lower floor of the building, but it was a fruitless task. The fire was winning.

Claire raised her camera. She looked through the viewfinder and framed the scene. It was a good shot, even a great shot, but not the one. *Tap, double tap.* The tangle of hoses writhed and slapped the road with a familiar rhythm. Children chanting. Hands clapping. She shook her head to clear her thoughts and put the camera to her eye again. No. Nothing felt right. They moved on working their way round the group of vehicles.

Water soaked her feet. Debris made their progress uneven. The flotsam of once buildings and their contents now fought for space on the road with the fire hoses. The blare of a car horn forced Claire to look behind. A civilian car, small tender in tow, was making its way past on her right hand side. Half on half off the pavement, it crabbed its way forward.

The vehicle pulled to a stop alongside one of its fellows, joining the others battling against the demon enemy set on destroying St Bride's. The roof of the church had gone. The lead had melted and fallen in, taking the carved wooden ceiling with it. Claire ignored Tobias, as he shouted to her to keep moving. She squeezed her way down the side of the parked car. Water soaked the front of her woollen coat, increasing its weight. Claire only had eyes for the scene before her. Beams of coloured light streamed outwards from the remains of the church's stained-glass windows. It bounced off the remaining glass in the buildings surrounding the church. Yes. That's it. Here was her holy grail. Claire raised the camera to her eye and framed the perfect picture in the viewfinder. She went to press the shutter. A shout went up. One of the firemen bumped into her as he struggled with a hose. The church began to crumble inwards and vanished into the flames.

Claire screamed in frustration. She doubled up as if she had been punched in the stomach. She could not get her breath. *Hell and damnation.* The shot was gone. What had possessed that fool of a man? Could he not see what she was doing? "Damn you! All I needed was a couple of more seconds. You could have given me that, instead of pushing me out of the way." Claire rounded on the fireman, who ignored her. He was totally focused on helping one of his colleagues wrestle the fire hose to a new position. "Don't you dare ignore me! I was framing my shot and you ruined it."

"Claire, enough! They are just doing their job, it's not ours to get in their way. We need to keep moving. I need to get to St Paul's. You will get your shot." Tobias touched her hand to catch her attention. Claire looked down at his hand on hers, then at him. Tobias removed his hand, as if her gaze had burned him. His lip twisted. He made to speak, but just walked away. *God*, he was angry at her? No, of course not.

"I had my damn shot. Those stupid –" She drew in a breath. The air was hot and damp. "All right," she muttered, and began to follow him.

Slowly they made their way across Ludgate Circus and up Ludgate Hill towards the Cathedral. The streets took on an eerie familiarity. Knots of vehicles surrounded by a web of hoses and clusters of men. Only the nature of the buildings changed and the degree to which they were aflame.

Again and again Claire put the camera to her eye trying for that certain shot. Each time it did not compare to that lost one. The one that damn fireman ruined. Sweat began to run down her right cheek. She wiped at it, staining her fingers with black. For a moment she looked at her hand confused as to where the smuts had come from. *God*, she was covered in them. That's it for the coat. It was already sodden with water. The hem knocked against her legs sending runnels of soot stained water down her legs. Not that the coat or her state were important any longer, nothing was. Only the matter of the illusive photograph was. It gnawed at her thoughts.

St Paul's seemed to be no closer than it had when they started out. It was a fool's errand going there. "Tobias, I have changed my mind. I am not going to get any good shots here. We need to move further that way." She waved in the direction of Stationers' Hall. Tobias did not answer. She looked round. He was walking quickly down the side of a fire engine. A man in a tin hat was by Tobias' side. What was Tobias up to and why had he abandoned her? She followed him; increasing her pace as best she could. Tobias nodded to the man as if agreeing to something. Then out from shelter of the rear of the vehicle a group of bedraggled figures emerged. She watched as Tobias picked up the smallest. The child put its arms round his neck and buried its head in his shoulder. She could see Tobias say something to the woman who was tucking the edges of the child's coat round its legs. The woman stopped what she was doing and looked in Claire's direction, then called to her. What she said was lost in the roar of water and flames, yet there was something familiar about the woman's voice. The woman beckoned Claire forward, urging her to join them. Claire just stood there. It was plain where they were going. To a shelter. Well, no way was she going to one. Did Tobias take her for a fool? The woman called again. Tobias shook his head and turned, joining the others now hurrying down the street. The man in the tin helmet followed, shooing the small crowd as if they were wayward ducks towards...

There in front of them looming out of the smoke and surrounded on all sides by the bright bitter glow of burning buildings was the dome of St Paul's. Claire felt her breath hitch. Oh *God*, there was the shot. She raised her camera again the cold metal almost biting at the skin of her cheek. *Tap.* Her head began to ache. The beat of that children's rhyme began again to niggle at the back of her thoughts. Hands clapping. Voices chanting. No. The angle was wrong. She got down on one knee, angling the camera upwards. This time. Yes, this time. *Tap...*

The woman turned round and called again. She took a step forward, beckoning at Claire with both hands. Her figure filled the centre of frame. It was so perfect. A woman and her child. Others fleeing the flames. The dome of St Paul's looming over them. The white light of the fires, the ragged edge of which blended into the bleak winter night sky. Then the wonderful sight was gone.

Tap, double tap.

The camera was knocked from her hands. Lost. As was the vista of St Paul's. She tried to shout her frustration and anger at again being robbed of the very thing she desired. But no sound came. The white hot air she drew in scoured her throat. She had been jolted sideways and to the ground as the wall on her left exploded down to the street and buried her legs. The sodden wool of her coat hissed as it was flash dried, and burned into her flesh. The pain was nothing compared to the loss that was all-consuming. Her shot. The one perfect picture. She tried to crawl forward and find her camera. She refused to accept that she would never have what she so coveted. Her breathing became more difficult. She saw through the dust mote-filled air figures trying to reach her. She heard their voices calling, but they became lost in the, *tap, tap… double tap,* rattle of falling masonry hitting the road all around her. It mimicked the children's rhyme. She now remembered the words. Her lips began to repeat them as the chant filled her mind.

Our blood, our bone: push the stone.
Our St Paul's from east to west.
In its shadow we take our rest.

Tap.

Fragments of flak rattled on the underside of the long slender fuselage of the Heinkel. The constant barrage set up by the ack ack guns ringing London forced them to fly high, and of late more and more of their fellow crews had fallen foul of the guns. Luck on the gunners' part or improved detection apparatus? That latter was the most likely. "Advantage Tommy tonight," Dieter, muttered, as he turned the aircraft, trying to spiral upwards. He didn't need the Knickebien to guide him any longer. Below and to his left an expanding haphazard pattern of light illuminated the city. He could see the simmering reflections in the wide bend of the river.

Rainer, his bomb aimer, lay beside him. He had slipped off his heavy fleece-lined outer gloves and now, his fingers clothed in the fine silk inner gloves, gently altered the focus on the bomb sight. Dieter could hear Rainer's breath through the intercom rasping in and out. The tube of Rainer's oxygen mask gently knocked against the side of the bombsite. The soft *tap…* lost among the roar and vibration of the Heinkel's twin engines, yet Dieter swore he could hear it.

It felt like the aircraft was carefully tiptoeing towards the increasing white blossoms appearing below, then suddenly the aircraft lurched upwards. "Bombs gone!" Dieter instinctively reacted to Rainer's words over the intercom. He hauled hard on the column as the Heinkel, now free of its bomb load of incendiaries, began to rise in the air. Dieter knew the higher they were the less chance of –

A Flash. His night vison gone. Shattered perspex flew inward, penetrating the remains of the Heinkel's nose cone. Voices screamed over the intercom. The aircraft started to bank to the right. Fractured metal and bone, blood and oil tumbled round Dieter. He automatically pushed at the control bars with his feet, but the rudder did not respond. He cursed and continued to push, unaware that his ankles were shattered. His legs felt heavy. Cold. Numb. His hands slipped on the control stick slick with blood. The screaming in his ears turned to curses, then silence. He called to his crew, but they did not respond. His vision began to clear. Black spotted. A raw, bitter wind tore down the length of the stricken bomber. His fingers began to stiffen. The blood coating them froze. The aircraft jerked; responding to his continued pulling on the stick. It drunkenly righted itself then began to fall away to the left. The headless remains of Reiner rolled against Dieter's leg and for the first time he became aware there was something wrong. The numbness began to change to a hot rush of pain. It increased as did the speed of Renier's corpse as it slithered backwards towards the gaping hole in the front of the aircraft. Reiner's parachute harness caught on the broken machinegun hanging from its stanchion. The bent barrel swung into remains, *tap, double tap.*

Dieter screamed and tried to rise. The movement completed the severing of his right ankle. Blood poured out his artery, floating upwards. *Meat grinder.* The aircraft continued to veer to the left, spinning down towards the river. For a fleeting moment Dieter caught sight of the dome of St Paul's as the left wing of his aircraft caught on the thick wire of a barrage balloon. It swung the aircraft round. The Dome flashed by, once, twice. Dieter screamed. Damn Dome. Bloody city. Damn Dome.

Tap, tap… tap, double tap. The wild flapping of the balloon as it was pulled down towards the aircraft echoed through its shattered remains

The rhythm increased; invading Dieter's thoughts as his brain struggled to stay alive.

A fading vision of children playing. Hands clapping. Together. Apart.

Chanting.

Unser Blut, unser Knochen: Erhebe die Kuppel. (Our blood, our bone: raise the dome.)

Unser Knochen, unser Blut, schützt unsere Kirche vor Feuer und Flut. (Our bone, our blood, protect our church from fire and flood.)

Suddenly the aircraft was free. The thick cable had sheered through the metal of the wing. The balloon bounced back up into the fiery night sky. The aircraft plunged on into the darkness of the River Thames.

Luke heard the air raid siren roughly fifteen minutes after the dean had and ensured that word of a yellow warningwas passed on. A yellow did not always mean that the city would soon be bombed. But tonight as the eerie wail of the siren penetrated the stone of the great building, Luke knew people had, with luck, five to ten minutes to find shelter. For him and his fellow members of the St Paul's Watch there would be no running for shelter. In fact the opposite.

As he picked up his bucket and stirrup pump Luke knew that if a large high explosive shell hit the Cathedral then there wasn't much he or his fellows could do. But against the 1kg incendiary, packed with thermite, they stood a bit of a fighting chance. Though the watch was made up of volunteers its approach to the defence of the building was anything but amateur. This was down to Mr. Godfrey Allen, the Cathedral Surveyor. In fact it had been back in April 1939 that Allen had begun his planning. He also knew at the outbreak of war that the 62 strong volunteers made up of Cathedral staff would not be enough to mount a twenty-four hour watch. And with many of the younger men being called up a request was made to the Royal Institute of British Architects for help. This is how Luke had become a member of the watch, along with his employer, Mr. Thomas. Luke was exempt from military service due to having failed his physical examination. Mr. Thomas due to age. And it was Luke who puffed and wheezed far more than Mr. Thomas when climbing among the small corridors of the upper building, but they made a good team.

As they made their way to their station a sound like a scuttle full of coals being spilt on the kitchen floor echoed from above them. *Tap*. An aircraft had loosed its payload onto the city.

"Here we go," Mr. Thomas said, and squared his shoulders, as if bracing himself for the coming onslaught. Luke could feel the building around him hunching down, defiant, like a child poking its tongue out at the bigger child threatening it. By 7.00 pm men were fighting a dozen or more fires on the various roofs of the Cathedral. The bright metal cylinders had bounced across the long stretches of roof over the nave and clattered down into the 'pocket roofs,' the lower roofs over the aisles.

"Shit! Bugger! Damn! Go out will you."

"That's fairly mild for you, Fred," Mr. Thomas joked, as he worked the stirrup pump, for Luke, who was aiming the spray of water upwards towards the flames trying to take hold in the roof timbers five feet above his head.

"I'm in church," Fred, the senior warden in their section, replied, as he shifted his position on the beam. He was another four foot higher and to the right of the incendiary the men were trying to extinguish. It had lodged in an awkward position. Five of them had been at the job for over half an hour. The bugger was stubborn all right, Luke thought as he wiped the water out of his eyes. He was soaked to the skin. A mixture of sweat and foul black water. The run-off from the burning timbers above his head. His arms felt like jelly after his turn on the pump and he swore his joints creaked far more that Mr. Thomas'. The older man seemed to be made of the same stone as the building. He stood there solid, balanced on the beams. The bucket braced between his legs. His feet on the stand. Luke could see his lips moving as if he was praying. *Tap...* A clink of metal on metal joined the hiss of the pumps as the fifth member of their group filled Fred's fast-emptying bucket and then carefully inched his way back to the hose. At the moment there was enough pressure to force the water this high into the rafters. But that could change. The pressure could drop suddenly, or even worse the water supply to the cathedral could be cut. Anything that could hold water had been pressed into service and these containers placed at various stations across the building. At least he and Mr. Thomas were not on, 'top-up duty' tonight. Carrying buckets of water up the hundreds of steps, and through the narrow walkways.

Tap, double tap. "Fuck! Damn water's gone, fingers crossed for the electric." Fred gestured for their elderly water boy to call for buckets from the water station.

Luke looked behind him. The hose swelled, then went slack again, shuddering. Mr. Thomas kept on pumping. It would take just over a two minutes to empty the bucket. Luke inched his way closer to the seat of the fire. Suddenly the red glow of the wood dulled and turned to black streaked through with white. The flow of water from both pumps began to die.

"Stop pumping!" Fred shouted, and leaned forward, inspecting the blackened area of timbers. "Right. We will stay for a bit and damp it down. You two take a break for ten minutes and write up the damage for the dean."

"You sure, Fred? Luke asked. Fred nodded. Luke felt a wave of relief. Just that short time would allow him to catch his breath.

"That was a close one." Mr. Thomas said, as they inched their way back across the beams. "I could murder a cuppa."

"So could I," Luke agreed.

"You write up the report while I go in search of some tea," Mr. Thomas said, as he straightened his tin hat.

Luke just nodded. He was the younger man. It should be him clattering down the narrow staircase, but he doubted he would be able to bring it back in twice the time and with less than half a mug for each of them. His hands had begun to shake. Luke's boiler suit was soaked. The thick cotton hung in bunches round his hips. He was so cold. His teeth began to chatter. He set down the stirrup pump and looked round for the report book and pencil. Both were actually in their correct place hanging on a string from a nail driven into the stone wall. As he removed the string from the nail his fingers brushed the stone. Whenever he had touched the walls of the cathedral before, the sensation had always been one solidness. No matter what shape the building had taken in the past, it knew in its bones it had always been there and always would. Now there was a crack in the building's self-belief. Luke pressed his right palm to the damp stone. The blood pulsed in his fingers, echoing what he sensed. He swore the building doubted it would survive in this form or another. The conviction was stupid. He withdrew his hand, but the feeling remained.

Tap.

Luke heard something like the clap of hands.

Tap...

A memory of a rhyme.

Tap, double tap.

He heard the words echoing up the narrow staircase.

Our blood, our bone: push the stone.

Our blood, our bone: raise the dome.

Our bone, our blood, protect our church from fire and flood.

Our St Paul's from east to west.

In its shadow we take our rest.

He knew the voice. It was Mr. Thomas. Luke knew that rhyme. He had heard it sung in the street as children played.

Palms together.

Luke clapped his hands.

Right palm on your partner's left palm. Tap

Luke reached out with his right hand and slapped the stone wall.

Left palm on your partner's left palm. Tap...

He reached out with his left hand and again placed it on the stone. The chill of the wall made his fingers twitch.

Both your palms on your partner's palms. Tap.

Two hands now against the stone.

Again twice more on both your partner's palms. Double tap.

Both hands twice more. He could feel the warmth left by his previous slapping of the wall. He pushed against the stone leaning towards the wall. The rhyme began again. But the words were different. The language old, yet recognisable.

Our blood, our bone: pusheth the stone.

Our blood, our bone: raiseth the dome.

Our bone, our blood, protecteth our church from fireth and flote.

Our St Paul's from east to west.

In its shadow we taketh our rest.

And with it he heard not the slapping of children's hands, but the tap, tap... tap, double tap of metal on stone and wood. *Blood and bone.* A chisel sculpting away at limestone. A saw slicing through oak. The voices of the men and women who had worked, prayed, and lived, in and around this building, and its predecessors for over thirteen hundred years. The current incarnation was drawing on the memories of these people. Their belief in the permanence of the building. How its shadow had always been there as a backdrop to their lives.

He pushed harder. His shoulder and elbow joints began to ache. He needed to know. He drank in the images; a flickering kaleidoscope. People at prayer. People being laid to rest in the crypt, under the floor of the nave, or side chapels. People celebrating and mourning. People now moving through flaming streets in the belief that this building would give them sanctuary. And there was the kernel of the building's doubt. It was afraid it could not fulfil that purpose this night.

Why? Luke pushed harder. His muscles bunched in his upper arms. His feet began to slip on the damp stone. So many images. So many memories. So much past. He began to chant the rhyme, hoping it would help him focus on the present. Once. Twice. Three times.

Our blood, one bone: raise the dome.

The dome. It was the dome. Something was wrong with the dome? Was it on fire? He pushed harder. His knees gave way and he fell against the wall, his forehead grazing the stone. Blood ran down into his right eye. Yet he still kept his hands pressed against the wall. He could sense the fear of his fellow members of the watch. He knew what the danger was. A call had been received from Cannon Street fire station saying the dome was on fire. The Dean had sent men to deal with it. They found the dome was not on fire, yet, but an incendiary bomb had lodged halfway through the lead roof which was beginning to melt. The men could not reach it, and if it fell inwards...

No. It can't. It must not. But what could he do. He was just an observer. It was all in his head.

Our bone, our blood, protecteth our church from fireth and flote.

The chant rattled in his thoughts, changing as it did so:

My bone, my blood protect my church from fire and flood.

Luke could see the bomb in his mind. His hands pushed harder. He reached out. His blood, bone and flesh became part of the Cathedral's fabric. His fingers touched the edge of the burning bomb and he closed round it. He screamed. His hands were melting like the lead. He recoiled. His grasp on the device slipped. Then it tightened. He pushed. Flames coursed down both his arms. The bomb moved out of the lead and fell onto the Stone Gallery. Luke's vison began to blur. His body shook. He slumped against the wall curled in a foetal position cradling his smouldering hands. His eyes began to close. His breathing hitched. Heart fluttered.

"By hell, you're frozen," Mr. Thomas said, shaking Luke's right shoulder.

"My hands…" Luke began, half opening his hands not wanting to look at crooked cooked flash.

"Aye, they are blue. Get them round this." Mr. Thomas began to press a tin mug into Luke's open hands.

Luke's eyes snapped open. His hands they were not burnt to the bone. Unable ever again to practice his profession. He blinked unable to comprehend what had happened. Had he imagined it? No. His blood and bone throbbed in time with the heart of the building and that of the city in which it sat. He struggled to sit up against the wall.

"I know it's not tea, but beggars can't be choosers," Mr Thomas said, winking at Luke and offered Luke the tin mug again. A rich smell of chocolate rose from the mug.

Luke gave his employer a smile and took a sip. He leant his head back against the wall. There was no longer any self-doubt running through the building's veins. In fact if he had to attribute a feeling to the building now it was akin to a stiffening of its resolve to continue to stand.

"They got that one stuck in the dome. Damn lucky it over balanced and fell down to Stone Gallery," Mr Thomas said, as he sat down beside Luke.

"I know." Luke replied, as he sipped his cocoa.

On the 144th night of the Blitz, December 29th-30th 1940, the chief photographer of the Daily Mail, Herbert Mason, was fire watching on the top of his newspaper's building. German bombs had destroyed a large part of the city and for a number of hours St Paul's was surrounded by smoke. Herbert was determined to get a shot of the Cathedral. Mid-morning the smoke cleared for a few minutes and Herbert took, what was later called one of the War's greatest pictures. In England and many other parts of the world when it was first published it was seen as a symbol of defiance. When it was published on the cover of Berliner Ilustriete Zeitung in January 1941 it was depicted as a sign that the German bombing campaign was working.

BEHIND THE SHADE

Arthur Morrison

The street was the common East End street – two parallels of brick pierced with windows and doors. But at the end of one, where the builder had found a remnant of land too small for another six-roomer, there stood an odd box of a cottage, with three rooms and a wash-house. It had a green door with a well-blacked knocker round the corner; and in the lower window in front stood a 'shade of fruit' – a cone of waxen grapes and apples under a glass cover.

Although the house was smaller than the others, and was built upon a remnant, it was always a house of some consideration. In a street like this, mere independence of pattern gives distinction. And a house inhabited by one sole family makes a figure among houses inhabited by two or more, even though it be the smallest of all. And here the seal of respectability was set by the shade of fruit – a sign accepted in those parts. Now, when people keep a house to themselves, and keep it clean; when they neither stand at the doors nor gossip across back fences; when, moreover, they have a well-dusted shade of fruit in the front window; and, especially, when they are two women who tell nobody their business – they are known at once for well-to-do, and are regarded with the admixture of spite and respect that is proper to the circumstances. They are also watched.

Still, the neighbours knew the history of the Perkinses, mother and daughter, in its main features, with little disagreement, having told it to one another, filling in the details when occasion seemed to serve. Perkins, ere he died, had been a shipwright; and this was when shipwrights were the aristocracy of the work-shops, and he that worked more than three or four days a week was counted a mean slave; it was long (in fact) before depression, strikes, iron plates, and collective blindness had driven shipbuilding to the Clyde. Perkins had laboured no harder than his fellows, had married a tradesman's daughter, and had spent his money with freedom; and some while after his death his widow and daughter came to live in the small house, and kept a school for tradesmen's little girls in a back room over the wash-house. But as the school board waxed in power, and the tradesmen's pride in regard thereunto waned, the attendance, never large, came down to twos and threes. Then Mrs. Perkins met with her accident. A dweller in Stidder's Rents overtook her one night, and, having vigorously punched her in the face and breast, kicked her and jumped on her for five minutes as she lay on the pavement. (In the dark, it afterward appeared, he had mistaken her for his mother.) The one distinct opinion the adventure bred in the street was Mrs. Webster's, the Little Bethelite, who considered it a judgment for sinful pride – for Mrs. Perkins had been a church-goer. But the neighbours never saw Mrs. Perkins again. The doctor left his patient 'as well as she ever would be', but bed-ridden and helpless. Her daughter was a scraggy, sharp-faced woman of thirty or so, whose black dress hung from her hips as from a wooden frame; and some people got into the way of calling her Mrs. Perkins, seeing no other thus to honour. And, meantime, the school had ceased, although Miss Perkins essayed a revival, and joined a Dissenting chapel to that end.

Then, one day, a card appeared in the window, over the shade of fruit, with the legend 'Pianoforte Lessons'. It was not approved by the street. It was a standing advertisement of the fact that the Perkinses had a piano, which others had not. It also revealed a grasping spirit on the part of people able to keep a house to themselves, with red curtains and a shade of fruit in the parlour window; who, moreover, had been able to give up keeping a school because of ill-health. The pianoforte lessons were eight-and-sixpence a quarter, two a week. Nobody was ever known to take them but the relieving officer's daughter, and she paid sixpence a lesson, to see how she got on, and left off in three weeks. The card stayed in the window a fortnight longer, and none of the neighbours saw the cart that came in the night and took away the old cabinet piano with the channelled keys, that had been fourth-hand when Perkins bought it twenty years ago. Mrs. Clark, the widow who sewed far into the night, may possibly have heard a noise and looked; but she said nothing if she did. There was no card in the window next morning, but the shade of fruit stood primly respectable as ever. The curtains were drawn a little closer across, for some of the children playing in the street were used to flatten their faces against the lower panes, and to discuss the piano, the stuff-bottomed chairs, the antimacassars, the mantel-piece ornaments, and the low table with the family Bible and the album on it.

It was soon after this that the Perkinses altogether ceased from shopping – ceased, at any rate, in that neighbourhood. Trade with them had already been dwindling, and it was said that Miss Perkins was getting stingier than her mother – who had been stingy enough herself. Indeed, the Perkins demeanour began to change for the worse, to be significant of a miserly retirement and an offensive alienation from the rest of the street. One day the deacon called, as was his practice now and then; but, being invited no further than the doorstep, he went away in dudgeon, and did not return. Nor, indeed, was Miss Perkins seen again at chapel.

Then there was a discovery. The spare figure of Miss Perkins was seldom seen in the streets, and then almost always at night; but on these occasions she was observed to carry parcels of varying wrappings and shapes. Once, in broad daylight, with a package in newspaper, she made such haste past a shop-window where stood Mrs. Webster and Mrs. Jones, that she tripped on the broken sole of one shoe, and fell headlong. The newspaper broken away from its pins, and although the woman reached and recovered her parcel before she rose, it was plain to see that it was made up of cheap shirts, cut out ready for the stitching. The street had the news the same hour, and it was generally held that such a taking of the bread out of the mouths of them that wanted it by them that had plenty was a scandal and a shame, and ought to be put a stop to. And Mrs. Webster, foremost in the setting right of things, undertook to find out whence the work came, and to say a few plain words in the right quarter.

All this while nobody watched closely enough to note that the parcels brought in were fewer than the parcels taken out. Even a hand-truck, late one evening, went unremarked, the door being round the corner, and most people within. One morning, though, Miss Perkins, her best foot foremost, was venturing along a near street with an outgoing parcel – large and triangular and wrapped in white drugget – when the relieving officer turned the corner across the way.

The relieving officer was a man in whose system of etiquette the Perkinses had caused some little disturbance. His ordinary female acquaintances (not, of course, professional) he was in the habit of recognising by a gracious nod. When he met the minister's wife he lifted his hat, instantly assuming an intense frown, in the event of irreverent observation. Now he quite felt that the Perkinses were entitled to some advance upon the nod, although it would be absurd to raise them to a level with the minister's wife. So he had long since established a compromise. He closed his finger and thumb upon the brim of his hat, and let his hand fall forthwith. Preparing now to accomplish this salute, he was astounded to see that Miss Perkins, as soon as she was aware of his approach, turned her face, which was rather flushed, away from him, and went hurrying onward, looking at the wall on her side of the street. The relieving officer, checking his hand on its way to his hat, stopped and looked after her as she turned the corner, hugging her parcel on the side next the wall. Then he shouldered his umbrella and pursued his way, holding his head high, and staring fiercely straight before him; for a relieving officer is not used to being cut.

It was a little after this that Mr. Crouch, the landlord, called. He had not been calling regularly, because of late Miss Perkins had left her five shillings of rent with Mrs. Crouch every Saturday evening. He noted with satisfaction the whitened sills and the shade of fruit, behind which the curtains were now drawn close and pinned together. He turned the corner and lifted the bright knocker. Miss Perkins half opened the door, stood in the opening, and began to speak.

His jaw dropped. "Beg pardon – forgot something. Won't wait – call next week – do just as well." And he hurried round the corner and down the street, puffing and blowing and staring. "Why, the woman frightened me," he afterward explained to Mrs. Crouch. "There's something wrong with her eyes, and she looked like a corpse. The rent wasn't ready – I could see that before she spoke; so I cleared out."

"P'r'aps something's happened to the old lady," suggested Mrs. Crouch. "Anyhow, I should thing the rent 'ud be all right." And he thought it would.

Nobody saw the Perkinses that week. The shade of fruit stood in its old place, but was thought not to have been dusted after Tuesday. Certainly the sills and the doorstep were neglected. Friday, Saturday and Sunday were swallowed up in a choking brown fog, wherein men lost their bearings, and fell into docks, and stepped over Embankment edges. It was as though a great blot had fallen, and had obliterated three days from the calendar. It cleared on Monday morning, and, just as the women in the street were sweeping their steps, Mr. Crouch was seen at the green door. He lifted the knocker, dull and sticky now with the foul vapour, and knocked a gentle rat-tat. There was no answer. He knocked again, a little louder, and waited, listening. But there was neither voice nor movement within. He gave three heavy knocks, and then came round to the front window. There was a shade of fruit, the glass a little duller on the top, the curtains pinned close about it, and nothing to see beyond them. He tapped at the window with his knuckles, and backed into the road-way to look at the one above. This was a window with a striped Holland blind and a short net curtain; but never a face was there. The sweepers stopped to look, and one from opposite came and reported that she had seen nothing of Miss Perkins for a week, and that certainly nobody had left the house that morning. And Mr. Crouch grew excited, and bellowed through the keyhole.

In the end they opened the sash-fastening with a knife, moved the shade of fruit, and got in. The room was bare and empty, and their steps and voices resounded as those of people in an unfurnished house. The wash-house was vacant, but it was clean, and there was a little net curtain in the window. The short passage and the stairs were bare boards. In the back room by the stair-head was a drawn window-blind, and that was all. In the front room, with the striped blind and the short curtain, there was a bed of rags and old newspapers, also a wooden box, and on each of these was a dead woman.

Both deaths, the doctor found, were from syncope, the result of inanition; and the better-nourished woman – she on the bed – had died the sooner; perhaps by a day or two. The other case was rather curious; it exhibited a degree of shrinkage in the digestive organs unprecedented in his experience. After the inquest the street had an evening's fame; for the papers printed coarse drawings of the house, and in leaderettes demanded the abolition of something. Then it became its wonted self. And it was doubted if the waxen apples and the curtains fetched enough to pay Mr. Crouch his fortnight's rent.

SOUTHALL TANTRA

Paul StJohn Mackintosh

"Eww, look, he's carrying his head."

Derek Clare looked up from the reproduction of Rubens's *Miracle of Saint Justus* in the chapter on the iconography of cephalophore saints. Ealing Art College library didn't carry the volume, and he'd had to order it in specially. The Indian girl looking over his shoulder evidently wasn't impressed.

"You know that's pretty disgusting, with his windpipe gaping like that," she commented, head cocked on one side. "Are you into that stuff or what?"

"It's for my dissertation," he replied hastily, shutting the book. "Motifs of self-sacrifice and martyrdom in Western art."

"Oh, that makes it completely all right," she said, smirking. "Plenty more of this kind of thing to keep you busy, is there?"

"There's a whole tradition of it." He thrust the book away and pushed his chair back from the table, praying that the flush he felt in his cheeks didn't show too much. "There's even a word for it: cephalophore, Greek for head-carrier. That's what I came here to study."

"Yeah, thought I'd seen you at the first year meet and greet." She paused reflectively, then stuck out her hand. "Anika Chowdhury."

He shook her hand, noticing the soft brown skin. "Derek Clare. Pleased to meet you. You can call me Clare: everybody else does."

He'd been called Clare rather than Derek at school, and it had stuck. Better to be a Clare than a Derek, he always thought.

"So, don't you need to be just a little bit kinky to be interested in this?" she chuckled, looking at him out of the corner of her dark eye.

"No, no, not at all." He hoped the red flush wasn't rising over his collar. Why on earth was she being so cool and ironic asking him about this? "It's all about the psychology of belief, and the evolution of iconography."

"Ooookay." She sucked her lip and nodded. "Want to tell me all about it then?"

"Huh?" Surprise momentarily overcame his chagrin.

"College has an okay café. Go on: I'll stand you a coffee. Convince me."

Put like that, he didn't have a choice. He slipped the precious volume into his Crumpler knapsack, and followed her sheepishly to the cafeteria.

"So, where are you from, Mister Clare?" she asked, after she'd brought their coffees from the blocky server at the counter.

"Um, St Albans?" he admitted, accepting his espresso like a challenge. "Not London exactly, but just on the outskirts, you know?"

"Not from around here, eh?" Anika sipped from her paper cup, then licked the froth off her lips. "Southall born and bred, me. Just a little bit west of here. This is my home turf."

"So, what's your subject?" Clare asked, although he guessed she must be taking one of the few art history and criticism courses, just like him.

"Critical Writing in Art and Design," she explained. "And I'm doing my dissertation on Indian religious art. And let me guess: you're doing History of Art, right?"

"Right." He nodded. "You know how good a rep the College has." Actually, the College's academic reputation hadn't been so much of a draw for him as its roster of alums: Freddie Mercury, Ron Wood, Pete Townshend, Robert Rankin, Alan Lee. Clare had hoped that this kind of ambience would somehow unlock his own creativity.

"I want to focus more on contemporary stuff than history." She shrugged. "There's a whole vocabulary of classical Indian aesthetics I want to bring to art criticism. The tradition goes all the way back to the Natya Shastra, before the foundation of Rome. You've got the rasas, or essences, that each work of art tries to capture and embody. There are nine of them, the rasas of love, humour, anger, compassion, disgust, horror, heroism, wonder and peace. You can see how all of that might freshen up and vary the old Western categories like Romanticism and the sublime."

Anika's accent stepped up a level along with her diction as she detailed her credo. Clare nodded, a little awed. "How did the faculty take to that?" he asked.

"Oh, they love it," and she giggled. "Even got special grants for it, from Indian foundations and the local authority. You know, all the local community expression thing. I'm not going to have to worry much about repaying my student loan, me; I'm flush."

Clare was enchanted despite himself, contemplating her slightly smug pout, those rounded caramel cheeks. "Going to be an art critic or art administrator one day, then?"

"Maybe; we'll see." She turned her gaze back on him, cooling and calming. "How about you?"

"Oh, probably an academic," he deflected. "Keep up with the research, take it further."

"Okay, then you might be interested in this." Anika took out her phone and laid it down on the café table, fastidiously avoiding the coffee rings. She opened the gallery and brought up a picture. "Take a look," she said, turning the screen toward him.

Clare squinted at the screen. The small indistinct image, almost woodcut simple and garish in its forms and colours, showed a scarlet female nude wearing a necklace of heads, standing on a naked couple, with two similar attendants on either side. Only, the central figure was carrying a scimitar in one hand, and in the other, her severed head. Gouts of blood gushed from her neck like tentacles, landing straight in her own detached mouth and the waiting mouths of her two acolytes.

Clare pulled back from the screen, shocked despite himself. "Who or what is that?" he asked.

"Thought that would get you. It's Chhinnamasta, the Hindu goddess, one of the ten Mahavidyas, or aspects of the primal mother goddess. Right up your street, isn't she?" Anika pulled her phone away like a conjurer concluding a particularly impressive trick.

Clare stared at her, wondering what point she was trying to make. "You've definitely got me there. Care to tell me more?"

"Well, what would you like to know? She's a Tantric deity, also appears in Tibetan Buddhism. She's supposed to typify self-sacrifice, renewal, and female energy, as well as just about any opposition and contradiction you can think of: life and death, passion and self-control, sexuality and spirituality, the mind and the body, destruction and creation. She's one of the more... heh, striking combinations of those essences I was talking about."

"Well, it's definitely interesting, and relevant to what I'm doing. Can you tell me where I can find out more about it?"

She lowered her head slightly and looked at him from under her dark lashes, almost demure. "I can show you. Come along with me and see the South Asian gallery at the V&A and we can take a look?"

Clare's eyes widened. "Er... Yes, sure. Tomorrow afternoon maybe? I've got a class, but I can easily beg off it and claim I'm on a study trip. It'd be true after all, wouldn't it?"

"It would," and she nodded, gathering her things and getting up from the table. "So I'll see you here tomorrow after lunch, right, Mister Clare?"

He watched her receding back, her long dark and slightly frizzy hair, her firm hips in her jeans. Did he now have a date?

South Kensington was a straight haul from South Ealing. They rode together on the Piccadilly Line, straphanging to leave space for the tourists and backpackers, exchanging intermittent small talk. The wide pavements of Cromwell Gardens were mercifully empty. At the Victoria & Albert Museum main entrance, Anika paused and laid a hand on the foundation stone.

"This stone was laid by Her Majesty Queen Victoria Empress of India, on the 17th day of May 1899, in the 62nd year of her reign," she recited, reading the inscription. "There you go, that's what we're here for. The V&A's got one of the finest collections of South Asian art in the world; outside the Subcontinent that is. Did you know that?"

"No," Clare admitted. Up till now, his studies had completely bypassed South Asia.

"London's just one massive pile of loot from the Empire, like

Smaug's treasure horde," she giggled. "Sod your Elgin Marbles; feast your eyes on this haul."

She led the way in, under the main dome and tentacular chandelier, then left to the Nehru Gallery.

"You know I got a study grant from the Nehru Trust?" she remarked. "Just a small one, but looks good on the CV."

Under the spotlights of the exhibition space, they stopped before a display cabinet showcasing another, more sophisticated version of the same picture that Clare had seen on Anika's phone.

"She looks pretty grim," Clare opined, suppressing an urge to step back from the case.

Anika bent closer to the glass, twining her hands sinuously around each other in the small of her back as she leant forward. For a moment, Clare thought of grabbing her wrists with one hand and holding them there, letting his other hand roam over her.

"Oh, she's scary, but she's not dangerous," Anika mused, half to herself. "She's not a destructive form of the Mother Goddess, like Kali or the war goddesses. Her rasas are bhayanaka, for terror, but also vira for heroism and sringara for love. In one of the original legends, she's bathing with her two attendants, Dakini and Varnini, when they get hungry and beg for food. She promises them she'll feed them when they get home, but finally she beheads herself with her own nails and feeds them with her blood. She sacrifices herself out of love of all, and turns all her fury and aggression in on herself. It's a very female thing."

"And yet she's nude, and stands on top of a copulating couple? Don't tell me that's all about heroic self-denial."

Anika glanced back at him and snorted. "Typical Western attitude: always fixating on the sex. Well, unlike the Christian tradition, Hinduism doesn't reject the body as evil or sinful, and it treats sex as another divine natural force, to be channelled and balanced. Chhinnamasta embodies desire, but also mastery and control over desire: that's why she stands on top of the... er, coupling couple, and cuts off her own head, signifying ego and selfish desire. The energy she releases and channels is kundalini – spiritual energy, not sexual passion. She transmutes negative energies by sacrificing herself to regenerate the world. Remember that line from *The Witches of Eastwick*, about a woman being a hole with all the futility of the world pouring into it? That's what she's swallowing, and transmuting. In other versions, she rides on top of Shiva, her consort and the archetype of elemental power. Her self-control shows in her self-sacrifice. She's the sacrifice, the sacrificer and the dedicatee who receives the sacrifice, all in one."

"That's a very female thing too: all those contradictions in one," Clare quipped, eliciting a giggle from Anika. "Still, I'll give you one thing: divine power through self-sacrifice shows up in the Western tradition too. St John Chrysostom said that a martyr's severed head terrifies Satan more than when it could speak, and that the martyrs presenting their heads to Christ are like soldiers displaying their battle scars. *The Golden Legend* claimed that St Paul's severed head said 'Jesus Christ!' fifty times."

"There you go: quite the cross-cultural critic already," Anika snickered. "Want to get another coffee?"

They picked up the debate in the café, surrounded by the mirrors and glittering majolica of the Gamble Room. "All of it paid for by the fruits of Empire." Anika sniffed, gazing around her.

"Back on to politics now, are we?" he niggled.

"I never left it," and she shrugged. "Cultural politics at least. You know that Chhinnamasta even has a political significance? One English critic compared her to India, beheaded by the British, but still surviving by drinking her own blood."

"Well, I'm not going to cut off my own head and offer it up to you as a gesture of restitution," he assured her. The momentary tension broke, and they both laughed.

"Nah, don't do that: it'd be a shame." She smiled, and for an instant she reached across the table and brushed his collarbone with her fingertips. Clare felt his skin tingle after she withdrew her hand.

"So, are you from India originally?" he asked, after a moment.

"No, Southall girl, like I said," she corrected him. "Though I admit, I've dug into my roots quite a bit. You should come over and see it some time: it's only a bit west of here."

"I'd love to."

"Well, how about this weekend?" She gazed at him with her calm brown eyes. "Unless you've got something else on, that is."

"No, nothing else on: that'd be fine." He nodded, his neck pivoting on that warm place where her fingers had lingered.

Despite himself, Clare went to Southall with some trepidation that weekend. It wasn't helped when he found Anika waiting for him outside the station with two other, younger girls, both decked out in heavy bangles, lurid blusher and eyeshadow, patterned tights, and highlighted big hair. They both giggled and fluttered their eyelashes at him when he came up to greet Anika.

"This is my sister Anuja and her friend Swati," Anika introduced them. "Now why don't you two tarts fuck off to Tottenham Court Road and do some shopping there? I won't tell Mum. Just get out of my hair for once, will you?"

"Oh sure, sis," Anuja giggled. "Enjoy yourselves." And with a broad wink at Anika, she took her girlfriend by the hand and sashayed into the station entrance.

"So what was that all about?" Clare asked as they walked up South Road over the railway bridge, towards the golden domes of the Gurdwara Sri Guru Singh Sabha temple.

"Oh, my parents sort of rely on my sis to keep an eye on me, and vice versa," Anika shrugged. "It's not very serious, but it needs a bit of quid-pro-quo, that's all."

"Should I be worried, then?" he said casually, glancing at the headscarves and turbans on the indifferent passers-by.

"Oh yeah, you took your life in your hands coming down here," and she chuckled. "Gangs of vengeful relatives prowling the streets to defend my virtue."

Clare tried to laugh along with her, and failed. "Bit of a Sikh neighbourhood for you, isn't it?" he remarked, as they passed the scrubbed facade of the Sikh temple.

"Oh, Southall is a total melting pot," Anika told him, seemingly more open on her home turf. "You've got Hindus, Sikhs, Muslims, Jains, Pakistanis, Bangladeshis, Nepalis, all living cheek by jowl: just like Mother India herself, really. Sometimes you get sectarian flare ups, but mostly we just stick together. The way that Mum and Dad describe it is that we don't belong to any special caste or creed, just to Southall."

"And are they Chhinnamasta worshippers?"

Anika paused in her stride and looked at him critically. "That's a weird question. You know that in Hinduism you don't exclusively worship one god or goddess or another. You venerate any deity in the pantheon, more or less, at some time or other. Besides, Chhinnamasta is one of the more obscure ones, most popular in the esoteric Tantra traditions. I don't think she has a shrine or a temple anywhere round here."

"Oh, okay, just wondered."

They walked on between the two-storey brick semis and terraces with their white window sills and plaster string courses, and the brightly painted shops, with their memorial pictures to Tej Ram Bagha, 50th Mayor of Ealing.

"You've got something on your mind, haven't you?" she asked, and led him into a café beside the defunct King's Hall Methodist Church. "Come on, sit down and tell me about it."

Over cups of masala tea, he pulled out his phone and showed her the links and web pages he had downloaded.

"I did some research on Chhinnamasta earlier, before I came over," he explained. "And this is what I found."

Anika squinted at the screen, her frown deepening as she read through the clippings. "What the fuck: you've been collecting this stuff?"

The reports, some from Indian newspapers and at least one from a UK tabloid, concerned the death of a man in northeast India who had slit his own throat in a temple to Chhinnamasta, apparently as an offering to the goddess. The temple buildings themselves were predominantly blood red, variegated with brightly coloured stripes and bands. At the end of the tabloid article was an image of a long scythelike blade, lying in a pool of blood.

Anika was predictably annoyed. "You shouldn't take this kind of shit seriously. People go crazy all the time. It doesn't mean anything."

"But I googled it, and that came up," he protested. "You must admit, it's pretty graphic, and it's exactly like the pictures themselves."

"It's a report in a fucking tabloid: what else do you expect?

They're just looking for the most lurid and eye-catching ways to traduce ancient beliefs: of course they're going to sensationalise it. Faith can show itself in all kinds of weird ways. Is this any worse than US evangelicals going on shooting sprees or wrestling rattlesnakes, or suicide cults offing themselves because of some comet? Don't make such a big thing of it."

Clare was at a loss for words. "Sorry," he finally said, lamely. "I wish I'd never brought it up now."

She studied him for a moment, before evidently coming to a decision. "All right, forgiven. But next time you come across something like this, just ask me, okay? I'm not trying to hide anything. Fuck, I want you to learn and understand, not run away from stuff."

"Okay, I promise," he answered, still a little stiffly.

"Look, no hard feelings." She reached both her hands across the café table and clasped his, looking warmly into his eyes. "It's all right, I understand, really I do. It can be a shock crossing the cultural divide and all that."

He soon calmed and settled again. After that, they just sat there, holding hands across the table.

They took one more week before deciding to spend the night together. Fellow students were already treating them as an item, winking and giggling in the halls. Anika still went home dutifully to Southall after class every evening: "Got to keep up appearances for the folks," she explained. But she spent her days beside him, holding and kissing him when she could, laying plans with him.

"I'll tell Mum and Dad I'm doing a sleepover with a friend," she explained, beaming up at him as he held her in the corridor by the lockers. "She's someone who's covered for me before: we've been tag-teaming this way for years. It'll be fine."

"So I'm your dirty little secret, am I?" he chided, kissing the tip of her nose.

"What Mum and Dad don't know won't hurt them," she demurred, lowering her dark eyes. "Besides, I want you to try my cooking. A boy student looking after himself, I bet your cooking sucks. You need feeding up." She pinched his lean waist.

"Oh, and you're the girl to do that, are you?"

"Show me any other girl who wants to try, and I'll scratch her eyes out." She raised her own eyes to his again, and kissed him.

They arranged to meet at Northfields Station early that Saturday afternoon. Clare was renting a studio apartment in a semi belonging to the College off Northfield Avenue. At least it had a separate bathroom and kitchenette besides the main room, and the mousy nerd downstairs hardly disturbed him at all. He wasn't ashamed to invite Anika back there.

"Not bad," she mused, pursing her lips as she gazed around the small room. "I was expecting it to be a real mess."

"I do try to look after myself," he grumbled. In fact, he had spent the morning frantically tidying, bundling away all his dirty laundry in the shared washing machine downstairs, stowing away anything he thought might not appeal to her. The kitchenette for once was almost spotless, with every surface wiped clean.

Anika had brought a packsack of gear for the night with her. They left it in his apartment before walking out together to Lammas Park and Walpole Park, to catch the best of one of the last fine days of the year. With cold beers from a corner store, they lay down on the grass across the ornamental pond from Soane's Pitzhanger Manor, with families and weekenders strolling and playing around them.

Anika snuggled back against his chest.

"Warm enough for you, my tropical beauty?" Clare asked her.

"I'm as British as you are, white boy." She nudged him in the ribs. "I've never actually been to India. Yeah, I'd love to some time, but I'm in no hurry. I've got all I need here."

"Aren't you curious, though? Wouldn't you like to experience all that warmth and colour?"

"I guess." She stared up into the pale autumn sky, where faint jet contrails were threading the blue. "One thing I will say about the UK: now and again it feels ever so slightly bloodless. I'll admit I wouldn't mind something a touch more gutsy for a change."

"Yeah, I know what you mean." He hugged her to him. "One advantage of being here: you've got Heathrow Airport just to the west. Not hard to do a getaway."

"Getaway my arse. It's hard enough to get one evening alone with you."

When the sun slipped down behind the autumnal trees and the shadows lengthened, they strolled home hand in hand, and picked up some supermarket wine from Tesco. Anika was clearly a practised and dedicated cook, and had even brought her own favourite utensils with her: an emaciated-looking roller, long metal tongs, a wooden spoon strainer, a crescent-shaped mezzaluna chopper. "Got to use the right tools to get the right taste," she explained, pulling a few Ziplock bags and sachets out of her pack.

"I didn't have you pegged as the housewife type," he said, craning over her shoulder as she busied herself in the kitchenette.

Anika shrugged. "It's just another traditional art. And you know you'll enjoy it, so don't snark."

The first dish she produced was deep-fried capsicum and chicken. "No beef, I'm afraid; I am that much of a Hindu at least," she admitted, as they clinked glasses over the first course. The main dish was a Dover sole curry with parched grain and eggplant and potato.

"I was expecting pilau rice?" Clare remarked, as he probed the spiced grain.

"It's one of the oldest and most widespread forms of cereal cooking in the world. It even pops up in the Bible. Now hush up and eat."

After they finished the meal and put the dishes to soak in the sink, they retreated to the couch with the rest of the wine and lay there together watching Netflix. Clare's couch was also his bed, covered with rugs and cushions during the day, and with only the small dining table and desk against the walls, it dominated the room. Anika lounged back against him as they watched the screen on his desk, and soon curled round and started kissing him deeply mouth to mouth, as he stroked and squeezed her full, heavy breasts.

"You know I'm not a virgin," she breathed, eyes heavy with the arousal building in her.

"I know," he reassured her. Actually, he had only guessed, but he relaxed a little more once it was confirmed. He checked his bedside clock: already close to midnight.

"Just let me clean up a little, and I'll be right back." Anika kissed him hard, pressed her body against him, then slid off the bed and picked up her pack. "Could you get the bed ready?"

Clare pulled the covers off the bed and rearranged the cushions while she went to the bathroom, then stripped down to t-shirt and boxers. He turned off his PC and made sure the blinds were closed; the muted street noise of traffic and passers-by reached him from the lane outside. Then he lay back on the bed and waited for her.

Anika had undressed, and now wore just a light cotton wrap, tied shut. She pulled her bag with her bundled clothes across the room and laid it on the floor beside the bed. The bathroom light cast a golden halo round her dark hair before she turned it off and lowered herself onto the bed beside him, unbelting her wrap. She gazed deep into his eyes as she pushed her warm body against him.

"Lover," she sighed, then added a couple more half-heard words in what he guessed was Punjabi. As she kissed him, she pushed his t-shirt up and off over his head, so that within moments they were naked and flesh to flesh, in the warm light of the bedside lamp.

"Don't worry, I'm safe; and I trust you," she sighed, as she slid down his chest and kissed him hard. As soon as he was erect, she straddled and mounted him, taking him inside her with the slightest catch in her breath, riding his erection. Clare caught the briefest glance at the alarm clock: it was 11.59.

Anika spread her hips wider to take him in deeper, arched her back to show her temple statue figure at its fullest, panting slightly with each push and thrust. Then she gathered up her hair and pulled it back behind her head, reached down beside the bed, and produced the crescent mezzaluna knife from her pack. As Clare watched, she lifted the blade and poised it against her neck.

ABOUT THE AUTHORS

Edward Frederic Benson (24 July 1867 – 29 February 1940) was an English novelist, biographer, memoirist, archaeologist and short story writer. He is best known for his four Mapp and Lucia books, set principally in a town named Tilling, which is recognisably based on Rye, East Sussex, where Benson lived for many years and served as mayor from 1934.

Rose Biggin is a writer and theatre artist living in London. Her fiction has been published in *Irregularity* (Jurassic London), *The Adventures of Moriarty* (Constable Robinson) and *Creatures: The Legacy of Frankenstein* (Abaddon Books). Her first academic book *Immersive Theatre & Audience Experience* is published by Palgrave Macmillan (2017).

Susan Boulton, as the song by The Police says, was born in the 50s and had the distinction of arriving into this world 200 yards from where, thirty-seven years before, Tolkien spent time thinking about hobbits. She now lives in deepest darkest Staffordshire and has had two novels and a number of short stories published.

Paul Di Filippo lives in Providence, RI (USA), H.P. Lovecraft's old stomping grounds, with his partner of forty-plus years, Deborah Newton, a calico cat named Penny Century, and a cocker spaniel named Moxie. He sold his first story in 1977, and since then has sold over 200 more. He has over forty books to his credit.

George Robert Gissing (22 November 1857 – 28 December 1903) was an English novelist who published 23 novels between 1880 and 1903. Gissing's early life was mired in controversy after he was found guilty of stealing from fellow students at Owens College (forerunner if

Manchester University), purportedly to support a young woman he was besotted with. Following a month's hard labour in Belle Vue Gaol, he travelled to the USA before returning to settle in London. Here he earned a living as a tutor and writer, his literary efforts gaining considerable acclaim – George Orwell numbering among his admirers.

Terry Grimwood's work has appeared in numerous magazines and anthologies. While horror is his home, he ranges with mad abandon across literary borders into SF, romance, thrillers and, with his latest novella *Joe*, human tragedy. "Albert and the Engine of Albion" is his first NewCon publication. *Joe* is available as an eBook and as a paperback later in 2019.

Sir Thomas Graham Jackson, (21 December 1835 – 7 November 1924) was one of the most distinguished English architects of his generation, contributing significantly to many of the colleges at Oxford, including the Bridge of Sighs over New College Lane. He published the volume *Six Ghost Stories*, which includes the story featured here, in 1919.

Juliet E. McKenna has been fascinated by fantasy, myth and history since first learning to read. Her debut novel, *The Thief's Gamble,* was published in 1999, the first of *The Tales of Einarinn,* followed by *The Aldabreshin Compass* sequence, *The Chronicles of the Lescari Revolution* trilogy, and *The Hadrumal Crisis* trilogy. Her most recent novels, *The Green Man's Heir* and *The Green Man's Foe*, are contemporary fantasies drawing on the myths and folklore of the British Isles. She writes diverse shorter fiction, from contributions to themed SF anthologies and forays into steampunk and dark fantasy, to stories for licensed properties such as Doctor Who, Torchwood and Warhammer 40k. She reviews for web and print magazines and has served as a judge for the James White, the Aeon, the Arthur C Clarke and the World Fantasy Awards. In 2015 she received the British Fantasy Society's Karl Edward Wagner Award.

Paul StJohn Mackintosh is a Scottish writer of weird and dark fiction, a poet, translator and journalist. Born in 1961, he was educated at Trinity College, Cambridge and has lived and worked in Asia and Central Europe. Paul's first story collection, *Black Propaganda*, appeared from H. Harksen Productions in May 2016. His second story collection, *The Echo of the Sea & Other Strange War Stories*, was published by Egaeus Press in October 2017. His novella *The Three Books* was published by Black Shuck Books in March 2018. His fiction and criticism appears regularly in a broad range of publications.

Henry Mayhew (25 November 1812 – 25 July 1887) was an English social researcher, journalist, playwright and advocate of reform. He is probably best known as co-founders of the satirical magazine *Punch* in 1841 and was the magazine's joint-editor in its early days. One of seventeen children, he attended Westminster College before escaping education by running away to sea. His four volume (the final one co-written) *London Labour and the London Poor* provides a remarkable record of London street life in the 1850s. "Watercress Girl" is taken from Vol I (1851).

Arthur George Morrison (1 November 1863 – 4 December 1945) was an English writer and journalist known for his realistic novels and stories about working-class life in London's East End, and for his detective stories, featuring the detective Martin Hewitt. In the 1970s the BBC produced a seven-part TV series of his novel *The Hole in the Wall*, which focuses on a young lad raised in a shady docklands pub.

James Hume Nisbet (8 August 1849 – 4 June 1923) was a novelist and artist born in Stirling, Scotland. He moved to Australia at the age of sixteen, living there for seven years. Nisbet produced many volumes of verse and books on art and fiction, but he is best remembered for his ghost stories, of which "The Phantom Model" is a standout example.

Reggie Oliver is an actor, director, biographer, playwright, illustrator and award-winning author of fiction. Published work includes six plays, three novels, and eight volumes of short stories, including *Mrs Midnight* (2011 winner of *Children of the Night Award* for best work of supernatural fiction) His stories have appeared in over seventy anthologies and three 'selected' editions of his stories have been published: *Dramas from the Depths* (Centipede Press, 2010) *Shadow Plays* (Egaeus 2012) and *The Sea of Blood* (Dark Regions 2015). His most recent collection is *The Ballet of Dr. Caligari and Madder Mysteries* (Tartarus 2018/9). Recently his story "Flowers of the Sea" was included in the *Folio Book of Horror Stories* among such classic luminaries of the genre as Poe, Lovecraft and M. R. James.

As well as writing short stories, **Bryony Pearce** is an award-winning novelist of fiction for young adults. Her novels include *Angel's Fury, The Weight of Souls, Wavefunction, Windrunner's Daughter, Phoenix Rising, Phoenix Burning and Savage Island.* She was raised on the science fiction and fantasy books in her parent's bookcase, and now lives in the Forest of Dean where she raises her own two children on a similar diet and enjoys gardening, theatre and cinema. Her husband likes maths. She puts up with his foibles.

David Rix is an author, editor and artist from London's East End, where the canals, railways and wild areas of street art and alt culture have been a major inspiration. His published books include the novelettes *A Suite in Four Windows* and *Brown is the New Black,* the novella/story collection *Feather,* which was shortlisted for the Edge Hill prize, and the novel *A Blast of Hunters.* He also runs Eibonvale Press, which focuses on unusual new writing in the area of Slipstream, Speculative Fiction and Horror. He has been designing the covers of Eibonvale Press books since the press started in 2004.

Ian Whates is the author of seven published novels, the co-author of two more, and has seen some seventy of his short stories published in a variety of venues. He has also edited more than thirty anthologies. His work has been shortlisted for the Philip K. Dick Award and twice for BSFA Awards and has been translated into Spanish, German, Hungarian, Czech and Greek. His latest novella *The Smallest of Things* was released by PS Publishing in October 2018. In 2006 he founded award-winning independent publisher NewCon Press by accident.

More New Titles from NewCon Press

David Gullen – Shopocalypse

A Bonnie and Clyde for the Trump era, Josie and Novik embark on the ultimate roadtrip. In a near-future re-sculpted politically and geographically by climate change, they blaze a trail across the shopping malls of America in a printed intelligent car (stolen by accident), with a hundred and ninety million LSD-contaminated dollars in the trunk, buying shoes and cameras to change the world.

Maura McHugh – The Boughs Withered

Kim Newman provides the introduction for this, the debut collection from one of the most exciting writers around. Twenty tales, including several original to this book, which represent the best short stories from an award-winning writer of fiction, non-fiction, comic books, and plays. A series of contemporary visions and murky pasts that draw upon the author's Irish heritage and so much more.

Simon Morden – Bright Morning Star

A ground-breaking take on first contact from scientist and novelist Simon Morden. Sent to Earth to explore, survey, collect samples and report back to its makers, an alien probe arrives in the middle of a warzone. Witnessing both the best and worst of humanity, the AI probe faces situations that go far beyond the parameters of its programming, and is forced to improvise, making decisions that may well reshape the future of a world.

Best of British Science Fiction 2018

Editor **Donna Scott** has scoured myriad books, magazines and webzines to identify the very best science fiction stories written by British and British-based authors in 2018. A bumper volume of twenty-six stories, by Alastair Reynolds, Lavie Tidhar, Aliya Whiteley, G.V. Anderson, Tim Major, Dave Hutchinson, Colin Greenland, Matthew de Abaitua, Natalia Theodoridou, David Tallerman, and many more.

Available now from: **www.newconpress.co.uk**

Immanion Press
Purveyors of Speculative Fiction

Strindberg's Ghost Sonata & Other Uncollected Tales by Tanith Lee

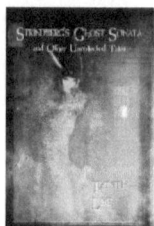

This book is the first of three anthologies to be published by Immanion Press that will showcase some of Tanith Lee's most sought-after tales. Spanning the genres of horror and fantasy, upon vivid and mysterious worlds, the book includes a story that has never been published before – 'Iron City' – as well as two tales set in the Flat Earth mythos; 'The Pain of Glass' and 'The Origin of Snow', the latter of which only ever appeared briefly on the author's web site. This collection presents a jewel casket of twenty stories, and even to the most avid fan of Tanith Lee will contain gems they've not read before. ISBN 978-1-912815-00-5, £12.99, $18.99 pbk

A Raven Bound with Lilies by Storm Constantine

The Wraeththu have captivated readers for three decades. This anthology of 15 tales collects all the published Wraeththu short stories into one volume, and also includes extra material, including the author's first explorations of the androgynous race. The tales range from the 'creation story' *Paragenesis*, through the bloody, brutal rise of the earliest tribes, and on into a future, where strange mutations are starting to emerge from hidden corners of the earth. ISBN: 978-1-907737-80-0 £11.99, $15.50 pbk

The Lord of the Looking Glass by Fiona McGavin

The author has an extraordinary talent for taking genre tropes and turning them around into something completely new, playing deftly with topsy-turvy relationships between supernatural creatures and people of the real world. 'Post Garden Centre Blues' reveals an unusual relationship between taker and taken in a twist of the changeling myth. 'A Tale from the End of the World' takes the reader into her developing mythos of a post-apocalyptic world, which is bizarre, Gothic and steampunk all at once. 'Magpie' features a girl scavenging from the dead on a battlefield, whose callous greed invokes a dire curse. Following in the tradition of exemplary short story writers like Tanith Lee and Liz Williams, Fiona has a vivid style of writing that brings intriguing new visions to fantasy, horror and science fiction. ISBN: 978-1-907737-99-2, £11.99, $17.50 pbk

www.immanion-press.com
info@immanion-press.com

www.ingramcontent.com/pod-product-compliance
Lightning Source LLC
Chambersburg PA
CBHW030106260626
47156CB00008B/2539